Searching for Summer

—— *A Novel by* ——

Christine Campbell

Thanks, Libby.

Christine

Published in 2015 by FeedARead Publishing

Copyright © 2015 by Christine Campbell

First Edition

A CIP catalogue record for this title is available from the British Library.

Contents

For Gus

Thank you to all the friends and writing buddies who have beta read, critiqued, advised, and generally encouraged me in my writing, especially Sharon Scordecchia and Jane Blewitt.

Special thanks to Launie Lapp for proofreading, and Wendy Janes for beta reading and her great editing advice.

The cover of this novel has been a family affair, and my love and thanks go to Michelle Campbell for her amazing art work and Tim Pow, who converted her beautiful painting into a book cover.

Most of all, love and thanks must go to my dear husband who has always been a tremendous source of encouragement, and who helped and guided me as I edited this book.

Without him, I doubt I could write a word.

Chapter One

The letter had finally come and Mirabelle suggested they should go out for a meal and to the cinema to celebrate.

She gave Summer a quick one-armed hug while shoving her bare feet into floppy sheepskin boots and preparing to rush out the door to work. "After all, not every day a girl gets accepted into uni," she said, giving her daughter a kiss. "Imagine! A lawyer in the family."

"Yeah, well, don't count your chickens and all that. I might never graduate."

"You will, chicken. I know you will. You always finish what you start. Not like me," Mirabelle laughed. "Scatty as they come."

"And proud of it," Summer muttered. "That would really stick it to Aunt Hannah, though, wouldn't it?" It was said with a sneer. "Snotty besom!"

"Summer! That is my sister you're talking about."

"No worse than you think about her. And don't think I haven't heard you and Yvonne say more or less the same thing."

"That's enough!"

"What was wrong with your mother anyway? Three sisters, three dad's. And you bang on to me about morals."

"I said, that's enough! I will not have you talking like this about my mother or my sisters. Right?" She chose to ignore the sulky look she got in reply. Gathering herself and her bits and pieces together, she took a count of five and composed her face. "Anyway, honey, don't let's spoil the day." She gave her daughter a smile. "Celebrations are in order."

Summer scowled. "Yeah. Big deal."

"Now, you know I've never been much for throwing a party. Love them. Think it's the Jamaican in me. Always up for a bit of carnival." Hands in the air, bracelets scurrying down plump brown arms into the folds of loose sleeves, she gyrated her large hips to an internal rhythm of the Caribbean. "Love, love, love a party." The rows of beads trailing from her neck bobbed and swung, a colourful waterfall of sound. "Just no use at organising them." One last shimmy in defiance of the look of disgust directed at her wobbling boobs, and she handed Summer her schoolbag and urged her towards the door. "But we absolutely have to celebrate somehow."

"You'll definitely be home from work in time?" Summer asked with a sigh.

"Of course I will."

Summer stood her ground, blocking the doorway. "There's no of course about it, Mum. You're never home before eight o'clock. The film starts at seven-thirty. If we're to get something to eat, you need to be home six at the latest."

"Okay. Okay. I can do it. Don't get your knickers in a twist."

Summer gave her a scathing look. "Ugh! That's *so* yesterday."

"Well, I'm a yesterday girl. Could've been a great flower person in the sixties." She held out her long, multi-coloured skirt and spun around on the spot. Her many rings and bangles sparkled in the light cast by the ornate, crystal-encrusted chandelier in the tiny, over-bright hallway. "Being a teenager in the nineties just didn't have the same cachet."

"You didn't need the sixties." Summer scowled.

"True. Oooh," she cooed, stroking her daughter's cheek. "Look at your pretty wee freckled nose all scrunched up there." She tapped it gently. "Do I embarrass you, my petal?"

"All the time, Mother."

Mirabelle shrugged. "Well, get used to it, kiddo. I'm unlikely to change." Words tossed behind her with the kiss she blew as she grabbed a shawl from the back of the door. Draping the material round her shoulders, she picked up her big floppy bag and danced past Summer, out the door and down the communal stairs.

'Unlikely to change.'

Words she'd later long to take back.

To rewind that day, push herself away from her desk, away from the stack of papers. Step crazily backwards, her shawl flying from the back of her chair into her hand, draping itself round her shoulders. Retreat through the office door, pulling it closed in front of her, her feet faultlessly finding the flight of stairs behind. She'd back down them, seeming to sink into each step, her knees straightening and flexing, straightening and flexing. Then walking backwards out into the street, her head bobbing as she took back morning greetings from colleagues and strangers.

Press rewind again to speed it up. The bus rushing in reverse, passengers seeming to get on, flying effortlessly up the step, their backs to the open door, ignoring the ticket machine, ringing the bell as they sat in their seats. Passengers seeming to get off, seeing only what they were leaving, strange knee-bent drops from the opened doors, taking their money from the ticket machine, catching it as it was spewed up from the top of columns of coins to jump into their palms. Mirabelle herself taking the leap behind her, leaving go of the handrail as her feet found the pavement.

Back, back. A reverse salsa at the bus stop, taking back the sharing of her joy at the good news of her daughter's acceptance at Edinburgh University, smiles disappearing into closed, reserved strangers' faces.

Backwards, backwards. Dancing down the street and up the stairs, rushing, rushing, unusual lightness in the ascent. Up the stairs and through the door and, there and then, standing beside her daughter, "I'll change," she'd say. "If you want me to, I'll change."

But, with no rewind facility available, no benefit of hindsight in play, Mirabelle neglected to change old habits. She came back from the office, late as usual, with the customary flustered apology ready on her lips and a placatory tub of ice cream in her hands as she laboriously climbed the stairs to their flat. She had got lost in the clutter that was her desk at work, writing reports about the safety or otherwise of other people's children.

"Sorry, pal," she said as she pushed through the door. "Not too late, are we?" She didn't shrug out of her thick woollen shawl, though it was damp from the drizzle she'd hurried through. "Ready to go?" She pushed open the living-room door. "Summer? You there?" she said to the empty room.

Still holding the ice cream, a possible cause of the shivering tinkle her bangles made, she stuck her head round the door of her daughter's bedroom. "Summer?"

Expecting to find her lolling across the bed or sitting at her desk tapping away on her computer, Mirabelle walked in, the ice cream held out before her as a peace offering. But the bed, duvet neatly pulled up as Summer left it every morning, was untouched, the computer unopened. Summer wasn't home.

Mirabelle assumed she'd been in and had given up waiting; gone to the cinema herself or with a friend. She tried Summer's mobile number but wasn't surprised when it went straight to the message box since she'd probably turn it off in the cinema. Shrugging off the damp shawl and hanging it over a chair in the kitchen, she put the ice cream in the freezer and gathered herself some food: leftover pasta from the night before with a dried up chunk of pizza, the dregs of a pot of potato salad and half a tin of cold baked beans. Too hungry and too tired to bother heating anything, she settled in front of the TV to eat it and wait for her daughter to come back.

She expected Summer to be sulky and accepted the sullen looks and acerbic comments would be well deserved. Her seventeen-year-old daughter had, after all, won a University place. She'd been promised a treat; assurances it would happen had been demanded and given. Mirabelle knew she'd fouled up again.

When she finished eating and had made considerable space in the ice cream tub, she turned the TV off and checked Summer hadn't come in quietly and gone to her room, having had the sudden thought maybe it was some game Summer was playing. On tip-toe, she crossed Summer's bedroom floor, throwing open the wardrobe door: "Got you!" Pushing skirts and trousers along the rail, looking between them as though her eyes might have deceived her, feeling behind them just to make sure. Crossing the hall to the bathroom, she swept aside the shower curtain with a loud, "Ta-ra!" then felt foolish, staring at the empty bathtub as though it was capable yet of concealing her daughter.

Chuckling to herself, she set about decorating the flat, stringing toilet paper across the rooms, draping it over the many pictures, round the sagging sofa, round the mismatched comfy chairs, a big soft bow finishing it off on each one. She made a huge toilet paper flower and stuck it on the lid of the toilet cistern. Dancing to the reggae music she'd put on the CD player, she gyrated to her bedroom and back, lipstick in hand, to write 'Well Done!' and 'Congratulations!' on the mirror, on the fridge, even across the doors, with no thought as to how it would be removed tomorrow.

"Party dress," she decided, searching through her chest of drawers, scattering underwear, socks, scarves and gloves around her like the flutter of autumn leaves. Finding what she knew was buried in the depths of one of the drawers, she threw the bright pink feather boa round her neck on top of the strings of beads she already wore, made some soft, floppy toilet paper flowers, clipping them into the tight curls of her black hair, and added some more bangles to the ones already jingling on her wrists.

Dancing through to the kitchen, she dug out a box of little flower candles, designed to float on a lake in a bowl, and sat them on top of a sponge cake from the freezer, unable to resist scooping some of the frozen cream from between its layers with her finger. It felt icy on her teeth, sweet on her tongue.

Confident Summer would be accepted at Edinburgh University, she had bought an iPad thingy from a catalogue and it had been delivered, wrapped and hidden days ago. She brought it out and gave it centre stage on the kitchen table in front of the cake, sweeping the resident clutter off onto a chair from which most of it cascaded onto the floor.

There were some sparklers in the drawer beside the matches and she stuck them in the cake, ready to light at the first sound or sight of Summer.

"She's gonna love this," Mirabelle sang, her finger scooping out more cream. "She's gonna love it."

She looked at the clock.

Half-past nine.

The film would be over by now. The cinema was only at the top of the road.

She draped herself in the deep, old armchair they kept in the kitchen, turning it so she could see the look of delight on Summer's face as she came through the door.

Ten o'clock, Mirabelle tried Summer's mobile again. Still turned off. She thought about going up the road to check if Summer was in one of the after-theatre coffee shops in the Omni Centre, but thought better of it, knowing how well that would be received.

"Grief, mother! I'm not a kid," she'd hiss, moving *Mirabelle away from the table, away from her friends.*

She thought about phoning Shana, thought better of it for the same reason. If Summer was with her friends, she'd be mortified if Mirabelle phoned someone else's phone to get hold of her.

Instead, she phoned her sister, Yvonne, but it was Yvonne's husband who answered. "Hi Hugh, Vonnie there?"

"Who, er, who?"

"Sorry, Hugh, Mirabelle here. Yvonne there?"

"No, er, no. She's not, not, em, home."

"Summer with her?"

"I, em, I don't think so. I …"

"Thanks, Hugh. Bye!" She had no patience for Hugh's bumbling tonight.

After wandering about the flat for a bit, feeling adrift, anchor-less, she decided she didn't really care if she embarrassed her daughter, she needed to know where she was. So she phoned round Summer's friends, or at least any whose numbers were listed on the paper Summer had pinned to the noticeboard in the kitchen. None of them had Summer with them.

She must be with Yvonne.

Mirabelle paced through the flat, paper decorations drooping sadly round her, not sure how to occupy herself, feeling useless and slightly uneasy.

She made herself a cup of tea, tried to pretend it was all right, Summer would walk in the door at any moment. She'd laugh when she saw the impromptu decorations, would love the fuss Mirabelle had made. They were going to have a party after all.

Music.

Her reggae CD had long since run out. A party ought to have music. Scattering CDs across the floor, Mirabelle shuffled through them till she found one of Summer's favourites. "Rhianna. That'll do nicely." Mirabelle danced through the hall and across the kitchen floor, the varnished floorboards deliciously cool on her bare feet, remembering how Summer slagged her for her moves. "Old fashioned they might be, my girl," she said. "But hot! Hot! Hot! Hot! Mmmm." Another scoop of cream filling, leaving the sponge cake decidedly askew, and the dance took her round the table.

Another cup of tea and a stack of biscuits, all danced out and feeling flat, Mirabelle opened the door and listened. She might be at the foot of the stairs right now. Her ears strained to catch a footfall, but there was none.

Summer's bedroom was always neat and tidy, an oasis of calm in the riot of living that prevailed in the rest of the flat. Yet another look into it revealed no change.

Unable to settle to anything more productive, she lifted the scatter of dirty clothes in her own room one by one, dropping them into the waiting laundry basket and straightened her own bed. She ran some hot water into the sink to soak the dirty dishes, washed a cup or two, left the rest, nipped a few dead leaves off the plant on the kitchen windowsill, shifted a pile of assorted bumf from one bit of the worktop to another.

What had been a flutter of anxiety in her chest, became a thudding beat.

Mirabelle phoned her sister again.

"Hi, hon. You okay?" Yvonne's voice was sleepy.

"Sorry, sis. I've disturbed you."

"S'okay. What's up?"

"Summer. She's not home yet. I'm getting worried."

Yvonne yawned. "What time is it?"

"Midnight? Maybe after? I don't know. Late."

"Where'd she go?"

"The flicks, I think. She didn't leave a note."

"Tried phoning them? Maybe a late showing?"

"This late?"

"Sometimes have an eleven or eleven-thirty showing. Phone them."

"Yeah, I'll do that. Just thought she might be with you?"

"Not tonight," Yvonne said on a yawn. "Sorry, sis. Let me know she's okay? I leave for work seven-thirty, but you could get me on my mobile?"

Covering her mounting panic, Mirabelle said goodnight and let Yvonne get back to her beauty sleep.

Not at Yvonne's. She's not at Yvonne's. How can she not be at Yvonne's? Mirabelle asked the mirror in the wee cloakroom by the door as she washed her hands after using the toilet. She'd been sure she'd be at Yvonne's.

With Yvonne eight years younger than Mirabelle, she and Summer were more like friends than aunt and niece. *"She's just cool's all,"* Summer told Mirabelle when she'd asked what they talk about. *"Not lost in a time warp like some folks."*

When Yvonne married, Summer was her bridesmaid, choosing her own dress, returning from the shopping trip with her aunt, flushed and excited. *"Look, Mum,"* she said, holding the bags aloft. *"Vonnie says I can keep the dress. I'll be able to wear it again."*

Time-honoured words, "You'll be able to wear it again," of bride to bridesmaid, usually about a dress that no bridesmaid would ever want to wear for any other occasion, except, in this case, Summer did want to wear the dress again. And she did. She wore it at every opportunity, loving its soft, flattering drape, its funky cut and colour.

Mirabelle picked up the frame from the sideboard, smiling back at the beaming nine-year-old Summer, proudly showing off the purple and white mini-dress. *"Unconventional for a bridesmaid, is it not?" she'd asked Yvonne when Summer ran off to try it on to model for her.*

Yvonne laughed. "Since when did you give houseroom to convention?"

"True. But I thought you might, at least for your wedding."

"Stuff convention. Stuff tradition. Happiness is what it's all about."

And there was no denying Summer's happiness. It radiated out from the photo. She loved that dress.

"Pity about the marriage though," Mirabelle muttered now as she replaced the photograph beside the phone. Yvonne was already on her second husband. "And I've not bagged the first yet." She sighed and dusted the top of the sideboard with her sleeve. Nights like this could bring Mirabelle down if she let them. There were so many longings in her heart.

She gave Summer's mobile one more try then looked up and dialled the number for the cinema, without much hope they'd still be open but intending to double check the time of the first and second showings if they were. Perhaps, by the time she'd waited for her mother's no-show, she'd missed the first, gone to the second, or even, as Yvonne suggested, there'd been a late showing. Perhaps a pizza or something till it started. When there was no answer, only an automated message, she shoved her feet back into her slippers and hurtled out the door and down the stairs, out onto the street.

She no longer cared whether she caused embarrassment or not.

Panting, her chest tight and heaving, she struggled as fast as she could, so much faster than she should given her weight and lack of regular exercise, up the hill to the roundabout at Picardy Place. Looking across to the Omni Centre, it was clear there was no-one about, but she crossed the road anyway, went to the locked glass doors, peering through to assure herself the cinema was irrevocably, indisputably, crushingly closed. Too late now for even the latest of late shows. Too late, too, for the after theatre cafés.

Her breath ripped through her chest and throat like broken glass. Her legs threatened to buckle beneath her. Unable to walk any further for the moment, she sat on the shallow steps, her head in her hands, her shoulders heaving with hard, unshed tears. "Summer. Summer," she whispered.

Then, standing, trying to catch her breath, searching the night, she looked up at the inscrutable faces of the gorgeous metal-work giraffes standing guard outside the centre, incongruous in the winter of a Scottish city.

She loved these proud sentinels, their beautiful heads way above her own, sharing the pavement with passers-by, looking South rather like tourists wondering which way was home, remembering things she'd never see: African skies; lions; leopards, and hyenas. Remembering places she'd never visit: savannah; grasslands; watering holes, and open woodlands.

A mother and her calf, not quite full grown, the equivalent of a teenager she often thought. So many times she lingered near them, feeling a kinship. Like her, this mother bore sole responsibility for her young one. "Summer?" she asked them. "Have you seen my daughter, Summer?"

Stroking the calf's leg, accepting the silence. "Thanks anyway," she said as she moved away.

The loneliness of loss was seeping into her with the light drizzle that fell.

"Summer!" she howled to the almost empty, darkened streets fanning out from the roundabout.

A taxi slowed, ready to stop, assuming she'd hailed it. Moved on again when she turned to walk away. A drunk muttered, swore when she got in his path, leant against the leg of the taller giraffe to regain his balance and gather his energy for the shuffle home.

Mirabelle hugged her arms about her and stumbled home herself, the wet pavement licking the soles of her slippers, the door of the property yawning, the flights of stairs stretching before her, more daunting than any mountain she would ever encounter. Weariness adding to her already considerable weight, she pulled herself up flight after flight and entered the open door of the flat, holding her breath for a moment, hoping, praying to hear her daughter's reproachful, *"Where on earth have you been?"*

Silence.

Only the overloud ticking of the over-ornate clock on the kitchen wall marking off the seconds of her disappointment.

She could imagine her daughter staring at the clock earlier, booted foot tapping, painted fingernails clicking on the table-top till the time had come and gone for the promised special meal, the promised trip to the movies threatened yet again by the more-important-than-her demands of work. She would have been furious by the time she'd flounced out the door, no doubt slamming it heartily behind her.

By three o'clock, after another futile try of the mobile number, Mirabelle gave up and lay on her bed, where she fretted and dozed for a few hours, guessing, hoping, praying Summer had decided to go stay with her pal, Shana, after all and hadn't bothered to let her know. She accepted the reprimand.

Summer was right. Sorting out other people's problems,

helping them make sense of their lives, looking after their kids — it should all come second to looking after her own.

Five am. Too early yet to phone Shana, still no answer from Summer's mobile, Mirabelle made herself a cup of tea and sat at the kitchen table, poking at the dried up sponge cake, talking to herself in harsh censure, promising to be a better parent from now on.

Chapter Two

"Lena?" Mirabelle's hand shook as she held the phone.

"Hi, Belle. What's up?"

"Lena, it's Summer. She hasn't come home. She's not answering her mobile." Her voice broke on the tears. "I've phoned Yvonne and Shana. I've phoned all her friends. She isn't there. She's not with any of them. I don't know where else she'd be. I don't know what to do."

"I'm on my way."

"We were supposed to go to the cinema last night. I didn't get home. She wasn't here." She glanced at the clock. "It's half-seven. She's been out all night. I don't know what to do, Lena. I'm frantic."

"Right. Just let me get my clothes on," she said, and Mirabelle could hear the change in her friend's voice as she dressed. "I'll stop by the station first. Check if there's been any incidents. You have a look in her room, make sure she took her mobile, then stay by the phone in case she calls. And, Belle," she said, her voice softening from Woman Police Constable mode to friend.

"Yes?"

"Try not to panic. Remember, she's done this before."

Three times before. Each time a different excuse, each time a grudged apology, each time a promise she'd always let Mirabelle know if she was not coming home when expected. And each time an argument about why she bothered coming home at all.

"You're never here. You're always working," Summer accused.

"Not all night," Mirabelle defended. *"Anyway. When I do*

25

get home, I expect you to be here."

"Why?"

"Because it's your home. It's where you live."

More often than not, the argument ended with Summer turning from her, her rigid back giving eloquent reproof. And Mirabelle's guilt would drive her home from her desk at five o'clock for the next few weeks, or days.

But now, she shook her head. "No," she said to Lena. "Not all night. She's never stayed out all night. Only if she's been at Yvonne or Shana's and then she usually phones to let me know. We've had so many rows about it in the past, she always phones now. Always."

"Could she not have forgotten this time?"

"No. I phoned them both, and everyone else I can think of. She wasn't with any of them."

"I'll be right over. We'll find her. She's probably sulking with another of her friends, someone you don't know, hoping to teach you a lesson in punctuality."

"Uh-huh," Mirabelle sniffed. "You're probably right."

By the time the day had properly wakened and had its breakfast, Summer still wasn't home and there was no word from her.

"Her father? Could she be with her father?" Lena asked as she took off her coat.

"No."

"You're sure? Have you checked?"

Mirabelle slammed down the kettle. "I said, 'No.' I don't need to check. She's not with her father. Okay?"

"Okay!" Lena held her hands up. "As long as you've checked. There's no point us calling out the troops if she's just nipped round the corner to stay the night with her dad."

"Trust me. She hasn't."

"Okay." Lena sighed. "Neighbours? Anyone she sometimes visits?"

Mirabelle shook her head.

"Maybe when you're not home? Working late?"

"I'm telling you, 'No.' We hardly see any of the neighbours. They're busy. We're busy. They work. I work."

Lena took out her notebook. "I'll talk to them later then. Give them time to get up and have their Saturday breakfast."

"I'm telling you. She won't be there."

"Yes. But they might have heard something. Seen her on the stairs. Whatever. I just need to build a picture of her movements last night."

"Oh, yes. Right. Sorry."

Lena took a breath. "Okay. What about friends?"

"I called all her friends last night, then again first thing," Mirabelle said, pouring hot water into a mug. "She didn't stay with any of them."

"Did you ask when they last saw her?"

27

"Well, no. But I imagine it was yesterday, at school."

"Yeah. Maybe."

"What does that mean? What's with the face?"

Lena shrugged. "Just, if she *was* at school yesterday."

"Why wouldn't she be?"

"Calm down, Belle. I'm only saying."

"Yeah, well don't. Summer isn't in the habit of skipping school."

"As far as you know."

Mirabelle lifted the teabag out of the mug and threw it in the bin. "And according to her last school report." She handed Lena the tea and pushed the milk towards her.

She caught the carton as it slid to the edge of the table. "Which was how long ago?"

"Mid-term? October?"

"And it's now late February."

"Your point being?"

"Meaning a couple of months can see a lot change in a teenager's life."

She shook her head. "Summer doesn't skip school."

Lena moved back a little. "Okay! Okay. So, if she's not with any of her pals, where d'you think she is?"

"You're the policewoman. I was hoping you'd help me work that one out."

"Right. Let's start by asking at the school. Find out if she turned up yesterday."

"I told you ..."

"What about exam leave? She'll soon be finished school. Do they not give them study leave these days? You need to ask at the school." She raised her eyebrows, her head on one side. "Well?"

"It's Saturday," Mirabelle said with a sulky pout. "No-one'll be there."

"You'll have the secretary's name though?"

Mirabelle shook her head.

"The Head Teacher's? We can call him at home."

"Her. The Head's a woman. Mrs Bell."

It took a while, but eventually, they tracked down the Head Teacher, then the School Secretary, who drove over to the school and checked the computer registers. Summer hadn't shown up at school the day before.

Mirabelle felt icy water in her veins.

"Okay," Lena said, giving her shoulders a squeeze. "Missing …" She looked at her watch. "Missing twenty-six hours. Let's make the search official." She lifted the phone again and dialled the number for the station. "I'll get someone over and we'll start taking statements."

Listening to the police in the stair was eerie. It was her daughter they were talking about, yet something in Mirabelle found it funny and she started to giggle, thinking how funny it was going to be when Summer came tripping up the stairs full of the joys, to find police in the stair. They might even ask her if she'd seen or heard anything, someone going in or out yesterday. She giggled again, deciding that's exactly what was going to happen. Summer would be home any time now. In fact, that might be her she could hear coming up the stairs.

She opened the door of the flat a little wider and listened. No, only her downstairs neighbour by the sound of it.

Leaving the door ajar, she wandered through to the living room and plonked herself into a chair to watch the news. No sense in everyone wasting their time looking for Summer. She'd be home any time. Trust Lena to panic and call out the squad.

Mirabelle felt the giggle rise in her throat again. It was all too silly for words.

It felt a bit early in the day to be watching the news. Saturday. She and Summer were more often than not out and about on a Saturday. Damn it! Summer better not have stolen a march and gone to that new bistro restaurant on Hanover Street without her. Wee minx. She knew Mirabelle fancied them going there for lunch soon. It was one of their things, a long lie for her on a Saturday until Summer came home from Shana's, then into town together testing out new eating places, pretending they were food critics, telling the chef how many stars they'd get. Wee minx. Bet that's where she is.

30

Mirabelle lay back in the chair and laughed.

What had started as a giggle had become a full-on belly laugh, and, when Lena came rushing into the flat to find the cause of the terrible howling that could be heard throughout the stair, she found Mirabelle holding onto her side, tears running down her face. She fetched a blanket to wrap round her friend and made her a hot, sweet cup of tea.

No-one in the stair had seen or heard anything unusual, no-one had seen or heard Summer since early yesterday when she and Mirabelle had left the flat, though there were still two tenants they had to interview.

"Your neighbour from across the landing says she heard raised voices," Lena said, her eyes not lifting from her notebook. They were sitting across from one another, Mirabelle in the armchair, Lena sitting on the edge of the settee, her back straight, her feet neatly together.

"Oh, it was nothing." Mirabelle dismissed it with a wave of her hand.

"What was it about?"

"Does it matter?"

Lena looked up at her, Woman Police Constable Lena Gillies now. "I'm afraid it does."

"Seriously?"

"Would you prefer if PC Elliot spoke to you? I mean, what with us being friends."

"Aw, come on, Lena. You surely don't think ..."

"I don't think anything. I'm only paid to gather evidence."

"Evidence of what?"

"You reported your daughter missing. We have no sighting of her since yesterday morning, since you both left the property after a heated exchange."

"We were talking about having a party, for heaven's sake. Look!" Mirabelle lifted her arm, indicating the improvised party decorations. "We were going to celebrate Summer getting accepted into uni."

"So what were you shouting about?"

"We weren't."

"Your neighbour says …"

"She's mistaken. We were just loud. I'm always loud. You know that," she said to Lena. "Besides, the door was open. We were just about to go down the stairs."

"Something about your sister."

"My sister?" Mirabelle thought back to the conversation of the day before. "Oh! I know what it was." She smiled, relieved to remember. "It was nothing. I just got a bit cross because Summer was speaking out of turn about my Hannah and her dubious parentage."

"How was the argument left?"

"How was it left? Well, it wasn't really an argument. Just a sentence or two. I got cross, she got sulky, I tried to lift the mood because I didn't want to spoil the celebration. That was it. That was all there was to it."

"And when did you next see Summer?"

"Aw, come on Lena. Relax. You know this. I told you, I came home and Summer wasn't here."

"And you had no contact with her during the day?"

"You know I didn't. I was at work. She was, well I thought she was at school."

"What time did you leave work?"

Mirabelle got up and started towards the door. "I don't believe this, Lena. You are interrogating me as though I was a suspect in a murder enquiry. I am going to put the kettle on and you and I are going to sit here with a cup of tea and wait for Summer to come home."

"What time did you leave your office?"

Mirabelle stopped in the doorway. "You're really going to do this?"

Lena's posture softened for just a moment. "I have to, Mirabelle. I have to do this properly, the more so because you're my friend. A neighbour reported an altercation between you and Summer. Summer has gone missing. I have to ask these questions." She looked at Mirabelle, mute appeal for co-operation written on her face.

With a sigh, Mirabelle sat down again. "Okay, I'm sorry.

Of course you have to do this." She smiled at Lena. "It's all going to seem like a colossal waste of time when Summer comes waltzing in that door, though."

Lena returned her attention to her notebook, pencil poised. "So what time did you leave your office."

"Haven't a scoobie!"

"Was there anyone else still working? Anyone who might know when you stopped?"

Mirabelle pulled a face. "Mmmm, nope, don't think so."

"Cleaner? Security?"

"Cleaner! I said goodnight to Magda as I left."

"Do you have Magda's surname?"

"Nup! Just know her as Magda."

"I'll be able to check that out."

After a few more questions ascertaining the times of Mirabelle's coming and going, Lena closed the notebook and sat back on the couch.

"Got all you need now?" Mirabelle asked. "Cup of tea?" when Lena nodded.

Conversation felt stilted and awkward all of a sudden and neither knew what to talk about, so they sat in silence, making much of sipping their tea.

"I'm sorry, Mirabelle. I'd better go now," Lena said as she finished her drink. She tapped the notebook in her pocket. "Report to write up and all that."

"Of course."

"Shall I get Yvonne over to sit with you?"

"Nah! I'm fine. Feel a bit silly calling you out actually. I was thinking of you more as a friend than a bobby. Didn't mean to make all this fuss."

"That's okay, pal. It's my job."

"Yeah. Summer'll be in anytime, probably laugh her head off when she realises anyone thought she was lost."

"Let's hope so."

"You get off now. I'm fine. I'll just potter till she comes in. And I'll give you a bell when she does." She shaped a phone against the side of her face.

Lena sighed. "Still, I'd feel a bit better if someone was with you."

"Don't be daft. Off you go. Catch a few criminals. I'll shout if I need you."

"Mmm, think I'll get Yvonne to come over anyway, soon as she can."

Mirabelle shrugged. "Whatever. She'll probably be looking in anyway, it being Saturday."

"Good."

The door closing behind Lena made an empty sound and it wasn't long before the silence filled up with doubts.

Mirabelle had been here before, in this no-man's land of doubt and fear. She visited it often, whenever she thought of her father, wondering where he was, if he was alive or dead. She sometimes missed him so much it physically hurt enough to double her over. It happened now as she wished he was here to soothe her with his gentle sing-song voice. To tell her it would be all right, she was not losing her daughter too.

Having Lena question her in such an official, interrogative way had made her feel sick in her stomach and very much on her own. She had called her as a friend and Lena came as a police officer, leaving her feeling bereft and alone, and sparking all sorts of scenarios in her mind. She knew she hadn't harmed Summer, but someone else might well have.

Her mind raced through every possibility, all of them bad. Summer had never reached school. She'd been abducted on her way there. Someone had grabbed her, dragged her into a dark place. Raped her? Oh, God, please no, Mirabelle prayed, please not that. Dead, then? NO! No, not dead! Her precious Summer couldn't, she just *couldn't* be lying in a ditch somewhere, cold and grey, battered and bleeding. NO!

It was inconceivable she had played truant. Not Summer. A straight A student — well not quite, but Mirabelle chose to waive the odd B or C.

Summer would never deceive her that way: go off as though to school but have another plan for the day.

And then, even if she had, she was still missing. Even if she'd taken the day off — to do what? Go shopping? the cinema? what? — that only accounted for the day. Where had she been all night?

She hadn't been at Yvonne's, her usual refuge in times of domestic disagreement. She hadn't been at Shana's, her buddy, her pal, her special friend. They'd been almost inseparable all through school. If anyone knew Summer's secrets it was Shana, but she didn't know where Summer was.

Anxiety surged through her.

'Too soon to panic,' Lena had said. 'Too soon to assume the worst. Wait till we know a bit more.'

What if there wasn't more to know? What if they couldn't find her? She had been unable to find her father. In all these years, she had been denied the closure of knowing if he was dead or alive. What if it was all happening again? Mirabelle shuddered. What if they didn't even find her body?

STOP! She had to stop this. She had to stop thinking like this.

Of course they were going to find her. Of course they were. This time was different. This time she was an adult, able to do something about the search before the trail went cold.

Mirabelle put the kettle on. A nice cup of tea. She'd have a nice cup of tea and wait to hear what Lena finds out from her further investigations. She took a cup from the draining board and rinsed it under the tap.

But what if she couldn't find anything out?

No! She shook her head, determined not to start along that road again. Not yet. Not until there was something to fret about. She threw a teabag in the cup.

The phone rang and Mirabelle started so violently she sent the cup spinning across the worktop and crashing to the floor.

She snatched up the receiver. "Yes?"

It was Yvonne. "Summer turned up, then?"

"No." Tears of disappointment rushed to Mirabelle's eyes. "Oh, Vonnie, I don't know what to do. She never came home. I don't know where she is. Something awful must've happened to her."

"Hey. Hey. Slow down. What d'you mean, you don't know where she is?"

"I DON'T KNOW WHERE SHE IS."

"She's not at Shana's?"

"No. I'm telling you, I don't know ..."

"Okay! Okay, Belle. Don't get upset. I'm sorry. I just thought ..."

"I know. I did too. But ... but ... something..."

"No, Belle. Don't even go there. You'll go mad if you think like that."

"Too late."

"Have you asked around? Some of her other friends?"

"Lena's doing that now. Trying to get a picture. You know, when she was last seen, things like that."

"Okay, sis. That's good. That's good. I'm glad you've got Lena onto it. She'll sort it out, if anyone can. It'll be all right, Belle. Really. There'll be some simple explanation. She probably told you she was going somewhere and you've forgotten. You know what your memory's like."

Despite her tears, Mirabelle managed a laugh of sorts. "True. True."

"Look, I'll not stay on the phone in case Lena's trying to reach you. But I'll come round soon as I've finished work. And I'm here, if you need me before that." Yvonne's voice was insistent, reassuring. "You know I'm only a heartbeat away."

Mirabelle smiled as she put the phone down, trying to allow her sister's platitudes to calm the frantic beating in her throat. She picked the phone up again to check there were no missed calls, no messages. Yvonne could be right, maybe Summer had told her she had plans.

The level on which Mirabelle knew she hadn't had such information lay beneath a very thin veneer of carefully forming self-delusion. She swept up the debris of the shattered cup with great care and attention, sweeping the entire kitchen floor with slow deliberate strokes, holding tightly to the broom to stop herself falling through the ice.

Chapter Three

"Any idea why Summer Milligan skipped school yesterday?" WPC Lena Gillies asked one of Summer's classmates.

"Double Maths and Science, man." Shana waved her hand in front of her face. "Heavy day. You know? Great day to bunk off?"

Lena smiled. "Yeah, not much of a mathematician myself. Did you know she was going to bunk off?"

Shana shrugged. "Sort of."

"Is that a yes, then?" Lena asked. "Yes that you knew beforehand?"

"She got her letter, like, into uni? Texted me first thing. Said she'd 'had it' with school. But I didn't believe she'd do it, you know? She was always saying things like that. Never usually did half what she said she'd do. She was gonna go shopping, like. Wanted to get a dress."

"Something special?"

Another shrug.

Lena sat beside Shana on the couch. "Do you know if she'd something planned? A party maybe?"

"Maybe."

"But you weren't invited?"

"It wasn't like that." Shana's chin went up.

"Oh, I can't imagine one of them would have a party without the other," Shana's mum said as she carried in a tray of tea and biscuits. "They were very close. More like sisters." She placed the tray on the coffee table and handed them each a drink. "Which is why Mirabelle must be losing her mind with worry. She probably thought Summer was here last night."

"Yes," Lena said, taking the tea. "Thanks. Yes, she did."

"Was that the plan?" Lena's companion, PC Elliot, asked.

But Shana shrugged. "Not really. We didn't have a plan."

"But Summer wanted a new dress?"

Shana nodded.

"Did you fall out?"

Shana turned to PC Elliot, her face colouring. "No! I told you, I didn't see her yesterday."

"Before that?"

"Oh, I really don't think …"

"Sorry, Mrs MacIntosh, but I'd like Shana to answer for herself."

"But I really think it unlikely …"

"Shana?"

"No. We didn't fall out," she said to PC Elliot, then turned to face her mother. "But we're not joined at the hip, like."

"So," Lena put her cup on the table. "Is there anyone else she might be with? Best friend?"

Shana shrugged. "S'pose that would be me really."

"Boyfriend?"

She shook her head. "Just broke up with Dirty Drae."

"Drae?"

"Dermot Wilson. But they only went out for coupla weeks, like. She wasn't really into him, you know?"

"D'you have his address?"

Shana pulled a face. "Somewhere off the Walk? Balfour Street maybe?"

PC Elliot exchanged a glance with the WPC beside him. "Think we might know, Master Wilson, eh, Gillies? Bit old for you girls is he not?" he asked Shana.

"Dunno." She pulled on the hem of her short skirt, tugging it down a fraction. "Bout twenty-five?"

He nodded. "Like I say, bit old for you girls."

"Nuthin' to do with me. Couldn't stand the skunk."

"No one else?"

"We kinda hung out as a gang, five of us like, you know?"

WPC Gillies took their names and addresses.

40

school friends

Like Shana, none of the other three believed she'd really do it, thought it all just talk, the same discontent they felt with life put into the same words of make-believe intent. They all talked about having had enough of school. Talked too about what they'd do and where they'd go when their acceptance letters came in. When Summer hadn't turned up at school yesterday morning, after disclosing on Facebook she'd got her acceptance letter and had 'had it with school,' they all thought she was playing truant for the day, to make a point, to make the token rebellion, show her disgruntlement with life. She'd get over it, settle down to hum-drum again until the end of term, just like the rest of them.

Suddenly, their Saturday got interesting. They could forgive the police banging on their doors on a weekend.

While WPC Lena Gillies and another WPC questioned the girls, PC Elliot and DI Sam Burns banged a different door: Dermot Wilson's. "No-one home, sir," Elliot said after a few minutes and a few hefty thumps.

"Bang again." Sam had taken up the case when he realised Dermot Wilson was involved, giving the case a new status, one with a little more urgency. "Bang again," he instructed PC Elliot. "Louder."

When he did, the door across the landing was thrown open. "Hey! Hey! Hey! What's all the racket about?"

"Sorry to disturb you, sir. I'm PC Elliot and this is DI Sam Burns."

Sam showed his badge.

"We were hoping to speak to Mr Dermot Wilson?"

"Aye? That's where he bides, right enough."

"But he doesn't seem to be home."

"Naw? Probably sleeping yet. It's Saturday. Doubt he was in afore five this morning. He's no usually on a Friday/Saturday. Does the clubs an' that, ye ken?"

Sam nodded and Elliot hammered on the door again.

"Does he live alone, do you know?" Sam asked the neighbour.

"Naw. Wi' his mother, ken. But she works Saturdays. The supermarket down the road."

"Thank you, Mr ...?"

"Murray. Jock Murray." The man offered his hand.

"You've been very helpful, Mr Murray."

"Shall I let him know you're looking for him when he surfaces?"

"No. Thank you," Sam said. "We'll catch up with Mr

Wilson later. No need for you to mention we were here."

Jock Murray gave a rueful grin. "Fraid he'll do a runner on you?"

Sam smiled back. "Got it in one." He nodded, tipping his finger to the side of his nose.

"No bother." Jock chuckled. "He's no pal o' mine. More trouble in the stair than he's worth. His mother's okay though, ken?"

"The supermarket, you say?"

"Aye. The one on the corner. Works on the checkouts."

"Thanks."

"Mrs Wilson?"

Dermot's mother looked up from the till. "Yes?"

"DI Sam Burns." He showed his card again. "And PC Elliot."

She closed her eyes and bowed her head. "Okay. What's he done now? That boy's killin' me."

"Home, is he?"

"Doubt it. Never came in last night. Probably sleeping the drink off in some bird's place." She looked at her watch. "If he's no back by four or five this afternoon, doubt I'll see him till Monday."

"That his regular routine?"

"More or less. High time he had a place of his own, if you ask me. Uses me like a laundry service and restaurant."

"Mr Wilson?"

She sniffed. "Long gone."

"Okay," Sam said. "Thank you for your help. We'll try at the house again later."

"So, what's he done?" She looked tired. Tired and defeated.

"Nothing as far as we know."

"What are you wanting him for?"

"Just some questions. You know who he's seeing just now?"

"As in girlfriends, d'you mean?"

43

Sam nodded.

Mrs Wilson shook her head. "Not a clue. Doesn't exactly bring anyone home for tea, if that's what you're wondering."

Sam left PC Elliot in the unmarked car outside the flats. He indicated his mobile phone. "Give me a bell if he shows up. As soon as he shows up. I'll get someone over with a sandwich and some tea for you. PC Craig can spell you and I'll be back when Mr Wilson deigns to come home."

"Think he's with the girl, sir?"

"Can't rule it out. Distinct possibility." He closed the car door. "Remember." He raised his mobile. "As soon as he shows."

The house was full. There was nowhere to escape to. Mirabelle shut herself in the toilet to get away from their kindness but it wasn't long before she was discovered to be missing and Yvonne sent to see if she was all right.

"Just wanted a bit of peace," she said as she unlocked the door. She'd been sitting on the lid of the loo making toilet paper flowers. "I'm getting quite good at these," she said. "What d'you think?" She held the soft, blue flowers up for Yvonne's inspection.

"Seen worse," Yvonne laughed. "You okay?"

"Wish they'd all go home." She left the flowers on the cistern.

"Everyone wants to help. To let you know we care." She led Mirabelle back to the kitchen where her family were gathered round the table and leaning against the worktop.

"Cuppa?" Hannah offered.

"Scone?" Gran produced a plate of her home-made cherry scones.

Mirabelle shook her head. "Nothing, thanks."

"She'll be back, love. You see if she's not," Gran said. She turned to her husband. "Won't she, Harry? I said, 'She'll be back, won't she?'"

Harry nodded from behind his mug of tea. "We'd best be getting that train home now," he said. "If there's nothing we can do for you, love?" he asked Mirabelle.

"No, thanks, Gramps. It was good of you to come."

"Where else'd we be when there's trouble, pet?" He gathered his wife and their coats and headed for the door.

"Teenage rebellion," Gran said over her shoulder as they left. "You all did it, one way or another."

Hannah sniffed. "Well mine would never do anything like this."

Mirabelle and Yvonne exchanged a look.

"Yours've not reached their teens yet," Yvonne pointed out. "They're still toddlers. How can you possibly know what they'll be capable of in their teens?"

"I do know they'll not pull a stunt like this."

"Oh? And how are you going to ensure that?" Mirabelle asked. "Implement a Nazi regime? Lock them in their rooms?"

"Yeah, yeah. Very funny. Kids need to know their boundaries."

"Yeah, but is the electric fence *really* the way to go?"

Hannah gave a long-suffering sigh. "Clever, Belle. But it's not a joking matter."

"Who's joking?"

She turned away, reaching for her coat. "You're too soft on Summer. If you ask me ..."

"Thanks, Hannah, but I'm not asking you."

"Okay, girls," Yvonne stepped between them, just as she'd always stepped between them: her older and her younger sisters never did manage to become friends. "This is not the time." She looked around, started shepherding everyone towards the door. "How about if we all get home and give Belle a bit of space. She looks exhausted. Probably could do with a bit of an early night."

Mirabelle nodded, accepting the hugs and sniffles of their goodbyes with more than a little relief.

"I'll stay a bit and clear up for Belle," Yvonne told them at the door, refusing all offers of assistance with the task. "Can you organise something for dinner when I get home?" she asked her husband as she pushed him out at the tail end. "Ready meal or something," she responded to the panic in Hugh's face.

"I ... I, em ... Tesco? Asda?"

"Your choice."

"I ... but ... I..."

46

Yvonne sighed. "M&S, then. They do some nice steak dinners." She located her bag, rummaged through it for her purse and handed him some money. "Okay? You manage that?"

Hugh nodded. "Of, eh, of course." He pecked her cheek and allowed himself to be bundled out the door.

"Phew," she said as she filled the basin with hot water and a squirt of washing-up liquid. "Save us from our loved ones. You okay, Bellabear?"

Mirabelle put a hand each side of her head. "So many suggestions. So many theories. 'Ma heid's birling like a peerie,' as Gramps would say."

"You go lie down for a bit, while I wash these cups and stuff."

But Mirabelle lingered, lowering herself into the old armchair. A tide of weariness washed over her, dragging her strength like shingle from a beach as it ebbed. "D'you think Hannah's right?"

"Is Hannah ever right?"

Mirabelle laughed, a weak and tired laugh, but welcome relief just the same. "There has to be a first."

Yvonne scrunched up her face and shook her head. "Naw!"

"Probably not."

"Poor Hannah. Don't know where Mum found her." Yvonne came over to the table to gather some of the dirty cups. "Sometimes it's hard to remember she's not the oldest, she's so bloomin' bossy. And, well, she's so *different* from the rest of us."

Mirabelle held her plump, chocolate-brown, Caribbean arm next to Yvonne's slim, white Scottish one. "Not like you and me, eh?" she chuckled.

Yvonne gave her arm a friendly push and laughed too. "You know fine what I mean." She lowered the cups into the sink and stood, her hands also in the soapy water. "Hannah's not ... well ... She's sort of ..."

"Snooty?"

"Yes!" She started to wash the dishes. "So where did that come from?"

"Perhaps her dad worked in the bank?"

"Belle! Go wash your mouth out." Yvonne offered Mirabelle the wet washing-up sponge, pretending to be shocked.

"All joking aside," Mirabelle said, her smile fading. "Was she right about Summer? Am I too soft on Summer?"

Yvonne shrugged. "What would I know? I've no kids."

"But what d'you think?"

"I think you do your best. No-one can ask more than that."

"Trouble is, I don't know how to be a good mum, really. Don't know how to be a mum at all."

"No role model."

"Yeah, Mum didn't exactly set a good example, did she?"

"Five kids to three, possibly four, different fathers? I'd say not. Think you did most of the bringing us up bit. You and Gran and Gramps," Yvonne said. "Not that we saw them all that often. Think Gran found it too distressing to come to our house and there was no way Mum could organise us all to go to theirs." She stood at the sink, her hands in the soapy water as they each thought about those days, when they could only watch with helpless fear as their mother sank deeper and deeper into alcoholic depression and ineptitude. "No, it was mostly down to you."

Mirabelle pulled a face. "I was only a kid myself." Her face clouded over. "Didn't do so well with the wee ones, eh?"

"Don't let's go there," Yvonne said, wiping her hands on the dishtowel and giving her sister a hug. "Not today. 'Sufficient for each day' and all that."

They stood for a moment, clasped together, breathing as one, grieving as one, releasing as one.

After a while, Yvonne went back to the dishes and left Mirabelle to her thoughts, then, just as she was getting her coat on, Sam arrived. Yvonne held the door, barring his entry, waiting, a question in her expression.

"Sam Burns, Detective Inspector Sam Burns," he said.

"Oh." Her brow cleared. "I'm Yvonne, Mirabelle's sister." She held out her hand. "You'd best come in. Piccadilly Circus in here tonight," she told him. "Everyone and his auntie offering a take on things."

He shook his head. "Poor Belle. But at least they care."

Yvonne raised an eyebrow. "What I said." She looked at Sam. "Still, not easy for Belle. Think she just wants left in peace."

"I won't stay long."

Yvonne laughed. "I didn't mean you. She'll be delighted to see you. You're her 'friend,' aren't you?" She drew quotation marks in the air. "The one she meets sometimes for lunch?"

Sam smiled and nodded.

"Yes, well, like I say, she'll be pleased to see you. At least you can actually tell her what *is* happening." She nodded towards the door behind him. "Instead of all their guesses."

Sam shook his head. "Not much to tell yet." He held up his mobile. "Waiting for a call from my PC." He shrugged. "Maybe something, maybe nothing."

Chapter Four

Sam had never met Summer. He and Mirabelle had only met up a couple of times for coffee in the police canteen, more or less by accident, and a couple of times for a stroll in the Botanic Garden, more or less by design, before he found out she had a daughter.

"You do know I've got a kid, don't you?" she said when he asked her out on a proper date.

"No, I didn't know." He stopped walking and turned to her. "All these weeks we've been seeing one another, you never said. I can't believe you never said."

"I kinda thought you knew." She twisted the bracelets on her wrist one way, her face the other.

"How would I know if you didn't tell me?"

Mirabelle shrugged, her face still screwed up in an expression of doubt mixed with embarrassment. "I just kinda thought you did."

"No," he said. "I didn't." He looked at her discomfort. "Why? Is it a problem?"

"I'm, ehm, I'm not sure. I just kinda thought you knew."

"So you keep saying, but I ..."

"And I kinda sorta assumed you didn't want to talk about her."

"Her? You've got a daughter?" Sam smiled. "Is she like you?"

She thought of Summer's red hair and pale skin, her hazel eyes and slim figure. "Not particularly." She fingered her tight, black curls and knew Summer inherited none of her own Jamaican colouring. "In fact, not at all."

"Like her dad?"

"Sort of, I suppose."

He hit his hand off his forehead. "You're married! Oh, hey! I didn't know, had no idea. I would never have asked ..."

"It's okay. Don't get yourself all worked up about it. I'm not married."

They were walking through the Botanic Garden and had paused beside one of the enormous hothouses. "I think I need a seat," he said, ushering her past the door to one of the benches outside. "You're not married. Course you're not married. You're still a Milligan. Divorced then?"

"Single parent."

"The father?"

"Didn't want to know."

Sam shook his head. "You told him though?"

"Wrote him a letter." She picked at the fringe of her shawl. "More than one, actually." She remembered the hope with which they'd been sent, could almost smell the lilac-scented stationery she'd used, a gift he'd given before they'd parted, before she'd known she carried his child. 'No excuse for you not to write,' he'd said. But excuse enough for him not to reply, it seemed. Months later, she'd tipped the remaining envelopes and paper into the bucket in a ceremony of tight-lipped tears.

"How old is your daughter?" Sam was asking.

Mirabelle pulled the shawl close round her shoulders, rubbing her arms. "Just turned seventeen."

"That's ni ... Hey! Wait a minute." He jumped up from the bench.

"No, she's not."

"Not?"

"Not yours."

"Seventeen when?"

"February."

He counted it out on his fingers. "June ... July ..."

"I said, 'She's not yours.'"

He sat beside her again, shaking his head. "You're sure? It'd be about the right time."

51

"No need to look so panicked. She's not yours."

"I'm not panicked. It was just, well, I just kinda thought…"

"You just kinda thought you were her father?"

He nodded.

"You're not."

"So you said." He looked at her. "Who is her father then?"

"None of your business."

"Well, I think maybe it is. We were together…"

"Huh," she said. "Don't flatter yourself we were anything more than a summer fling."

"Thanks! I suppose that explains a few things then. Like why you never phoned, never wrote."

"Neither did you."

He shook his head, leaning back on the bench, stretching his legs out in front of him. "Uh-uh! No, you can't put that one on me. I seem to remember that particular ball was in your court, since you didn't know where you were going to be." Drawing his legs in again, he turned to her. "You said you'd have no fixed address, no phone number till you got a flat."

Mirabelle twisted the bracelets round her wrist, watching how the light caught the beads, giving some of them an iridescent glow.

"I watched for a letter, a postcard, a phone call. Nothing," he said, spreading his hands wide. "Not a word."

She looked up, the challenge on her face. "Sit by the phone did you?"

"Checked the hall table very day when I got home. Nothing. No letter, no phone message."

"Your mother would have told you, I suppose if there'd been one."

"Yup! So don't pretend you called, because I know you didn't." He got up and walked away a bit.

Mirabelle's brow wrinkled. "So you think I broke up with you?"

"By default, yes."

"And I thought you broke up with me — by default."

They looked at one another, eighteen years shimmering between them in uncertain light.

"Well, like I said. A summer fling," Mirabelle said with a shrug.

He pulled a face. "And now?"

Matching his expression with an equally questioning one of her own, Mirabelle got up from their bench and they started walking together. "Let's just enjoy the gardens, shall we? It's a lovely day for a walk."

By the time they had wound their way back to Sam's car, things had thawed a little between them, though they had finished their lunch break in silence.

"Can I meet her?" he asked as they got in the car.

"Maybe. Not yet. I'm not ready for that yet."

"Okay. I can wait," Sam said as he started the engine. "But I would like to meet her."

"And you shall. Just not yet."

That had only been a few weeks ago, and now, if Lena was right and Summer was teaching her a lesson, Mirabelle knew she was likely to meet Sam when she arrived home. She wasn't sure how she felt about that. And, more importantly, she wasn't sure how Summer would feel about it. The few times over the years Mirabelle had brought someone home and introduced him to Summer, it hadn't gone well.

When Summer was a toddler, two, three at most, Mirabelle found herself with an admirer whose attention she enjoyed, a workmate, a kind, gentle man. After a few weeks of shared lunches and after-work drinks, Mirabelle invited him round for dinner.

"Say hello to Uncle Alec," she said, pushing Summer forward.

Scowling and whimpering, Summer retreated behind her legs, clutching her mother's skirt, and no amount of cajoling and wheeling would persuade her to come out of hiding.

"Come on, honey. Alec's not going to hurt you."

Summer looked unconvinced. When Mirabelle bent down to persuade her, naked fear was written on her daughter's face.

"She's not had much contact with fellas," she explained to Alec. "She'll come round as she gets to know you."

But she didn't. Over several weeks and several difficult attempts to share a meal with what he described as 'a recalcitrant toddler,' Alec gave up, explaining to Mirabelle he couldn't take the fear in Summer's eyes, the constant clinginess, and the resentment emanating from her. He lost interest in the relationship.

Things didn't improve over the years, each attempt at introducing a man into the house failing at the same hurdle, and when Mirabelle tried again when the toddler was a teenager, Summer sulked and pouted, called her mother a slag and made 'new uncle' comments. To say she didn't take kindly to the idea of Mirabelle dating was more than a slight understatement. Mirabelle tried to reason with her, tried to assure her she'd still be number one.

"Number two at best!" Summer shouted back. "If he comes here I'll be straight down to number three."

"No." Mirabelle opened her arms wide. "No, honey-bun, you're my number one girl."

"Yeah, but not your number one priority." Summer declined the embrace. "That's your precious social work. And, if you were to count up your 'clients' individually, God knows where I'd come in the charts."

"Watch your tongue, girl!"

"And I'm not your honey-bun." Her face contorted in distaste at the sticky illusion, her hands wiping the sweetness on her jeans as she slammed off into her room.

Mirabelle would let her go, chastened by the accusation. The budding relationship with potential paramour plucked and discarded.

But this time, Mirabelle wanted it to be different. She'd said nothing about Sam. Had mostly met him at lunchtimes so Summer didn't know they were seeing one another.

Mirabelle had been choosing her timing carefully. Choosing words too, sifting through available information, selecting appropriate revelations. It was important Summer liked Sam. This time it mattered.

This time she herself really cared about the outcome.

And now, it looked as though control had been wrested from Mirabelle. Sam was here. Summer could walk in any moment, her own explanations pushed aside by her demands for theirs.

Sam didn't get the call he was waiting for till early next morning, having left Lena staying over with Mirabelle, *"Just for company," he told her. "I'll feel better knowing someone is here."*

"Seems he went in the back, across the gardens, sir," Elliot told Sam as he got out of the car. "Jock Murray, the neighbour, tapped the car window not more than half an hour ago. Says he heard 'them through the wall' shouting around midnight, the lad and his mother. Thinks there was a bit of a tussle as well."

"Did he not think to let us know earlier?"

Elliot shrugged. "Just turned up his telly, he said. Guessed they'd gone to bed after a bit, when it went quiet."

"Right. Let's go visiting."

They walked across the street, into the stair and banged on the door.

"Ah! Dermot Wilson."

"Aye?" The young man slumped against the doorframe, hands in pockets.

"DI Sam Burns," Sam said, showing his identification. "We've met before."

"Aye."

"And this is PC Elliot."

"Aye."

"Okay if we come in?"

Dermot shifted uncomfortably, his lanky body still barring the door. "What's it about, like?" He wrapped his arms round his body, the thin, grubby tee-shirt pulled tight against him, exposing the frailness of his chest.

"Or perhaps you'd prefer to come down to the station?"

Sam turned towards the unseen police car parked in front of the flats.

Dermot indicated his bare feet, the tattered jeans pulled on to answer the door. "It's only eight o'clock, man. I've no had ma breakfast or nothing yet."

"That's okay, son." Sam stepped forward, forcing Dermot to stand aside and let them enter the hallway. "Tea 'n' toast sounds good to me. What about you, Elliot? Tea 'n' toast for you?"

"I'll put the kettle on then," Dermot muttered.

"That's okay, son. PC Elliot here'll do that. You can get out the marmalade while we chat."

"What's to chat about?"

"Summer."

Dermot looked out the kitchen window at the sparkle of a Scottish winter day. "Aye, it's no here yet."

"And Summer Milligan? What about her? She here yet?"

Dermot's head snapped up from his rummage through the breadbin. "What?"

"You heard me. Summer. Summer Milligan. She here?"

He shrugged, his face contorted into a grimace. "Sunshine? Aye, sure. She'll be doon the hall, in bed wi' ma mother."

"Seen her recently, have you?"

"Who? Ma mother?"

"Yeah, son. Right. Summer? You seen Summer recently?"

Dermot looked towards the window.

"And we'll do without the seasonal references. Right?"

The breadbin raid continued, accompanied by another shrug.

"So? You seen Summer Milligan recently?"

"Only when ah walked by the school."

"When?"

"Dunno. Yesterday? Day before? Just in passing, like." He slipped a couple of slices of bread into the toaster. "We don't speak much."

"Dumped you, did she?"

"Mutual."

"Aye? Now why would that be? Something you're not telling us?"

Dermot pulled a face. "Nuthin' tae tell." He reached the pot of marmalade down from the kitchen cupboard. "We went out coupla times. We broke up. She's a slag. Got the picture?"

"She's missing. Know anything about it?"

"Missing? What d'ye mean 'missing'?"

"Missing, as in didn't come home yesterday or the day before."

"Well, dinnae look at me. Ah don't even pass the time o' day wi' her anymair."

"Yesterday? Did you see her at all?"

Dermot frowned in concentration. "Yesterday?"

"Aye, yesterday. Saturday. Anywhere? Did you pass her in the street? See her on the bus?"

He shook his head. "Nuh."

"Friday night? Your mother says you didn't come home?"

"So?"

"So, where were you Friday night?"

"Here 'n' there."

"Anyone vouch for you 'here' or 'there'?"

"Probably." Dermot scratched his ear, rubbed his hand over the top of his shaved head. "Mates, bouncers." His fingers traced the length of the lightning flash marked out under the stubble.

Sam nodded to PC Elliot. "We'll get a note of where was 'here' and where was 'there' when we're done. Right?"

"If I can remember."

Sam smiled. "Oh, I think you'll remember, son. Don't you? If you set your mind to it?"

"Hmmh."

"Who were you with?"

"Look, what is this? Am I being fingered for something?"

"Summer? Were you with Summer Friday night?"

58

"Look, I telt ye. No."

"Meet up with her outside school Thursday? Friday?"

"Look, ye're no listening. Me an Sunshine, we dinnae talk anymair. Why would I want tae meet up wi' her?" Just as he turned away with a dismissive gesture of his shoulders, the toast popped up. Dermot jumped and clutched his chest.

"Oh, aye," Sam said. "Thought that was a gun, did you, son?"

"It jist gave me a fright."

"And why would that be, eh? Something to hide? Something you're not telling us?"

"It was jist the toaster."

"Well I know that, son. But it didn't make me jump. Did it make you jump, PC Elliot?"

Elliot looked up from the steaming kettle he had in his hands, halted in the act of pouring hot water into the teapot. "No." He shook his head. "Didn't bother me."

"Ah jist wisnae expecting it, like."

Sam moved towards the kitchen door. "Mind if we take a look around?"

"Aye ah mind! Ma mother's in her bed. Ye'll scare the life oot o' her."

"You'd best go wake her up then, eh?"

"Dae ye no need a warrant for searchin'?"

Sam put his hands up and smiled. "Only if you don't show us round, son. Why? Is there something you don't want us to find?"

Dermot shrugged. "Naw." He stood aside. "Be my guest. Jist dinnae bother ma Ma."

Chapter Five

It rained all night.

Mirabelle lay listening as heavy showers battered against her window, and feelings of helplessness battered her soul. It was so hard just to lie here, unable to do anything while someone you love might need your help. Her mind flitted between thoughts of her daughter and thoughts of her father. Both hidden from her, possibly vulnerable, in need of her help.

She felt adrift in the sea of her own emotions, rudderless, unable to steer towards either of them. Anchor-less, unable to be content without them.

Sleep driven away, she gathered the duvet round her and stood in the dark watching for moving shadows, watching the rain curtain the street lights, tracing the drops that ran down the other side of the glass.

So much water, the kind that stings, that soaks through clothes, making them heavy and cold. That reddens the nose and deadens the fingers. That bruises treetops and flattens snowdrops. Ice in it, needle-sharp.

It wasn't a night you'd want to be a cat or a cow left out to prowl or pasture.

Who was waiting when Summer slipped through the flap?

Was she safe? Was she being fed? Being cared for? This Dermot boy didn't sound the caring type, but at least if Summer was with *him*, she'd be with *someone* and possibly warm and dry.

Steady rain drummed on car bonnets, sprayed from tyres, puddled gutters.

But, if she wasn't with him, then where was she? Who was she with?

Mirabelle adjusted her position, resting her face against the cold glass, listening to the rain so close to her cheek she could almost feel it pock her skin. She stayed like that until the side of her face felt flat and cold. A shiver ran through her and she hugged the duvet closer.

Was Summer cold? Was she dry? What coat was she wearing?

Seized with a need to know if her daughter was adequately clothed for the weather, Mirabelle abandoned her window vigil, letting the duvet fall in a frilly, floral snowdrift and rushed to the closet in the hall. She raked through the coats and scarves and assorted rags and tags hanging there.

She herself hated coats, never wore one: too restrictive, too formal. Instead, no matter the weather, she would wrap a poncho or some soft, colourful material around her shoulders. Two layers if it was cold, three if it was colder. When heavy with rain, she'd hang them around the house to dry: multi-hued banners proclaiming her artless individuality. When the fringes frayed and tattered, she'd discard the shawl and use another. The same with bags. The ones she favoured were large and fancy, made from canvas or linen, always bright and soft, the kind she imagined Jamaican women might carry for transporting mangoes, papaya and other exotic fruits home from market. She stuffed them full with her treats and treasures, rummaged through them for papers she'd filed in their depths then hang them behind her bedroom door when worn into holes and no longer useful.

The coats in the closet all belonged to Summer. Mirabelle tried to work out which one was missing. Damn! Not the waterproof. There it was, slick and shiny, mocking her from the cupboard. But why would Summer have taken her waterproof coat? The one Mirabelle found in the Cancer Care shop. The one Summer refused to wear.

"Mum! It's pink! It's meant for a kid. Look! There's love-heart pockets on it, for crying out loud." She stuffed her hands in them and pulled the coat away from her body.

"But it fits you."

"So? A bin bag would fit me. Doesn't mean I want to wear one." She unbuttoned the offending garment and handed it back to Mirabelle. "Thanks. But no thanks."

No, she didn't take the waterproof.

Or the anorak provided a couple of years ago from a similar source.

"Nice one, Mum! I'm fifteen, remember? Not fifty! No wonder the shop's called flamin' Help The Aged."

It hung beside the waterproof, its muddy purple brightened by its neighbour.

As far as Mirabelle could see, all that was missing was what Summer always wore. The only thing Mirabelle had bought for a long time at full price, brand new, from a high street store: her blue denim jacket.

Blue denim bruised to black if she had no shelter.

It rained all night.

Mirabelle's bed was hardly slept in when Sam came by in the morning, after he'd spoken to Dermot, and Lena had gone.

"What d'you mean does she do drugs? Of course she doesn't do drugs. Summer knows how I feel about the whole drug thing." Mirabelle threw down the box of teabags she had in her hand.

Sam side-stepped as teabags cascaded and flapped to the floor at his feet. "Calm down, Belle. I'm only asking."

She picked up a spoon and wagged it at him, rings glinting, bracelets scurrying down her arm to hide in her loose sleeves. "You know nothing about my daughter. Nothing! How dare you come in here and suggest she was on drugs."

"I didn't Belle. I was only asking."

"You were only asking if she could have been taking drugs."

"Yes, but I wasn't saying she *was*. Just that it was a possibility. She'd been hanging out with …"

The spoon was pointed straight at him. "Well I'm telling you it's not a possibility."

"This guy she's been seeing …"

"*And* she hasn't been seeing any guy." She stirred the tea, the vigorous motion slopping it over the mug.

"You don't know that, Belle. You can't possibly know that. You're not with her every minute of the day."

"I *do* know that. She would have told me." The soggy teabag hit the sink with a muted splash.

"Another thing I have to ask …"

Mirabelle held out the mug of tea.

"Thanks." He took it from her and looked for somewhere to put it. Gathering up a pile of junk mail and stacking it on top of more of the same, he made room on the table beside him. "Did Summer have a computer?"

"What's that to do with anything?"

He sighed. "Just, was she on any of the social networking sites or anything?"

Mirabelle pulled a face. "Doubt it. She knows I disapprove of these things. They're dangerous. Cause a lot of trouble. People can say anything and you've no way of checking it's the truth." She moved the days-old, dried-up sponge cake to another part of the table and put her cup down.

"Thought so." He sat down. "You really won't know that, will you?"

"What are you talking about?" Mirabelle sat opposite him.

"You'll not know if she was using social media."

"Like I said, she knew I disapproved."

Sam opened his mouth, then seemed to think better of it and closed it. Shaking his head, and sighing, "Do you have internet access in the house?" he asked instead.

"Through the phone company. Yes." She shrugged. "Summer said she needed it." Mirabelle poked at the cake, her finger making a hole in the dry sponge. "School projects and things, she said."

"So, you're saying you don't know if was Summer on Facebook or Twitter or anything like that? Did she chat to her friends online at all?"

"That I don't know either. You'd have to ask them. I always just assumed she was on the phone anytime I heard her chatting with them."

Sam did the fish impersonation again, opening and closing his mouth. "Right," he said, controlling his smile. "I'll take her computer when I go. Okay?"

She shrugged, not curious enough about what he nearly said to bother asking, and nodded.

"I'll get someone to check what she's been up to online."

64

"Whatever." She shrugged again. "Didn't know you could do that. Makes you think. If all your calls on the internet are recorded, it's like Big Brother listening in, monitoring all your conversations, isn't it?" She shuddered. "That's why I don't like computers."

This time, Sam smiled. "It's not quite like that, Belle. When I say she chats with her friends online, I don't mean she actually talks to them."

"Make up your mind, then. Do they chat or don't they?"

"It's messages. They type messages back and forth."

"Oh! Of course. I suppose I did know that. Just wasn't thinking."

He shook his head. "I really can't believe in this day and age ..."

"Anyone could be so ignorant?"

"Well, I wouldn't have put it quite like that."

"But it's what you meant. Told you. Don't like it. Causes too much trouble. I do what I have to for work, emails and stuff, leave the rest to the admin." She waved her hand, dismissing the undesired technology. "If I want to socialise, I'll meet someone and talk face-to-face, thank you very much." She took a sip of her tea. "Ouch! Too hot." She pushed the mug of tea away then looked up at Sam, the meaning of his words belatedly registering in her brain. "Anyway, what are you talking about? What could Summer have been up to online?"

"She might have talked to her friends about things she would've found hard to talk to you about."

"Meaning?" Mirabelle was on her feet, reaching for the milk. "She knew she could talk to me about anything, anything at all." She slopped some into her tea and onto the table around it.

"Kids seem to find it easier to open up on these sites. No holds barred with their friends."

She slapped down the carton of milk and leant across the table. "I told you, she knew she could talk to me. No holds barred."

"She might've said something about planning to run away, the boyfriend, whatever."

"She didn't."

"Plan to run away? Or talk about it to her friends?"

"Either. I'd've known." Mirabelle walked over to the worktop beside the sink, snatching up the dishcloth.

"Talk about the boyfriend? Or have one in the first place?"

"How many times do I have to say it?" Mirabelle turned back and leant down, putting her face close to Sam's. She spoke very slowly and carefully and with a lot of emphasis. "I would have known."

Sam sat perfectly still and stared her down. "But you don't know, Belle." His voice was soft, calm. "You don't even know if she was on Facebook."

Mirabelle straightened up, threw her hands in the air, her bracelets ricocheting down her arms. "We talk about everything."

"When, Belle? When would that be?"

"We do." She turned away, busying herself with tidying the tea things away, wiping the worktop. "Of course we do."

"I don't doubt you do talk, Belle. You're good at it."

She threw the dishcloth into the sink as she swung round. "What's that supposed to mean?"

Sam got up and stepped towards her.

She looked away, snatched up the dishcloth again, wringing the water out of it, her face set and angry.

He reached to touch her arm, to turn her back to look at him. "Only that you love to talk. You're a great story teller. You know how to entertain." He paused. "But, I just wonder, do you know how to *listen*?"

"I'm a social worker. Of course I know how to listen!"

"When was the last time you sat down and listened to Summer about what was on her mind?"

Her body crumpled into a chair, the beads still clutched in her hand. Heavy air entered her chest.

"I don't mean to be cruel, but you said yourself you work

too hard. Never home till late. Never here for Summer. How would you know what she was doing, Belle? How would you know?"

"I'd … I'd just *know*."

Sam sat down again. "You think you would. Every parent thinks they would know whether their kid has a boyfriend, where they go with their friends, whether they're doing drugs. But, the fact is, they don't. Most of them have no idea what their kids are up to."

"Meaning?"

"Meaning, Summer might've had a boyfriend, might've been experimenting with drugs, might've told her pals she was going to leave home."

Mirabelle put her hands over her ears. "Summer hasn't left home. She's missing. Lost. She hasn't run away."

"We don't know that yet."

"*I* know that! And, anyway, why would she choose *now* to run away? She's just been accepted to uni. She's just got what she wanted."

"What *she* wanted? Or what *you* wanted for her?"

Mirabelle's eyes flashed. "Like I said, you know *nothing* about my daughter, Sam Burns. *Nothing!* And you know nothing about what she, or I, want."

"She was seeing this guy who hangs around the school gates. Her pals gave us his name. They reckon she's been going out with him."

"They've made that up."

"Why? Why would they make that up?"

"Drama. Teenage girls love a bit of drama." She was up again, pacing the kitchen. "I don't believe them." She felt for her knicker elastic through the folds of her dress and pulled the offending garment to a more comfortable position.

"She's been seeing him, Belle."

She wet the dishcloth.

Wrung it out.

Wiped the worktop, scrubbing at it hard.

She threw the dishcloth into the sink, water spraying up.

"He's lying."

Sam shrugged. "He's known to us, Belle. He's no good. Dangerous to a young girl like Summer. Been picked up before for possession. He's into drugs."

Mirabelle turned away, her shoulders dropping. She reached behind for the edge of the chair and lowered herself into it. "That doesn't have to mean Summer is."

"No, it doesn't." Sam drew his chair over to sit closer, reaching forward to touch her hand. "But it *could*."

She drew her hand away. "So what's next?"

"Next, Lena talks to her friends again. See what they're *not* saying." Sam sat back and sighed.

"I could do that."

"What?"

"I could talk to her friends."

"Oh, I don't think ..." He leant forward again.

Mirabelle stared him down. "Summer is *my* daughter. These are *her* friends. I know them. I'd know if they're holding something back."

"But ..."

"No buts." Mirabelle stood up and walked to the door. "No offence to Lena. She's a good friend and a good polis, but, I'll do better with these kids. You know I will."

Sam raised his hands in acquiescence as he also stood up. "Okay, Belle. Okay. You may be right."

"No." She turned to face him. "I *am* right. You know I am."

"Well, I can't stop you talking to them, Belle. But as far as I'm concerned, we're investigating the disappearance of a young girl, and my officers will be interviewing her friends."

more than she wanted to know

Mirabelle knew a lot of things: she knew she'd have to dig deeper, push harder than Lena probably would when questioning Summer's friends. Teenage girls can be incredibly loyal to their friends, stunningly cruel to their enemies. But she reckoned she was a match for them. Through the years, she'd got to know some of them pretty well — or so she thought.

She soon found out the kids who say 'Please!' and 'Thank you!' are the same ones who shrug and pull a face when put on the spot. The teenage girls who traipse through your kitchen on their way to your daughter's room via the biscuit barrel only let you see what they think you want to see: nice polite girls, suitable company for your own teenage tyrant. You don't really *know* them. Mirabelle began to doubt even their mothers really *knew* them.

Certainly, she was fast realising she didn't know Summer. Oh, she knew the minutiae of her life, more or less, but she realised now she didn't know the big stuff. Now, hitherto unsuspected facts rained on her like bullets.

Seems Summer was no longer the quiet, compliant little girl waiting at home for Mum, living by the rules of her mother's preaching.

"You're saying she hung out with this boy. What does that mean? What does hung out mean?"

Shana shrugged. "You know. He was like, sort of, like, her boyfriend for a while."

"And what does that mean? She went on dates with him? To the cinema? For walks?" Mirabelle threw her hands in the air.

"Och, you know."

"No. I'm asking."

"Look, I'm sorry, Mrs Milligan. I'm sorry you're so angry. I didn't know you didn't know."

"So tell me. What kind of relationship did my daughter have with this slime-bag?"

"You know. The usual kind of thing." Shana picked at the sleeve of her cardigan, pushing her body deeper into the chair, turning away from Mirabelle.

"Like?"

She shrugged again, looking down at her lap, tears glistening on her lashes.

Mirabelle saw them and a little of the fire went out of her. "I'm sorry, Shana, pet. You know it's not you I'm angry with, don't you? It's just, well, I'm worried. In fact, I'm crazy-scared. Don't know what to think. What to do." She was pacing from the window to the door and back again, stopping at the window, looking out, almost expecting to see Summer coming to call for her friend. Listening at the door, hoping for the knock. Now she sat down opposite Shana. "I'm sorry," she said again. "There. I'm calmer now. Please, tell me about this boy Summer was seeing."

Shana rewarded her penitence with a watery smile. "You know she'd chucked him, like?"

"Yes, Sam told me. So how long had she been going out with this boy?"

"He wasn't really a boy."

Mirabelle sighed and wiped a hand across her forehead. "Sam said. He's what? About twenty-five, twenty-six?"

Shana nodded. "But she's not seeing him any more, like."

"And you're sure about that?'

"Well I think so, like. She chucked him."

"Yeah, you said. But before that. What did they do?"

"Dunno. Snogged, I s'pose."

"Snogged?"

"You know, Kissing and stuff."

"Yeah! I do know, and it's the 'and stuff' I'm worried

about."

Shana ducked her head.

Mirabelle leant back in the seat and passed a hand over her forehead, wiping the clamminess from it onto the skirt of her dress. Taking a deep breath, "Is that all they did?" she asked.

"S'pose. And they went dancing and stuff. You know, in clubs and that."

"Clubs!" Mirabelle was up again, another bullet striking home. "What kind of clubs?"

"You know, nightclubs and that."

"Nightclubs?" She paced. "Nightclubs? She's only seventeen." Stopped in front of Shana. "How could she have been going to nightclubs?"

"We … she…"

"You? You as well?"

Shana put her hand to her mouth. "Oh, please don't tell my mum. She'll kill me."

"Of course I'm going to tell your mum. In fact, *you're* going to tell your mum. Have you any idea the danger you've been putting yourselves in?"

She started to cry. "Please. I can't. I don't go any more. Not after, not after …"

"Not after what?"

"Not after Summer had the fight with Drae. He got us thrown out. He grassed us. Told the bouncer we were under-age."

"When was this?"

"Two, three weeks ago."

"How could you be going to clubs without me knowing? Without your parents knowing?"

"Summer told you she was staying at mine and I told Mum I was staying at yours."

"How long had this been going on?"

Shana shrugged, pulling a face. "I don't know. Maybe … about a year?"

Mirabelle stood, staring at the girl in front of her as

71

though she'd never seen her before. "This is unbelievable! Incredible!" She shook her head, feeling the bullet burn in her chest. "I can't believe this. I just can't believe it."

"I'm sorry, Mrs Milligan. I'm really, really sorry." Tears were flowing now, coursing down Shana's anguished face. "I didn't know anything would happen to her. Honest, I didn't know."

Chapter Six

It used to be Mirabelle's idea of a good night out: loud music, flashing lights, too much to drink. Though she still loved dancing, she now preferred it to be less frenetic. And she liked to remember she'd done it.

The nightclub was heaving, strobe lighting picking out bodies gyrating in ritualistic, tribal war dance. Another nightclub, different décor, same scene. She had been spending every evening visiting the local nightclubs. This was the third she'd tried tonight. Friday night, a week since Summer had gone missing, possibly her best chance to find someone who'd remember seeing her, assuming many of them would be regular Friday night customers. She moved among the dancers, Summer's photograph in her hand. "Have You Seen My Daughter?" she asked. "It's okay. She's not in trouble. I just need to contact her. Have you seen her?"

Those who bothered to notice, shook their heads, pulled negative faces, turned away. She could have been offering gold, it would have made no difference. They were living in a world beyond her reach, their eyes red-rimmed and glazed. "Have You Seen My Daughter?" she begged anyway. "She used to come here. You might have noticed her. Long hair?" She touched her head. "Not curly like mine." She'd laugh. "And not black. Red. Redder than it looks in the photograph. Quite distinctive."

There were few things Mirabelle felt like doing these past few days: dancing was not one of them. But dance she did. Wanting to fit in, gain credibility, release any inhibitions remaining in those she moved among, hoping their memories could be jogged to recognition. Dancing the only way she knew how, with arms snaking and weaving as her overweight body twisted and turned, she could close her eyes and imagine the look of embarrassment on Summer's face if she saw the out-dated moves, the clumsy lack of co-ordination.

When the beat began to bore her and she became increasingly aware she'd need to do more than wobble around a bit to fit in with this these people, she bought a soft drink and sipped it as she sauntered between the tables, showing her photograph, asking her question: "Please! Have You Seen My Daughter?"

If anyone had, what would it have proved? That Summer had been there weeks ago? She knew that already. Knew too she was engaged in a pointless exercise, born out of desperation.

With heavy heart, Mirabelle took her warm wrap from the back of the chair where she'd left it and headed for fresh air. Pausing at the door, she looked back one last time, scanning the tables and the dance floor before she turned away with a sigh and stepped outside into the night.

"Hey, Mirabelle! What you doing here? Not your usual scene." The huge hand laid in friendship on her shoulder could have crushed it in anger.

"Hey, Robbie. Long time no see."

"Was down the club the other night. Got to thinking about your dad." Robbie, the nightclub's doorman, shook his head. "The best."

"Yeah? Haven't seen him since I was a wee girl."

"Went back home, d'you think?"

Mirabelle pulled a face. "Think so. According to my mother anyway. But I've not been able to find any record of him leaving the country."

"Bit young, weren't you to check that out?"

She smiled. "Well, I was at the time, but I started trying to trace him once I was old enough."

"Any joy?"

"Nothing." She fingered the beads that lay on her chest.

"Gone now you reckon though, eh? Got back into the ring, rumour was?"

Mirabelle nodded, holding the beads close against her.

"One fight too many, they tell me? Haemorrhage?"

"That's the rumour, Robbie," Mirabelle said. "But I've no proof of that either. If he did fight again, I've no idea where or when. Wish I could find who started the rumour, get more details from them. Any idea who told you?"

He shook his head. "Too long ago, Belle." He tapped his forehead. "Memory's gone."

"No bother." She touched his arm.

Robbie looked at his feet and shuffled for a bit.

Mirabelle pulled her wrap closer round her shoulders, preparing to go.

"So, what you doing here?"

She reached into her bag and brought out the photograph again. "I'm looking for my daughter, Robbie. You seen her?"

He shook his head. "Not tonight, Belle. Mind, I wasn't here till later. She could've gone in before my shift on the door."

"Yeah. Don't see her though."

"Let me get another look at that picture." He took it from Mirabelle's hand and held it to the flickering light flashing from the doorway of the club. "That your girl, Belle? Seen her before. It's the red hair I remember. Like my mum's used to be."

"You've seen her?"

Robbie closed his eyes and put his mammoth hand to his forehead. "Give us a minute, Belle. Let me think." He put all his concentration into the exercise. "Got it!" he said, clicking his fingers, the sound a deep thud of flesh on flesh. "Underage, isn't she?"

"Fraid so, Robbie."

"Thought so." He handed back the photograph. She's the one used to come here with Big-shot. Sorry, Belle. Didn't know she was your daughter. I threw her out a few weeks ago."

"Please! Don't be sorry. Just wish you'd never let her in."

"He vouched for her you see. Big-shot."

"Big-shot?"

"Aye. That's what all the bouncers call him. No sure what he cries hisself, but we call him Big-shot. He's such a pain in the backside. Swans about like he's somebody."

"Skinny guy? Shaved head? Lightning tattoo on his scalp? Wears a short, black leather jacket?"

"Sounds like." Robbie nodded. "You know him?"

"Sort of. Not personally, but had him described to me."

Robbie shook his head. "You want to watch your girl with that one, Belle. He's a piece of filth thinks he's clever." He cursed and spat on the pavement. "Carries more than his wallet."

"Yeah, I heard. You saw him with Summer?" The beads were cool in her hand, something to hold on to as her world slipped out of balance.

"Quite a few times. Bit of a regular. Told me she was nineteen. Had an identification card an' all. Had to throw her out one night. Coupla weeks back. Been drinking. Sorry, Belle. Don't suppose you want to hear this."

"It's okay. On you go. Maybe I don't want to hear it, but I think I need to all the same."

"Aye, well. She'd been drinking, and more I suspect. Started to get loud, cursing and swearing. Look, you sure you want to hear this?"

"If I don't, it won't mean it didn't happen."

"Just, you don't look too tidy about it."

"It's okay. On you go. She was cursing and swearing." Mirabelle closed her eyes, her hand flat against her chest, pushing the rows of beads hard against the pain, unable to even begin to picture the scene: her lovely, sweet Summer, drunk and foul-mouthed. She shuddered. Not that she hadn't heard her swear before. But Mirabelle always thought it was just something brought home from school by mistake, not belonging to her, not part of what she was about.

"Yeah. Then she threw up over his shoes. He fair screamed at her. 'You've barfed on my new trainers,' he yelled. Allie and me, we was on the doors that night, we were loving it. Till he hit her. Smacked her right in the face, so he did."

Mirabelle flinched, clutched at the beads.

"We cut in then. Sent them both packing. 'She's only seventeen!' he telt us. 'She shouldnae be here. And she shouldnae be drinking.' We was going to get the polis to them, but her pal came and pulled her away, said she'd see her home, so we left them to it. Threw a coupla buckets water over the pavement to clean up the mess. Haven't seen her since. Mind, you might want to try The Blue Chip Casino. You know the one? Down off the Road?"

Mirabelle leant against the wall, letting the cool brick absorb some of the heat of her shame. She felt such a fool. To have known her daughter so little. To have assumed she would be wise just because she told her to be. To have assumed what she saw was all there was to be seen. Another bullet exploded in her chest.

"You all right, Belle? Want me to call you a cab or something?"

She shook her head. "Thanks, Robbie. I'd rather walk. Need the air. Just need a minute."

"She okay? Your girl?"

She knew the bouncers at The Blue Chip too. They'd all known her dad.

He'd worked his way from Jamaica in his twenties, come to seek his fortune as a fighter. He'd heard there was a strong boxing fraternity in Scotland, thought he'd try his fists as an amateur, hoping to be spotted by one of the big promoters. And he did well at first. Won a few big bouts, was drawing a bit of attention. Then he met and married Mirabelle's mother and lost his concentration and one too many fights, took one too many punches to the head. *"Made me a bit forgetful,"* he'd explain. *"Keep repeatin' meself. Keep repeatin' meself,"* a twinkle of mischief lighting his eyes.

He turned to coaching other young hopefuls in the 'noble art,' trying to content himself with the role but missing the blood and sweat of participation. He taught Mirabelle the rudiments of the game, letting her swing her tiny padded fists at his jaw, falling prostrate from his knees to the floor, counting to ten, allowing her to feel the jubilation of victory. She still felt it rise in her breast with the memory.

He taught her to play the kettle-drum too, his fists flattened out into instruments of beauty, the same speed of hand and grace of movement employed in a more rhythmic pursuit. His intention had been to play and sing in pubs and clubs to fund his fighting, and he did for a while, but he found he was unwelcome, his music unappreciated. Once he married, he stacked shelves in the supermarket instead.

When Mirabelle was a toddler, he took her along with him to the gym of an evening, where he trained what he called 'de up-an-comers.' An unusual environment in which to nurture a child, but better than the option of the pub with her disenchanted mother. As Mirabelle grew from toddler to girl, the boys became men and she made firm friends in the boxing fraternity, friends she never lost and could still call on for help and information. She was still welcome in the gym, though she seldom lingered long there. Unlike her father, or perhaps because of him, she was no lover of pugilism or any other violence.

They had been on their way home, late one evening, Mirabelle and her dad. She remembers yet the song she was skipping along to: "Mary, Mary, quite contrary," she lisped, her eyes over-bright the way it is with children out too late at night. They were going to fetch her mother home too.

"You wait here, me flower," he said at the door of the pub.

She was jumping on and off the doorstep in time to her song when two men rolled out of the door. She drew into the shadows, hoping not to be seen, instinctively afraid of their drunken voices.

"Aw, hen," one of them said. "Gonna gie us a wee dance?"

She drew further back.

"C'mon, hen." He did a wobbling step or two of a jig, grabbing her arm, pulling her into his embrace. "Gie's a wee dance. You lot are supposed tae be guid at the dancin'. Nat'ral rhythm yer supposed tae have." He didn't see her father come through the door at his back, didn't see the punch that landed squarely on his jaw as he turned in response to the tap on his shoulder.

Fortunately, the man recovered or Mirabelle's father would have been on trial for manslaughter. As it was, because he was a boxer, her father's fist was designated 'a deadly weapon' and he served two years in prison for Serious Assault. Too young to understand why her father was taken from her, she felt lost and abandoned, missing his company and his music as well as his care and protection. Every night, she pulled out his kettle-drum from its corner and dusted it down, longing for his hands to caress and thrum a tune from it, until her mother snatched it from her and delivered it to the pawnshop: *"At least the damn neighbours'll be happy,"* she muttered. *"Bad enough you've got his colour. Ye can do without his music."*

That was when Mirabelle first realised she was different.

Her father had brought his culture and his music to Edinburgh at a time when Edinburgh had not learned to loosen its stays. He didn't hang around long after he was released from prison: his wife having decided he was not worth waiting two years for; his bed occupied by her latest boyfriend, and his spirit dull and disillusioned. His aura stayed longer and lived on in Mirabelle.

When she was old enough, Mirabelle tried to trace her father, longing to reconnect with him. As far as she understood from her mother, he had 'scuttled back home to his mammy' in Jamaica. It was always said with such derision that Mirabelle stopped asking after a while, hating to see the sneer on her mother's face. He deserved better.

When she was alive, her mother hinted at further trouble, but refused to explain what she meant, saying only, "Good riddance to bad rubbish." He deserved better.

It had been difficult to get information from Jamaica without going there and Mirabelle lacked the money and the time to make the trip, but as far as she could find out, there was no record of him going back there. Nor could she find him on census forms or anywhere else here. Rumours abounded: her mother, Rose, had killed him; he'd fallen from the boat on the way to Jamaica; he'd killed a man, and was in hiding, and most ridiculous of all, he had become a millionaire and was living a life of luxury in Barbados.

Whatever the truth, Mirabelle felt sure it was none of those.

Her biggest fear was, not that he had died, but that he was alone, unloved and lonely. He deserved better.

Many of the lads he'd coached became bouncers: doormen at the various clubs and casinos of Edinburgh's night-life. They remembered him fondly and regretted he was no longer around. Remembered too, the bright wee girl who used to hide behind his legs, though it must now be more than thirty years ago. Mirabelle had been their mascot then and became their champion now, helping them out with life's bigger bouts.

She'd been Davy Eskdale's social worker when his wife left him and his kids five years back. He hadn't forgotten her kindness and his face showed his delight when he saw her approach the casino. "Mirabelle! Cold one the night." He rubbed his hands together to warm them a little before he offered one in greeting. "You coming in?"

"No, Davy. Least, I don't think so."

"Didn't have you down as a gambler."

Mirabelle shook her head. "No, thanks. Not me."

"What can I do you for then?"

She brought out Summer's photo. "Any chance you've seen this girl? She in tonight?"

He took the picture. "Red?" He pointed to her long, wavy red hair. "Gorgeous that. Fiery." His face folded in on itself in concentration. "Comes in pretty reg'lar. Doubt she's the age she claims." He shook his head. "Kids get false ID cards easy these days. Too many o' them clever wi' computers and the like, ken. Flash their cards as they go by in a crowd an' it's hard tae tell."

"Not in tonight, though?"

"Nup. No the night. She was in last Friday but, ken."

"You sure?"

"Pretty much. Aye. Must've been last week, ken."

"You remember her?"

"Red?" He winked. "Always remember a pretty face, especially one I had to throw out."

"You had to throw her out?"

"Aye! These young lassies cannae haud their bevy, ken? Make a right fool o' theirsels."

"She'd been drinking?"

"And some. Turned up here ready for trouble. No good for custom. Punters get put off. Like to think they're more sophisticated than that. I sent her packing."

Ice-cold prickles down her spine made Mirabelle shiver. Last Friday, the Friday Summer disappeared. "Don't suppose you saw where she went?" She could hardly get the words out. Her teeth rattled together, her tongue froze to her palate.

"Wandered off." He shrugged.

"Was she alone?"

"Bunch o' guys hanging round her. Waitin' to see who'd get takin' her home, maybe." Broken teeth and golden fillings flashed in a lop-sided grin. "She one o' your clients down the Social Work?"

Mirabelle couldn't move, couldn't speak. The pain in her chest took her breath and twisted it four different ways. Davy's aftershave was acrid in her nostrils as he leant to support her.

"You okay, Mirabelle? Not going to faint, are ye?" His woollen jacket was rough against her face, his hand cold on her neck. "Hey girl. You okay?" He cradled her against him, taking her weight easily as he whistled for a taxi.

taxi for vernon

One of his mates from the boxing had brought Vernon home in a taxi. When her dad was released, his mate was the one who took Mirabelle to meet him at the gate, who wrapped his muscles round him in a bear-hug, and paid for the taxi to take them home. "Aye, yer welcome, man," his reply when Vernon tried to thank him. "We had a whip round down the club," he said, handing Vernon a bag of new clothes and a pair of shoes. "Jimmy says tae tell ye, there's a job waiting for ye down the gym. No much, like, just sweeping up and that, but enough tae get ye back on yer feet."

The kindness overwhelmed Vernon and he nodded his thanks, tears straying from the corners of his eyes.

"Look after yer da'," the mate said as he closed the taxi door and waved the driver off.

Look after yer da'.

Oh, that she had been old enough. Oh, that she had understood, had warned him, had seen the inevitable result of his homecoming. But she was a child, and, with a child's innocent enthusiasm she had ushered him in and presented him to her mother.

Rose looked over the rim of a glass and swore.

The letter announcing his release lay unopened on the sideboard along with every other letter he had written in two years.

When Vernon stepped towards her with his arms open for her embrace, she hurled the glass at him, its amber liquid soaking his clothes as it emptied when it hit his chest.

Vernon hurried Mirabelle from the room and, taking the few coins he had in his pocket, he put them in her hand and *sent her to fetch him some chips.*

When she came home, he was gone, her mother too. The house was empty, the bag of new clothes lying on its side in a corner of the couch, the new shoes standing to attention on the floor beside it.

Mirabelle waited in silent expectation until the room was cold and dark, and she fell asleep on the couch, her head on the clothes, clasping the cold, greasy chips to her chest.

She never saw her father again, and her mother had nothing to say about what had taken place while Mirabelle ran the three blocks to the chippie, took her place in the queue, and ran back with a bag of chips for her father's homecoming celebration dinner.

Sam followed up the slim lead Mirabelle uncovered at the casino, questioning Davy again the next night.

"Red? Gone missing. That's a sod, eh?" Davy scratched his head and handed back the photograph. "Nice looking kid."

"The men who watched her leave?"

"Aye, well, they were hanging about outside, ken."

"Did they follow her?"

Davy shrugged. "Look, I had other things to see to. After I threw Red out, there was others needin' sorted."

"But did they seem to be waiting for the girl?"

"Dunno. They was watching her, that I know. Waiting for her?" He shrugged again. "Who's to say?"

"And you didn't see if they followed her?"

"Maybes aye, maybes naw. Like I say, I had other stuff going on, ken."

"But you think they might've followed her?"

"Aye, maybes. They had a bit o' a crack with her, like. I saw that. One of them wis helping her walk, last I saw."

"She went with them?"

Davy looked round, stepped in closer to Sam. "Look! I dinnae want to get anybody in bother. But, aye, she went with them. In as much as I saw them move off with her. After that corner," he pointed to the end of the building, "your guess is as good as mine."

"That the last you saw of them?"

"More or less."

Sam waited.

"One of them came back in later. Back into the tables, like."

"Name?"

Davy pulled a face. "No good wi' names. Just faces."

"He a regular?"

He nodded. "He's in the night."

"Show me."

Davy whistled and another bouncer appeared from inside the casino. "Watch the door," he told him. "Back in two shakes."

Sam followed Davy inside. The evening's entertainment was in progress: a female singer making a tolerable job of a blues number Sam was unfamiliar with. Few of her audience seemed captivated by her performance. Most were engrossed in their play. There was a bit of movement over by the bar and Sam couldn't quite see what was going on, but it looked like someone was trying to pay his tab, the barman taking his time getting to the customer. Sam decided that's where he needed to be. Find out who was in a hurry to leave and why. He'd often found his entrance precipitated someone else's exit. Always interesting.

By the time he reached the bar, the transaction had been completed and the customer had slipped away unseen.

Sam held his badge for inspection. "Guy just here, where'd he go?" he asked the barman.

He shook his head. "No idea. Back to the tables?"

"Description?"

The barman pulled a face. "Wasn't paying attention. Just a guy."

"Rewind, pay attention, have a think about it. Right?"

"Got it," the barman said in response to the look on Sam's face.

"Right!" Sam slapped his hand on the bar and turned to survey the room.

Davy walked through the main room, scanned the tables, went into every alcove, every side room. "Nuthin'. Punter's gone," he informed Sam as he joined him at the bar.

"Damn!" He turned back to the bartender. "Captured the memory?" he asked. "Description?"

"Close-cropped hair, black leather jacket, nothing remarkable. Except he didn't wait for his change." He held up a twenty pound note.

"His tab?"

"Twelve quid."

"Good tip? Better than usual?"

"You bet. He's not known for his generosity."

"A regular, then?"

The barman shrugged. "Could be."

"Is there another door?" Sam asked Davy. "Somewhere he could get out without passing you?"

"Fire exit, s'pose."

They made their way through between the tables to a corridor at the back where the toilets were.

The urinals were in use, but Davy shook his head. "Nane o' them," he said.

They pushed open each stall door in turn, but they were all empty.

The last of the men at the urinals was zipping up and scurrying away.

"Hey!" Sam shouted.

The guy turned, his eyes large, caught in the headlights.

"Don't forget to wash your hands," Sam said with a smile as he walked past him to go out the door.

Having checked the toilets, there was nowhere else left, so they spoke to the bouncer who guarded the back exit.

"Anyone leave by this fire door?" Sam asked him.

"Aye. Ten minutes ago? Lad wi' a splittin' headache. Reckoned he couldnae take the lights. Asked tae get oot here. Ah checked wi' the boss." He held up a two-way radio. "Naeb'dy doing a runner, so ah let him oot."

"Description?"

"Skinny, shaved head sorta growing out, know what I mean, stubbly? Leather jacket."

"Aye," Davy turned to Sam. "Yon's yer guy."

"Okay. Thanks. I'll get someone over from the station. See if we can mock up a decent picture between you two and the barman."

"We done?" Davy asked.

Sam interviewed one or two of the casino regulars as he wove back through the place, but the trail fizzled out. No-one owned to having seen the unidentified man, either tonight or any other night. Neither had any of them seen Summer last Friday night after she staggered away from the door, a predatory pack hot on her heels.

Vernon
sunk without a trace

Vernon never appeared down the gym to take up the proffered job. When Mirabelle tried to find him there in the days and weeks following his release, there was no sign of him. When she asked his mates if they'd seen him, they had no idea what to say to her other than tell her the truth. No-one knew what happened to Vernon after she left her home to fetch him something to eat.

No-one heard word of him, nor caught sight of him since then. They must have been relieved when she stopped looking in every day on her way home from school, her anxious brown eyes pleading with them for news they couldn't provide.

"Ye've a new dad now," her mother said, nodding in the direction of the boyfriend who had already supplanted her father. Paddy was an ugly man to start with, but his face had been well mashed in some fight or other, though he wasn't a boxer or any other sort of athlete by the look of his paunch and weedy arms. The red and black track of recent stitches did nothing to enhance his slack jaw and rubbery mouth.

'Uncle Paddy' had moved his kit in weeks before her dad had come home. Mirabelle had expected him to remove it that day. Instead, he had brought another case-full, his record collection and his football boots. "Aye!' He winked at her mother. "Yer old man's in the river. Sunk without trace," he laughed.

Worst of all, he wore the new shoes.

Chapter Seven

Monday. "That's close enough for me," Sam said, throwing down the identikit picture. "Elliot!" he shouted from his office door. "You, me, car."

"Where to, sir?"

"Think it's time for another chat with Mr Dermot Wilson." Sam tapped the picture on his desk. "Looks like he was holding back a bit of information from us."

This time, when they caught up with Dermot, they brought him in to the station for their chat.

"You arrestin' me or what? What'm ah s'posed to've done?"

"Just some questions, son. Just a chat."

Dermot leant back in the chair and crossed his right foot over the knee of his left leg.

"Nice trainers," Sam remarked. "They go through the washing machine okay?"

"Aye. No bother. Why? Ye got a pair?"

"How long've you had them?"

Dermot uncrossed his legs. "Whit is this? A bloomin' fashion show or somethin'?"

"A week? Two? When d'you buy them?"

"Look! They're legit. I bought them down Leith, the Paki store, Constitution Street."

"When?"

"Ah dunno. Two, three weeks about. Why? Fancy a pair. They've maybes still got some."

"Four weeks and already through the wash?"

"Aye, well. Stupit bird barfed on them."

"Summer?"

"Aye! I mean … wait a minute …"

"Three weeks ago?"

Dermot wiped his hand across his mouth. "Y-yeh. Coupla weeks ago. Yeh. That's about right."

"Thought you broke up?"

"Aye, we did. Efter that. Yon besom had ruined ma trainers."

"But you saw her again a week past Friday?"

He shuffled in his seat, wiped his hand across his mouth again. "Maybe," he said slowly, as though searching his memory. "Possibly. Round and about. We frequented some of the same joints."

"Frequented!" Sam turned to PC Elliot. "Frequented, Elliot. Bit of class we've got here."

"Why? What's it to you?"

"Last Friday?"

"Nup."

"Not Friday there, the one before? Blue Chip Casino?"

"No me."

"You were seen there."

Dermot shook his head. "Week past Friday? No. Wasnae me. Wasnae there."

"I have two witnesses who say you were."

"Two witnesses, eh?"

Sam waited.

"Week past Friday? Friday. Let me think now …" Dermot stroked the short stubble of his hair back from his forehead.

"You and a few friends?"

He shook his head. "Naw. Couldnae be me."

"No friends?" Sam turned to PC Elliot. "Sad, eh? No friends?" He spun back round to Dermot. "So who were they, if not your pals?"

"Just some guys."

"Names?"

Dermot sat back in the chair, re-placing his foot on the opposite knee. He shook his head. "Now there you've got me. Not a clue. Could a been Jack the Ripper an' his mates for all ah ken. Met them inside the casino. Did a bit of business outside, no questions, no names. Sunshine came along, been thrown oot, couldnae get back in, wanted me tae help. Guys took a shine tae her. Ah left them tae it."

"And you can't give me some names?"

"Didnae ask for introductions."

"You seen them before?"

"No tae ma knowledge."

"Since?"

"Naw." Dermot shook his head. "A once off."

"Want me to book him, sir?" PC Elliot asked as they closed the door of the interview room.

"Nothing on him," Sam replied with a sigh.

"Pimping?"

"Proof?"

"Trafficking?"

"No evidence. If he says he was putting on a bet, he was putting on a bet."

"Doubt it, sir."

"Yes. But it's proof we need, not doubts. Let him go, Elliot, but put a watch on him. Wherever the others went with Summer, he wasn't with them at that point. Let's see what he gets up to in the next day or two. And let's get a warrant. Do a more thorough search of his flat. Meanwhile," Sam stretched and yawned. "I'm off to the pub. Need something to take the bad taste from my mouth. Then I'm taking this laptop back to Mirabelle."

"Good luck with that, sir," Elliot said with a grin.

"Yeah. She's not going to like it much is she?"

"What? That her daughter was talking on Facebook about running away from home, tracing her father? What's not to like?"

Sam tried to show Mirabelle some of the comments he'd found on Summer's Facebook page but she pushed the computer away.

"I really don't want to know," she said. "You're telling me she said these things, or wrote them, anyway." She shook her head. "I don't need to see them."

"Suit yourself."

"I intend to."

"Pity. You could maybe find out what was in her mind before she left."

"You've told me. She wanted to find her father. Tough. She didn't. She was busy making plans to go. She's gone. Tough on me." She slammed the lid of the laptop shut. "Is that not enough? Besides, that might've been all talk. About leaving home, I mean. Doesn't mean she did it."

"And I'm not saying she did."

"All girls talk about leaving home. It's part of growing up. Wanting to be independent. Rebelling against authority. It's only fools like you believe all that." She waved her arm in the direction of the laptop. "All that fiction. Daydreams. Silly 'what if' talk, that's all it is. Doesn't mean anything."

"Look, Belle, it's no good being angry with me. We need to do all we can to find Summer. Together."

She spun round to face him. "You think I don't know that! Instead of tormenting me with… with all this…" She shoved the laptop further away from her, "… this *stuff,* why are you not out there looking for her?" She started pushing him to the door. Then, "Please," she said, bending her head, her hands clutching his jacket. "I'm sorry, Sam. It's just… it's just…"

"I know, Belle," he said. "I know." He held her against

him. "I will go now but I'll see you later. And, Belle," he said, turning in the doorway. "Try not to give up. Remember, no news is good news."

"Yeah, sure." She nodded. "That's what they say, isn't it?"

Words. It's all just words, she thought, closing the door behind him. Empty, stinging words. She stroked her daughter's laptop, wishing she hadn't had to hear the news it had brought.

In her father's case, no news had been just that. No news.

When Mirabelle told Jimmy, the owner of the gym, and the others what 'Uncle Paddy' said about her dad being, "In the river, sunk without trace," their reaction was predictable. After they interrogated Paddy in their own fashion, they marched him to the police station to see if more orthodox methods of questioning could elicit information their fists could not.

"It was a joke," he claimed. "Yer man's got on a boat. Said he'd work his passage back to Jamaica."

"And why would he leave the new shoes behind?"

"Dey're not like us, those native folks. Do they not run about in der bare feet over there? With hoolie-hoolie skirts on an' all?"

"So what boat did he get on?"

"Well now, we didn't go all the way to the dock with him. Did we not say our fond farewells outside the house when we waved him off."

"And the fight, Paddy? When did you have the fight?" The detective nodded at the stitches tracking across Paddy's face, the purple bruising round his eyes.

"Ah, now, and wasn't that a scrap I got meself into down the pub the other night."

"Witnesses?"

"Well, it was round the back dere, so I doubt there was an audience at all."

"So who was the fight with?"

"Was it not some passing itinerant or other. Maybes a gypsy man or such. I didn't know the man but he invited me

to part with my wallet an' all."

"You know we can check at the hospital when you were there to get the stitches?"

"Right, and so you can, sir. Yes, well, let me think then." Paddy closed his eyes and leant back in the chair, making it creak with the pressure. "I do believe it was right after we waved yer man Vernon off on his travels."

"But it wasn't Vernon you had the fight with?"

"Not at all, sir. Didn't we wave him off afore all that."

"And where did you go after you waved him off?"

"Well now, did we not go off to the hospital, me and Rose, to get all this embroidery done." He winced as he touched the stitches on his lip. "Next thing, we had to take a wee look in at the pub to medicate the pain. Sure, ye can check that out with Tam in the very pub. Did we not go and send Vernon off in his absence. Lifted a glass that he'd have a rare trip."

"You and?"

"Me and his missus. Rose and me."

"And after closing time?"

"Ah, well now, we raised a few shouts from the neighbours as we sang our way home. You can check it out when you're ready. You'll find it's the God's honest truth."

And as far as they could find out, it was.

With no witnesses to misbehaviour down the docks, and plenty to misbehaviour in the pub and on the way home after closing time, there was no case to answer. The police let Paddy go.

Paddy didn't hang around much longer himself. Jimmy and the boys were less forgiving than the police force and Paddy found it best to don the new shoes and hoof it.

For the next few days, after Sam had talked about the correspondence on the laptop, when she couldn't stand the emptiness of the flat any more, Mirabelle roamed Edinburgh, searching the faces of strangers, seeking a clue, traces of Summer. The rational part of her mind told her it was futile. What were the chances Summer would be strolling through The Gardens or along Princes Street in the middle of the afternoon? Why would she be sitting in the window of this tearoom or that fast food joint?

Mirabelle wandered into music shops and bookstores without any pretence of looking at CDs or books, asking assistants if they'd seen her daughter, showing them a photograph. "She loves books, loves to read. Perhaps just browsing? No?"

Friends, relatives, people she knew would ask, "How are you?" They'd say it with a sad, pitying look, almost embarrassed but feeling duty-bound to ask, "How are you?"

"Fine," she'd say. "I'm fine."

What else could she say?

Tell them she felt like a child's rag doll? Her seams splitting, coming apart, stuffing oozing out through the rupture. That she'd find herself propped up against the wall, the door, the window, unsure how she came to be there, unable to move away. Or sitting, her arms on the kitchen worktop or the table, her head lolling on her arms, forgotten, discarded: the once-favourite toy.

That nothing had any meaning any more.

There was nothing she wanted to do, no-one she wanted to see, didn't care about work, workmates or clients. Hadn't given them a moment's thought since walking into an empty house that Friday night.

That there was no comfort, no words, no arms that could stop the pain.

That the sun didn't shine any more, the rain wasn't refreshing, the sky always dark.

That food stuck in her throat, like dry clumps of bitter grass.

She could tell them she felt numb, frozen into a time warp. The hands of the clock never advanced. It was always quarter to. Quarter to tomorrow. Quarter to yesterday. What did it matter? Time meant nothing. It was only a way to mark the duration of pain.

Or she could tell them she felt rotten, her body gangrenous, filled with canker, giving off a stench of decay.

The thought that Summer had even had the fleeting idea of running away, that it had even entered her mind — though she knew that wasn't what happened — the very thought was eating away at her. A voracious maggot.

Knowing her daughter had a false ID card, where she got it, how long she'd had it, maggots.

Picturing her daughter drunk and vomiting, another maggot.

Imagining her daughter lying in a cold grave, another.

Every picture, every imagining, another maggot. Maggots eating their way to her core, leaving her rotten and dead.

She could tell them that's how she felt.

But that was on a good day.

Other days she knew she was alive. The pain reminded her.

Easier just to say, "I'm fine."

Easier yet just to avoid them.

losing things

It wasn't difficult to get used to losing things. Some things seem so trivial, as though they're meant to get lost and not be missed when they're gone. Like the paper slip that flutters from a box of chocolates, its information repeated inside the lid or on the bottom of the box.

She was used to losing her door keys. It used to be a frustration, the hour lost every day hunting them down in the chaos around her. She'd found a way of coping with that: she stopped locking her flat door, leaving it open in case Summer had lost her key, leaving the stair door on the latch too when she went out, buzzing a neighbour to open up if it was closed on her return.

She learned to cope with other losses: people, places, names, what you went through to the other room for, what you meant to get at the shops.

She even learned to cope with bigger losses: when her baby sister died, then her brother, her mother. She missed them, though she found the passing of years had softened the losses. Or maybe it was just she had learned to live with the pain.

But she doubted she'd ever get used to losing Summer, any more than she had been able to get used to the loss of her father. How does someone come to terms with such huge losses? In her father's case, perhaps if she knew what had happened. The how, the why and the where of it. Maybe she could have processed the information, made sense of it, accepted it and moved on.

Of course she had moved on.

There was little alternative.

But she wore her father's unexplained loss like an undergarment, rarely seen by others but there all the time, moulding her into the person she had become with all her fears and insecurities hidden under layers of colourful eccentricities and bravado.

Chapter Eight

Detective Inspector Sam Burns warmed the glass of lager with his hands. He didn't care for ice-cold lager. It gave him hiccups.

While he waited, he scanned the room. Occupational hazard: never could be in a room without checking it over, mentally noting everyone in it, what they were doing, who was with whom. Tonight he was relieved to see there was no one he'd rather avoid.

It wasn't a fashionable pub, not full of the in-crowd, or whatever they called themselves these days, the eternally popular, well-heeled, young people about town. Sam closed his eyes, content to endure the smell of stale sweat and dirty feet. Unfortunately, the landlord had aspirations that required he served ice-cold lager. Sam turned the glass in his hand. If the owner hoped to change his clientèle, he'd need to smarten the place up a bit. The cosy brown leather benches and well-worn tables seemed at home with the dark, scuffed wooden floor; the wide-screen plasma didn't. How long before this became just another characterless, modern parlour for those with smaller screens at home?

He checked his appearance, the mirror above the bar assuring him he was still neat and tidy despite the rigours of the day. He knew his colleagues thought his soft, dark-brown, leather jacket and brown cord trousers old-fashioned, but he didn't care: they were comfortable. They were vaguely in fashion when he bought them. Sam plucked at a loose thread hanging from the seam at his elbow, looking up as the barman wiped the counter in front of him. "Any good with needle and thread, Tam?"

"Better with hammer and nails. Any good to you?"

Sam smiled and lifted his hand. "P'raps not."

"Staples?"

"Mmm! Worth a thought," he said, lifting his pint and heading for a table. With a sigh of resignation, he ignored the loose thread, opting not to pull it. "Could do without the whole thing falling apart," he muttered, remembering a time when his mother would've had the jacket off his back and stitched it up neatly before he'd noticed the need. He vaguely wondered whether the thread had already been a subject of ridicule and speculation down at the station. They probably ran a sweepstake: 'How long before the seam unravelled?' and 'Would Sam notice before the sleeve actually flapped open?'

His tweed tie and checked shirt came in for silent criticism too, he guessed, but he'd always worn a shirt and tie to work, didn't see reason to change: they were comfortable too, the brushed material of the shirt, soft and warm. Couldn't see himself in jeans and tee-shirt any more than sharp suit and starched collar. Even after his promotion to DI, he saw no reason to revamp his wardrobe. He smoothed his hand across what was left of his faded sandy hair. Wouldn't know what on earth to shop for nowadays anyway; what would tone with his rustic colouring.

It had been some years since he could've looked to Mother for advice, though she'd never been one to hold it back. But he did the shopping now, buying her slippers and stockings, flannel and frumpery. Her needs were few since she'd been in the nursing home and she paid no heed to what he brought her. Scant attention to his visits at all in fact. He doubted she remembered who he was. He shook his head, sadness covering him like a heavy rug, and turned his mind to other things.

Trying not to think too much about the various case files that sat on his desk, the court appearances to make, the leads to follow, the criminals to question, he allowed his mind to wander through the Scottish highlands. He had a yearning to go walking in the hills, always did around this time of year, when spring was melting the snow, making the burns run full and fast. Given the chance of a few days off work, he'd pack a rucksack, head off in the car and pitch his tent at the side of a stream or the foot of a mountain. Not being stupid, he took care where he walked when on his own, not going too high into the snow, nor too deep into the gullies. The weather up there had a habit of making sudden changes and he had no fancy for getting caught in a white-out or lost in the fog. There were places enough where it was safe to walk unaccompanied.

Thinking of company, he wondered if Mirabelle still liked to walk the hills. Wondered if she'd be up for a few days camping once they'd found Summer and made sure she was safe. Perhaps best not to ask till then. No point in courting a negative response.

But it would be nice, to walk on springtime grasses and hear the rush of water and the call of birds. It would be good to breathe fresh, mountain air.

Taking a long, deep breath, he sat back, eyes closed and imagined himself walking in Glencoe or the Cairngorms with Mirabelle.

Sam knew he'd end up waiting. Always did, even having arrived fifteen minutes after their agreed rendezvous time. But he didn't mind. It was pleasant enough to sit here dreaming, watching the world go by, or stop for a pint if it pleased.

There'd be no apology when she breezed in. There'd be no need. He knew he'd happily wait a lot longer than the usual twenty or so minutes for Mirabelle. He knew he'd have to.

They'd arranged to meet here, rather than Mirabelle's flat, because she didn't want to tie herself down to being back from her wanderings at a specific time. *"In case I turn something up,"* she'd said. *"You know, someone who saw Summer. But we can get together in the pub, right? Pool info? Right?"*

He'd nodded.

"Save me hanging about in an empty house," she'd said. *"And at least you can enjoy a pint if I'm late."*

He took another swallow of his drink and sat back with his eyes closed again, though the dreams had shattered. He hated cases like this. He knew he'd have one of his sick headaches for days now till the kid showed up.

"Hey, Rip-Van-Winkle, you gonna buy me a pint, then?" Mirabelle plonked her bags and shawls on the chair beside her and sat opposite him. Leaning across the table, she lifted his glass and took a sip. "Mmm! Same for me," she signalled to the barman before turning back to Sam. "So? Any news?"

"Trail's gone a bit cold, I'm afraid," he said. "Had a word with Davy Eskdale and it looks like she went willingly with the guys who were hanging about outside the casino."

Mirabelle's shoulders sagged and her head wilted, her neck a weakened stem. "No clues as to who they were?"

"Not even a decent description at this point. But we'll keep digging. Might turn something up."

"She can't just disappear like that. Can she?" Mirabelle said.

"I'm afraid it happens all the time."

"I'm getting desperate, Sam. With each day that passes, I just feel further from her. As though she's moving away." She looked up at Sam, her eyes glistening, red-rimmed. She nodded her thanks as the barman placed her drink on the table, then continued explaining to Sam, "Like she's on an escalator, a moving pavement thingy, you know? Being carried away. And I can't get on it. There's nothing I can do to stop it."

Sam reached across the table and put his hand over hers.

"I've been calling in to see some of my clients. The ones I know are doing drugs. They're always a bit unreliable for information, I know, but so far, none of them have seen or heard anything of Summer in those circles." She looked up at Sam. "See, I do listen to you. Even when I don't like what you say."

"And I'm not saying …"

"I know. I know. Oh, Sam, I'm just so scared something

awful has happened to her," she said looking down at their hands. "Maybe these men, even if she went willingly, maybe …" Her voice broke and her head dropped further, her face pale and drawn.

He sighed. "I know, Belle. I know. But we've no reason to believe she's come to any harm. Maybe it wasn't empty talk. Maybe she did plan to go."

She shivered. "Cold comfort, that." Pulled her hand away.

"Sorry."

"I just don't believe she'd run away. She must know how frantic I am."

"Not the way it works, I'm afraid. If she thinks you don't care."

"Of course I care!"

"*I* know that, Belle. But maybe *she* doesn't. Teenagers often get into that whole 'Nobody loves me' mindset."

"That's when she usually goes to my sister's."

"Well, maybe this time she wanted to get further away. Maybe she was afraid Yvonne'd turn her in, phone you, let you know she had her there." He paused, swirling the last of his lager round the glass, watching the foamy trail the liquid left on it. "There's something I need to ask you, Belle."

Mirabelle sighed and took a swallow of her drink. "Fire away."

"You might not like me asking this."

"Then don't," she said, placing the glass firmly on the table in front of her.

"I have to." He took a deep breath. "I know you said she wasn't with her father."

"She's not."

"And that you'd checked."

"I don't need to check. She's not."

"And you know that because?"

"I know that because she doesn't know who her father is."

"Ah!"

"Yes, ah!"

105

Sam took a long time to think about what he was going to say next.

"Let me spare you the embarrassment," she cut in. "Yes, I do know who her father is. But I have chosen not to tell her. That's not to say I didn't intend to at some point."

Summer had asked about her father. Of course she had. Mirabelle knew she would some day. And she had — repeatedly. It had been her favourite torture for a while: goading Mirabelle.

"You must know something!"

"It was a holiday romance. A one night stand."

"But he must have told you his name."

"Probably. But I don't remember," Mirabelle lied. "He was nobody special."

"Thanks! That's half my gene pool you're dismissing so casually."

"I didn't mean it like that. Of course he was special. You're special. I just mean we didn't have that sort of relationship, a proper relationship."

"And you honestly don't even remember his name?"

Mirabelle shook her head.

"You slept with this guy. You got pregnant. And you really can't even remember his name?"

"Sorry!"

"Grief, Mother! You're pathetic! No wonder you're always losing stuff. Your mind's like a great big tub of popcorn. One shake and everything's on the deck." Summer stormed out of the room and threw herself on her bed. "How the hang am I supposed to know who I am if you can't even be bothered to remember something as earth-shatteringly important as who my father is?" she shouted, punching a hollow in her pillow before burying her face in it.

Mirabelle followed her into the room and sat on the bed. "But you do know who you are." She stroked her daughter's hair, lifting the weight of it aside, exposing the soft vulnerable skin. "You're my lovely, special Sunshine Summer."

Summer growled.

Mirabelle bent and kissed the nape of her neck.

Shaking off the intimacy and rolling over to look up at her, "That might've worked a few years ago, Mum, but it's not enough now," Summer said. "It's just not enough." She got off the bed. "I'm going out."

The same scene played out a dozen times. Mirabelle sighed. It would be easier to tell her. But then what? Maybe she'd find him.

"I just hadn't got around to telling her," she said.

"Ah!" Another long pause. "Is there any way Summer could've found out?"

"No."

Sam waited. "No? That's it?" he said, spreading his hands, palms up. "You know for sure?"

"Absolutely."

"She couldn't have gone in search of him?"

"No." She shook her head. "She'd nothing to go on. She'd have nowhere to begin."

"Nothing? You're that sure? What about her birth certificate?"

"No."

"Let me guess. You didn't put his name on it."

"He didn't want to know about her. I didn't want her to know about him. To have the hurt and resentment of feeling unwanted."

"And there's no other way she could have found out? Yvonne? Your grandmother?"

"No-one knows who her father is. No-one but me."

"And her father, presumably."

Mirabelle leant forward, her forearms on the table, her face set. "There is no way she has found her father. There is no way she could. There is no way she will. Subject closed."

"If he …"

"He hasn't."

"But if he …"

"He hasn't."

"And you know that because?"

107

"Because I know that. He has not made contact with her."

"Yet you don't use Facebook, Twitter, email …"

Mirabelle sighed. "I don't need any of these gimmicks. Summer has no contact of any sort with her father. Trust me on this one, Sam. I know."

"If she …"

"No, Sam. You're right. I don't like this line of questioning and it's over now. Understand?"

He nodded and shrugged. "If you say so."

"Oh, I do, Sam. I do say so."

He drained his glass. "Then why is her laptop search engine history filled with sites about tracing birth parents?"

It took Mirabelle a while to make sense of what Sam was saying. "Search engine? History? I don't know. Oh! Are you saying she's been …"

"Actively looking for her father? Yes. That's exactly what I'm saying."

"But how? How could she do that?"

"Online? Easy. All she needs to know is his name, her date of birth."

"She doesn't. She doesn't know his name."

"Then she won't have had a lot of joy tracing him, will she?"

Mirabelle shook her head.

"And we'll just have to assume she's hiding out somewhere else." Twirling his empty glass in his hand, pushing it away, Sam started to rise.

She leant across and put her hand on his arm. "No," she said, her eyes begging him to understand. "We'll have to assume something must have happened. I don't, I can't believe she'd do this to me."

So Sam tried to keep the search going, but, since there was no evidence to suggest foul play, and plenty to corroborate the fact she planned to go, the police were slowing up the operation. Seventeen: already an adult under Scots law. Another runaway teenager. So many on their caseloads.

he can't have planned to go

There was no evidence of foul play, but nor was there evidence of Vernon's return to Jamaica. How many years could it take for him to work his passage across the world? Two? Three? Ten?

As soon as she was old enough to work out how to do it, Mirabelle started making enquiries about him: at the docks, immigration control, the Jamaican embassy. Allowing several years to pass, she tried them all again.

The police had no interest in finding him, certainly not enough to institute an international search. When Mirabelle asked, they assured her their budget didn't run to looking for random folks who chose to leave the area, even though they'd served a prison sentence. He wasn't on parole, he was not required to hang around if his wife had moved on.

The only thing Mirabelle felt sure of was he could not have planned to go wherever he went. He would not have gone without saying goodbye to her. He would not leave her fretting about his safety.

Mirabelle was sitting on Summer's bed. She had been sitting there some time, lost in a world of conjecture and pain, touching Summer's pillow, feeling the dip her head had made during years of sleep, when something caught her eye: something peeping out from under the chest of drawers. She thought at first it was a spider and got up carefully, intending to fetch her feather duster, but then she realised it was no living thing creeping out from hiding. It was plastic, black plastic, pushed under the furniture. Down on her knees, she coaxed it out with her finger, the bit she saw attached to a length of black flex. She pulled, then realising it would be plugged into the wall socket, she reached in behind the chest of drawers, unplugged it and retrieved the attachment at the other end of the flex, taking a moment to understand the significance of her find.

Summer's mobile phone charger.

Mirabelle hated her mobile phone. Rarely used it other than to do with her work, and even then would often forget to keep the battery charged.

"Technophobe," Sam had called her.

"Don't believe it's progress," she retorted. *"Just another invasion of privacy."*

"Allows you to keep in contact, wherever, whenever," Yvonne tried.

"Precisely my point. There are times I don't want to be in contact."

She didn't have a personal computer either, and never opened Summer's laptop.

"You're not on the internet?" Sam asked.

"I am at work."

"But not at home?"

"Summer is."

"But you're not?"

"Should I be?"

"Well, nowadays, everything's so much easier."

"So you say. But then you keep moaning about frozen screens and crashed programs."

"Small price to pay for progress."

"Huh! Progress. I don't think so. What if there's a power cut?"

"Batteries."

"What if there's a power cut and your batteries have run down?"

Sam had looked at her. "Really, Belle? That's your argument? An unlikely scenario?"

She'd shrugged. "I know I have to use the blessed thing at work. It sits there on my desk leering at me till I feed it some information, then it spits information I don't even want back at me. I'd rather go to the library, or use a pen and paper."

Another time.

"I'm being disenfranchised," she complained. "Telephone banking, internet banking, online shopping, cheaper to buy online, cheaper on ebay. I'm fed up hearing all the reasons why I should be glued to an office chair or walk with a piece of plastic stuck in my ear."

No. Mirabelle didn't enjoy using a computer. Or a mobile phone.

But she knew how they worked.

Knew the phones needed regular recharging. Knew the chargers were not uniform. You couldn't use just any old charger. It had to suit the phone. Which meant it was necessary to access your own phone's charger at regular intervals. Like every week, sometimes every few days.

Mirabelle looked in all the obvious places. No phone. Summer must have taken her phone. But not the charger.

By now, the battery would certainly be dead.

111

A spider of fear crept over Mirabelle's skin.

Summer *couldn't* phone.

If she'd been in trouble. If she needed help. She couldn't phone.

Would Summer really have planned to run away and not pack her phone charger? What would be the point in that? Why would she take the phone but not the charger?

The spider grew. It spun sinister webs of imaginings in Mirabelle's mind.

She sat back on the bed and rolled the trailing flex round the plug of the charger. She was not by nature a tidy person. Her own room usually resembled the inside of a shaken snow-dome. But Summer's room was always tidy and uncluttered so she looked round for where to tidy the charger away. Opening the drawers one by one, it occurred to her here was another reason to distrust the theory that Summer had run away. Not only did she not take the charger, but each drawer was perfect in its orderliness and nothing looked to be missing.

Mirabelle thought about what else Summer would not want to be without no matter where she was going, looked for her hair dryer and straighteners. They were still plugged in to the wall socket beside the wee table Summer used as a dressing table. A shudder passed through Mirabelle. Summer hated having curly hair, looked with disdain at Mirabelle's curls as though they had infected her, and always dried it as straight as she could, going over every strand with the electric straighteners, making certain there was not so much as a hint of a kink.

What else? What else? The spider grew, spinning tremulous alarm in Mirabelle's heart.

Clothes: no underwear, no clothes, nothing gone as far as Mirabelle could see. She lifted out a fistful of folded panties, clasping them to her as a wave of panic chased the spider of fear down the dark abyss into which she felt herself fall. Summer would *never* go *anywhere* without clean knickers. Mirabelle used to complain about the amount of washing generated by Summer's standard of personal hygiene.

"Three pairs of knickers a day? Is that really necessary?" she asked.

"Well, I like to change after school."

"Right down to your knickers?"

"Yes."

"And the third pair?"

"I put fresh ones on under my pj's. Anything wrong with that?"

"You're obsessive-compulsive. You know that? You need to see a doctor or someone."

"Look, what's your problem, Mum?" She snatched the washing basket from Mirabelle's hands. "I'll do the stupid washing if it bothers you so much."

She put the underwear back in its place. No way Summer intended to go away. Not without clean underwear.

Chapter Nine

Mirabelle lay on top of Summer's bed and descended into the abyss.

She fell apart.

Staggering to the kitchen, amid incoherent sobbing, she phoned Sam about the phone charger, and managed to make him realise the significance of the untouched underwear.

Faced with the irrefutable truth that Summer had done no packing, no visible preparation to carry through on her chatter about leaving home, Sam had to start taking Mirabelle's concerns seriously, as she had no hesitation in telling him when he came to the flat to comfort her. "You didn't even have someone search her room," she accused. "I'd have thought that was standard procedure."

"Well, yes, when we suspect foul play."

"Hah! And you'd made your mind about that before you stepped over the threshold," she screamed at him. "Judged me and my daughter. 'Oh, she'll have run away from home. Let's just go through the motions to keep old Belle happy!' That's what you were thinking."

"You know we've been doing all we could. Questioning her friends and …"

"Yeah, sure, you've been questioning her friends. But you've been doing it with your mind already made up about what their evidence would tell you."

"That's not true, Belle."

"No? Coming round here sticking her laptop in my face, telling me she talked online about leaving home." She stepped in closer to him. "You'd rather believe the idle chatter of teenage girls on social media, than put one ounce of faith in the fact that a mother knows best."

"Come on, Belle, you know that's not true."

Mirabelle beat her fist on her chest. "I know, I tell you. I know something has happened to my daughter. I feel it in here. So what are you going to do about it now, Detective Inspector Burns?"

To his credit, and Mirabelle's satisfaction, Sam accepted her reprimand and stepped up the search, his officers making house-to-house, shop-to-shop enquiries in the vicinity of the casino where Summer had last been seen the Friday night she disappeared.

Dermot Wilson's flat was searched, this time with a warrant, and he was invited down to the station for questioning. Sam had hoped to find him at least in possession of drugs to have an excuse to arrest him and hold him while they continued to search, but there was nothing. The flat was clean. And they had found no-one who would testify he was 'recruiting' young women as prostitutes, though they were pretty certain he was.

"Saw us coming, I reckon," PC Elliot said. "Tidied up, by the look of it. No drugs and no sign of the girl."

"Don't worry, Constable," Sam said as they entered the interview room. "We'll find his stash. *And* we'll find he was selling drugs to Summer Milligan."

Dermot shook his head. "Now why would I give a young girl drugs?" he said. "That would be against the law. That would be supplying."

"We'll get you on possession."

"How come? You've found nothing."

"We got you the last time."

Dermot put his hands in the air. "I'm a reformed character, DI Burns. Law abiding citizen, so I am."

"Good! Pleased to hear it. Because if I find you're supplying again …"

"Uh-uh! Not supplying. I think if you were to check it out, DI Burns, I was done for possession only."

"So the drugs we found in your flat the last time were

115

purely for your own use?"

Dermot nodded. "Guilty as charged."

"Enough there to keep any hardened user happy for weeks."

"That's right. Plan ahead. That's my motto. Don't like to get caught short."

Sam threatened and questioned to no avail. Dermot maintained he never supplied drugs to Summer and had not seen her after she left the casino that Friday nor anytime since and Sam was unable to prove he did.

"This case is on-going, son," Sam told him as he let him go.

"Harassment. Police harassment, that's what's on-going, DI Burns." Dermot smiled. "But I'll not press charges this time."

"Don't worry, sir. We'll watch him," Elliot said as the door swung to behind Dermot's swagger. "He'll want to get back to business soon and then we'll have him."

"Yeah, but it's not just him we want, is it, Elliot? So don't follow him too close. Give him room to lead us to the girl."

"Or her body."

Mirabelle appealed to Summer's friends and they gathered in groups after school each day and helped Mirabelle comb the city, knocking doors, entering shops and businesses, showing Summer's photograph, asking if she'd been seen. They went online to every forum they could, asking for information, appealing to Summer to get in touch if she could.

Then they waited, sometimes in hushed groups making candle-light vigils, sometimes one or two together, staring at the screens of mobile phones, tablets and laptops, watching for tell-tale signs of activity from Summer, looking for tell-tale traces of red hair on Instagram or Facebook.

Mirabelle made the rounds of her old clients again, teenagers and older, all those she knew had drug problems. All those who might know if Summer had been using drugs too. She didn't tell them it was her own daughter she was looking for, just showed them Summer's photo and asked if they'd seen her.

Police teams were formed to search, inch-by-inch, plots of waste ground and derelict buildings. Mirabelle knew it had become a suspected murder enquiry, though Sam didn't ever say as much.

There was a press conference and Mirabelle made an impassioned television appeal for Summer, or anyone who knew anything about her whereabouts, to come forward. A telephone number, designated to the search team, was shown on the screen.

The police suggested she should stay at home in case Summer responded to the appeal, or they received information and needed to contact her. Sam encouraged her always to carry her mobile phone to make that part easier, but Mirabelle no longer had the energy to remember to keep it charged then remember to put it in her bag or her pocket, so, still on sick leave, she opted to stay put by the house phone.

Then she did nothing; let her life fold about her like a shroud.

Night after night, she sat in the armchair, staring at the empty chair across the fire, the bare coat hook behind the door. She knew every swirl and curlicue of the hook's wrought-iron design. If she stared hard enough, she could almost see Summer's denim jacket hanging from it. Or she would stand for hours gazing into the unoccupied bedroom, the teenage posters on the wall mocking her with their bright colours and strangers' faces.

She stopped going to bed: didn't bother to try. The effort to get undressed or washed was too much, not that the idea of doing so crossed her mind most nights. She would doze in the chair, starting awake as her head lolled to the side or the pain and stiffness in her neck intruded on her feverish dream-search for Summer.

In her dreams they were together: Summer and Vernon. Floating on tranquil sea-green water in a small rudderless boat, drifting, drifting away from her where she lay drifting too, her long dress flowing out around her, her legs caught in seaweed strands of helplessness, a tenuous anchor at best.

Disappointment flooded over her with each new wakening. Despair dug deep into her consciousness.

The feeling of being adrift was a familiar one to Mirabelle, awake or asleep.

Sometimes it felt more as though she was walking on shifting sand, her feet slithering and sliding down sand dunes, hampered from reaching solid ground by half-truths and lies. Then Mirabelle felt she didn't know who she was, felt disconnected from her grandparents and her sisters because her mother had cast so much doubt in her mind about her heritage.

Tales of finding her under a bush morphed to tales of

being handed a bundle of rags by a gypsy only to find it was a baby when the gypsy had gone. Or being handed the same bundle by her father: take me, take my child. What choice did a woman have but to mother such a baby? For many years, Mirabelle wondered if the last story was true, but she knew her father and her instinct told her the story was yet another yarn her mother spun in her fragile mind.

Certainly, she felt no connection to her mother. Difficult to form a relationship with a woman who only ever saw you through the bottom of a glass or a bottle.

Mirabelle was a colourful, glorious flower planted in a rock crevasse, blooming only till the winds of misfortune exposed her roots and ripped them away.

Mirabelle was withering.

Yvonne got the doctor in to see her and she prescribed sleeping tablets. At first, Mirabelle resisted taking them, afraid to sleep, afraid to miss the sound of Summer's key in the door. Eventually, exhaustion overwhelmed her, body and mind craving rest, and she took the medication.

Next morning, there was that soft, liquid moment when everything feels molten and warm. When, with eyes glued shut, it's impossible to know if dawn has broken or the darkness deepened. Mirabelle lay still and listened. Faint murmur of cars on dry roads, footsteps passing the shops below, the postman's whistle: these were the sounds she listened for and found missing. Early yet, she concluded. No sighing wind, no pitter of rain. Just her own breathing, deep and rhythmic. A time of choice: to drift gently downstream on the river of dreams or to kick up through them to the surface.

She floated a little longer, allowing herself the luxury of comfort, hugging the duvet closer and snuggling down the bed. When sleep declined to overtake her again, she stretched her legs, her feet searching for a cool spot, flipped onto her back and let her bare arms find the chill of smooth sheets. She had no idea what day it was, and didn't care.

Summer would wake her when it was time to get up.

An electric shock of pain jolted her eyes wide open.

Summer!

Mirabelle rushed from bed, the duvet tripping her, wrestling her to the floor. Sobbing, she fought it off and crashed through to Summer's room.

Empty.

Disoriented and weak, she stumbled back to her own bed and crawled into it, dragging the duvet in a heap on top of her.

No rush to get up.

Mirabelle no longer jumped out of bed every morning, pulled on comfortable clothes, rushed out the door, a spring in her step, eager to put the world to rights. Yvonne had phoned Mirabelle's boss, explained the situation the Monday after Summer went missing. Mirabelle's colleagues had been sympathetic, understanding, wished her well.

The fit notes signed by her doctor declared her to be suffering from depression. These, Yvonne delivered to her work, returning with many more kind wishes for Mirabelle and assurances that they were looking after her clients since she had not managed to do so herself since Summer went missing, since her world had turned upside down and all that had been top of her priority list slithered to the bottom.

Years of study, years of dedication to her work had become ethereal. All that was real was wrapped up in one fact; Summer had disappeared as surely and comprehensively as Vernon. Mirabelle had been abandoned again.

She burrowed under the duvet.

No rush to get up.

No-one to get up for.

No-one to waken for school.

No-one to make breakfast for.

Only, she didn't get Summer up for school. Didn't make her breakfast. To her shame, Mirabelle realised she should have. A proper mother would have. That's what mothers do. Summer had taken care of her own morning routine far more capably than Mirabelle ever did or would have.

Since that very first day of school, when Mirabelle allowed them to oversleep and they had arrived at the classroom door, Summer's hand in hers, long after the other children had taken their seats and the teacher had introduced herself. Since that day, Summer took control. Without any discussion, at only five years old, Summer listened for the alarm clock Mirabelle ignored. It was Summer who roused her mother every morning. As a little girl, she would pull the covers from Mirabelle's face, press her lips against her mother's cheek: a tender call to arms. In her teens, Summer banged her mother's door as she passed on her way to the bathroom and shouted it was time to get up.

Drowning now, not floating. Gone the comfort. Gone the warmth. Only cold reality and an empty room next door. Mirabelle knew Summer was dead. It was a matter of waiting for her body to be found. With a mother's instinct, she knew Summer's heart had stopped beating and she ordered hers to stop too.

Mirabelle took another sleeping tablet.

Days and nights merged together. Each time she woke up, she'd stumble to the bathroom, find her way to the kitchen, take a long glass of water and another sleeping pill. When the small supply was exhausted, she wept like a baby, afraid of the nights without them.

Yvonne refused to help her get more. "I'm scared for you, sis. You're taking too many. You're just blocking out the pain instead of dealing with it."

"And?"

"And it's not good to do that all the time. You have to eat. You have to move about. You have to be awake at least part of the day."

"Because?"

"Because you have to. You have to look after yourself."

Mirabelle pulled the duvet over her head.

"Like I said, I'm scared for you, Bellabear." Yvonne picked up the empty foil strip that once held sleeping tablets, tapped it against her other hand. "I'm scared of what you'd do with them," she said to the heap on the bed.

Sam tried to rouse her and was unceremoniously thrown out of the flat. "And don't come back until you've found my daughter!" shouted after him as he trudged back down the stairs he'd climbed only a minute before.

Mirabelle crept back under the duvet.

Day followed on day. Mirabelle didn't know why.

Unblocked, pain and regrets surged through her with unexpected violence, crashing into her, crushing her. Sometimes she'd march about the flat, muttering angry words, railing against Summer's inconsideration. Then she'd dissolve into a puddle of remorse for her own. She sat, holding her daughter's clothes, burying her face in them, inhaling her daughter's scent, clinging to her essence. Every scarf, every button that had touched Summer's precious body became a treasure to be fondled and cried over.

Summer was missing. And it wasn't just teenaged Summer she'd lost. She'd lost her girl, her toddler, her baby, and she mourned for them all.

She took Summer's childhood out of her memory box and examined it: compared her view of it to what may have been Summer's. The trip to the zoo when Summer was six. She wondered now, did Summer notice her impatience? That she hated standing watching caged animals? Did Summer share her longing to unlatch the gates and set them free? When Summer tugged her hand, pulling her over to search for animals either hiding in bushes or non-existent in vacated pens, did she feel her mother's reluctance, her unwillingness to waste the minutes? Did Summer count how often Mirabelle checked the time? Asking strangers, peeking at the watch on some other parent's wrist, seeking the clock in the café, the gift shop and, at last, the foyer as they finally escaped.

"Oh, God," she prayed. "If I had those days again."

All of it. If she had all that time again, the whole childhood, she'd take more holidays, have Summer at home all summer. With her. Not childminders, relatives or friends. Take her wherever she wanted to go. Stay for as long as she wanted to stay. She'd not care what time the next bus was. When she could get back to work. When she could follow up on this school-age mum, that Giro. She'd not care about University, Social Work Degrees. Social work at all. Any job: she'd take any job that paid enough for them to have a home and food for their bellies. Enough. That would be enough.

Remorse rose in her throat: acid, bitter gall.

But then she remembered other days, better days. What about the Saturdays they'd spent on the beach? Taking the bus to Portobello, North Berwick, Dunbar. Shoes off, they'd push their toes into the sand, splash through shallow water, rock pools. Had Summer remembered those times? Times when they laughed together. Played crazy golf, ate ice cream, had fish and chips for tea before getting the bus home, sticky, sleepy and happy.

Or the Sunday walks up Arthur's Seat, or through the Botanic Garden. Or round Duddingston Loch, feeding the swans and the geese that cackled round their feet, greedy for every crumb, making them laugh with nervous fear and glee. How would Summer have remembered those days? As the happy, bonding times Mirabelle thought they were? Or as something else altogether? Something Mirabelle enjoyed and Summer endured?

No!

Mirabelle shook her head. No! Nothing could, nothing should soil those crystal-clear moments sparkling through murky regrets.

She wandered the house, sorrow following her like the train of a dress: heavy, sweeping behind her. Swishshsh! Swishshsh! The rustle of pain surrounded her. It was in the catch in her throat. The sniff of her tears.

Crying, she clutched the drooping bows of toilet paper that had fallen from the chairs, the loops of it that had drifted down from the walls, remembering the crazy, joyous hope with which she'd hung them weeks ago. She had not allowed them to be removed, though both Sam and Yvonne had tried. Now, she left them lying in crumpled heaps in the corners of the room: sad, coloured snowdrifts.

Frantic, she scanned the bookshelves in Summer's room, found her scrapbook. Dunbar, on the beach. There it was, the seven-year-old-Summer's matchstick people that were 'me' and 'Mum' — and they were smiling. Summer was smiling. Page after page of laboured writing labelling carefully drawn memories of things they'd done together. Page after page of smiling Summers.

Mirabelle stroked and wept over every one of them. It was all she looked at, all she read.

Summer was smiling.

'abandon all hope; ye who enter here'

For weeks, she slept with the scrapbook under her pillow in Summer's bed, in unwashed sheets until Sam gently helped her strip them off to wash when the smell changed from eau de nostalgia to something rather more pungent and less pleasant.

Sam had appeared at the flat, clearly anxious about her, not knowing what else to do. He hadn't been in her home for weeks. She had fended him off with polite phone calls until she stopped making any and stopped answering the insistent ring. She reckoned Sam would come in person when he found Summer's body.

Yvonne had phoned Sam, asked him to check in on her sister. "She won't let me help her. Just keeps telling me to b-off," Yvonne told him. "Like a bear with a sore head, so she is. Threw me out last time I went round. Hurled a plate at me. Don't know what I'm supposed to have done."

"She's just venting anger and frustration. You happened to be there, I guess."

"Maybe she'll let you near?"

He found the flat cold and untidy, dishes lying unheeded by the sink, uneaten food congealed on them in dry, mouldy lumps. Mirabelle herself unwashed, her nightclothes stained and crumpled, her short curls matted and thatched to her scalp. He'd pushed open the unlocked door, having received no answer to his knocking, and walked into her desolation.

She allowed him to bathe her and wash her hair, responding to his tender care with silent tears, leaning against him like an invalid, unable to help with the task. Having changed both beds, he led her to hers and read to her until she slept. Then he left her while he tidied the flat, washed the dishes and made a pot of soup. When she woke, he sat her up and spoon-fed her like a baby, coaxing nourishment into her wasting body.

"She's dead, Sam. My baby's dead."

"You don't know that, Belle."

"I do know that. Don't you understand mothers know these things? If she was alive, I'd feel it here." She put her closed fist to her chest. "Empty. It's empty inside here. My baby's gone."

Sam held her close and said nothing.

During the next few weeks, Sam and Yvonne took turns nursing Mirabelle, coaxing her to eat, helping her to wash and care for herself. With infinite patience they teased her back to life, like the green-thumbed gardener might a plant traumatised by unseasonable weather.

Then a body was dredged out of the water of Leith.

Chapter Ten

She read it in his face as he came through the door. "It's Summer, isn't it?"

Sam couldn't look at her. "I just thought I'd pop by."

"Why?"

"No reason. Just to see how you are." He still couldn't raise his eyes to hers. "Do I need a reason to look in?"

"No, but something's wrong. isn't it? It's written all over you, Sam Burns. What have you found out?" Then, when he still couldn't answer her, still couldn't meet her eye-to-eye, "You've found her body." It wasn't a question.

He looked up, reluctance in his movement. "They've found *a* body."

"Summer."

"They don't know that yet, Belle. She's been in the water."

"She. It's a girl then."

"Or a woman. They've not even established her age. Difficult. The water."

Mirabelle took a wrap from behind the door. "Let's go."

"Where? Let's go where?"

"To wherever this body is. I need to see if it's Summer."

He stood in front of the door. "No, Belle. That's not wise."

"So what do you suggest?" She was eerily calm. No panic. No fear. "My daughter's body has been found. I need to go to her. I need to claim her."

"We wait until forensics have at least given us more idea as to age, height, things like that. We need to rule out the possibility it could be Summer."

"Or the certainty that it is."

128

Sam shook his head. "No, Belle. You mustn't think like that."

"Why not? Isn't it better to accept what's happened and move on? Get the identification over so we can hunt down her killers?"

"Belle, you're jumping to all sorts of conclusions here. Until they can identify the body and establish how it came to be in the river and for how long ..."

"Let's do it then?"

He looked at her, the question in his eyes.

"Let's get down there. Leith is it? Or wherever. Let's get ourselves to the scene and identify her."

"I told you. We need to wait."

"So why did you come?"

He held up his phone. "To be here. I got a phone call ... I wanted to be with you ... I thought, when I get the forensic report ... In case, in case you need ..."

"Comforting?"

He nodded.

"Well, as you can see, I'm perfectly calm." And she was. Calm, composed. Cold even. "I told you, I know Summer is dead. I've come to terms with it."

Sam looked at her. He didn't move to let her pass. "We stay put for now."

They were still standing in the hallway. A face-off.

"Would you like a cup of tea? Coffee?" Mirabelle turned and walked to the kitchen.

"Coffee would be nice." Sam stayed a moment longer at the door.

"Do come in then," Mirabelle called through. Polite. Good manners. So important. She filled the kettle. Flicked its switch. Took two mugs down from the cupboard.

Sam lifted a couple of mugs from the worktop, started to rinse them. "These would do," he said. "Save the washing up."

"Not at all, DI Burns." And she took them from his hand and put them on the drainer. "Milk? Sugar?"

"The usual, thanks."

She stared at him, her hand poised over the packet of sugar.

"Milk. Two sugars," he said.

Mirabelle put coffee and sugar in two cups. She opened the biscuit barrel and arranged a few biscuits on a plate. "Please, do help yourself," she said, offering the plate.

Sam frowned at the plate. "Are you all right?"

She sat at the kitchen table. Invited Sam to join her. "Perfectly. Why do you ask?"

He shook his head. "No reason."

"What did you expect? That I'd fall apart at the news my daughter is dead? I told you. I knew she was. It's not news to me." She smoothed her skirt around her legs then folded her hands in her lap, her fingers bare of rings, her wrists empty of bracelets and bangles. All the joyous adornments of her adult lifetime had been cast aside since her certainty of Summer's death. Strings of beads, earrings and bracelets, everything lay in a jumble on her dressing table. She had no heart for such frivolity now.

She examined her fingers, the paler, newly exposed skin above her knuckles. Her fingers looked so thin and frail without an assortment of metal splinting them. They didn't look as though they belonged to her. Perhaps they didn't.

And her arms. She pushed her sleeves up. Stared at the strangeness of them; still brown, still hairless, but thinner than she remembered. If they were hers. Bizarre. Unreal. The air around her was becalmed and heavy, loaded with certainty. Her spirit flightless. Gravity sucked her energy, compelled her to sit motionless. Waiting.

When the kettle boiled, she sat listening to it bubble and hiss, clicking off, steaming on. It had settled into silence again before she got up and had to reboil it to make the coffee.

Sam's mobile phone started to ring. They both froze, Mirabelle with the steaming kettle poised above the mugs, Sam with his hand lifting a biscuit.

It rang again.

Mirabelle put the kettle down.

Sam put the biscuit down.

They looked at one another.

The phone rang again.

With a strangled cry, Mirabelle sank onto a chair. She started to shake uncontrollably. Her teeth chattered together.

Sam answered his phone.

Mirabelle waited, hugging her shawl round her, her knees shaking up and down, making her feet tap on the kitchen floor. She still had her slippers on and they were flapping against the painted floorboards and then against the soles of her feet. Tap-flip. Tap-flip. She concentrated on the noise. Tap-flip. Or it could be flip-tap. Flip-tap. Sam was listening on his phone. She didn't look at his face. Just concentrated on the noise of her slippers against her feet and the floor. Flip-tap. Flip-tap.

"Thank you," he said, before putting his phone away.

He moved towards her. Knelt in front of her, prising her hands from the shawl, taking them in his. "It's not Summer," he said, looking into her face.

She couldn't stop shaking. Her teeth rattled against one another.

"Can you hear me, Belle?" He squeezed her hands, lifted them to his lips. "It's okay. It's not Summer."

The shaking got worse. She started to whimper.

"An older woman, with marks from a wedding ring on her finger. Much older. Grey hair." Still holding her hands, he shook them gently. "It's not Summer, Belle. Do you hear what I'm saying to you? It's not Summer."

Mirabelle closed her eyes, nodded almost imperceptibly, leant forward, her head bowing over their clasped hands and she started to fall.

Falling, falling into merciful blackness.

Sam cushioned her, lowering her onto the floor. He went to her bedroom, pulled the duvet from the bed and lifted the pillow.

She moaned as he placed the pillow under her head, and again as he tucked the duvet around her and rolled her onto it in the recovery position. Her arm was limp as he lifted her wrist to check her pulse. Her breathing began to regulate.

Sam lay behind her, holding her to him, whispering nothing and everything as he rocked her till the shivering stopped and her breathing settled to that of sleep. They stayed that way for a long time.

Sam hated that part of his job. He hated it anyway, even when it wasn't Mirabelle's daughter they were looking for. He guessed every policeman did, reckoned you'd have to worry about someone who took pleasure in it. Telling a family their kid's turned up dead, a wife that her husband's not coming home. Waiting to identify a dead body, watching the pain of the mother, the father, the wife or the husband till they knew it wasn't their missing loved one, their relief tinged with guilt because they knew someone else wasn't going to feel it tonight.

No, that was not a part of the job he enjoyed.

Locking up criminals might be some folks idea of what the police force was all about, but that wasn't what it was like for the most part. Foot-slogging, paperwork, court appearances, reports, case notes, detective work, it all had to be done, it was all important, all part of the jigsaw that made up a policeman's life.

Community work. He quite liked community work. Working with kids. Visiting schools and youth clubs. Prevention is better than cure. Sam firmly believed that, and was happy to do his share of whatever came his way in the form of talks or whatever. All good.

But, and he knew this surprised a lot of his colleagues, what Sam enjoyed most about being a detective was detecting. Some of his team thought he liked catching the bad guys. And he did, of course he did. Some of them went through the motions, viewing it as a job, a more interesting one than walking the pavements or cruising in cars, but a job just the same.

Sam viewed it as a puzzle. A puzzle he needed to solve. He loved gathering the pieces and watching how they fitted together to build a picture.

Solving The Times crossword; rattling off a Sudoku while he waited for the kettle to boil for his wake-up cup of coffee, feeling wide awake when he completed it before the kettle clicked off; digging his Rubik's Cube out of the top drawer of his desk, completing it in record time before anyone even noticed that's what he was doing; beating the contestants to the answers on University Challenge: that's how he felt when he got to the bottom of a difficult case.

He knew his colleagues likened him to a terrier, laughing that he couldn't let go once he got his teeth into something. And they were right. He'd wrestle till his teeth were loose rather than give up something that mattered.

He'd been slow believing there was a puzzle to be solved here and he was ashamed of that. Familiarity got in the way of good practice. Mirabelle had been right, he should have taken more notice of her fears and placed less faith in words tossed casually into cyber space. Had it been a stranger, he wondered if he'd have taken a more objective look at the facts. He knew he'd have had someone search Summer's room. They could have gained precious days if they'd realised she'd packed nothing.

Sam felt chastened by his lack of humility. He had let Mirabelle down.

So he lay there on Mirabelle's hard, cold kitchen floor, cradling her until she slept as long as she needed to, until he was certain she was comforted.

Every day, he returned to nurse her through her mourning, updating her on the state of the search, encouraging her to see it as good when there were no results. "There's every chance Summer's still alive," he said. "Every chance. We're finding nothing to suggest otherwise. As I say, no news is good news."

Mirabelle turned away.

He coaxed her to eat a little, and she would try, but the food had no flavour. It was dust in her mouth. He opened her windows. "You need fresh air if you won't go outside," he said. She shivered no matter the temperature.

But she acknowledged his kind attention by making an effort to wash and dress. Be up and about when he knocked the door. Smiled at the pleasure it gave him.

She even managed to tidy round a little from time to time, recognising he really didn't have the time to do it if she neglected to. There was a certain satisfaction in hearing his 'Well done!'

He probably thought she was getting better.

Chapter Eleven

As she allowed herself to be nursed through her grief, she did start to get better, slowly at first, but, yes, she did begin to feel alive again, and she succumbed to Sam's pleas that she get out and about in the fresh air. Sam was right, of course, it did help. It didn't kiss away the hurt, but it certainly eased it.

Mirabelle loved living in Edinburgh: loved the atmosphere created by a city whose main shopping street looked across the road to a castle, Edinburgh Castle standing guard over Princes Street, its severe façade softened by the gardens skirting it, the gardens themselves cocooned from the bustle and noise, folded into their own tree-lined valley, with paths dipping into and out of its depths.

Almost daily, she lingered in the gardens on one or other of the benches tucked neatly against the edges of long stretches of grass, sometimes with tears coursing down her face as regrets stung her consciousness. Her need to turn back time was a fierce, swirling whirlpool that could never be satisfied.

But she was getting better. She was beginning to eat again, beginning to smile, laugh even at some of Yvonne's stories of her colleagues. Yvonne was a great story-teller. Really knew how to laugh at herself, how to turn an ordinary day into a hilarious tale for Mirabelle's amusement, how to lift Mirabelle's spirits. How to make her feel alive again. Alive and able to look around herself and enjoy the city of her birth, and Mirabelle was thankful for that.

Still signed off by her doctor as 'unfit to work,' Mirabelle had plenty of time to look at Edinburgh, to see what tourists saw, what made people from all over the world tarry here, find somewhere in the city to put down roots for a year or two, or stay indefinitely, and she was struck anew with the beauty of her home.

She knew the adage, Edinburgh was 'all fur coat and nae knickers.' She was well acquainted with its underbelly, its darker side, saw its dirty linen, but loved it anyway.

Up the Bridges and down the Cowgate, Mirabelle showed her photograph, got to know homeless men and women, young and old, asked her question, listened to their histories, knew their routines and territories.

As she went, she would stop and rake through second-hand shops for scarves and shawls, bags and boots, sandals and skirts, showing her photograph, asking her question. The volunteers who staffed the charity shops became her friends.

"Hi, Belle. See what I have for you today," said the young woman who stood behind the counter in the Help the Aged shop. She went into the back shop and brought out a neatly-folded bundle: a colourful Indian shawl of painted silk, its pattern intricate with reds and golds, greens and yellows. "Guessed you were due in about now."

"Oh, Irma, it's beautiful!"

Irma beamed. "Knew you'd like it. Be good for the summer, don't you think?"

Mirabelle accepted it gladly, paying over her money, her bright smile and banter a poignant mask.

Before she left the shop, she checked the side window, made sure the little poster was still in place, hadn't slipped down, become obscured by bric-a-brac.

Irma shook her head with a sad smile and a sigh. "Sorry, Mirabelle. No news for you. No-one's seen her."

Draping the shawl over the one she already wore, Mirabelle trundled on.

Always on the lookout for more.

Always on the lookout.

Often, she'd sit deep in conversation with the friends or strangers she met in the parks or gardens of the city. "Have you seen this girl?" the invariable opener followed by the reluctant return of the photo to her bag.

Today, it had been Peter she'd found shuffling past the bandstand in Princes Street Gardens, his dad's oversized coat buttoned carefully, his hands stuffed deep into its pockets. His grey head was down and she had to step into his path to gain his attention. "Hi, Peter," she signed next to his chest, shaping the words with her lips, though he didn't look up. "You hungry?"

"Hungry," he signed back, nodding. "Thirsty."

Mirabelle held up a carton of juice. "Orange?"

Peter reached for the fruity drink.

"And your favourite," Mirabelle signed before dipping into her bag and producing one of the packets of crisps she always carried in the certainty she'd bump into him before many days passed.

He took them greedily, accepting her offering with the familiarity of friendship and hurried, in his own distinctive fashion, to the nearest bench.

Mirabelle smiled to herself as she watched his arthritic shuffle speed up with anticipation for the welcome treat. She sat beside him, not even trying to make further conversation until he'd finished the crisps and taken his first few gulps through the straw in the carton of juice.

"You look tired," she signed.

"Lookin' for Da."

Mirabelle sighed. "I know. You still miss him, don't you? It's been a long time." Five years since his father died of a heart attack. Five years he'd been wearing the coat and walking the walk: a curious man-child, forty-eight with the mind of a toddler.

Peter slurped the rest of the juice and handed back the carton, saying his thanks without looking at her, and they sat for a while, Peter wriggling uncomfortably on the bench.

"Need to be moving on?" she signed in front of his bowed head.

"Yeah," he said. He pointed through the trees in the direction of the Castle.

"Royal Mile, today, is it?" she signed, mouthing the words in case he ventured a look at her face.

Peter nodded, already on his feet, his shuffle resumed.

Mirabelle took the photograph from her bag and held it for him to see, a futile exercise, she knew, yet still she compulsively did it every time.

He shook his head. "No see," he said. "Peter no see girl."

She watched him go, his gait shortened by imaginary shackles, his back bent under an unseen load. He would walk through the rest of the park, out at the West End gate, down Lothian Road to King's Stables Road, trudging slowly past the back of the Castle and up to Castlehill. He'd rest there the first time and the second but, later in the afternoon, after his third round trip, he'd lean out over the battlements of Castle Esplanade, watching the ant cars of the city below him until his mother finished her part-time work and came to take him home.

Mirabelle often found him there or at some other point on his circuits of the Royal Mile and Princes Street Gardens and had come to realise he must know intimately every cobble, every kerb, every grass verge of his chosen route. She doubted he'd recognise many of the buildings though he must have passed them every day for much of his adult life. The shops, the offices, the museums and even the cathedral didn't seem to exist for him. All he saw was his own feet on grey stone or green grass.

She, on the other hand, never tired of the secrets hidden in the Royal Mile, high above the gardens, its cobbles leading from Castle Esplanade to Holyrood House.

Sometimes its secrets were the colour of Summer.

One day, she was halfway down the Mile when a girl caught her eye. A young, flame-haired woman who quickly looked away, head bent, and increased her pace. The colour of Summer.

Mirabelle felt her heartbeat stutter.

"Excuse me!" she called, boldly following her through one of the archways into a tiny, paved courtyard, bumbling out in embarrassed confusion when the person turned a stranger's face in enquiry. "Can I help you? Are you looking for someone?" Mirabelle shook her head in apology, tumbled back into the High Street and continued down the mile of history: the Via Regis.

From Lawnmarket to Cannongate, the Royal Mile buzzed with visitors, students and lovers. She barely noticed the tourists; studied the students and lovers. As she searched their faces, looking for that one special one, they'd sometimes turn, a smile warm in their eyes, happy to share their glow with someone they must have imagined a tourist herself, her colouring declaring her part Jamaican, her loose, colourful clothing more suited to the Caribbean than Edinburgh's austere Calvinism.

Should she walk its length every day of her life, she reckoned she'd uncover something she'd missed before: wynds snaking behind old buildings, ancient doors leading who knew where, tiny stairways spiralling up into special places. Tourist shops and museums served those without time or inclination to wander from the street, tiny theatres and history rewarded those who did.

And shades of Summer that failed to yield her daughter.

the wash-house

At night, more often than not, she'd lie wide awake, unable to let go of the day. Then, she'd wander the house on one of her night-time vigils, standing at the window, watching the darkness deepen then lift into morning.

Summer's room was at the back of the flat, its window overlooking the small courtyards and gardens that chequered the area between their flats and the ones in the street over the back. Backyards divided up by fences and palings, walls and wash-houses. Here and there an effort had been made: a few vegetables, a row of flowers, a climbing rose. But mostly, the rectangles were criss-crossed with washing lines or dotted with patio chairs or litter.

Mirabelle stood, staring down at the silvered scene, unable to associate the concrete slabs or grey, grassy patches with any sort of humanity. Moonlight lent them an eerie stillness. Like a foreign land. Come the morning, colour would be born to them and she'd recognise them for what they were.

Who cut the grass? Swept the patio? Who planted the flowers? Ate the vegetables? She'd never seen anybody move about down there, yet often, in the summer, sheets would hang limply or waft in the draught that sneaked past the shelter of the tall buildings.

She and Summer used to pretend the space was an alien planet, populated by invisible people. *"Look!" she'd say, pointing to an old, rusting bench. "That young couple are there again. See they're having a picnic."* And they'd play the what's-your-favourite-sandwich game until, giggling together, sandwiches had to be made and they'd jostle one another for the peanut butter or the chocolate spread, the empty

141

courtyards forgotten again in the clutter of their kitchen.

Sometimes, they even put their sandwiches and some biscuits, together with a bottle of lemonade, into a bag and became the picnickers on the old bench.

"What's that building?" Summer asked her once.

"It used to be a wash-house."

"A wash-house?"

"Yes. All the housewives would gather there on a Monday — washday was always a Monday — and they'd fill the boilers and boil the sheets, lifting them out with great wooden tongs. They'd rinse them in the big stone sinks, then wring them through the old mangles and peg them out here in the yard."

"What's a mangle?"

"A mangle? It's a sort of a wringer."

"A wringer?"

"Instead of wringing the wet washing in your hands." Mirabelle demonstrated, using the paper towel she'd used to wrap their sandwiches, twisting it round and round with both hands. "You know, so you get most of the water out? Yes? Well a mangle is a machine that does it for you. It has two big rollers and you push the wet sheets and things through between them and they sque-e-e-eze all the water out." She screwed up her face, squeezing the onomatopoeic word out, her hands held flat and slowly pushing forwards through the invisible mangle. "It has a big handle on the side you have to turn to make the rollers go round as you feed in the washing."

"Wow! Sounds like a lot of work."

"Hurrah for automatic washing machines, eh? Mind you, I bet they had some fun too. A whole bunch of women working together. They'd gossip and chat. They'd maybe even sing while they worked. The wash-house would've been all hot and steamy."

"Can I see inside it?" Summer was trying to climb up to peep through the grimy window. "What's it used for now?"

"Storage, I think." Mirabelle punted her up. "I used to

have an old key. I'll look it out for you."

"Can it be my secret cottage?" Summer asked as *Mirabelle lowered her back to the ground.*

They'd put an old stool in it, a cardboard box to serve as a table, and her doll's tea-set. For a time, on an occasional summer evening, while Mirabelle sat in the yard, work files scattered around her feet as she wrote up case notes, Summer entertained her imaginary friends to supper.

Mirabelle had checked it out. Right after Summer disappeared, she found the huge, old rusty key in the kitchen drawer and went to check there were no signs of a lodger among the broken lawnmowers and rusty spades. Then she dug out one of their old sleeping bags from the hall cupboard and left it just inside the creaky old unlocked door with a few tins of beans and a tin-opener. They were still there.

Chapter Twelve

Mirabelle was sitting at the kitchen table, a cup of tea cooling beside her hand, the biscuit tin open behind it. Sam had placed it there, hoping to tempt her. He still came by every morning his shifts allowed, made sure she was getting up and made her a breakfast she would later scrape into the bucket under the sink. And every evening, to check she had something to eat, had been out and about during the day, was settled for the night.

Sometimes, he'd stay for a while and they would talk or listen to music, or occasionally pretend to watch a film. Sometimes, like tonight, he had to work in the evening, so he'd pop in early and make her some supper. He sat and watched her struggle to eat the cheese on toast he had grilled for her, leaving only when the plate was empty and he'd made the cup of tea. She was sitting as he left her more than an hour earlier.

When the phone rang, it took her a moment or two to recognise the sound. She had been lost, totally absorbed in a day-dream of her and Summer sailing a yacht on a wide blue lake surrounded by trees. Her father was at the helm. He'd come to take them to his home in Jamaica. The dream had felt so real she was reluctant to leave it.

"Yes?"

"Mirabelle, it's me. Davy."

"Davy?"

"Aye. Davy Eskdale."

"Oh, Davy. Yes. How can I help you?"

"Think I can help you. Y'know Red, that missing girl you were looking for a while back?"

Mirabelle held her breath. "Yes?"

144

"She still missing?"

"Yes."

"Aye, well. One of thae guys that was hanging about yon night waiting for her, ken?"

"Yes?"

"Well, he's inside now."

"Inside?"

"The casino? The Blue Chip? He's on the roulette. I've someone watching him for you. D'you want I should keep him here till ye can get a word?"

"Yes! Yes! Oh, yes, Davy." She was off the chair, grabbing her bag, pushing her feet into a pair of ankle boots. "I'm on my way." She only paused long enough to phone Sam after hanging up on Davy. Up Broughton Street and along Princes Street, paying no heed to the Castle, floodlit and majestic up on the hill. Usually, this was the time she loved Edinburgh best: when the shops were closed and the city began to party. Tonight she allowed no distraction as she hurried towards the West End and Lothian Road.

Sam arrived at the casino first and, after checking the man was still playing the tables, he waited outside for Mirabelle.

"Right, Belle," he said as she puffed her way up to the casino door. "Here's how we're going to play this. I am going to do the questioning. You are going to wait here, by the door till I'm done, right?"

"Wrong!" Mirabelle tried to push past him.

"No! Right. Davy here ..." He nodded to Davy who stepped forward and laid his hand lightly on Mirabelle's arm. "Davy'll look after you in the meantime."

"But ..."

"No buts, Mirabelle. This is *my* job. Not yours. Let's not fall out over it, eh?"

Davy put a protective arm round Mirabelle's waist. "Come on, girl. Let the man do his work."

With a toss of her head, Mirabelle allowed Sam to go in. But there was no way she was going to wait outside. With

Davy close beside her, she sat on a stool at the bar where she could see, though not hear, the conversation as Sam approached who she'd decided was the prime suspect. "If he laid one finger on my Summer," she muttered, her face mutinous as she sat on the edge of the stool, ready to pounce at any moment should the need arise.

From her vantage point, she could tell the conversation didn't start well. The suspect, as Mirabelle thought of him, a man of about thirty or so, an ugly, mean looking fellow in her eyes, was clearly uncomfortable when Sam showed his badge and positively shifty when questioned. Sam must've asked him to accompany him to the station but the suspect was reluctant. He indicated the tables. He was on a winning streak, the pile of chips he lifted to show Sam evidence he was playing well. Mirabelle started to get off the stool to add encouragement to Sam's polite request.

"Uh, uh!" Davy laid his hand on her knee. "No time tae move yet, ma darlin. You just bide a wee bitty."

But Sam was persuasive enough without her help and soon had a result, leading the man from the casino and out to his car. Davy allowed Mirabelle to follow them and summoned a cab when Sam decreed she should not ride in the police car with him.

Mirabelle was furious. Sam was insistent, Davy firm.

Mirabelle rode to the police station in the taxi, but she made Sam pay the fare when she arrived, striding past him with her lips pursed and her back cold as he held the door for her.

Ricky Horner, Sam told her, was in an interview room and she would just have to be patient while he asked him a few questions.

"Patient!" Mirabelle fumed. "I've already been more than patient. Wish I'd never called you. I could've got the slime-bag to talk myself."

"No doubt, Mirabelle," Sam said with a smile. "But let's do this right, eh? If he knows anything, we'll get it out of him, don't you worry."

146

Mirabelle paced the waiting area with all the tension of an expectant father. She knew Sam was right: it was better to let him get on with the work at hand. But it was so hard not to be able to roll up her sleeves and weigh in.

And what did she know of him? Of Sam? This echo from the past who had the task of finding her daughter's murderer? She didn't even know if he was good at his job.

She threw herself into a chair.

She knew he was kind, she knew he was patient, shy, self-effacing.

She jumped to her feet again.

But she needed him to be forceful! Her fist punched the air beside her thigh. To be strong! Her face tightened round her clenched teeth. To blast information from this man he had brought in for questioning.

She looked at the clock, wondered if it was working.

She sat again, throwing herself into the chair, ignoring the self-inflicted pain in her hip, holding her head in her hands.

At least he was persistent. Didn't give up easily. She knew that from the patient way he'd waited for her initial antagonism to wear off. She'd been so rude, so deliberately rude. Yet he kept returning her bad behaviour with good, a kind word for a caustic remark, a polite gesture for an ignorant disregard; softening her until she relented, until she would throw a hint of a smile his way as they passed.

Mirabelle's work had meant she was often in the police station for one reason or another, she also often used to meet Lena there and they'd lunch together, so it was no surprise she and Sam would bump into one another from

147

time to time. But that wasn't how they *met*.

Mirabelle remembered how they met years ago, when they were both students: he at the end of his studies, she starting out. She closed her eyes, remembering Sam as a young man: his seriousness, his neatness, his disciplined study regime.

She sat back, reluctant to recall too much of that time, reluctant to recall how he'd dumped her. Though Sam disputed that interpretation of how they'd lost touch with one another, that is how she remembered it, that he dumped her.

She turned her attention back to his time in the police force. He probably was good at his job. He was a Detective Inspector. He'd have to be pretty good at this stuff to make DI.

She looked at the clock.

She shifted her weight, crossed her legs.

Uncrossed them.

Tugged at her dress to loosen it.

Got up again.

Rubbed the pain in her hip.

Walked across the room.

"Is that clock working?" she asked the desk sergeant.

He looked at his watch and then at the clock. "Think so," he said.

She walked back to the row of chairs.

Sam had been married. Didn't like to talk about it, but she knew he'd been married and divorced. Was that a good sign? What did it mean? That he was weak? Let his woman get away?

Mirabelle folded her arms across her chest. She should be in that room. She should be making sure he was being firm: getting the job done.

He'd told her it hadn't been much of a marriage: had only lasted eight years. *"I suppose you could call it a marriage of convenience,"* he told her in a rare moment of revelation. *"It suited both of us. Sheila wanted to get away from her father's over zealous parenting and I wanted — well, it doesn't matter what I wanted,"* he said. *"We parted amicably*

148

enough once the arrangement ran its course. After that, I applied for a position in Edinburgh. Made a new start."

Mirabelle rummaged in her bag for some coins. She fed them into the machine at one end of the room and got herself a plastic cup of tea: weak and insipid, but at least it was hot. And it passed a minute or two. Because, yes, the clock did seem to be working. The hands had moved. They'd marked off five or six minutes while she'd been thinking about Sam's marriage.

She sipped the tea.

Burned her lip.

Swore under her breath.

Put the cup down on a table.

Paced some more.

Why did she care he'd been married before? What did it matter? He had made it clear he wanted to be with her now. She picked up the cup.

If he played this right, if he got the truth out of this guy, if he found Summer's murderer, then who knew where this relationship was heading?

Mirabelle smiled. Took another sip of tea.

Burned her mouth.

Swore.

Put the cup away from her again.

What was she thinking? Why was she thinking about Sam? It was Summer she needed to be thinking about.

A new thought.

What if Summer is alive?

What if this man knows something about where she is? That could be possible, couldn't it? Did he look like a murderer?

What does a murderer look like? Joe Bloggs, she supposed. The man next door. Every murderer must live next door to someone. Every murderer had a mum. Every murderer had a gran.

But maybe he wasn't a murderer.

Maybe he knew where Summer went.

Maybe he took her somewhere.

Maybe they're living together. She's making his supper right this very minute. Chopping carrots and onions on a wooden chopping board. Dropping them into a pot. Another pot alongside, potatoes newly peeled, the water coming to the boil. Perhaps it's chops tonight. Or minced beef. She was a good wee cook, Summer.

She could be standing there, in some kitchen Mirabelle had never seen, her face flushed from the heat of the stove, an apron covering her clothes. Summer always wore an apron, hated her clothes to get splattered, hated them to smell of cooking. Mirabelle used to rummage through the odds and sods boxes in charity shops for old-fashioned aprons. Summer liked the long ones that went over her head, tied at the back of her waist. They covered more of her, protected her from splashes and spatters.

Sometimes, when Mirabelle puffed and panted up the stairs, realising she'd forgotten to shop, trying to remember what bits and pieces of this or that or leftovers there might be in the fridge, her heart would lift at the sound and smell of cooking as she opened the door. Chicken and Garlic. Beef Hot-pot. Fish Pie. Home-cooked, hot food. Money found, shopping accomplished, preparation done, cooking in progress. The table would be set, knives and forks neatly aligned, plates warmed and ready.

What a star!

Her heart was pounding in her chest, fresh hope pulsing through her. She quickened her pace, walking back and forth, exultation lightening her steps.

She *knew* Summer was alive.

Didn't she feel it in her very being?

Didn't she know all along her daughter couldn't be dead? Not when she felt her heartbeat alongside her own.

Mirabelle took a deep, shuddering breath.

Another, calmer one.

Sam would find out where they lived. He'd get to the bottom of this whole business.

She almost felt like laughing, the relief was so great.

She sat down, her hand straying to the cup, its heat

reminding her of the sting of her lip.

She rummaged once more in her bag, found some lip salve and smoothed it on.

Time stretched out like a long strand of elastic. Let go of one end and it would ping back and you'd find the clock had hardly moved at all though it felt like hours.

Feeling calmer again, she allowed her thoughts to stray back to Sam. It had taken her a long time to allow herself to warm to him, second time around. Thinking it was his fault they'd lost touch, she didn't share his sentimental regard for the old days, led him to believe they had meant nothing to her, though, back then, they had seemed filled with promise and possibility. When he found her again, she felt it was the proverbial, 'too little, too late.'   She reckoned he hadn't wanted her when he had her. Why should she fall at his feet now?

He had knocked on her door. After all those years, he had knocked on her door. Just like that! Mirabelle marvelled at his audacity. One evening, just after eight o'clock. Mirabelle hadn't even divested herself of shawls and shoes. Hadn't even read the note chalked up on the kitchen blackboard that would tell her where Summer had skedaddled off to.

"Hi!" he said. As casual as that. "Hi!"

She stared at him.

"Remember me?"

"No! Should I?"

A pink flush spread across his face. "Oh … I felt sure … I thought you might."

"Well you thought wrong, didn't you?" She started to close the door.

"Mirabelle! Wait! It's me. Sam Burns."

She closed her eyes and took a deep breath. "Burns … Burns … Sam Burns." Her eyes snapped open.

He smiled.

She shook her head. "No! Sorry. Means nothing. Now, if

you'll excuse me." She made to close the door again.

He stepped forward, his hand reaching out to stop the door. "Sam Burns! You remember. We ..."

"I'm just in from my work and I need to eat and I need to pee. Not necessarily in that order, but both with some urgency. So, unless you have some reason for knocking on my door other than to convince me we've met before — bit clichéd as a chat-up line, by the way — I have to go."

"But we have met before. A long time ago, granted, but we were, how shall I put it, something more than friends." He smiled at her.

A nice smile, she had to admit to herself. He always did have a winning smile. "Well, sorry," she smiled back, pretending she hadn't already noticed him in the police station when she'd been in and out a couple of times. "It can't have meant as much to me as it did to you, because, how shall I put it, I have no memory of it. Now, if you'll excuse me, I really have to go." She crossed her legs and hopped about dramatically.

"Ok," Sam grinned. "I can see this isn't a good time for you. I'll be in touch."

And he was gone.

She'd leant against the closed door listening to his footsteps as he went down the stairs, her heart thumping in her chest, her legs weak.

She reckoned she didn't need Sam Burns. Not after all this time. He'd had his chance and he'd let her go.

She had Summer. She didn't need anyone else.

master or lover
drudgery or joy

She had Summer and she'd let her go.

She'd let her down.

And now Sam was interrogating someone who might well know where her daughter was, someone who may have been kind to her.

She shook her head.

Or this guy may not have been kind.

It didn't bear thinking about, but he may have taken her by force. Seduced her away from her mother somehow. Installed her in some crummy flat somewhere. She was probably scrubbing the floor or standing, hot and tired, doing a great pile of ironing this very minute. There'd be crisp, clean shirts buttoned onto hangers hanging from the door knob beside her. Trousers pressed, steam rising from the last pair as she laid them over the airer. Sheets and towels in a neat pile on the table, waiting to be carried through to the airing cupboard.

Mirabelle, who'd never ironed a shirt in her life, and certainly not a sheet or a towel, laughed at herself, recognising the scene as one from Hannah's immaculate laundry routine.

It was Hannah who taught Summer to iron.

"Every girl should know how to iron a man's shirt," she said. *"No wonder you've no husband, Mirabelle."*

As though an ironed shirt could miraculously conjure up a man.

"Domesticated! That's what a woman should be. That's what's important in a marriage," Hannah said.

Love? Mirabelle questioned silently. Didn't I read

somewhere, 'All you need is love, love. Love is all you need?'

No, it was a song.

The Beatles.

A radio appeared in the vision.

There'd be a radio playing in the kitchen where Summer was practising her domesticity. Radio One: pop music. Or it might be Classical Radio. Summer's musical taste was pretty varied. Something soothing as she worked.

Mirabelle smiled.

The music made it better, the work less arduous.

Did she slave willingly?

For love?

This guy Sam was questioning, was he her master or her lover?

Mirabelle's heart quickened. She needed to know. It changed the picture. Changed what was happening to her daughter from drudgery to joy.

She held her head in her hands, forcing the noises to stop, the pictures to fade. Sam would suss out whatever and whoever this guy was: good guy or bad.

She needed to leave it to Sam.

Sam would sort it out.

He knew how important a child was to a mother.

Mirabelle knew he was fond of his own mother.

His mother had followed him to Edinburgh after a few years, not to care for him as she'd have liked, but to be cared for as she needed. She'd become confused and infirm with the relentless cruelty of early-onset Alzheimer's.

At first, she'd tried to fight it, to hold on to memories and routines, but, like many before her, she was defeated.

After his father died, Sam knew his mother could not be left to care for herself on the croft. When she joined Sam in his house in Edinburgh, she tried to share in the cooking and cleaning, ironed his shirts with love and pride.

It was only when she kept forgetting to turn off the cooker and started leaving empty pots on the rings that Sam realised she needed more care than he could give while working full-time. Since detective work tended not to be nine-to-five, never mind part-time, eventually he had to find a suitable alternative: a Care Home for the elderly, though Ella was far from elderly at only sixty-five. Though she rarely recognised him, he still visited regularly.

Lately, he'd sometimes take Mirabelle along with him.

She imagined she would have liked Ella Burns if she'd known her before the Alzheimer's. Sam painted her as a kind woman: kind, but forceful. Knew what she'd wanted for her son.

Mirabelle remembered Sam telling her how, as a young man, he'd been on automatic pilot: flying blind towards an unknown destination, until his future was mapped out for him. Mother had decreed he'd follow his grandfather's trail. He'd be a policeman, not a crofter as her husband was, but an upholder of the law as her father had been.

Allowing his mother to dictate his destiny was not a capitulation or a compromise, it was a resignation.

Nothing else would make her happy and he had no one else but his parents to make happy.

To please his father, he went to Stirling University first and got a Degree in Sociology to fall back on since his father was quietly less certain of his son's future career than his mother.

"Another string to your bow," was how his father saw it. "You need to study, to know how to study," he told his son. "To be on the land with me will not help you to have a career. To study and to learn, that will help you."

A veritable speech from his father: a rare insight from Sam into his own past.

Yes, Sam understood the importance of family.

He'd sort this whole mess out.

She smiled again.

If Sam could help her find Summer, perhaps she could have them both.

Perhaps, this time, she would be there for Summer and Sam would be there for both of them.

She looked at the clock again, willing it to retreat, the

hands to spin round and round anti-clockwise, turning back the minutes, the days, the weeks. Let her have that fateful morning again. Invite Sam along to celebrate with them, introduce them, watch them click. Because she was sure they would. Once Summer got to know him, Mirabelle felt certain she'd like him, approve of their growing courtship.

Mirabelle laughed out loud. "Courtship!" she muttered. Courtship: such an old-fashioned word. Yet that's the way she thought of it. A sedate, old-fashioned courtship, starting slowly and building gradually.

The first time she agreed to share a cup of coffee with him, she'd been in the station with a minor who'd been helping with enquiries regarding a stolen car. She had gone along to the canteen to get a coffee while she waited for the boy to come back from the gents toilet after the interview.

Sam had asked to join her at the table.

She'd given a please yourself shrug, hardly an invitation, but he'd sat down anyway. It was only a week or two after he'd turned up at her door and she hadn't seen him since, and hadn't wanted to.

"Is it something I said?" he asked. "Can I just apologise for whatever it was? And can we try to be civil to one another?"

Mirabelle couldn't tell him what he'd done. She chose to try the civility thing. She had always enjoyed his company. He was still a quiet, peaceful man though not as shy as she remembered him.

This time it was he who did the running, he who nourished the relationship. And he had the sense to proceed with caution.

"You have real trust issues, don't you?" he'd asked one day.

She couldn't deny it.

But she was having to trust him now. No choice. She could hardly go barging into the interview room and demand to interrogate the prisoner. In her mind, the man had fluctuated from 'the prime suspect' to 'some guy in a casino' to 'Summer's live-in partner' and now back to 'the prisoner,

157

the kidnapper, the murderer,' tried and found guilty in the time it had taken so far. Much longer she'd have him sentenced too.

She took a long gulp of tea. It didn't burn this time. Nor did it quench her thirst.

"Come on, Sam," she muttered as she paced. "Come on."

"Dear, oh dear, oh dear, Mirabelle, I've never seen you so impatient," the desk sergeant said.

She stopped and looked at him.

She'd forgotten he was there.

"It's never been about my daughter before," she said.

Ricky Horner travelled over from Glasgow every month or two to visit his brother. While waiting for his brother to join him, he'd play the tables, build a pot if he could. Together they'd have a few drinks, smoke a joint or two, hit the clubs and casinos and end up in some unsavoury hotel room with any women they could persuade or pay to join them. With little persuasion other than the promise of another bottle, Summer had accompanied them to a sleazy room off Constitution Street a little over three months ago.

Sam had promised to tell Mirabelle what he elicited from Ricky's interview, but he decided to give her information on a need-to-know basis and skipped over that particular piece, minimising the graphic details Mr Horner seemed intent on providing, including the interesting fact that Dermot Wilson took money for introducing them to Summer, telling her instead about what followed.

"Apparently, they had the decency to pay for a room for her to pass out in, down Leith."

"You believe him?"

"His brother's being brought in right now for questioning. See if their stories match." Sam nodded to the two detectives as they passed on their way out. "It's all being looked into as we speak."

Mirabelle closed her eyes against the pain.

"He claims not to have known she was only seventeen, and not to have seen her since that night. Claims too that she was alive and well."

"But unconscious?"

Sam shrugged. "Sleeping. He has an alibi after that."

"Huh!" Mirabelle snorted. "His brother?"

159

"And the bouncers at a couple more clubs they hit after leaving her. And, yes, we're checking that too."

"It was definitely Summer?"

"Description fits. He identified her from the photo you gave me. Picked hers out from dozens." Sam sat beside her and took her hand. "You all right, Belle? Need a drink of water or something?" He turned to the constable on duty at the desk. "Any chance of a cup of tea? Hot, sweet and strong."

you can't eat stubbornness

By the following day, when Sam called at the flat to give her an update, Ricky Horner's story was verified, his alibi sound.

When last seen, the night she went missing, Summer was alive and vomiting.

"The next day, the hotel guy says he had to bang the door all morning and half the afternoon to waken her," Sam read off the Constable's notes. "But waken her he did." He looked across the hearth at Mirabelle. "Remembers her because he'd been at the point of calling the police when she surfaced. The room was only paid ahead for the one night and he'd someone else waiting for it. His cleaner couldn't get in to change the bed."

"And it was definitely Summer?"

Sam nodded. "Remembers her red hair. Says, 'She looked like death,' or words to that effect, but she was definitely alive. Stumbled out, shielding her face from the light, and shuffled off to find breakfast," he ad-libbed as though reading from the much more colourful account in the notebook: bubble-wrapping the sharp reality of the facts. "So, on the Saturday afternoon, two-thirty, she was definitely alive and functioning."

Mirabelle tried to find comfort in that. She sank back into the armchair in her living-room, her head resting against its back, trying to stop the thumping pounding through her body.

"Summer is probably alive, Belle. Summer is alive!"

She nodded, tried to smile.

Not in another kitchen somewhere then. Not preparing supper for this man who'd discarded her daughter when no longer of interest. No wooden chopping board. No pretty apron. No neat pile of clean, pressed laundry. The picture fragmented and fell from her: ten thousand jig-saw pieces tumbling to the floor.

But alive. Seen alive that Friday night. Even better, still alive the next afternoon.

Mirabelle thought back to that Saturday afternoon three months ago. What had she been doing while Summer slept off her alcohol?

All that energy wasted pacing the floor.

She saw herself instead, walking to the top of the road, turning down Leith Walk, past the eclectic mix of shops: restaurants, furniture shops, charity shops, the Chinese supermarket, the Polish deli, bed shops, carpet shops, the Turkish restaurant.

Past all the pubs, the betting shops, pawn shops, tattoo parlours. Past the junkies who hung out at the foot of the Walk.

Past all of them and down to Constitution Street to take her daughter home. A short taxi ride and she could've had Summer tucked up in her own bed with a basin beside it and a cold flannel on her forehead.

Yes, they'd have had a row about where she'd been, who she'd been with, what she'd been doing, but she'd be safe.

"We're going to find her, Belle." Sam shook her gently bringing her back to the moment. To her own living room, to the empty, cold fact that Summer was alive then, but where was she now? "You do know we're going to find her?"

And it should have been easy.

Where could a seventeen-year-old girl go, with no money, no job, no clean knickers? Mirabelle ticked off the things Summer didn't have.

Yet was shocked to think of what she had.

Courage?

Shame?

Fear?

Which was it that kept her away?

Determination?

Stubbornness?

162

One thing Mirabelle knew: you can't eat stubbornness.

It wasn't hard to work out where Summer got her stubbornness. It was a trait her mother had often remarked on in Mirabelle. When she stubbornly refused to stop asking about her father. When she stubbornly refused to believe her father had left without so much as a 'Goodbye!' When she stubbornly held on to the belief he would come back for her. He would take her away with him once he had a place to live. He would be her knight in shining armour.

So much hope, based on so little evidence. Just the sure and certain knowledge that her father had loved her.

Throughout her childhood, Mirabelle held on to her dreams. Stubbornly.

Chapter Thirteen

Mirabelle tried to establish a routine of sorts. Anything to keep her sane.

Morning stretches at Sam's insistence. "Ten of each," he said, demonstrating the half dozen stretches he wanted her to do. "Every day."

"Every day?"

He nodded. "Every day. Ten of each. At least."

"But what if I'm too tired?"

"Doesn't matter. It'll wake you up, re-energise you. And you drink this," he said, putting a litre bottle of water on the table. "This amount every day. At least. Next week, we'll add in some actual exercises. And you can do it to music, if you like." He selected one of her favourite CDs and popped it in the machine.

"I know what you're up to," she said.

"Fine." He hit the button to start the music. "Do it anyway. Just to please me?"

So she did.

Anything to keep her sane.

To keep her mind from straying down the cul-de-sac of fear just around every corner. That Summer had survived the night she went missing was something. But it wasn't enough. That she'd been seen alive one day did not mean she was alive the next. That she had been 'sold' to Ricky Horner and his brother did not have to mean she was used that way again, but she feared it. Feared the kind of life her daughter might be living. Feared she might not be living at all.

Ten stretches this way. Ten stretches that.

Anything to keep her sane.

The University term had started now, but Summer hadn't

taken up her place, had never acknowledged the acceptance letter. Mirabelle had checked.

"No," the secretary said, shaking her head. "No Summer Milligan on any of the registers." She indicated the computer screen. "If she was on any of the courses, I'd know."

"Could you check, please, for any student with the first name Summer," Mirabelle asked. "In case she's adopted another name."

"She couldn't really do that on a whim," the secretary assured her. "Not to enrol as a student here. She would need her birth certificate, her examination certificates, the paperwork registering a change of name." She looked at Mirabelle. "But I'll check anyway," she said. "Just to be sure."

There was no other Summer and no other Milligan.

"Sorry!"

"Thanks for looking anyway."

All Summer's dreams, all the hard work she'd put into getting the grades she needed, the subjects she chose, all wasted. All lost. The pain in Mirabelle's chest intensified every time she allowed herself to imagine what that must mean. There didn't seem too many alternatives to consider.

Ten stretches this way. Ten stretches that.

Anything to keep the panic at bay.

Walking was not only good exercise, but good therapy too. It helped her not to feel quite so helpless. While she was searching for Summer, at least she was doing something. So she walked every day, choosing a different route, a different area, scanning faces, watching passers-by as she rested on a bench here and there.

Then it occurred to her, if Summer was still alive, and not confined in some dungeon, not shackled to some cellar wall, if she was roaming free, not wandering somewhere confused with amnesia, but had all her faculties and plain didn't want to be found, she was hardly likely to casually stroll past her in the street. She would surely about-turn when she saw Mirabelle sitting here, standing there.

Mirabelle started watching distant street corners for the figure that advanced then retreated, looking for someone who looked as though they were lost.

The house phone was ringing as she walked in the door of the flat after one of her daily walks, her face glowing from fresh air and exercise. Feeling ready for something to eat for a change, something 'proper' as Yvonne would call it, she lifted the phone and started to rummage in the fridge to see what Sam had left for supper. "Hello."

"Mirabelle? It's me, Doreen. Peter's mum?"

"Oh, hi, Doreen. What can I do for you?"

"It's Peter. He's not here."

Mirabelle looked at the clock on the wall. Six-fifteen.

"He's always here! Five o'clock, on the dot. He waits for me here."

"I know, I know. On the battlements, Castle Esplanade. I've seen him."

"He's always here," Doreen repeated. "He's autistic. He's had the same routine for fifteen years. He's never not here." Her voice was rising through the octaves of anxiety.

"I'm on to it," Mirabelle said, retrieving her bag from the chair beside her. "You stay put. I'll walk his route. Have you called the police?"

"Not yet. I just keep thinking he'll be here. Keep checking my watch. Do you think I should?"

"Ask for DI Burns. Tell him Mirabelle told you to. Sam'll know what to do."

"Right! Thanks, Mirabelle. I didn't know who else…"

"It's okay, Doreen. It'll be okay. Just stay put in case he gets to you."

Mirabelle was out the door and down the stairs before she thought again about food. Good thing she always kept a Mars or two in her bag: sweet dinner on the move.

Peter's walk took her longer than ever. She looked in every doorway, every wynd. She spoke to strangers, friends, acquaintances: anyone who might have noticed him. "Small man, head down, shuffling. He's autistic, you see — and deaf."

166

By the time she'd reached Castle Esplanade, she was exhausted and sweating but still on the move. "Not turned up?" she asked Doreen.

Doreen shook her head, unable to speak.

"Hold tight, love. Police onto it?"

Doreen nodded.

"Right! I'll finish the circuit. Be back." Her breath was coming in harsh painful rasps now. Her usual sauntering pace had quickened with every empty doorway, every negative response to her enquiries. Her heart was beating out her fears as she ran down the stairs to Johnston Terrace.

He's autistic.

In his own world.

Vulnerable.

A man-child.

Rocky heights rose above her as she ran along the Terrace, rushing past lingering tourists staring up at the back of the Castle.

Not till emergency, realise how fond.

Something happened.

Must have.

Past the entrance to the car park and on to Castle Terrace. Up Lothian Road, past St Cuthbert's and St John's.

Mirabelle had to lean on the barrier between the pavement and the road. She had to get her breath. The pain was crushing. Tea-time traffic easing now, but still people walking past, looking at her, walking around at a little distance. She guessed she probably looked drunk — or worse. Swaying against the barrier, sweat coursing down her face, her neck, her back, soaking through her clothes.

But she had to find him. She pushed off from the railings and started running again — or what passed as running. The strength was going from her legs. She was pushing through treacle now. With millstones strapped to her ankles.

Round the corner.

In at the West Gate.

Almost through the Gardens.

Almost out of puff.

Stars exploding in front of her.

And, at last, the old, threadbare coat.

His father's old threadbare coat.

She had done the circuit the long way round.

If she'd just come straight into the Gardens.

She ran to the bench in a last, superhuman gasp of effort.

He was sitting, asleep it looked. No-one would have come near him in hours. Probably assumed he was a tramp, a drunk, a down-and-out. His hands were cold as she took them in her own. She felt for a pulse. Thanked God, she found one. Weak, but there: his life blood still coursing through his huddled body.

"Help! I need some help here," she shouted, looking round for someone, anyone walking through the park. There was a girl, a young woman, hanging back, watching from a distance. "Please! I need help. An ambulance. Do you have a phone?"

The girl drew back a little; hesitant, unsure.

"He's unconscious. Something's wrong. Please, you have to help!"

With obvious reluctance, the girl took a mobile phone from her pocket and brought it to Mirabelle.

"You do it," Mirabelle said. "I won't know how to use yours."

"You still don't know...?"

"Just do it, will you? Please. This man's in trouble. He needs an ambulance."

The girl turned away a little and started dialling. "Here," she handed the phone to Mirabelle. "You explain."

After the ambulance arrived, the girl disappeared. She hung around after getting her phone back until the ambulance crew had assured them Peter was going to be all right — and that Mirabelle, herself, was going to be all right. After they'd seen to Peter, one of the paramedics insisted on taking her blood pressure while his colleague climbed into the driver's seat of the ambulance. "You want to watch

168

yourself, dear. Doesn't look like you're well enough for all that runnin' around."

"No, I've not been too great for a while," Mirabelle agreed. "Been trying to get healthy, though. Walk every day. Thought walking was supposed to keep you fit."

"Yeah! Only if you watch what you're eating too. Need a good balanced diet." He looked at the Mars bar she had taken from her bag.

"Don't *you* start!"

He laughed. "Been told that already, eh?"

"Ad infinitum!"

"P'raps time to listen. Blood pressure sky high. On any medication?"

Mirabelle shook her head.

"I'd get myself along to the doc's, if I were you."

With a sigh, Mirabelle acknowledged perhaps it was time she did.

She looked round to thank the girl. "Have you seen a girl? A young woman? She was just here," she asked the paramedic. "It was her phone."

The paramedic shook his head. "If you'd like to come with us …"

"No, no, it's okay. I got the girl to phone Sam — DI Sam Burns — after she phoned for you. He'll get Peter's mum to the hospital. They'll meet you there."

"Yes, but I'd like you to come anyway," he said. "You know Peter. If he comes round — a familiar face?"

"Oh, yes." Mirabelle sat down again. "You didn't see her, though? The girl? She was black. No, *she* wasn't black. She was all *in* black. Her clothes, her hair, her make-up. All black."

"A Goth, like?" The paramedic closed the ambulance door and sat by Mirabelle. Peter was lying across from them, the oxygen mask in place, the other medic monitoring his vital signs.

"S'pose." Mirabelle shrugged. "It's just, I feel I've seen her before." She shrugged again, as she brought her hand up to wipe perspiration from her forehead. "Oh, well. Never mind. Too late now. She's gone." She closed her eyes and relaxed into the motion as the ambulance cautiously wound its way along the paths of the park.

Thankfully, no need for sirens and panic.

Peter was stable.

Everything under control.

A happy mum waiting to cry her thanks on Mirabelle's shoulder.

"You okay?" the paramedic asked Mirabelle. He patted her hand. "He's going to be all right, you know. You did well. Found him in time."

She nodded. Tried to smile.

"Tears of relief, then?"

She hadn't known she was crying. "Something like that," she said, wiping her face. "Just tired."

So tired.

She almost fell asleep against the medic's shoulder but they arrived at the hospital and they had to move. Almost as soon as they'd stretchered Peter out and on to a trolley, the paramedic's beeper went and the ambulance prepared to leave.

Another call. Another emergency.

"No rest for the wicked!" he said, with a wry smile and a nod of farewell.

As soon as Peter was settled in a ward, his mother beside him, Sam took Mirabelle home and sat by her bed as she cried herself to sleep.

So tired.

So emotionally drained.

"You have to go to the doctor," Sam said when he looked in the next morning.

"So everyone keeps telling me," she said with a sigh.

"Oh?"

"Ambulance man. Took my blood pressure. Sky high."

"You'd been running?"

She nodded.

"You can't go on like this, Belle." He sat down beside her. "One day, you'll climb one hill too many. You really need to look after yourself. I know you're beginning to eat again, but you're eating all the wrong things. If Yvonne or I don't cook for you, you eat nothing but rubbish. Your body needs nourishment. You keep telling me you get light-headed sometimes. Seriously, Belle. That's not normal. Please, will you just go to the doctor."

So, to keep Sam happy, and despite feeling better now she'd recovered from her overexertion, Mirabelle reluctantly walked to the Health Centre a few days later, muttering under her breath about the lack of necessity.

"Hi, sis!" the receptionist greeted her. "What you doing here?" Concern shot across her face. "You're not sick are you?"

"Course not," Mirabelle said. "Just socialising with your employers."

Yvonne blushed. "Sorry, Belle! Course you must be ill if you've got an appointment to see the doctor. Just that you're never in here, apart from when you come for your fit note, and you're not due one."

"I know. And I wouldn't be here now but Sam put a headlock on me. Said if I didn't get a check-up he'd

171

confiscate my box of Mars bars."

"Ouch!"

"Exactly."

Yvonne scanned the computer screen. "Doctor Morrison, did you say?"

"Ten-thirty."

She clicked on the time. "Yep! There you are. If you'd like to take a seat, she'll see you in a mo. Think someone's in with her just now."

"You okay?"

Yvonne nodded. "You?"

"Lunch after? Catch-up?"

"Great, sis." She turned to take the next patient's name. "Hey!" she called after Mirabelle. "Don't suppose you're free Saturday for a visit to Gran? Thought I'd borrow Hannah's car and pop out there. Wanna come? Sorry," she said to the lady waiting at the desk, "She's my big sister," by way of explanation, a potentially puzzling explanation for the onlooker since Mirabelle's colouring was so obviously Caribbean and Yvonne's was so obviously not. But neither she nor Mirabelle favoured the 'half-sister' label and didn't mind creating a bit of mystery.

They made arrangements to meet for lunch and Mirabelle took a seat in the waiting room quite close to the desk so she could engage in intermittent snatches of conversation with her youngest sister until Doctor Morrison called her name.

Mirabelle was obese. The doctor's very words. "Morbidly obese." Hardly a cheerful diagnosis.

"Sounds gruesome," Mirabelle muttered, rubbing her arm where the blood pressure cuff had been.

"I want you to join our diet and exercise clinic." Doctor Morrison handed her a slip of paper with the details. "That is not a suggestion," she said, looking sternly at Mirabelle. "It is an absolute necessity. I can't help you otherwise. You may well have lost weight, as you say, but I'm afraid you need to lose at least another eighteen, nineteen kilos."

172

"What's that in real money?" Mirabelle asked, petulance pouting her lips.

"About forty pounds."

Her eyebrows asked the question.

"Coming up for three stones."

"Right!" Mirabelle laughed. "You're asking me, no, I suspect you're *telling* me I have to lose three stones?"

The doctor shrugged. "I'm *advising*."

"Huh! Not so long since everyone complained I wasn't eating."

"Mmm. The weight lost during times of stress is often quickly regained, I'm afraid. Once you start eating again."

Mirabelle looked down at her belly. "Which I obviously have," she said.

If anyone were to ask, Mirabelle would tell them, "I love being fat." But it wasn't true. She found her extra weight burdensome as she walked about in the streets of Edinburgh. It slowed her down, made her breathless, dizzy sometimes. She had an unpleasant tingling in her fingers and her toes.

"You're in danger of becoming diabetic," the doctor added. "I'd like you to make an appointment with the nurse for blood tests and to hand in a urine sample. But it's a fair guess we'll find your glucose levels bad — and your cholesterol."

Mirabelle scowled.

"Tell me about your diet."

Mirabelle never cooked: never had. And she hated salads.

"You're a fraud," Summer called her once. "Everyone thinks you're some kind of modern hippie. You dress like one, you act like one, but you're not. You're just some weirdo doing your own stupid thing. Real hippies eat raw vegetables and lentils and stuff. They're vegetarians, vegans even, some of them. They don't eat all this stuff," she said pushing away the greasy kebab Mirabelle had brought in for her supper. "You're just a great big fat fraud!"

173

Junk food, that's what she liked: pizza, pies, pastries and chocolate.

Hardly a balanced diet, she knew, but what she was used to, what she was comfortable with. Only, she was no longer comfortable. It was becoming difficult to find knickers. Knickers never lasted long. The elastic always failed quite quickly nowadays. Mirabelle remembered a time when elastic seemed indestructible. The knickers would wear into holes before the elastic went. Not any more. Within weeks, it seemed, she would feel the offending undergarment slipping down her body. She would have to feel through the folds of her dress, find the failing band and haul the pants up. *"You know,"* she'd say, *"they just don't make things like they used to. Shoddy workmanship! I blame the telly."*

She blamed the telly when she found herself unable to get up in the mornings too. *"Up too late last night,"* she'd say. *"Watching rubbish."* But she wasn't. She wasn't watching anything, rubbish or otherwise. She'd doze off in the chair half-way through the evening and drag herself through to bed hours later, sluggish and un-refreshed from her uncomfortable half-sleep. Then she'd rise again before the clock had ticked off many minutes and, pulling an A4 pad towards her, she'd write feverishly until her hand cramped and her brain fogged. She had decided to record everything she could remember about her life with Summer, make some sort of journal after the event. The need to relive and re-examine their life together drove her from her bed.

She also recorded everything she had found out about where Summer had been, what she had been doing, what she herself thought, what she felt. The journal was messy, with changes aplenty, almost indecipherable in parts, night-time ramblings of a desperate mind.

The couple of hours sleep she stole as the street lights dimmed was enough to sustain but not enough to restore.

The problem wasn't the telly. Never had been. The telly was there for Summer; company when Mirabelle was late home from work. She'd always had a dodgy diet — good when Summer cooked, dreadful when up to her to feed

174

herself. Over the years she had managed to be active and alert, feeling no need to change the habits she'd formed. True, since Summer went her diet was worse than ever, but too many late nights and a bad diet were not really the problem. They were symptoms. Symptoms of a state of mind, symptoms of depression and despair.

"Do you want me to prescribe some anti-depressants for you?" Doctor Morrison drew the prescription pad towards her.

Mirabelle shook her head. "No," she said. "I'm not a great one for pills and stuff."

"Sometimes they are very necessary."

"I don't doubt it. But not for me. I really don't need anything, thanks. I'll be fine. Just need to sort myself out." She sat up straighter.

"Just to tide you over for a month or two?"

She laughed. "Then what? No." She shook her head again. "Thank you, but no."

She'd be fine. Like she said, just needed to sort herself out. Been scouring the streets of Edinburgh now for too long, that's all: staring into the faces of strangers, the faces of young women in their late teens/early twenties, following them, finding excuses to speak to them, looking for Summer. The problem was her hope was dimming, becoming ethereal, intangible, harder to grasp. Foods, in the shape of chocolate bars, on the other hand, were real, they were right there: solid, dependable, her friends.

"Okay. Tell me about your diet," the doctor said, pushing the pad away. "For instance, what's for dinner tonight?"

The dreaded sentence.

what's for dinner?

Mirabelle saw herself, sitting with an array of takeaway menus on her lap and wondered how many mothers, how many wives, husbands, fathers, partners heard the request and felt the thump of their self-esteem hitting the floor.

"Nothing. I forgot to shop."

Or, "Oh-oh! Is it that time already?"

Or, "Drat! I meant to pick up a ready meal."

Whatever.

It's not what you want to say.

You want to say, "Are you hungry, darling? I have a shepherd's pie in the oven. It's almost ready."

Or, "Ooh! I bought some lovely pork chops from the butcher today. I've done them with a cider gravy and roast potatoes."

Or, "Smells good, doesn't it? Braised steak with onions and garlic. Been in the slow cooker. Ready when you are."

Saw herself pick up the menus with a sigh …

Why couldn't she be the kind of mum who made the dinner every night from fresh, healthy ingredients, bought on her way home from work, rustled up into varied, nutritious, delicious meals? Many women worked and still performed the magic. Supermarkets stayed open late. It would always be possible to stop and purchase what was needed. Many households tolerated a late supper.

… fanning out the menus.

Ah! Here was another problem.

Choice. Too much choice.

"Indian or Chinese? Or the deli?" she'd ask Summer if there'd been nothing in the fridge for Summer to rustle into a meal for them, and no money lying around for her to use to

176

get something. She'd ask the question, knowing what Summer was going to say.

"Whatever! You decide." She'd eaten by that time, her appetite dulled by the cheese on toast or pots of yoghurt, whatever she found in the kitchen that would stave off the hunger pangs till her mother came home. *"I don't care."*

'I don't care.' What she really meant was, "*You* don't care." Mirabelle knew that now. Each time she ordered-in food for herself, she saw a little more of Summer's life: what it had been like to be a latch-key kid. Just because she'd been capable of improvising to fill her wee belly doesn't mean she should have been left to do so.

"Or the chippie? D'you want me to run up the road for fish'n'chips? A sausage supper?"

Often met with snorted laughter. "Run, Mother? You'll run up to the chippie?"

Mirabelle would look at her fulsome figure and remember she meant to do something about it. "Not the chippie, then."

Summer had her tagged. She was a fraud. Not just as a hippie, but as a mother, as a human being really. A fraud, that's what she was.

She stared at the doctor. "Oh, I haven't decided. Maybe a wee bit of fish?"

But she knew — and the doctor's face registered she knew too — she was going home to scan the fan. Choice. Too much choice. And, when she couldn't make the choice, she'd settle for a Mars bar.

Perhaps if someone told her what to cook, what to buy.

Was there a handbook she'd missed out on somewhere?

When she'd lain on that narrow couch in that dingy bedsit and got on with her daughter's birthing alone, did she miss out on some handbook handed out by some midwife in a crisp uniform with a starched apron, in a sterile hospital ward somewhere. "Here you are, Ms Milligan. *How To Be A Mum.* Everything you need to know in one nice thick volume." She'd flick through the pages. "See? Here's a chapter on how to burp your baby, how to change her nappy, cope with

177

colic. And here, further on, *Preparing For School*, *Helping With Homework*." She'd proffer the book. "And this one, *Cooking Nutritious Meals*." She'd leave it open on the bed. "There you are, dear. You browse through that while I flick that switch you have that makes you a real mum."

Or was it a pill she had missed? A motherhood pill?

Or an injection? An injection of maternal instinct? Essence of maternal instinct in a tiny dark-blue vial.

Whatever it was, Mirabelle had missed out on it.

"Hey, sis! You okay?"

Mirabelle leant on the desk. "I've to make another appointment."

Yvonne logged in to the computer. "So, when d'you want?"

"I don't!"

Yvonne's hand hovered over the mouse.

"Diet and exercise clinic."

"Ah! Hence the doleful-donkey look!" Yvonne handed her a card with the appointment details. "Never mind. We'll have a last fling at Gran's, Saturday. She doesn't believe in diets."

Chapter Fourteen

She had only popped out for a minute or two, dropping into the smallish supermarket down the hill to pick up a few mushrooms and a nice piece of salmon for her dinner later.

It had been Sam who suggested she think of something she might enjoy, something that might tempt her to eat properly. "Come on, Belle," he said. "You need to look after yourself."

"So you keep telling me."

"And so does everyone else. You're a terrible colour. Your skin looks like rough parchment and you're sore and stiff all the time."

Mirabelle shrugged. "Thanks a bundle. But it's my problem, not yours."

"It's mine too, Belle. Don't you see that? We're in a relationship. I happen to care about you."

She shrugged again.

"You've been to the doctor. You heard what she said. You need a proper diet. With fruit and vegetables, fish and meat." He opened one of her kitchen cupboards. "Not all this rubbish," he said, looking at the stash of chocolate bars and candy it contained. He opened another. "Grief, Belle. There's not even a tin of sweetcorn in here."

"I'm okay," she said, weary resignation in her voice.

"No." He shook his head. "You're not."

Mirabelle shrugged.

"You're eating worse than you ever did. At least when Summer was home you'd have some decent food now and then."

"Yeah! When she made it," Mirabelle muttered.

"All these carry-out meals are not good for you."

179

"Yeah, well! My cook's gone walk-about, or hadn't you noticed?" she mumbled.

"And so-called 'treats' that don't even make you feel any better."

"They do!"

Sam gave her a scathing look. "Oh yeah! Can you tell me they don't make your joints ache? That the high they give you lasts for more than a few minutes then you crash and feel rubbish?" He waited.

She didn't answer, just walked out of the kitchen and through to the living room.

"Right. As I thought." He slammed the cupboard door shut. "You don't deserve this, Belle," he said as he followed her through. "Bad enough Summer is punishing you for whatever sins she imagines you guilty of, without you punishing yourself."

"I'm not punishing anyone. Just can't be bothered cooking."

"Well it's time you were bothered."

"Anyway, it's stupid to say that Summer is punishing me. Until we know where she is, what's happened to her, you can't make that call. Neither can anyone else. Anything could have happened to my daughter. And, if you were half the detective you think you are, you'd have found out what by now."

Sam sighed deeply. "No, Belle. There is just no evidence anything has happened to Summer she didn't want to happen."

Mirabelle closed her eyes and put her hands over her ears. "Just because you haven't found evidence, doesn't mean there is none."

"Come on, Belle. You know I'm doing all I can do."

"Why haven't you arrested that so-called boyfriend, then? That Dermot person. Good grief, Sam. If ever there was a guilty man."

"There is no proof. Nothing."

"He's a drug dealer. And a pimp. You know that. He probably gave her drugs. He sold her services to those men. Is that not enough?"

"Not if you want us to find Summer, it's not, Belle. We need him out there, doing what he does, dealing with who he deals with."

"Huh!" Mirabelle flung herself into the armchair. "So you can get the man further up the food chain. I know. I've watched plenty detective dramas."

"No. So we catch him supplying Summer. Follow him, we find Summer."

"Oh."

"She's out there somewhere, probably needing her next fix. We just have to catch him supplying it and we've got them both."

"Oh. Right." Mirabelle sank back into the chair. "Always supposing she is actually hooked, of course."

"Yeah, Belle. Always supposing." Sam's mobile beeped in his pocket and, after consulting it, he started to put his jacket on. "Anyway, I've got to go to work," he said with a sigh. "Just remember what I said."

"You said a lot, Sam."

"I'm telling you. Summer is alive and well and is staying away for reasons best known to her. I reckon she's punishing you, and you just don't deserve it."

"Maybe I do deserve it."

Sam reached down to her in the chair, held her arms and turned her to face him. "No, you don't. There are few mothers who would deserve this kind of treatment from their daughters, and you are certainly not one of them."

She pulled away from him. "How do you know? You weren't around to know what kind of mother I was."

"But I know you, Belle. I know you would not, could not, have deliberately hurt or mistreated Summer. Any sins you were guilty of were of omission. Okay, so you were too preoccupied with your work, you maybe didn't give her enough attention, whatever. It still doesn't deserve what she's doing."

"Maybe she's just trying to give me a taste of my own medicine."

"Don't you see how cruel that is?"

Mirabelle began to fiddle with the television remote, flicking the set on, flicking through the channels. "She's only a kid," she said as she turned in the armchair to face the screen.

"Yeah! And what she's doing now is certainly immature, but it's also cruel."

She turned up the sound, a street dance crew strutted their stuff on the screen, their music making further conversation almost impossible.

Sam sighed and rested his hand on her shoulder. "Okay. Okay. I'm going, but, please, Belle. Just think about what I'm saying?" He bent to drop a kiss on her head. "Give yourself a break, pal." He'd bought a magazine full of recipes for delicious home-cooked meals and succulent foods, glorious full-colour photographs of enticing delicacies on every page, and he laid it on the arm of the chair.

"I am partial to a nice bit of salmon," she admitted, looking up at him.

"Good." He smiled.

She turned the sound down. "I'll buy some on my way home tonight."

"Promise?"

"Promise. and lemon and pasley."

"A few carrots? Or sprouts?"

She grinned. "Don't push it, pal."

The street dancers disappeared with a click of the remote as the flat door closed behind him.

And now her taste buds tingled in anticipation.

She was heading through the supermarket car-park, the pink salmon tantalisingly close, when her steps faltered, her mouth dried.

Without thought or care, she dumbly shadowed a young woman who walked from her car carrying a couple of clinking bags.

Halting, unable to move away, she watched as the woman threw bottles in the recycling bin, Mirabelle flinching with each crash as they smashed on top of the pile. The uniform jeans and tee-shirt gave nothing away and she couldn't see her face properly, but there was something about her movements, the way she held her head, the way she walked. And she looked the right age, seventeen, eighteen or thereabout.

Mirabelle took from the depths of her bag the same tattered photograph she'd been showing around and studied it again, though she hardly needed to, she knew it so well. The photograph was old and crumpled but the features were clear. With little imagination, it was possible to age the sweet young fifteen-year-old face looking back at her by two or three years. She replaced it in her bag and continued her observation.

The girl's hair was almost the right colour, the colour Summer's hair could be now, assuming it had darkened and dulled with the months and the lack of care and nutrition Mirabelle assumed her to be suffering: not the vibrant red it used to be, more reddish-light-brown, but that didn't count. Hair colour was unreliable for identification, it could be changed on a whim. And the loose curls falling round her shoulders, they could be manufactured too. Height about right: father tall, mother average. At an estimate, the young woman she had followed in the supermarket car park was slightly above average, about five-six or seven.

Mirabelle sighed. She'd need to see her face properly, study it up close. It was not enough to approach her just because she had a *hunch.*

"Do I know you?" the woman asked.

Mirabelle stepped back, startled.

"Only, you seem to be following me or something?"

"No ... no ... I ..."

"Tommy!" the woman called. "Gaunae git yerself over here. This wuman keeps starin' at me."

"Sorry! Sorry," Mirabelle stuttered, dropping her bag, her hands raised in front of her face, her flight hindered by the van she'd loitered beside. "I thought you were someone else."

Tommy placed his bulk between Mirabelle and his partner.

"I thought she was someone else."

"Why? H've ye lost someone?" The woman looked around.

"It's okay. I'm sorry. I didn't mean ..."

"Aye well, ah jist dinnae like being followed or anything, ye ken."

With a sigh of relief, Mirabelle picked up her bag and retreated from the car park, watching as the couple gathered their kids and headed for the shop. She shuddered, realising the woman was far older, probably mid-twenties, Mirabelle suddenly aware she could be losing her touch, losing the subtle skills she usually employed. She'd have to tighten up. Be more careful.

Having completely lost her appetite, she didn't bother going into the shop, but shuffled up the hill, past her stair, and started wandering the streets of Edinburgh, as she had so many times before, going far afield, unable to settle, unwilling to go home to the empty house, asking in various hostels and shelters if they had seen her daughter.

"Who's looking for her?" the duty warden of one of the hostels asked.

"I'm her mother," Mirabelle said.

He handed back the photograph. "You don't look like her. Got the ginger from her father's side, did she?"

"Certainly not from me."

"No, but she got your eyes. The shape of them. Not the colour. Yours are darker, eh?"

"Yes, hers are more sort of hazel."

"And yours are like delicious big pools of molten chocolate."

"Umm! Not sure what to say to that."

The warden grinned at her. "Take it as a compliment, love. Just don't tell the wife I noticed."

Mirabelle made to put the photograph of Summer back in her bag.

"She might've been here, you know. Months ago. Four months, five at most."

"She was? You're sure? But I've asked here before."

"Ah, but you'll not have spoken to me," he said. "Was down-under for couple of months."

"Down-under?"

"The wife and me, we were off in Australia visiting her brother. Been back a month now, but you've not been in lately have you?"

"No."

Pointing to the photograph, "But I think I remember this lass," he said. "She was in here a bit before we went."

"You're sure?"

"Certain." He walked through to his office, motioning for Mirabelle to follow him. "I've a great memory for faces. See?" He flipped back some pages and pointed to an entry in his visitors book, right after Summer went missing. "Sally Red. Not her real name, of course. I knew that. But it served. She was here three nights. See? Paid her fee too."

"Oh!" Mirabelle reached out to touch the page. "Her writing." She stroked the page, her fingers trembling, trying to feel the indentation, follow the writing back up the pen to that precious hand. "I'd know it anywhere." Her voice was hoarse. Came out as a whisper. "That's her writing."

"Aye. Sally Red, that's what she signed. It was after I'd remarked on her hair. Said she preferred to be called red than ginger." He laughed. "I let her off with the false name since she had a sense of humour." He started to tidy away the ledger. "Bright wee thing. Plenty spirit. Hope you find her."

Laughter leapt into her mouth. She couldn't stop it. It bubbled out and spilled all over the street as she walked home. People looked at her. Someone asked if she was all right. She couldn't answer through the tears streaming down her face as she laughed and laughed and laughed. She couldn't stop. Though her body hurt with it, her head ached with it, her nose ran, her eyes watered, she couldn't stop laughing until she cried.

"Don't call me ginger," Summer used to shout at anyone who dared to when she was little. *"My hair's not ginger, it's red!"*

"Ginger's a biscuit," she'd say when she was a little older. *"Or a cat. I'm not ginger."*

Mirabelle was heartened she still wouldn't allow it. Heartened Summer still knew how to make light of her situation. It showed spirit. Survival spirit. Maybe Summer was going to be all right after all. If only she'd just come home now.

"A joke's a joke," she said to Yvonne the next day.

"Have you told Sam?"

"No, but I will. Not that it tells us anything about where she is now."

"Still, he'll want to know."

"Yes."

"Why don't you get one of those whiteboard things," Yvonne said. "You know? Like in the detective programmes on the box? Make a timeline of where and when Summer was last seen."

"Yeah, but that was just a few days after she went missing."

"Still, it'd be good to see it on a timeline."

So Mirabelle did. Trouble was, after the first flurry of sightings, the line stretched long and empty across the board on her kitchen wall.

Chapter Fifteen

Even with all Sam's encouragement and ministrations, Mirabelle grew bent and stiff, her weight continuing to yo-yo and her colour bad, needing no mirror to tell her she aged more in the first eight months of searching for Summer than the thirty before.

She'd never been thin. Always curvy, her figure had blossomed with the years into voluptuous. For a while, after Summer went, her dresses hung looser, like semi-deflated umbrellas. Her skirts belted in folds at her hips instead of straining over them. In other circumstances she might have been pleased she'd lost some of her excess weight, but Sam was right, the doctor was right, that hadn't been a healthy weight loss. Her skin had an empty look. It had been dry and itchy, and, like her clothes, it had folded around her bones. There had been no firmness to it, no glow.

Then she'd started eating to please Sam, but not healthy eating. Fast food, sweets, whatever was easiest. Constant nibbling on cheese and chocolate. Curries and Kebabs delivered late at night. Weight piled back on quickly, just as the doctor had said.

She started going to the diet and exercise class at the doctor's instruction, but after weeks of dismal failure to keep up with the exercises and keep the weight down, she stopped attending.

"I'll sort myself out," she told Yvonne. "I don't need someone else to tell me how to jump up and down and bunny-hop." She picked up the diet sheets and waved them in Yvonne's face. "And you can have these if you like. I'm not going to cook all this stuff. I know what I should and should't be eating."

"Knowing isn't the problem."

"Yeah. Okay. Gonna get off my back?"

"I will, just as soon as you start doing something about it," Yvonne said, taking the diet sheets from Mirabelle and putting them on the worktop.

"I will. I will. Just need to get my head round it. Trouble is, once I start nibbling, I can't stop."

"Then don't start," Yvonne joked, giving her sister a hug as she left to go to work.

"D'you know, that's not such a bad idea."

So Mirabelle did. Almost. For weeks, she almost stopped eating altogether, starving herself, only eating the occasional chocolate bar or slice of cheese when her stomach gnawed. Avoided going to Yvonne's for a meal, or having Sam come and cook for her. "Too busy," she'd tell Yvonne. "Won't be in," she'd say to Sam. Stopped phoning for food to be delivered late at night. Neglected even to drink unless Yvonne or Sam came round and made a cup of tea.

"Yeah, you're losing weight," Yvonne said. "But look at you. You look awful. And you've no energy. I know you want to diet, but what exactly are you eating?"

"I'm eating."

"Yes, but what? When? I haven't seen you eat in weeks."

"I eat."

Yvonne opened the fridge. "There's nothing in here but a dried up piece of cheese."

"I've not done my shopping yet." MIrabelle draped a huge colourful triangle of material round her shoulders. "Which is what I was just about to do before you turned up, sticking your nose in my fridge."

"Yeah?"

"Yeah!"

"At ten o'clock at night?"

"Best time to go to the supermarket. It'll be nice and quiet."

"Come on, Belle," Sam said another day. "It's been more than eight months since Summer went. You have to sort yourself out, get your life back."

"Eight months? It's nothing." She clutched her belly. "I carried her for nine."

"I know, but …"

"I'm up and about, aren't I? What more d'you want me to do?"

"I want you to start eating properly. Put cream on your face. Wear your jewellery again. Look like you. Do things. Go places."

"I do go places. I'm out all the time."

"Without looking for Summer."

Mirabelle shook her head. "No can do."

"Come on, Belle. Summer's gone. That was her choice."

"You don't know that. You don't know she made that choice."

"All the evidence …"

"Oh, sod you and your evidence! You're a detective. How come you can't find my daughter?"

"Maybe she doesn't want to be found. In fact, clearly she doesn't want to be found."

Mirabelle ignored him, dismissing his logic with a wave of her hand. "Maybe she's locked up somewhere, being held in someone's cellar, some sex fiend's spare room."

"Don't, Belle. Don't do this again."

Mirabelle threw her empty mug at him, missing him and sending it crashing against the wall, smashing to smithereens. "Don't do what? Don't think about what's happened to my daughter? Don't think about whether she's alive or dead?"

"She's alive, Belle."

"You don't know that."

Sam put his hands over his ears. "Belle …"

"What? Calm down? Be quiet? What, Sam? Worried about the neighbours?" She stomped over to the sink, lifted another mug and hurled it after the first one. "Well, they're my neighbours, Sam. And I don't care what they think." She was yelling now, her voice hoarse with angry tears. "My daughter's missing," she shouted, throwing a third mug, and a fourth. "My daughter's missing!" Quieter now, the words strangling in her sobs. "My daughter's missing." She crumpled to the floor.

Sam tried to lift her.

"No!" she spat at him. "Leave me alone. Go find my daughter."

He backed off, scratching his head. "Come on, Belle. I'm on your side."

"Huh!"

"I've followed every line of enquiry, every clue. You know I have. Even since the case was closed, I've kept going in my own time. She's alive. I'm sure she's alive. Maybe she's just not ready to be found yet."

"Maybe, maybe, maybe. Maybe you don't know what you're talking about, Sam Burns." Mirabelle pulled herself to her feet. "How can I possibly stop looking for Summer? I'm her mother."

"I know, Belle. And I know I've never had children. But I'm not stupid. I can see what's happening to you. You're becoming obsessed with the search."

"Oh! Just get out if that's how you feel." She started pushing him towards the door. "Leave me alone. If I'm obsessed, then so be it. I'm obsessed." She flung his jacket at him. "All I know is I can't just pretend nothing's happened. I can't just 'get on with my life.' Summer *is* my life." And she slammed the door behind him.

But she knew he was right. And she knew if Summer had always 'been her life,' been *first* in her life, there'd be another 'maybe.' Maybe Summer would not have gone.

She'd taken a good look at herself in the mirror and didn't like what she saw. And she didn't mean her pallor or her droopy boobs.

Obsessed? She probably was obsessed. But was there a correct, a normal amount of time a mother should look for her daughter before accepting her daughter didn't want to be found? Was there a time limit on love?

After more than thirty years, she still wished she could find her father, still longed to see his face, hear his voice, be enveloped in his arms. Knowing that would never change, the longing would stay with her forever, she doubted it would be different with the loss of a child. Obsessed? So be it, she had said to Sam. So be it.

The echo of the slammed door still resounded when she accepted and embraced his diagnosis.

Sam walked down the stairs, wondering what else he could do. He reckoned he'd been pretty patient with Mirabelle. After all, there were kids out there who were being mistreated, who didn't have the choice to run away from home because they were too young or too cowed. He knew. He dealt with some horrendous situations all the time. And this was not one of them.

Summer was just a typically selfish teenager who had taken herself off, getting up to no good, he reckoned. The fact she'd stayed away this long showed her to be rather more selfish than average. She must know her mother's world had imploded. He shook his head. Selfish, selfish, selfish …

Sitting in the car, he couldn't quite bring himself to formulate the words he would normally use for someone like that. After all, it was Mirabelle's kid, and, by extension, might one day be his step-kid. Though, right now, any offers of marriage to Mirabelle were strictly off the table. Like he said, he'd been pretty patient up to now.

It had been a puzzle at first, Summer's disappearance. But it had gone long past that now. It was obvious the kid had done a disappearing act by choice. No puzzle there. Nothing for him to solve. Certainly nothing he could justify spending the force's resources on.

A bit like when he was a kid and used to play hide-and-seek with his mate. Basically, Danny McLeod was a cheat. As soon as Sam got close to finding him, he'd scarper off and hide the last place Sam had already looked. There was practically smoke coming out Sam's ears before he gave up on the game, Danny declaring himself the winner by default.

"You cheated!" he'd accuse.

"That's not cheating. It's the game," Danny would reason.

"No, it's no. Yer supposed tae stay put until yer found."

"No in ma rules," Danny would say as he walked away.

Good grief, it was irritating!

Every time they played the damn game, he swore it'd be the last time, but Danny had a way of getting what he wanted, and he liked hide'n'seek.

Their disagreements over the rules of the game could have ruined the friendship — if Danny hadn't fallen from the hayloft in his father's barn and landed badly.

Friendship.

Sam remembered the lesson his mother had taught him about the meaning of friendship. Actually, he'd never forgotten it, and it pushed its way out from his subconscious onto centre stage as he sat and thought.

Danny had broken his leg and was laid up in the house. It was summer, they were ten years old, and Sam was hanging about the kitchen, bored, missing his pal. He'd done his chores on the farm, it was a warm afternoon and he was without a playmate.

"Why don't you go knock on Danny's," his mother suggested.

"He's broke his leg."

"Aye, ah know that. But you could still knock see how he is."

"Why?"

"Because he's your friend."

"But he cannae play nothing."

"He's still your friend."

"It's nae guid if he can't play fitba'," Sam sulked.

"You could do something else."

Sam looked at her with scepticism. "But we always play fitba'. Or hide'n' seek. An he canna dae neither."

"Maybe he'd like to see you anyway."

"But why? If he canna come out tae play?"

194

His mother set aside the chicken she was plucking and wiped her hands on her apron. "Dae ye like having a friend?" she asked him, sitting beside him at the scrubbed wooden table. "When Danny's no hurt and ye can play, dae ye like having a friend?"

"Aye."

"Aye, well, if ye want to have a friend, ye've got to be a friend. And to be a friend, ye have to be there at the bad times, no just the good times. Dae ye understand?"

"I think so."

"Ye have to forget what you want, and work out what they need. Right?"

"I think so."

"Why don't ye tak yon stamps ye got from Uncle Tam and show them to Danny. Maybe he'd like to have some of yer doubles. Maybe he'd enjoy to collect stamps tae, specially while he's laid up."

After a lot of grumping and muttering, Sam did as she suggested.

He now remembered how much it had meant to Danny that summer, to have a friend come visit and sit with him till he was able to hobble about again.

They grew closer that summer, and remained good friends, still talking stamps and examining one another's collection whenever they met, no matter how infrequently.

He thought about his mother's words: if you want to have a friend, you've got to be a friend. You have to be there at the bad times, not just the good times, forget what you want, and work out what they need.

"Aargh!" he growled, thumping the steering wheel with the side of his fist. Mirabelle hadn't broken her leg, but she sure as heck was broken, she sure as heck was going through bad times.

Okay, so he thought it was time she got over it and chirped up, but, really, who was he to make that diagnosis?

Just as every broken leg took its own time to heal, and Danny's had been a bad break, needing pins and stuff,

195

keeping him immobile for weeks, so every broken heart would take its own time too.

He thumped the wheel again, setting off the horn. "Sorry," he mouthed to the woman passing the car when she turned to see if it was her he summoned.

It was Yvonne.

He wound down the window. "You going up to Belle's?"

She nodded.

"Sorry again, then," he said with a grimace. "Don't think I've left her in the best of fettle."

Yvonne smiled. "I'll take my chances," she said, turning to go into the stair.

With a huge sigh, Sam started the car, deciding he'd let Mirabelle cool off with Yvonne's help before apprising her of the fact that he would hang around and chum her through this hard time for a bit longer. Always supposing she wanted his company.

Yvonne took a deep breath as she opened the door of the flat. "I'm worried about you, Bellabear," she said as she put her coat over the back of a chair.

"Oh, not you as well."

"As well?"

"Sam was round." Mirabelle shot the last of the broken crockery into the pedal bin. "Tried to get me to get on with my life." She put the dustpan and brush into the broom cupboard. "What does he know?"

"He knows he cares."

"Huh!"

"What is it with you and Sam? He could hardly be more attentive and yet you keep pushing him away."

"Mmm. Literally today. I told him to get lost, or words to that effect."

"Why?"

"Oh, he just annoys me sometimes."

"Yet other times, you seem very cosy with him. Just when I think I'll need to go trying on hats, it's all nothing doing again."

"One thing for sure, you'll not be needing a hat. Whatever."

"Pity," Yvonne said, preening in front of the mirror. "I rather fancy myself with one of those wee fascinator thingies."

"With feathers sticking out all over the shop, no doubt."

"Absolutely! So, when can I start looking for one?"

"Forget it, Vonnie."

"Aw! Why? You not going to bag this one? He's good, you know. A keeper."

"That's as maybe, but I'm not looking to keep anyone. Least of all Sam Burns," she added under her breath.

But it didn't go unheard by Yvonne. "Why not? Why not Sam Burns? Like I said, what is it with you and Sam? He's gorgeous. Like one of these lovely cuddly mixed breeds. You know. A mix between a golden retriever and a terrier. Strong and dependable with a hint of rough."

"Okay. Enough." Mirabelle started pushing Yvonne to the door. "If you don't change the subject right now …"

"But …"

"No more." She held her hand in front of her face, palm out to Yvonne. "Stop now, Yvonne. Or you can follow him down the stairs."

"Okay. Okay. Look, what I actually came to say is, why don't we go visit Gran again? You need a break," Yvonne said. "You can use the journey to calm yourself down."

"I'm perfectly calm, thank you." Mirabelle closed her eyes. "In fact, I'm exhausted." Leaning against the worktop, her head drooping, she sighed. "You're right, I do need a break."

"And you need some good, home cooking. Get some veggies into that belly. Look at you, one month, you're all bloated and flabby, the next, there's nothing of you." She prodded Mirabelle's side. "Look at you. When's the last time you ate properly. Last Friday, when you came to me? And you didn't eat much then."

Mirabelle opened her mouth to protest.

"And don't think I didn't see half your dinner hidden under that paper napkin. You need to be careful or you'll lose all your cuddly, teddy bear softness."

"You and Sam been conferring on this or something? I have a distinct feeling I'm being picked on."

"Well, if you'd just give in and let folks look after you. Come on, get your glad rags on."

Mirabelle lacked the will to resist and found herself swathed in shawls and bundled onto the train to Linlithgow. She sat, not really listening to Yvonne's chatter, not really seeing the autumn countryside slide past the window, only vaguely aware of the train stopping and starting, the doors hissing open, flumping shut, people getting on and off.

Mesmerising electricity pylons, like skeletal extra-terrestrials with six arms, wrists shackled and linked together in chain-gang formation, marched across the landscape. Telegraph wires stretched for miles, strung between upright tuning forks with stunted tines: birds bobbing on the horizontal stave, chirping quavers and crochets.

De-de-de-dah, de-de-de-dah, de-de-de-dah: the joints in the tracks punctuated the whizz of the train.

Hypnotic.

She almost slept.

"Come on, sleepy-head. Our stop." Yvonne shook her arm.

Mirabelle let herself be led from the train like a sleep-walker, only waking up properly when they were outside the station and had walked down the road to catch the small local bus that would take them deeper into West Lothian to the row of farm cottages where Vi and Harry Baxter lived. The hard, uncomfortable bus seats brought her back to full consciousness quickly enough.

"Oh my!" Vi said when they came through the back door of the cottage. "You don't look well." She gave Mirabelle a hug. "You look proper peaky." She touched her hand to Mirabelle's cheek. "When did you last have a good square dinner?"

"That's what I said, Gran. She needs your home cooking." Yvonne lined up for her cuddle.

"You're in luck. It's steak and kidney pudding tonight. I'll peel some extra tatties and put a few more sprouts in the pot. But first, come away in and sit down. I'll put the kettle on." She bustled about the cosy kitchen, producing a plate of home-baked scones and pancakes from the cupboard. She placed them in front of the girls alongside a big jar of jam — "Last year's strawberries," she told them — and a slab of butter. Plates and knives were laid out and Vi indicated, with a flick of a wrist, they should help themselves.

"Mmm. Yummy." Yvonne put butter and a generous dollop of jam on one of the scones and pushed it to Mirabelle, where it sat untouched while Yvonne devoured hers.

"Where's Gramps?" Mirabelle asked.

"Oh, he'll be in in a bit. He's up the farm mucking about with tractors, no doubt." Vi shook her head. "Come in filthy and happy as a kid in a sandbag."

"Ach, you don't mind really, though, do you, Gran?" Yvonne said, smiling at Gran's almost-there-but-not-quite metaphor.

"Keeps him out from under my feet." She rolled up her sleeves and started peeling extra vegetables. "Stops him moping about looking miserable."

"Aw, you know you love him really."

"And he loves being miserable," Mirabelle said. "It's his default setting. We used to call him 'Grumpy', remember, when we were kids?"

"Until he started calling us the dwarves."

"Yeah, I didn't mind 'cos I was Happy," Mirabelle said.

"Yeah, but I did. I was Dopey."

"Well you did put his slippers away in the coal-box."

"It was a joke!"

"Not for Gran, it wasn't, was it Gran? Not when he trailed coal dust all through the front room."

"I was just thinking," Gran said as she popped the extra vegetables into the pots. "Have you spoken to Lexie?"

"Lexie?"

"Well, yes. I just thought, you know, since she and Summer were friends …"

"Of course! Lexie!" Mirabelle jumped up from the chair. "I should have thought of Lexie."

"Where are you going?"

"You're right, Gran. I should've talked to Lexie."

"Hang on." Yvonne crammed the last of a pancake into her mouth. "I'll come with you."

Alexandra Maxwell, or Lexie, as she preferred to be called, was Summer's summer friend. Since she was five years old, and until she was a teenager old enough to look after herself, Summer had stayed with her great-grandmother during school-holiday weekdays while Mirabelle worked. She and Lexie had become close friends over the years. They spent the long summer days wandering the countryside together or horse-riding at Lexie's uncle's farm; the evenings playing Monopoly and Ludo, the nights in sleepovers with one another. They were inseparable during school breaks when they were kids.

"I can't believe I didn't think of Lexie," Mirabelle said as she hurried down the lane that led to the Maxwells' cottage. "All these months I've been so focussed on Edinburgh, I didn't think of Lexie."

"I don't get it," Yvonne panted beside her.

"Don't you see? If Summer is hanging out anywhere, this is where it'll be."

"You can't really think she's here," Yvonne said. "Wouldn't Gran have known if she was?"

"Only if Summer wanted her to."

"But it's been eight months. Could she have kept in hiding from Gran all this time? Just a stone's throw from her back door?"

"Maybe she hasn't been here all the time. Maybe she came after she … When she had nowhere else to go." Mirabelle shrugged. "I don't know. But I mean to find out. I can't believe I didn't think of it before." She shook her head and pursed her lips. "If I find that wee besom is hiding here, right under our noses …"

"You'll be so relieved you'll hug her to death."

"Huh!" She knocked on the cottage door. It was nearly teatime, so they guessed the chances of someone being home were high, but still it was some time before the door was cautiously opened by Lexie's mother.

"Yes? Hang on a minute." And the door closed again.

They looked at one another.

"Sorry. Come in." Mrs Maxwell opened it again. "Stupid bitch is in heat. Don't want her to get out." She was holding onto a young terrier by the collar. "A wee mongrel up the lane's got the hots for her. Get more for thoroughbred puppies," she said as she held the door wide for them.

"Is Lexie about?" Mirabelle asked. "Or Summer?"

"Lexie's up in her room," Mrs Maxwell said. "But why on earth would you think Summer'd be here? Didn't your gran tell me she's still missing?"

Mirabelle nodded.

Betty Maxwell patted Mirabelle's arm. "Sorry to hear about that. Awful for you. Dreadful. Don't know what I'd do if it was my Lexie."

"It's just … I know how close they are."

"Thought she might be hiding here?"

Mirabelle nodded again.

Betty shook her head. "You really think I'd let her do that? While you break your heart? No, Belle," she said. "Too cruel. You should know that."

"I know. I do know. It's just …"

"Desperation? Clutching at straws?"

"Yes."

"Come on. Sit down. I'll put the kettle on, give Lexie a shout. She can tell you herself if she knows anything, anything at all, about Summer."

But she didn't.

"She hasn't had a word from Summer. Nothing," Yvonne told Gran when they got back for tea.

"Or so she claims," said Mirabelle.

"Don't you believe her?"

"Not sure. I mean, I know Summer's not *there*, but I don't know, I didn't feel Lexie was totally honest when she said there'd been no contact. Did you?" She turned to Yvonne.

"W-e-ll, she did seem a bit cagey. Especially when you asked about emails and phone-calls."

"You think she knows more than she's letting on?" Gran asked.

Mirabelle sighed. "Oh, I don't know. Maybe it's just wishful thinking on my part. If she has been in touch with Lexie, at least I'd know she was still … she was still …"

Gran put a steaming steak and kidney pudding on the table. "Of course she's alive. Don't you give up hope now. We'll find her. You see if we don't." She cut into the pudding and started spooning it onto their plates. "Tell you what. I'll keep my eye on that young lady down the lane. Make sure she's not up to anything."

"Thanks, Gran."

"Now, get yourself round that dinner." She pushed the dish of vegetables to the girls and walked to the door. "Harry!" she called through to the other room. "It's on the table. It's history repeating itself, that's what it is," she said as she sat down at the table. "Eh, Harry? Déja review." She served the hot food onto his plate. "You mark my words, Belle. She'll be back, tail between her legs. Summer'll be back. Just like your mum." She wagged the serving spoon at Mirabelle. "Only sixteen she was when she went off the first time."

"But you knew where she was, Gran."

"Not right away we didn't, did we, Harry? Three days she left us worrying before she phoned."

"Summer's already been missing eight months." Eight months. Mirabelle felt again the clutch at her belly. "More. Two hundred and fifty-seven days to be exact."

"She'll be back, you'll see. Just like your mum."

Mirabelle closed her eyes. "Please God, not *just* like her. I mean, I hope you're right and she'll be back. But preferably without the drink problem."

"Your mother didn't have a drink problem. Not back then. Not when she was sixteen, did she, Harry? That came later."

"Och, Gran! She'd been drinking in secret since she was fourteen," Yvonne said. "Proud of it she was. Used to brag she could down three beers without you even smelling it on her breath."

Vi sniffed and turned her attention to her food.

"She wasn't much more than sixteen when it really got hold, was she, Gramps?" Mirabelle turned to him but he was intent on his food and didn't answer.

"Of course, I blame your dad for that," Vi said.

"Aw! Come on!"

"Yes, we did, didn't we, Harry? She met him playing that … that tin bucket."

"His kettle-drum."

"His kettle-drum then. Playing it in the pubs, he was. He took her eye and she followed him from pub to pub."

"And, of course she had to buy a drink in each one. I know, I know, Gran," Mirabelle said. "But, honestly! You can't blame him. You can't really blame Dad for her drinking. He didn't ask her to fancy him. And she could've ordered lemonade, or fruit juice, tomato juice. She didn't have to buy shots."

Vi nodded as she collected up their plates. "True," she sighed. "But she got a taste for the whiskey, didn't she. That was the problem."

"And the vodka, and the gin," Yvonne chimed in.

"Where the hang did she get the money?" Mirabelle asked. "That's what I've often wondered."

"Pretty girl she was back then. Never had to have money."

"Yeah, well. Still doesn't make it my dad's fault."

"No, maybe not. Maybe not," Vi said, shaking her head. "But it didn't help he was in all those pubs."

"Sad really, isn't it?" Yvonne said. "One husband — *your* dad — who worked in pubs and never drank, and another — *my* dad — who drank in pubs and never worked."

"How is your dad, dear?" Vi asked Yvonne.

"Oh, you know. Maudlin as ever. Doing his best to drink himself into the plot next to Mum's."

"Talk about sad," Mirabelle said.

"It is sad. And she had a sad life, your mum," Vi said, scraping Mirabelle's barely touched meal into the scraps pail. "Not easy having two of your kids die as infants. No wonder she turned to drink."

Yvonne and Mirabelle looked at one another, the unspoken objection passing between them. The children had been sickly children, undernourished and neglected, born when Rose was well on her way to drinking herself to an early death.

Mirabelle, as the oldest, did her best to care for them, but she was a kid herself, had no idea how to mother a brood of sickly children from who knew what fathers.

"Not the way she was brought up, eh, Harry?" Gran said.

Harry turned from the sink where he'd already started washing their plates. "Right, dear."

"Anything you say, dear," Mirabelle and Yvonne chorused. "Oh Gramps! You weren't even listening, were you?"

"Deaf as a postie," Vi told them. "You're deaf as a postie, aren't you, love?"

"Right, dear. Anything you say, dear." And he turned back to the sink.

"History repeating itself. We were talking about déja review," Vi shouted to him. "Oh, never mind. He'd probably not agree anyway," she said to the girls. "Thought your mother could do no wrong, he did. Spoiled her. Anything she wanted." She leant closer to them and lowered her voice. "She was a late baby, of course. We thought we were never going to manage a family by the time she came along. I was older than most first mums." She mouthed the next few words with just the merest whisper of sound. "Thought I was going through the mental pause."

"The mental pause," Yvonne repeated with a giggle.

Mirabelle gave her a dunt in the ribs.

"Well, like I say, we were older parents. Older than most, especially for a first baby."

"A bit of a surprise, then, eh?" Yvonne gazed at Vi as though this was the first time she'd heard the story.

"Surprise! Shock more like. But we loved her, didn't we, Harry?" She raised her voice. "Our Rose? We loved her, didn't we?"

Harry showed no sign of having heard, so Vi tutted and continued. "Trouble was, we loved her, but we hadn't a clue what to do with her. Let her run wild. We were out here in the country. Didn't think she'd come to any harm." Her voice tailed off and she set out spoons and plates. "And *that* was her real problem, God rest her soul." Vi sniffed into a handkerchief taken from the pocket of her apron.

"Come on, Gran," Yvonne said, touching her arm. "You did your best. We know you did your best."

"Ah, well. Water over the bridge now, as they say. What's done is done."

"Exactly. I'm sure with hindsight, we'd all do many things differently."

"Amen to that," Mirabelle said, her voice hardly more than a sigh.

Vi stood poised at the end of the table, a jug in one hand, a cloth in the other, as though caught in the click of an old Brownie Camera, the pose of domesticity. But, instead of the proud smile of the thrifty housewife, it was a snapshot of a mother's pain.

Yvonne leant across. "Let's have that custard over here, then, Gran. Before it gets cold."

"History always repeats itself, you see," Vi said as she handed over the heavy jug.

"Yes, I'm sure you're right." Yvonne exchanged a look with Mirabelle and gave an apologetic shrug. "Summer'll turn up soon. None the worse."

"Especially if she smells that apple pie," Harry said. "Her favourite. Your Gran's apple pie is, you know."

Back home that evening, Mirabelle reflected it had been good taking the trip out to Gran's. Helped put things in perspective. Reminded her she needed to be functioning, to be alive herself, able to care for Summer when she came home — if she came home — but she mustn't think of 'if' — it needed to be 'when' or she'd go mad.

"'Life goes on.' Isn't that what they say?" Gran had said when they were leaving.

Mirabelle didn't like it much but had to admit it made sense. She had things to do. She needed to be able to sort things out in her head, work out a strategy for coping if history did repeat itself and Summer's drinking — and that was something she did know, Summer had been drinking — if it had become more than an experiment.

And what if history *did* repeat itself. *Her* history. And Summer turned up pregnant? What would they do then? Would Summer be stubborn, as she was, and try to go it alone? Or would she let Mirabelle help?

Mirabelle knew she'd want to.

Perhaps she'd make a better job of it this time, if that was the situation. Mirabelle sighed. She'd best pull herself together, stitch up her fraying seams. Push some of that stuffing back into the rag-doll she felt she was. Prop herself up. Get on with life, 'cos they do say, 'Life goes on!' And it seems it was going to, with or without her permission.

But she wasn't quite ready for steak and kidney pudding and apple pie.

Chapter Sixteen

Mirabelle had been nineteen, the winter she had Summer.

Summer: a gift given with early summer kisses, delivered with late winter pangs.

The February wind whistled through the crack under the door, lifting the thin rug, making it billow and slide across the wooden floor like waves surfing up to the foot of the sagging couch where she lay panting, braced against waves of pain, her cries stifled by the face cloth she'd stuffed in her mouth.

Sunday afternoon. She'd been listening to the UK Top 40 on the radio, singing along at first, trying not to focus on the spasms that came every eight minutes or so. By the time Bruno Brooks informed her the Alison Limerick record had dropped seven places, the space between contractions was six minutes and Mirabelle knew she, too, would have to *Make It On My Own.*

She turned the radio down for number twenty-six. *Thought I'd Died And Gone To Heaven,* seemed too poignant, too sad. It was hard enough without Mr Adams' commiserations. Sweat was breaking on her forehead, running down her neck. "Eeeee-owww!" she howled through gritted teeth, the sound squeezing through the barrier despite her best efforts at stopping it.

"Steady breaths," she told herself. "Try to relax." She paced the short distance between door and window, halting with the pain, clutching the back of the chair, doubling over it. She vaguely remembered seeing a film where the woman was told to pant through the contractions. She had little idea of how to do it but once the spasms became incredibly strong, she had a go.

Turned the sound up. "Oh God, oh God, I can't do this!" she cried out in a whisper, the pain bowing her back, her whole body soaked now in perspiration.

Collapsed in exhaustion on the couch. Wet Wet Wet's new entry, *More Than Love*, giving covering noise for her moaning.

It was imperative her landlady didn't hear her, alert the doctor or the police. If she was to keep this baby, it would be the end of her life as she'd planned it: her university education; all the scrimping and saving to pay for it; the hours of bartending, cleaning, studying. Everything would be lost. And for what? A scrap of a kid who hadn't been planned, hadn't been sought, but had foisted its pulsating life on her, had squirmed its way into her belly and was now thrusting its way back out, with searing, clenching waves of pain.

Panting through the final countdown, she bit down on the facecloth and Summer was born to the strains of The Temptations, *My Girl*, at number three.

Despite the tears that coursed down her face, mingling with her sweat, Mirabelle did what she had to do to sort herself out, laying the tiny scrap of life beside her on a towel as she worked as silently and efficiently as she could.

She had already decided what she was going to do with the baby. Knew she couldn't keep it: didn't want it.

She would bundle the child up in one of her collection of shawls. One, already chosen, newly purchased and washed, awaited its bloody, messy, wriggling stuffing: a bright, colourful paisley pattern and soft. She would at least make the thing comfortable, keep it warm. Also chosen, the hospital room where the bundle would be found: a cleaning cupboard, cosied by hot water pipes, a much used storage space, certain to be opened, its contents discovered within the hour after she left it there.

'No pets, no children,' it said on her lease.

With no morning sickness, no nausea or heartburn and none of the other tell-tale signs to catch her attention, she had sailed through the first four and a half months of pregnancy believing her periods to be even more erratic than usual. Having never paid them much heed anyway, she failed to note erratic had become non-existent.

She got on with her summer job, as a domestic in Edinburgh's Royal Infirmary, without a thought for the extra weight she was putting on, blaming all the bending and stretching of bed-making for the constant sore back. She had no mother to turn to for help or advice when the moving lumps and bumps in her abdomen began to kick realisation into her consciousness. And she couldn't foist such a burden on her grandparents.

As far as Mirabelle could see, she had two choices. Go it alone and do the whole single-parent-struggling-in-a-bed-sit-working-all-the-hours-to-make-ends-meet thing, or dump the baby and get on with her life as planned.

So, she had started her course at Edinburgh University, ensconced herself in an inexpensive bed-sit nearby, and had no time or inclination to give it all up to rear a love-child. If it *had* been love, which she now doubted since she'd had no answer to her letters informing her lover of his impending fatherhood.

It hadn't been difficult to conceal the unwanted tenant growing in her expanding belly. Mirabelle had a reputation for eccentricity, loose flowing clothes, flowers in her hair, rings on every finger: a sandal-wearing, lentil-eating, yesteryear hippie with a huge appetite and lust for life. She made jokes about having to cut down on the cream buns, stop buying chocolate bars and ice cream. "Putting on the beef," she said, working on the principle that, if she drew attention to her excess weight, her friends would think nothing of it.

When it was time to start her university course, on her last shift as domestic in the hospital, her last round of the wards with mop and pail, she chose the place she would leave her unwanted baggage. Even did some dummy runs in the months that followed, going to the hospital after her afternoon lectures, walking along the corridor with a batch of visitors, ducking into the cupboard when no-one was looking. Worked a treat every time.

Later, her own naivety stunned her. That she thought it would be as easy as that. That she could hold her baby in her arms, feed it from her breasts, then abandon it with no more difficulty than yesterday's garbage.

Having denied herself the joy and exultation that tried to overwhelm her when her unborn baby wriggled and kicked in her belly, having denied its right to her love, though it received her shelter, she unexpectedly found it claimed her heart in the brutality of its birth.

Tousled golden curls emerged from the towel she used to wipe the worst of the gooey, bloody mess from the baby's face and head. She had no intention of falling in love again but the same lop-sided smile in infant form caught her breath and won her heart. She had not believed new babies could see, didn't suppose they were able to smile, but she was certain Summer did.

When Mirabelle gently wiped the mucus muck from her baby's eyes, Summer looked straight back at her and smiled.

Perhaps even then, Summer knew she'd always have to produce that extra something to gain her mother's attention.

By pure coincidence, R&B singer Shanice, at number two in the charts, was singing, *I Love Your Smile*, and by the time the next record started playing, Mirabelle was humming it to the baby she held close to her breast.

Top of the Pops that week: Shakespeares Sister's long running Number One, *Stay*.

If Mirabelle's calculations were right and if Summer had left home because she was pregnant, it was about time, past time maybe, for the baby to be born, so Mirabelle started a tour of hospitals in and around Edinburgh, checking if any young, unmarried, red-haired girls had been admitted to the maternity wards within the past couple of months.

There was only Simpson's Maternity Unit at the Royal in Edinburgh, and the receptionist had not been too helpful, so she enlisted Lena's help before setting out to try Livingston, Falkirk, and wherever else they could imagine Summer might have gone.

"I can't do this officially without permission," Lena said.

"Then do it unofficially," Mirabelle said. "Just don't change out of your uniform first."

"Wouldn't it be easier just to ask Sam to make it official?"

"Probably." Mirabelle winked at her. "But there's no official search still going on for Summer, and I can't risk him saying no and scuppering the operation, can I?"

"I don't want to get into trouble, Belle. I'm hoping to take my sergeant's exam soon."

"You'll not be in trouble. Why should you be? All you'll be doing is asking an innocent question for a friend."

"Wearing police uniform."

"Exactly."

"Sorry. No can do. I'll help you, but unofficially — and not in uniform."

Mirabelle sighed, huffed and puffed, but Lena was adamant and questions were asked without uniformed aid.

The collaborators managed to get a little more information anyway, and Lena got a few promises from

213

receptionists, saying they'd let her know if anyone fitting Summer's description came in during the next few weeks, but it was beginning to look as though, if Summer had a baby, it was not delivered in Edinburgh or anywhere within a reasonable distance.

"Give the kid the benefit of the doubt, Belle," Lena said after speaking to what Mirabelle had promised would be the last receptionist she would have to question about this matter. "She might not have got herself knocked up."

"Or she might have moved somewhere else to have it."

Lena put her hands up. "Oh, no, Belle. Doing a bit of after-hours cloak and dagger stuff on my own patch is one thing …"

Mirabelle laughed. "Naw, you're all right, pal. I'm not thinking of sending you out on tour."

"Good, 'cos I wasn't for getting on the bus."

Chapter Seventeen

Vi smoothed her hand over the tablecloth then carefully placed everything on its snowy whiteness: one notebook, spiral bound; one pencil, with eraser; one magnifying glass, with handle; one pair of binoculars, polished; one newspaper, yesterday's, and a bag of sherbet lemons. She adjusted the lace curtains a little, stepped back, then readjusted them, stepped back and was satisfied. Picking up the newspaper, she sat at the table facing the window and waited.

She wasn't reading the paper, but peering over the top of it and over the top of her reading glasses. From time to time, she would reach forward to take a sherbet lemon from the bag, slowly unwrap it and pop it in her mouth. She would smooth its wrapper with her fingers and place it neatly beside the bag from which it had been extracted. From time to time, she would fold up the paper and lean forward to place it on the table. She would then pick up the binoculars, study something through them, lean forward to replace them on the table carefully — very carefully, they did not belong to her but belonged to her husband. She would then pick up the notebook and pencil, jot down a few words and replace them also, with less delicacy but still with care, positioning them exactly as they had been before. She would pick up the paper again and resume her non-reading of it.

She didn't bother to turn the page.

After a while, she made herself a cup of tea and brought it to the table. She didn't keep up the pretence of reading her paper while she had the cup of tea to drink, but took it up again after she'd finished drinking and had taken the cup and saucer back to the kitchen.

After a while longer, she sighed deeply and folded the paper, following the creases with methodical precision. Laying it on the table beside the sherbet lemons, she took up the notebook and pencil, made a few annotations, gave another long, shuddering sigh and stood up to stretch.

Just as she was about to resume her position, there was a tap at the back door and Yvonne called out as she pushed it open. "Hi, Gran! Anybody home?"

"Now, how did she get here without me seeing her?" Vi demanded of herself.

"What you up to?" Yvonne asked, coming into the room.

"How did you get to the back door without me seeing you?" Vi demanded of her granddaughter.

"We parked in the lane. Didn't you see the car?"

Vi picked up the notebook and, peering through her glasses, read what she had just written. "One jeep, dark blue. Oh! Was that you, dear?"

"Well, if by 'blue' you mean 'indigo' and by 'jeep' you mean 'four-wheel-drive,' then, yes, that would have been me," she admitted, giving her grandmother a kiss on the cheek.

"Oh! You know I'm no good with cars," Vi said as she returned the kiss and reached to hug Mirabelle as well. "A car's just a car to me."

"And a colour's just a colour. I know. You have mentioned that before," Mirabelle said.

"Well! All this indigo and cerise nonsense. If it's blue, it's blue! If it's pink, it's pink! Why can't people just say what they mean?" Her brow furrowed and she held Yvonne at arm's length. "Besides, you don't have a car."

"Borrowed Hannah's," Yvonne explained. "Cost me an evening's babysitting later, but hey!" She raised her arms and tilted her head. "Anyway, Gran, what you up to? What's all this?" She indicated the laden table by the window.

"Oh, just a few things I was dusting." Vi tried nonchalance but it didn't quite come off: more a sort of guilty, caught-in-the-act. "How is Hannah, dear?"

Yvonne chose to ignore the dusting. "I know what you're doing!" She picked up the binoculars. "You're snooping! You're a peeping Tom!"

Vi took the binoculars out of her granddaughter's hand and set them down carefully. "Nonsense! Like I said, I'm dusting." She rearranged the various items on the tablecloth, flicking them with the side of her hand as she placed them.

"Without a duster? I don't think so. No, you're spying on someone. Now," Yvonne said, picking up the binoculars once again, this time raising them to her eyes. "What can you see from here? Or, more to the point, *who* can you see from here?"

Vi affected indifference. But she craned forward to peer through the window, none-the-less, at the sound of an engine.

"Actually, who *is* that?" Yvonne wanted to know. "I don't think I know that car."

Her grandmother tutted. "There she goes again," she muttered.

"Who?"

"Lexie. Lexie Maxwell from down the lane." She turned to Mirabelle. "I told you I'd keep an eye on her."

"Yes, but that was weeks ago! Don't tell me you've been spying on her all this time?"

"Is she old enough to drive?"

Vi nodded. "Just passed her test."

"I always forget she's that wee bit older than Summer."

"She goes back and forth in that car all the time." She folded her arms across her chest. "Back and forth. Back and forth. Like a shufflecock. She's up to something, I'm sure of it. Just haven't worked out what yet."

"Has it ever occurred to you it's none of your business?" Yvonne asked.

"Loading stuff into the back of that car, she was. Saturday. And the Saturday before."

"How on earth do you see all that from this window?" Mirabelle strained to see down the lane.

"Oh, *I* can't! But Peggy Eaglesham can. From the bottom of the garden. If she goes up on her toes. Or stands on something."

"I don't believe you two!"

"Mmm, but something's going on. All those black bin bags. And a few boxes. Even a wee table last week."

"Probably having a turn out. She'll be getting rid of stuff."

"Or taking it to our Summer."

"So *that's* what you think," Mirabelle said. "She wouldn't. Would she? Be so cruel? To help Summer stay away from home?"

"I doubt it," Yvonne said, putting her arm round Mirabelle's shoulders. "I bet she's just having a jolly-good, old-fashioned clear-out."

"Anyway, dears, did you want a cuppa?" Vi said. "Your grandad's out at the bowling club this morning. Some big match or other this afternoon. He'll not be back till later, what with the socialising and all, so we," she patted Mirabelle's hand and nodded at Yvonne, "can have a nice cosy chat by the fire. You sit down and I'll put the kettle on. Then you can help me plot how we can find out what young Lexie is up to."

"How's your gran and gramps?" Sam asked the next day. They were on their way over to the nursing home to visit his mother. It had become part of their Sunday routine, sitting chatting with Ella Burns, though the conversation was rather bizarre. They'd tell her about their lives, what they were doing, how the search for Summer progressed, or didn't, and Ella would stare at them for a while then ask who they were and what they wanted. Very occasionally, she'd see something familiar in Sam or smile at Mirabelle with something akin to recognition. She seemed to enjoy their visits anyway, especially when Mirabelle was on form and 'put on a show,' even asking Mirabelle for her autograph one day.

"Gran and Gramps?" Mirabelle shook her head. "They're fine, but Gran is determined to play detective."

"Oh? Got competition, have I?" he asked as they turned into the stream of traffic going up Lothian Road.

"Absolutely. She seems to think her neighbour's daughter, Lexie — I've told you about Lexie, haven't I?"

Sam nodded.

"Well, Gran seems to think she's hiding Summer somewhere."

"Is that likely?"

Mirabelle pulled a face. "Highly *un*likely, I'd think, but Gran is adding two and two."

"And getting five?"

"Yup!"

"Is she likely to do anything about her suspicions?"

Mirabelle scanned the pedestrians crossing in front of them at the lights. It was automatic now. Whenever, wherever, if there were people, Mirabelle checked them out. "Don't think so," she said. "Don't know what she *could* do."

They drove on in silence for a while. Then, "You sure you're up for this," he said.

"From one old nutter to another, d'you mean?"

"Hey! What about political correctness?"

"Asterisks to it, I say! If I'm expected to deal with your mum and my gran, I intend to do it with good old-fashioned bluntness. Gran's getting nuttier every day."

"And my mother's somewhere on planet Zog."

"Yeah, well, it's them or us. Take it too seriously and we'll both be joining them."

But Mirabelle couldn't help but worry. Gran kept phoning her with all sorts of harebrained schemes, so, the following week, Mirabelle got on a train and popped out by herself to visit Gran. Yvonne had to work, so Mirabelle travelled alone this time.

Gran was not for putting her mind at rest.

"I think we should follow her."

"Gran! It's not really our business," Mirabelle said.

"Isn't it? Are we not public spirited citizens? Ought we not to find out about wrong-doing and report it?"

"You've no proof she *has* done wrong?"

"Exactly! We need proof," Vi said. "You said yourself there is something fishy about Lexie's behaviour, and I've had her under surveillance for quite a while now and I'm sure she's up to something."

"So you keep saying, Gran," Mirabelle sighed. She looked out the window. "But, even if she is hiding Summer, that's not against the law."

"But wasting police time is," Vi said.

"And?"

"Time they're spending looking for her when Lexie knows where she is."

"But the police are not actively looking for Summer any more. They've more or less decided she just ran away from home. They're not interested."

"Maybe so, but I am! Don't you want to find your daughter?"

"Of course I do, Gran. You know I do."

"Then let's follow Lexie. See where she takes all that stuff."

Mirabelle sighed. "Even if we did decide to follow her,

neither of us can drive. Have you thought about that?"

"Of course I have. We'll get your grandad to take us."

Mirabelle laughed. "Gramps? You have to be joking! He never drives further than the end of the village nowadays. What if she goes into Edinburgh? He'll never follow her into town. He hates driving in town."

"Let's catch him before he goes off to his pigeons. By my reckoning, Lexie's due a trip before lunch-time." She consulted the watch again. "It's my guess, she'll take off in an hour or so. That just gives us time for a quick cuppa and to persuade your grandfather."

Mirabelle shook her head. "You'll never manage to talk him into it."

"I can't *believe* I let ye talk me into this," Harry moaned. He was hunched over the steering wheel, his hands clutching it tightly, every muscle in his body clenched. "I hate driving in town."

"I know, dear, and it's wonderful you agreed to do your civic duty." Vi patted his hand. "They'll all thank you in the end."

"For a start, ah don't know who yer grateful '*they*' are, and ah don't give a damn aboot civic duty."

"Language, dear," Vi remonstrated. "Children," she hissed, nodding towards the back seat where Mirabelle sat miserably hunched, a perfect reflection of her grandfather's fear and tension, feeling as helpless as a child. "And you may not care about civic duty, but I'm sure you're happy to do your duty by your family."

Harry growled and clutched the wheel tighter.

To say Harry's driving was bad, would be unfair. It was horrendous. He'd never been a Stirling Moss or a Lewis Hamilton, and had not driven more than a few hundred metres for years now. His sole purpose when he did, was to keep the engine free. The girls used to urge him to sell the car, seeing the clear danger in any return to active service. But he loved his old Rover. It had been his treasured possession for *"nigh on thirty year,"* he'd remind them. *"Bought it for sixty quid from auld Maxwell,"* he'd chuckle. The Rover still gleamed with health and vitality, unlike its proud owner and carer. Harry was looking very old and very rusty as he tried to negotiate through the traffic.

"There she is!" Vi shouted, spotting Lexie's car up ahead as it took its turn to join the traffic on the roundabout at the bottom of Drum Brae.

"I see 'er. I see' er." Harry grumbled. "Hadn't lost 'er."

"Quick!" Vi urged. "You're going to lose her now."

Harry turned to look at her. "And jist what d'ye propose I do about it? Plough through the twa cars in front o' us and tak my chances wi' the bus coming up frae the right? Ye know nothing about your Highway Code," he mumbled. "Never bin a driver. Never stopped ye driving though — from o'er there." He nodded towards the passenger seat.

"Now! Now!" she shouted. "There's a space. Oh! You've missed it. Took too long. You're too slow, Harry. She's going to get away."

Harry clamped his teeth together, clenched his hands on the wheel and entered the fray. "Ah cannae *believe* I let ye talk me intae this," he said again.

"There she is! There she is!" Vi's head was out the window, her eyes scanning the cars in front for her quarry. "She's still ahead of us."

"Be a bloomin' miracle if she'd got behind," Harry muttered.

"I mean," Vi explained carefully, "she hasn't turned off." She stuck her head out again. "Oops!" she said as she retreated. "You're a bit close to those parked cars, Harry."

"Only if there's an eejit sticking her heid oot the bloomin' windae." But he moved over towards the middle of the road anyway.

"Careful, Gramps!" Mirabelle yelled. "Phew! That was close," as an oncoming bus skimmed past them, its driver judging the space to a millimetre. "Keep in a bit."

"Keep out! Keep in! Too many bloomin' drivers," Harry complained. But he moved back to his left anyway.

"Faster Harry! You're going to lose her if those lights change. Blast! They have. Keep an eye on her," Vi ordered.

"Keep your eye on the road. Keep your eye on the car. Keep your eye on the lights. How many eyes d'ye think ah've got?"

"Right," Vi said as the lights changed. "After her. Come

on, Harry. You'll have to go faster than that if we're to catch up."

Harry crunched up a gear. He winced at the sound. "See whit ye've made me do, wuman."

"I've told you, Harry. I am not a 'wuman.' I'm your wife, deserving of some respect."

"Aw, haud yer whesht, wuman. An' let me git on wi' the job in hand."

"Harry!"

"Gramps!" Mirabelle yelled, "Watch out! You're too close!" as Harry's wing mirror clipped the off-side wing mirror of a parked car.

"Careful!" as it hit a second.

"Move out!" as it tore off a third.

"Gramps!" as it mangled a fourth before dangling, useless, itself.

Four for the price of one.

"Now see what you've done," Harry said, glaring at Vi.

"Me?"

"Aye you." Harry stopped the car and turned to her. "Look, wuman. I never wanted tae dae this daft exercise in the first place. Ah dinnae like driving in the toun, ah telt ye. An' ah've had enough." He got out and walked round the car, ignoring the impatient tooting of the cars behind. Inspecting the damage to his wing mirror, he shook his head sadly. "Nigh on thirty year," he sighed.

"It was a nightmare," Mirabelle told Sam the next day. They were once more on their way to visit Ella Burns. "Poor old Gramps. I don't know if he'll ever get over the whole episode."

"Family, eh?"

"Yeah!" Mirabelle looked across at him. "But what would we do without them?"

Sam shook his head. "Speaking of which," he said as they drew up in front of the nursing home. "The nurse phoned me yesterday." He nodded towards the door of the building. "She's a bit worried about Mother. Apparently she's stopped eating. Keeps refusing to open her mouth. They reckon they can't force-feed her but don't think she'll go for long if they can't get some nourishment into her. There's not a pick on her and she's already had one stroke. Now, as well as food, she's refusing her medication."

"Oh, Sam. That's sad."

He sighed. "Yep. I'm afraid it is. But what can they do? She'll not tolerate being tube-fed either. Keeps pulling the tube out."

"Ouch."

"Don't know where they go from here."

Mirabelle held up the basket she had on her lap. "Maybe we can coax her to try some of this fruit. She'll maybe do it for you."

"More like she'll do it for you," he said. "She thinks you're 'It' with a capital I."

"When she remembers who I am."

"Just get that kazoo of yours out and she remembers quick enough."

226

Ella Burns had been a good wife and mother: she'd cooked and cleaned for her husband and son without complaint, listened to their dreams and their dirges, usually without comment or judgement. Sam found it hard to see her now, sitting in an upright armchair, pillows at her back, a blanket over her legs, immobile, nothing she wanted to do, nothing she could do. No cooking or cleaning. No words of comfort or advice. No needlework: darning or mending. No ironing, no baking. Just sitting staring vacantly out the window, aware of nothing, not the changing of the seasons or the daily passage of the sun across the sky.

Today, her posture was less upright. She looked smaller, weaker. And her colour was bad, somewhere between lavender grey and dirty yellow. Sam and Mirabelle looked at one another, unspoken worry shared.

"Hi, Mum," Sam said, stooping to kiss her cheek. "Some fruit for you."

"Fruit? Did I order fruit? What shop are you from? I don't remember putting in an order."

"No, Mum, it's me, Sam."

"Sam." She smiled. "I knew a Sam once, you know. Handsome lad, he was."

"And I've brought someone to brighten your day." He pulled Mirabelle forward.

"Hi, Ella. Love your cardi. You really suit that pink."

Ella fingered the pink buttons that closed the length of her cardigan. "Is it yours?" she asked. "I've never seen it before."

"No, it's yours, Ella. Sam bought it for you last week. It looks very fine on you."

"Don't know anyone called Sam." Ella took a tissue from the pink sleeve, sniffed and dabbed at her nose. There were footsteps in the corridor outside her room. She stiffened in her chair. "Is that you, Tommy?" she called. When there was no reply, she turned back to them. "Tommy should be back in a minute," she told them. "He'll know what to do."

Tommy Burns had been dead for the best part of twenty years.

He died in his bed late one Friday night after a hard day out on the croft.

"At least he saw you get your degree," Ella said to Sam after the funeral. "And that's what he wanted for you. He died happy, son. And quiet, just as he lived. A man of no sae many words."

Sam thought he'd have to stay home then, care for the land, support his mother, but she would have none of it.

"You'll go ahead as planned, son," she told him. "I'll no have this croft tak you like it took yer faither."

So, after months of intense, debilitating grieving with Sam caring for her, Ella Burns laid aside the mantle of widowhood and picked up the apron of motherhood, supporting and caring for her son.

"The land'll care fur itself," she said, and sold most of it to her neighbour, keeping only a few chickens and a vegetable garden for herself. "Aye, son," she sighed. "Just you an me now. And you, the man o' the hoose. Aye, and I'll just get on wi' ma life and you must get on wi' yours."

So he set his mind back on his career, joined the Police Force and studied hard to be the best policeman he could be.

"Aye, Tommy should be back soon," Ella said now, turning her face back to the window to watch for him.

The fruit basket sat, untouched, beside her. The kazoo remained buried in Mirabelle's voluminous bag. Ella had no wish for food or entertainment as she waited for the man she remembered marrying fifty years ago.

Chapter Eighteen

Lexie had been brought back into the frame by Gran, and Mirabelle had the feeling Lexie had not been totally honest with her right from the start. Her experience of questioning young girls had taught her loyalty between teenaged girls was stronger than common sense. She decided to have another shot at it.

"I'll chum you home, Gran," Mirabelle said after a lunch in town.

"Oh, that's okay, dear. I'm just going to hop on the bus."

"Yes. I'll hop on with you."

"There's really no need. I'm perfectly fine, dear."

"Oh, I know you are. In top form."

Vi smiled.

"But I want a word with Lexie."

"Oh, you're quite wrong about Lexie, you know. She's not up to anything. Just having a turn out, taking things to the charity shop, like I thought." Vi shook her head. "She's not up to anything at all to do with our Summer."

Once they disembarked from the bus, Mirabelle gave her gran a peck on the cheek and walked down the lane to the Maxwells' house, picking leaves off the privet hedge without thinking, rolling them in her fingers to make little tubes as she had always done, blowing through them out of habit. As she drew closer to the cottage, its garden subdued by winter, dull and unwelcoming under the dark sky, she found she was practising her lines, nerves drying her mouth.

"Oh, hi again, Mirabelle."

Caught off-balance straight away. For some reason, she hadn't expected Lexie to open the door. Mirabelle would just have to fall in and hope she remembered how to swim.

"Mum's not in I'm afraid."

"That's okay," Mirabelle said. "It was you I wanted to talk to anyway."

"Oh?"

"Can I come in?"

Lexie opened the door wider. "Sorry. Of course." She led Mirabelle into the living room. "Get down, you smelly bag of fleas," she said to the dog, pushing it off of the couch. "Please. Sit down. Coffee? Tea?"

"Nothing thanks. Just information. A few questions."

Lexie ruffled the fur at the back of the dog's neck, played with its ears. "Oh."

Mirabelle tried to sound casual, as though they were just passing the time of day, chatting about a friend they had in common. "I wondered if you'd heard anything from Summer?"

The dog rolled over under Lexie's hand and she slid onto the floor beside it. "She loves getting her tummy tickled," she said.

"I take it you mean the dog? Rather than Summer?"

Lexie laughed. "Sheba, yes."

"So? Have you heard from Summer?"

"Have I heard from Summer?"

"Yes. Have you?"

Lexie got up from the floor, leaving the dog rolling on the carpet. "No," she said, poking her gently with her foot.

"Don't, Lexie."

"Sheba loves it."

"Come on, Lexie. Please. Don't mess about with me."

"I'm not messing, honest, I'm not. I thought you were talking about the dog."

Mirabelle sighed. "I don't give a rat's tail about your dog, Lexie, as you well know. I want you to tell me what you know about Summer's disappearance."

"I told you already the last time. I don't know anything."

"I think you do. And I want you to tell me."

Lexie left the dog and walked to the window, a grey

230

silhouette against the darker trees outside the window.

Mirabelle took a deep breath. "I got the distinct feeling, when I was here before, you were not totally honest with me."

The dog finished rolling and followed Lexie, tail wagging, looking for more attention.

"Before you get your back up, it's not that I think you lied. I just don't think you told me the truth."

Lexie bent to fondle the dog's ears.

"You're determined not to make this easy, aren't you?"

Lexie looked up and shrugged.

"You know something. I can feel it in my gut." Mirabelle pushed her fist into her stomach. "Right here." She curled round the pain. "Come on, Lexie."

Lexie turned away, peering out into the garden.

"You don't have to tell me where she is. Please. Just tell me she's all right. She's happy. She's well. Something?"

Lexie didn't move a muscle.

"If you know something about what happened. Anything. Anything at all," Mirabelle said. "Please." Mirabelle's voice trembled. "Don't make me beg, Lexie."

Nothing.

Mirabelle closed her eyes. Blood whooshed through her head, beat in her chest, louder, it seemed, than the wind that rattled the window panes, than the tapping of a branch on one of them, and louder than the ticking of the big, old grandfather clock that stood in the corner of the room as it marked off what felt like an hour.

"I don't know."

Mirabelle jerked fully awake. "Pardon?"

Lexie turned away from the window. "Summer. I don't know how she is," she said a little louder. "But I did hear from her."

"I *knew* it!" Mirabelle didn't know whether to crow over the victory or wail over the lost months.

"She came here that Saturday. The day after she left home. She came for knickers."

"You saw her?"

Lexie nodded, her head bent as she picked at her nails.

"You saw her?"

"Just the once. The Saturday afternoon, late, just before tea-time."

"I can't believe you saw her and you didn't say. She came for knickers?"

"Mmm-hmm."

Mirabelle nodded. "Of course she did." She spread her hands out, palms up. "She came for knickers."

"Hey!" Lexie said, opening the door to her friend that Saturday afternoon. "You look awful."

"Thanks. Your mum and dad in?"

"No, both shopping."

"Good. You gonna let me in or what?"

"Sorry." Lexie held the door wider. "Just… You look…"

"Awful. Yeah, you said."

"Did you, like, sleep in your gear?"

"I need pants." Summer marched past her friend.

"What?"

"Knickers. I need clean knickers." She was already in Lexie's bedroom, rummaging through her chest of drawers, taking a fistful of pants from the top drawer. "Mind if I take a bra too? We're same size, yeah?"

"Hey!" Lexie snatched the bra from her hands. "Not that one. That's my Saturday bra."

"You have a Saturday bra?"

Lexie lifted her chin. "So?"

"So, why're you not wearing it, like?"

"Saturday night bra."

"Something you've not been telling me?"

Lexie turned slightly away.

"You're blushing, Lexie Maxwell! What's going down with you?" She snatched the bra back and held it across her chest over her clothes. "Mmm. Sexy lace. I smell a rat. A King rat."

Once more, the bra was snatched away. "Lid it."

"Give it up, then. Who is it?"

"You don't know him," Lexie said, looking round, lowering her voice. "He's at college."

"Ooh! I get it now. This is why you're not clubbing any more."

"That — and the fact you're being a total bam!"

Summer shrugged. "Aw, get over yourself, Lex. I'm not doing anything you're not." She stuck her nose up. "Just you think your boyfriend's classier."

"Yeah! And not into dealing."

"Drae, you mean?" Summer shook her head. "Chip paper."

"Good. You can do better than that loser."

Summer was stuffing pants into her pockets. "You got a back-pack or something?"

"Hey! Wait a minute. What's this about?"

"Taking a short sabbatical." Summer started looking in the cupboards, rummaging about on shelves. "Well? You got one, or what?"

"Here." Lexie pulled out a small, rucksack-style, fashion bag.

Summer took the black and red shiny bag. "Ooh! Dainty!"

Lexie grabbed it out of her hands. "I'll take it back if you're gonna be picky, like."

"No." Summer held her hand out. "No, it's fine. It'll do."

Lexie waited.

"Grief! You're as bad as my mother." Summer looked to the ceiling, sighed. "Please? Pretty, pretty, pretty please?" and was rewarded with the bag.

"About your mother."

"You never saw me." Summer filled the bag.

"If she…"

"You never saw me."

"Okay, okay. I never saw you."

"Right." Summer grinned. "Girlfriends rock?" She held up her hand.

"Girlfriends rock." Lexie went through the performance with her. "High five. Low five. Not gonna behive." They bumped hips together. "You do know this is a bit lame, like? We've been doing it since, like, since we were kids."

"Yeah." Summer walked out the bedroom and started down the hall. "And now's not the choice time to update it." She pointed a warning finger at Lexie. "Still holds."

Lexie nodded and sighed. "Still holds."

Summer came to a sudden halt. "Hell's teeth!"

Lexie crashed into her back. "What?"

There was a jangling of keys, almost drowned out by the barking of dogs, and the front door was being pushed open.

"Bedroom window!" Lexie pulled Summer back into the room and they raced over the floor, tumbling across the bed. Lexie lunged at the window and tugged it open.

"Remember," Summer hissed as she climbed through. "You ..."

"Never saw you."

"She came for knickers," Lexie told Mirabelle.

Another nod.

"You didn't see her again?"

"No."

"But you heard from her?"

"Just at first, like. Just a coupla times."

"You heard from her. I asked you and you lied to me."

Lexie walked over to Mirabelle and sat beside her. "I'm sorry. I'm really, really sorry. I wanted to tell you but she told me if I did that'd be the last I'd hear of her."

Mirabelle tried to speak but choked and coughed.

Lexie bit her lip. And turned away a little.

Mirabelle took as deep a breath as the tightness in her throat allowed. "And..." She swallowed. Tried again. "When?" she managed to ask. "How?"

"Email. Just the first month or two, but."

Tears started to roll down Mirabelle's cheeks.

Lexie put her hand out, touched her arm. "I'm so sorry, Mirabelle. I feel so bad. But I promised." She started to cry too. "If she thought she couldn't trust me she'd bomb out."

Mirabelle nodded.

"I didn't want her to totally disappear, like." She reached across for a box of tissues, pulled a handful from it and blew her nose. "I was that made up when she said she wanted to keep in touch."

Mirabelle made use of some tissues too. "I don't know what to say," she sniffed. "I'm, I'm trying to understand."

"I really wanted to tell you before." Tears built up in Lexie's eyes again. "But then Mum said your gran told her you knew Summer was alive?"

Mirabelle nodded.

"So it seemed easier not to say anything 'cos it wouldn't make any difference? You knew she was all right."

"Are you still … does she still … do you…?"

Lexie bent to play with the dog at her feet again. She shook her head. "No. I've no had nothing for donkey's."

"Nothing?"

"Don't know why, like, but she just stopped. I'd no done anything, or said anything." She shrugged. "They didn't bounce or nothing, but."

"Bounce?"

"Yeah, you know, bounce."

"No, I really don't know. What d'you mean? What didn't bounce?"

"The emails I sent."

"And?"

"It wasn't like they wouldn't go."

"Go?"

Lexie looked at Mirabelle, her face scrunched up. "You really don't know nothing about computers, do you, like?"

"Putting aside the double negative and your obvious incredulity, *like*, no, I don't know much about computers. Only what I absolutely have to. I know even less about email, only what I have to. Enough to send a few, read a few. So, walk me through this slowly. Summer emailed you?"

"And I emailed back," Lexie said as though she was talking to a child. "After a few went back and forwards, she just stopped answering mine. And what I'm saying is, it's not like they bou… sorry, wouldn't send or nothing."

"No?"

"Just that, like. I could still send emails to her, but she stopped sending any to me."

"Okay. I get that. So, what is it you're saying about them not bouncing?"

"Well usually when that happens it means the other guy, in this case Summer, has closed down their account." She frowned with the concentrated effort of explaining in words

Mirabelle might understand. "They've scrubbed that email address, like?"

"Why would Summer do that?"

Lexie shrugged. "No idea. Only I'm just saying, she didn't. Her account must still have been active."

"Otherwise your emails would've bounced. Ah. I get it."

"Right."

"So why did she stop answering?"

"No idea. Maybe it was 'cos I said you were here looking for her and I didn't know what to say if you came back and it was right after that she stopped answering and maybe she thought I'd crack and tell you something if she, like, dropped anything about where she was or anything?" She shrugged again. "Or ..."

"Or?"

"Or something maybe happened? She wouldn't be able to close down the account if anything had happened, like."

"No, she wouldn't." Mirabelle didn't know what to do with this information. Did it mean Summer was all right? Or did it mean she wasn't?

"You okay, Mirabelle? Only you look kinda not so good, like."

Sick. She felt sick. "And you've not heard anything since the early weeks?"

"Nothing."

Mirabelle looked at her. "She'd already been away eight months when I spoke to you the first time."

"Months then. Swear. Nothing since the first eight months."

"Right." Mirabelle started to get up, found her legs were shaking, her head spinning. "I don't really know whether to believe you."

Lexie put her hand up. "Guide's Honour. I swear that's the truth. Honest. She's no been in touch since then."

"Okay, okay, but, Lexie?"

"Yes?"

"If I find you've lied to me again ..."

"No. No. Honest. I haven't. Look, I'll show you." She went over to the laptop on a table in the corner of the room. Bringing it over and working so quickly and efficiently it made Mirabelle dizzy, she signed into her email account and showed Mirabelle the inbox. Scrolling down, she found the last email Summer had sent. "See? It's right after I told her you'd been here."

"And nothing since?"

"Nothing since."

Mirabelle looked deep into her eyes for a moment or two, searching her face for any signs of deceit, any flicker of embarrassment occasioned by a lie. "Okay. Thank you for being honest with me this time. Can I read her emails?"

Lexie shifted about on the seat. "Well. Not really. They're kinda private, like."

"But maybe they could help me trace her."

She shook her head. "I tried, but there's nothing. She didnae give nothing away about where she was, just that she was okay, like."

"You're sure?"

Lexie nodded.

With a shuddering sigh, Mirabelle heaved the dead weight of her sadness onto her back and prepared to rise from the chair. She knew she should be comforted by the knowledge Summer was now known to have been alive eight months into her disappearance. Another entry along the whiteboard timeline in her kitchen. But what now?

Knowing she was alive helped, but left her no closer to understanding why Summer left home in the first place. Why she felt she had to. Why she felt she had to stay away. How long had she been unhappy? Mirabelle wanted to find a quiet corner where she could weep for her daughter. Not weep for *her* loss, but for Summer's unhappiness. Her heart ached to make it okay again. That overwhelming desire to turn back the clock, to rewind her life washed over her again.

Closing her eyes, gathering all the hurt and pain to her centre, Mirabelle prayed Summer was somewhere safe and was happier now.

239

On another level, the scenario Lexie described felt like another betrayal, taking Mirabelle full circle to losing Summer all over again, plunging her back into the whole depressing cycle, doomed to experience the various stages of grief anew.

Hamster wheels in concentric circles. Empathy, longing, prayers. Understanding, hope, prayers.

Running alongside, another set of wheels. Loss, despair, grief. Abandonment, desolation, grief. With each new piece of information, instead of ripples spreading outwards through her consciousness, they contracted inwards to a central point, heavy with grief, a black hole swallowing hope and happiness.

Finish with one, coming to terms with the loss of Summer, straight into another demanding acceptance of Summer's unhappiness, but also her betrayal, highlighting the fact of her flight, but also her abandonment.

The circles spun.

Harsh glittering rings of pain.

Weariness threatened to engulf her.

"She nearly came home, you know?"

There was a long empty space between each beat of Mirabelle's heart. The room was shrinking around her, squeezing her chest.

Pushing against the weight, pulling herself forward in the chair, "Nearly came home?" she whispered. "*Nearly* came home?"

Lexie nodded. "Think she got cold feet or something, but."

Mirabelle groaned. Somehow 'nearly' made it worse: a weighed decision made, rather than an unavoidable circumstance.

The circles spun faster.

The room rushed away from her with a whooshing noise. It started to turn lopsidedly, tottering like a spinning top winding down. Lexie leapt from her seat and grabbed Mirabelle's arm, pulling her back down into the chair. She sank into it, deeper and deeper, never stopping, falling

240

through it, through the floor, through the earth, into deep, sucking, clinging mud.

"Here," Lexie said, holding out a cup of tea. "Hot, strong and sweet. Like what we learned in first aid class at school."

Mirabelle sat up, disentangling her hands from the blanket tucked around her. "What? I don't … I …"

"It's okay," Lexie said, proffering the tea again. "I think you fainted or something. I've called for our doctor and your gran's just coming too. She says she'll take you home."

"Home?" Mirabelle whispered. "Why didn't she come home?"

why didn't he come home?

"Why didn't Daddy come home?" she asked her mother the next day, after Rose had slept off her night at the pub.

Rose ruffled Mirabelle's hair. "Aw, did he no, pet?"

"No, he didn't come home for his chips. I bought him chips." She indicated the greasy paper bag of congealed chips sitting on the kitchen table.

Rose shrugged. "S'pose he went straight to the docks then, to catch the first boat outta here. Can you blame him? Look at that rain!" It was battering against the kitchen window, pouring from the gutter beside the door, gurgling down the drain. "Sky's fit tae burst. He'll be looking for some sunshine."

"But he didn't come for his chips. He didn't take his things." She indicated the bag of new clothes, the smart new shoes. Her face brightened with a sudden thought. "Oh! Maybe he'll come home today to get them."

Rose sneered. "Wouldn't count on it, pet. He's gone. He's fast-tracked it back to sunshine kingdom." She pulled her cardigan closer round her. "And good riddance to him. Loser!"

"Dad's not a loser!" Mirabelle flew at her mother, her small fists pounding into her mother's stomach. "He's not!"

Rose swatted her away with a smack round the ear. "That's enough of that, or you'll find yourself following him tae where he's gone." Pushing Mirabelle away, she picked the bag of chips up and threw them in the bucket. "Easy as that."

Mirabelle knew better than to tell her mother that would suit her nicely, guessing her mother would not come up with the money for her daughter's passage to Jamaica. It was yet

242

another empty threat, to be placed alongside the frequent threat to send her to boarding school or to a children's home. Both of which sometimes seemed better choices than staying at home.

Knowing her mother was barely on nodding terms with the truth, Mirabelle watched for her father every day, believing he would not have gone anywhere without saying his farewells to her and giving her promises of his return or of sending for her.

But he didn't come home.

With every setback in finding Summer, with every piece of information about how close she had been, how nearly she came home, Mirabelle suffered a double blow, reliving once again the pain of losing her father alongside the pain of losing her daughter. The two became increasingly intertwined, the pains indistinguishable, the circles no longer concentric but inextricably overlapping and locking together, creating bemusing spirals.

Logic dictated she needed to step off the treadmill, the circular searching, its crushing disappointments sending her spiralling into a meaningless half-life, but logic is rarely what dictates our actions when it comes to matters of the heart.

Chapter Nineteen

It had started snowing again. Large, fluffy flakes this time; not the tight, hard little balls of the earlier hail they'd endured. There hadn't been time yet for the pavements to clear even in the heart of town. People were walking on the road where the cars had made the snow slushy, taking their chances with the slow-moving traffic rather than risking the treacherous icy surface of their designated walkways — those who had ventured out at all. The city was eerily quiet, shop windows enticingly lit, displaying their wares to any who were brave enough or determined enough to be out shopping in spite of the biting cold.

Mirabelle trudged along the street, head lifted to the snow. She loved the softness of the new snowfall, how it landed on her tongue, refreshed her mouth then melted away leaving only the tingle of its icy taste. Her top shawl — she wore three today — was flecked with white, the flakes trapped in the stitches of the knitted fabric. By the time she reached home, she would be soaked through, the snow melting and seeping into the soft materials with no heed for her warmth or her comfort. She would hang the shawls around the house, on the backs of chairs, carelessly letting them drip onto her carpet. 'It'll dry,' she'd reason, placing a small convector heater nearby. She looked forward to the smell of the drying wool.

Her winter wanderings had taken her to Newington today. Much earlier, she had shown her bus-pass to the driver of the number 37 and enjoyed the luxury of the heated ride up the Bridges and all the way over to Cameron Toll, the sharp tinkling of hailstones on the windows making her glad of her decision.

It was busier inside Cameron Toll Centre; shoppers glad of the cosy shelter of an indoor shopping mall. They were unhurried too, not relishing re-emerging into the bitter Edinburgh winter. Mirabelle could scan the passing faces with casual leisure, standing at one shop front and then another, for all the world as though she was waiting for someone, a friend, a lover, a father, a daughter.

But Summer didn't show. No reason to suppose she would. Just the unflagging hope that, one day, Mirabelle would chance upon her, somewhere, sometime. The law of averages must surely dictate it.

Summer was in Edinburgh. She was as certain of that as she was of anything in her life. All Mirabelle's instincts told her it was so. Sometimes, she felt the hairs on the back of her neck prickle, and she'd swing round, expecting to look into Summer's laughing eyes, remembering the game they used to play.

"What's the time Mr Wolf?" Summer would chant from the far end of the room.

"One o'clock!" Mirabelle would shout, swinging round to try to catch Summer sneaking up behind her. "Two o'clock!" then "Three o'clock!"

Summer would almost fall over trying to stop and balance as though she hadn't moved, giggling herself off-balance the more.

The incremental chants would be repeated until the wolf would swing round, shouting, "Dinner time!" the object of the game being for the wolf to catch the sheep for his dinner, the sheep to reach the safety of the wall before the wolf could catch her.

The hairs on the back of Mirabelle's neck would prickle with anticipation as Summer closed the distance until, at last Mirabelle would turn and there she'd be, her sweet, laughing face so close, falling into the catch because it was more fun to be caught and tickled than to reach the cold, hard wall.

From time to time as Mirabelle trudged through the snow, she would swing round, afraid to breathe, hoping so hard it almost hurt physically, praying the prickle on the back of her neck was due to Summer's proximity.

She was walking all the way home from Cameron Toll, an enormous trek in weather such as this, but one she undertook in optimistic spirit, viewing it as healthy exercise rather than the obsession it was. It had been too long since she'd scoured this particular stretch of thoroughfare. She might've missed something; a clue, a shadow, a glimpse of that dear face, the colour of Summer bright against the white of the snow.

The snow was clinging to the branches of trees, turning their starkness into something graceful, the late afternoon light tinting them pretty in pink. Street lights began to twinkle. Cars, their lights appearing in reply to the prompting, slowed at traffic lights, their tyres muffled by the fresh snowfall. Everything seemed muted except for Mirabelle's senses.

She could be here: Summer could be here. She might live in one of those flats off Newington Road. She might shop here, along this very stretch of street. This might be where she buys her clothes, that might be where she buys her fruit. Even today, when the weather was cold and wet, she would have to feed herself, she would have to go about her everyday affairs.

Summer loved the snow. Mirabelle remembered her excitement at the first white covering every winter. A night's snowfall would be greeted in the morning by squeals of delight when she opened her curtains. Reasoning if there was snow here in town, there was bound to be more in the outskirts, they would play hooky and dig out the old sledge Mirabelle had rescued from a skip years ago, jump on the bus and head for Corstorphine Hill, where there was always good sledging.

Corstorphine Hill. That's where she should go tomorrow. Always supposing she didn't bump into Summer today.

And well she might.

It was the end of December, ten months since Summer left, and every evening for the past few weeks, Mirabelle would climb the steep hill that led her from Broughton Street to the Omni Centre, past the giraffes and on up to Princes

Street and the winter wonder of the outdoor ice-rink. Knowing her daughter's passion for skating, especially as day gave way to the magic of evening and fairy lights joined forces with street lights to create an atmosphere of delightful, twinkling mystery, Mirabelle ensconced herself on a park bench each day at twilight.

She shivered with anticipation: she had a good feeling about tonight. There had been so much snow today. It was irresistible. If Summer was in Edinburgh, she *must* appear tonight. As she walked along Mayfield Gardens, Minto Street, Newington Road and on down to the South and North Bridges, she had a spring in her step, a jauntiness that defied the cold, wet weather.

Summer watched Mirabelle as she made her way to the ice-rink. It was amazing how light she was on her feet, given she was still massively overweight, even though she'd lost tons. Made you realise how ginormous the woman used to be. Can't possibly be healthy to be that huge.

She looked stupid in her flapping dress and dripping shawls, her feet in big, furry sheepskin boots darkened by the snow that wet them. Summer tried to feel the old disgust at Mirabelle's unique, un-cool dress code but, instead, affection and tolerance filled her heart.

Why should Mirabelle conform? Why should she be as every other mother of her old school friends: either neatly turned out in their designer outfits, or sporting clothes that no longer suited them but made them feel young and fashionable? Mirabelle was different, all Summer's school friends had agreed on that. It used to matter, used to embarrass, frustrate, infuriate even. But now? Summer smiled. Mirabelle was exotic, even in her soaking wet state, she was bright and bouncy. Eccentric, yes, but so what? She was lovely.

Funny, she never thought of her as her mother any more. Just Mirabelle. This strange, exotic creature who had given her shelter and brought her up as her daughter. Summer alternated between feelings of affection for her and anger that she had withheld the truth from her all these years. Here Summer was, finding it impossible to find out anything about her birth parents, and there was this woman, Mirabelle, who probably knew all about them.

Summer knew she should be grateful to Mirabelle, but the anger had been stronger these past months. Tonight felt different. Perhaps because the snow softened everything it touched.

Tonight, she would walk up to her as she sat on her bench, no, she'd skate up to her. Tonight, the last night the ice-rink would be here this winter, she'd indulge her longing. She'd don hired skates, step out onto the ice, pirouette a few times, if she remembered how — she hoped it was like riding a bike, something you never forgot how to do — make sure she'd caught Mirabelle's attention, then she'd skate up to her just as she used to. "Did you see that? Did you see? It was perfect. Three rotations at least. Did you see?" she'd ask, breathless from exertion, her heart hammering in her chest, the fairy lights reflected in her eyes. How could Mirabelle resist? She'd surely clap with delight as she used to, her smile beaming bright enough to compete with the lights strung round the rink. They'd forget the intervening months apart, brush them away with the slush that formed on top of the ice, leaving a clean new surface for them to skate on.

She walked over to the kiosk, bought her ticket, hired her skates, all the while keeping her eyes on Mirabelle as she selected her usual bench, settled herself in, her big, soft, wet bag beside her. Tonight would be the night.

Summer had forgotten how uncomfortable hired skates could be and wondered if Mirabelle had kept her old skates. She frowned, suddenly doubtful. Why would Mirabelle have kept everything as it used to be? Would she really not have thrown it all out: the bits and pieces, CDs, DVDs, posters and clothes, the trappings of a teenager's life, the things she'd left behind, the things she was unable to carry with her? Why should she keep them? Would the skates really still be hanging there, behind her bedroom door, knocking against the paintwork announcing each entrance or exit?

Or would it all be gone in one angry gathering into big, black bin sacks to be hauled off to the charity shop where most of the rubbish came from. Would that be how Mirabelle saw it after Summer dared to take things from the house when Mirabelle was out? Not that she supposed Mirabelle noticed. She was so annoyingly untidy and scatter-brained at *home, keeping all her organisational skills for the benefit of her clients. Yet another reason to doubt Mirabelle was her birth mother. They were nothing alike. Nothing!*

Summer tried to remember what her room looked like the last time she'd been there looking for money and some underwear, but she hadn't taken time to look about, to check what was there and what was missing, because she could hear Mirabelle come back up the stairs, having not been out long enough for Summer to do much of anything. Stupid woman had forgotten her purse. Summer held her breath as she hid behind her bedroom door till Mirabelle left the flat. Part of her wished Mirabelle had found her and put an end to this stupid stand-off.

She sat back on the bench, one boot still poised above her foot, tears stingingly cold on her face. Oh God! She couldn't do it. Not tonight.

Her fingers stiff and cold, she fumbled with the laces of the boot she had already managed to get on, trying to undo the knot and bow she had so recently and joyously done up.

But, if not tonight, then when?

She should do it.

She should gather her courage and do it.

She didn't have to skate over.

She could just walk over.

Right now, before she chickened out again.

Teetering on the blades of the skates, laces loosened and flapping, she started to walk.

Mirabelle felt that prickle at the back of her neck again and looked up as a shadow fell across her face.

"Oh hi, Sam!" She slid along the bench.

"Thought you might need warming up," he said, throwing a heavy woollen rug across her knees, the topside of it covered with waterproof fabric of some sort. "You're probably already soaked to the skin, but better late than never, eh?" He sat beside her, the enormous golf umbrella he'd been holding in his other hand sheltering them both from the last of the lingering snow.

Mirabelle looked up at the deepening sky. "Probably going to stop soon. Look! There's definitely clear sky over there." She pointed to a growing break in the clouds. "Lovely though, isn't it?"

"Beautiful!" he agreed, admiring the reflection of the setting sun on the underside of the clouds and the rosy glow it cast over the snowscape around them. "Beautiful!" he repeated, turning to admire also the brighter warmth of Mirabelle's face. "You're the only woman I know who looks fabulous with wet hair dripping down her face."

Laughing, she shook her head, sending the melted droplets to shower him.

They sat and watched the skaters until the ice-rink closed and they could no longer feel their toes.

disappointment

As Summer neared Mirabelle, her heart thudding in her chest, her face flushed with anticipation, a man appeared.

"Thought you might need warming up," he said, throwing a heavy woollen rug across her knees.

From a short distance behind them, Summer watched the exchange. He was there again. Every day, just as Mirabelle got herself in position, he would appear. He'd sit beside her, his arm round her shoulders or offering some carry-out food or a treat.

Jealousy rose in her like bile. Whoever he was, they were obviously close. Summer swallowed the raw, green emotion of childhood and tried to grow into reality. Mirabelle had a right to be cared for, a right to be loved. But, despite it being her who had stayed away, she wished she was the one sharing the rug, offering the warm coffee, the bag of roasted chestnuts.

She returned the skates to the kiosk.

"Come on, Belle. Pull on a pair of jeans and a jumper. We're going out for a bit," Sam said one Saturday morning.

"Jeans? I don't have jeans." She hated jeans, found them too restricting, denim an unforgiving material. Mirabelle had always valued comfort above fashion.

"Whatever," Sam said, raking through the clothes on her bedroom chair, handing her the least crushed dress he could find. "This do?"

She nodded dumbly and he left her to put it on. "Where are we going?" she asked once she was dressed.

"Out. Just out," he said as he selected some bangles and beads for her. Her jewellery was tangled in a heap on her dressing table, neglected for so many months now.

"What've you found out?" excitement rose in Mirabelle as she pushed rings on her fingers. Excitement mixed with fear: a cocktail of dubious flavour. "Have you found her?"

Sam put his hands on her shoulders. "Hey! Hey! It's okay, Belle. This is not about Summer."

"Not about Summer?" Mirabelle shook her head, dropping bangles back onto the dressing table top. "But everything's about Summer."

"Not any more. This time, it's about you." He sat her down on the bed and sat beside her. "Listen to me, Belle." He made her look at him. "Summer left home. A year. It's been a year, Belle."

"You think I don't know that?"

"In Scots law she became an adult at sixteen."

"So?"

"She has the right to leave home. And that's what she did, Belle. She left home."

Mirabelle shrugged. "Maybe."

"Okay." He started again. "It would *seem* Summer left home — ran away, if you like."

"No. I don't like."

"You know what I mean. Summer went. It was her choice. As far as we can make out, she is alive and well and living who knows where, with who knows who and has left you to get on with it."

She closed her eyes. "Put like that ..."

"It's hard? Yes. But these are the facts."

"No. That is your theory."

"Okay. It's my theory, if you like."

"Not much."

Sam sighed. "Well, whether you *like* it or not, so far, the facts seem to bear out that theory. Summer has walked out on you."

"Ouch!"

"Sorry, but she has. She is probably making a new life somewhere. Will have no idea you can't do the same. She'll probably come back sometime. When she's ready. Meantime..." He squeezed her hands. "Meantime, you are here. You are alive. You are entitled to a life. And it's time, Belle."

"Time?"

"Time to start living that life. Your life. Not just marking time. It's time to turn the page. Start a new chapter of your life. I want you to have some pleasure. Something other than searching for Summer." He stood, picked up some bracelets again and held them out to her.

"But ..." She pushed the pile of baubles and beads away. It seemed wrong somehow to bedeck herself with the trivia of another life, the life before. "You're a good man, Sam Burns, and I know you mean well, but ..."

"No buts." He shook his head. "And don't worry." He put the jewellery he held down with the rest. "We'll take it slow. Easy stages." He held her face between his hands. "Baby steps." He wiped the tears from the corners of her eyes with his thumbs. "Today, we're going out for breakfast. That's all. Just breakfast. We're going to sit at a table with our coffee and bacon and eggs, and we're going to talk about the weather, the football, the tourists. Anything. But we're not going to talk about Summer."

Mirabelle looked up at him, at the gentle pleading in his eyes, the tenderness in his face. Sam was a good man, and he deserved better than she was giving him. She knew that. Knew he was right too. Perhaps it was time. Perhaps.

Little jaunts: to the shop at the corner and back, no photographs held out; to a coffee shop on George Street, no questions asked of anyone; to Yvonne's for dinner without discussion of how the search progressed.

Mirabelle's sick leave had finished some time ago, but she had no hunger for social work now, no desire to get back into the demands it of it. Her priorities had irreversibly changed, her focus shifted. Without a backward glance at all that used to be paramount in her life, she walked away from social work and decided to sustain herself with other, less demanding work, things she could enjoy doing but could drop when it suited.

When she had been at school, Mirabelle had an artistic flair her teachers expected her to develop, her craft teacher urging her to go to art college, but Mirabelle had been determined to set the world to rights through Social Work. The love of arts and crafts had never left her, despite a lack of practice or encouragement, so she turned to it now, making cards and collages, clothes and bags, all with her individual style and flair. Colourful, distinctive wares that she offered in shops and craft fairs.

It wasn't a great income, but it paid some of the bills. She no longer had a mortgage, her flat having been bought and paid for over a fifteen-year period, now complete, so gas and electricity were her main concerns, and she was managing to cover them with her variable income. Other things, she was learning to do without.

Time was not a problem for Mirabelle. She had more than she wanted, to do with as she wished, so, whenever

Lena, Yvonne or Sam were free, she would accept their invitations and encouragement to do things and go places.

One day, it was a trip to the Botanic Garden, to sit for a while in the tranquil setting, feel the balm of fresh air and silence — without stopping people, showing The Photograph, asking The Question. Holding hands, she and Sam walked through the gardens, past the duck pond, dipping under the weeping willows to stand at the edge of the water, watching a family of shell ducks preening themselves.

They found an empty bench set back a little from the path and they sat down for a while to breathe in the spring air, heavy with the scents of new life, budding trees and spring flowers, healing, soothing: she could feel it warm her soul.

"This was a good idea," she said, her face turned up to the sun, eyes closed.

"That's the most relaxed I've seen you for weeks. Months," Sam said, lounging back on the bench, his legs stretched out, his arm along the back of the seat and round Mirabelle's shoulders.

"It's the most relaxed I've felt in more than a year."

"I know, Belle." He squeezed her shoulder. "But don't get upset. It's okay to be here, to be relaxed."

"I feel almost guilty. Like I have no right to feel good."

"But you have. Of course you have. Summer's gone. We're still looking for her. We haven't forgotten her. But as the old saying goes, 'Life goes on,' and we have to go on."

Mirabelle sighed, a long shudder of a sigh. "Fed up hearing that. And it hurts so much." The pain was there all the time. It changed; went through various colours and tints, sadness, anger, guilt, shame, frustration, hopelessness, helplessness, a whole rainbow of suffering. Always there, always hurting.

Sam held her close against his chest.

"You're good for me Sam Burns," she said after a while. "I really don't understand how you put up with me. Why you keep coming back when I send you packing."

He kissed the top of her head. "Addiction," he said. "I'm totally addicted to you. Always have been, since the first day I met you. Tried to take the pledge. Didn't work," he laughed. "Still addicted." He pulled her closer.

She smiled, her cheek resting against his soft plaid shirt.

After a while, Mirabelle found pleasure and distraction in watching the little birds hopping about their feet looking for crumbs. "Must be lunchtime," she said.

"Hungry?"

"D'you know, I do believe I am. A little."

"Good! I'll treat you. The café here does a mean baked potato with salad."

a bigger step
a ballet step

Another Saturday afternoon, Sam managed to persuade her to accompany him to the ballet. It had been a long time since Mirabelle had been to the theatre and she only agreed to it this time because, back then too, it had been the Saturday matinee of Swan Lake — not that she shared that information with Sam.

Summer had been a little girl; Swan Lake, her favourite ballet. If it hadn't been her favourite before, it certainly became so that afternoon. *The production was glorious and the Festival Theatre seemed to glow with pride as it hosted it. The foyer was sparkling; fairy lights twinkled and winked at them as they were carried through the doors in a bright, laughing crowd of happy young theatre-goers. There must have been a party of schoolgirls sitting near them and their giggling joy was infectious. By the time the orchestra struck the first notes of the overture, Summer was lost in ecstasy. Eyes burning with excitement, she turned to Mirabelle and, putting her arms round her neck, "Oh! Thank you Mummy," she whispered.*

Sitting in that same theatre so many years later, Mirabelle closed her eyes and could almost feel again the softness of those beloved little arms, the earnestness of the hug and the moistness of the kiss.

The lights dimmed and the music started. It could have been the same costumes, the same dancers, the same backdrops for all Mirabelle knew: she watched the ballet through a mist of nostalgia.

When she turned her tear-stained face to Sam as the lights came up for the interval, he put his arms around her shoulders, a manly, harder hug, unwittingly dispensing today's comfort for yesterday's pain. "You're such a sentimental old softie," he said. "Mind you, it is beautifully done, I suppose." He gave her shoulders a squeeze. "Do you want ice cream?" He was already on his feet, feeling in his pockets for change.

Mirabelle let him go with a small nod of her head, not caring about ice cream but buying time to compose herself and look for Summer. If Summer was anywhere in Edinburgh, she should be here, right now, today, watching Swan Lake, her favourite ballet. At the Saturday matinee: her magical time.

A time when anything was possible.

The theatre.
The ballet.
The interval.
She'd looked for Mirabelle, knowing she'd be there, spotted her sitting alone.

So easily, she could have slipped into the seat beside her. So easily, slipped through the time warp of sorrow and regret, be a child again, swollen with pride as she sat by her amazing, funny, adorable mother. Is that not why Mirabelle was there? To find her? She'd know, if her daughter was anywhere in Edinburgh, that's where she'd be. There, in the Festival Theatre for the Saturday matinee of Swan Lake. Mirabelle was there to take her home. Maybe it was time.

Moving towards her from behind, threading through rows of seats, excusing herself to stumble past theatre-goers who stood or sat in her way, Summer never let the back of Mirabelle's head out of sight. Her hand tingled with remembered recognition of how those tight, black curls would feel.

She was no more than a few yards behind her, could almost have reached out to feel again the course, springy sensation, when someone handed Mirabelle a tub of ice cream.

That man again.

A look of familiar friendship passed between them. More than friendship, much more.

While Mirabelle opened her ice cream, Summer drifted past without sound or touch. Drifted past and out of the theatre. Drifted back into the streets of Edinburgh.

have you seen my daughter

Mirabelle saw no sign of Summer, though she sensed her presence in the theatre. That feeling you get sometimes when you turn round and someone ducks out of sight. Or you catch someone watching you, feel their gaze on the back of your neck. You spin round only to find them turned away, walking past. But never red-haired. No long red waves or freckled face.

So, on the way out of the theatre, despite Sam's injunction, she took The Photograph from her bag. "Have You Seen My Daughter?" she asked the girl at the door of the auditorium. "Have You Seen My Daughter?" she asked the girl who had sold her a programme earlier and held the theatre door for her now. "Have You Seen My Daughter?"

Distressed and defeated, Mirabelle would take a lot of coaxing before Sam could get her out of the house again.

"Sam," she said, her hand on his arm as they sat together on her sofa after the walk from the theatre. "I know you meant well."

He started to speak but she put her fingers to his lips.

"I know you want to help me. You think I can get over this. Get over Summer. Move on with my life. But I can't, Sam. I just can't."

"Are you not even a little bit angry Summer could do this to you?"

"Angry? Of course I'm angry. Sometimes I feel rage burning through me like a I'm going to explode. But then I remember she's my child, my baby, and I've loved her since the moment she was born and I can't stop loving her. I can't turn it off. No matter what she's done. No matter how angry I feel, it just fizzles out after a while and I want to find her. I

261

want her to come home."

Sam looked up from studying his hands. "What do you want me to do?"

"I don't know. Keep looking for her, I suppose."

"Belle, you know …"

"I know you can't, not officially. But I can't give up, Sam, and if you want to help me, then, not as a policeman, just as my friend, neither can you."

"Forget it!" her mother said when seven-year-old Mirabelle asked if she could write to her dad.

Learning to read and write turned lights on for Mirabelle: the realisation she had such an awesome tool of communication shone brightly for one so young. Stories in her childish printing lined the classroom wall, interspersed with those of her classmates, although praise and recognition had dried up at home since her father's departure. Writing made her feel good.

She instinctively knew she held in her hand the ability to reach other people, even her father in his distant home. She had looked at the map in the classroom, standing on a chair, her little finger tracing the distance from Scotland to Jamaica, her young brain computing, if the whole island in which Edinburgh was a tiny speck, smaller than the full stop she'd learned to put at the end of her sentences, if the whole island of Great Britain was narrower than her finger, then the large expanse of ocean wider than both her hands put together meant Jamaica was a world away. Out of reach of her presence but, thanks to the postal service she had learned about at school, not out of reach of her pencil.

"Forget it. He didn't leave an address."

"But I want to write to Daddy."

"Well you can't."

"Couldn't we find him? Perhaps he lives with his mummy again."

"Witch!" her mother muttered under her breath.

"Was she really a witch, Mummy?"

"Never you mind. None of your business." She picked up her cigarette packet, shook one out and reached into her

cardigan pocket for her lighter. "Hated me, if you must know."
She lit the cigarette and took a long drag on it. "Didn't want
your precious daddy to marry over here."

Mirabelle watched the smoke billow out with the words.

"Don't think it mattered who. She just wanted him home."

"To Jamaica?"

"Aye! And no doubt that's where he is now." She rose
from the table and walked across the kitchen to the
cupboard above the sink.

Mirabelle felt the flutter in her chest. She hated that
cupboard.

Rose reached down the amber bottle, selected the least
muggy of the glasses sitting by the sink waiting to be
washed and poured herself a generous measure. "And good
luck to him." She raised her glass.

Quickly, before her mother disappeared, before the
conversation disintegrated into angry, bitter words, Mirabelle
had one last try. "Please, Mummy. Do you have her
address? I want to write to Daddy."

"You're better off without him." She poked Mirabelle in
the chest, her fingers strong, sharp, scorching; the glow of
the cigarette between them threatening, menacing. "Let him
go. Just forget him."

"But I can't forget him, Mummy." Mirabelle remembers
the pain: stronger than her mother's words, sharper than her
fingers.

"Let it go, Bella. Stop your stupid moaning and go get us
some chips for tea." She threw the coins on the table. "Just
give up, will you?" She shook her little daughter by the arm.
"Will you just give up!"

At eight years of age, she gave up on her father. He'd been gone two years by then, but that's when she gave up. That's when she stopped picturing herself, all dressed up in her Sunday frock, standing on the deck of a ship, watching all the other passengers teeter down the gangplank and onto the dock. It would be busy. She was sure it would be busy. And colourful. Her country. Only not *her* country. Her father's country. One she had started reading about, dreaming about. Her father's home.

There'd be music. She was sure there'd be music. The same rhythms her father used to beat and tap on his shining kettle-drum. Music and noise. And colour. Not the greys and blues and sombre colours of Scotland's clothes but all the colours of the rainbow. Her father's people would open their arms to her, their black faces shining with welcome, their rainbowed clothes fluttering in the breeze, their bare feet tippety-tapping out their footsteps. She just knew their language would be music in her ears.

But, at eight years old, she made herself stop longing for the impossible. She stopped allowing herself the beautiful dream.

Besides, there was a new baby to care for.

Yvonne, or Y-vonne, as her mother pronounced it, the capital Y a whine in its alphabetic precision. Only when Yvonne went to school did they realise their mother may have been asking a question in choosing the name: 'Why? Y-vonne' instead of the 'ee' of pleasure. Rose was the only one who ever pronounced her daughter's name that way again. Yvonne had been mocked at school for the mispronunciation and demanded everyone say her name properly when she got home. *"Eeee-vonne,"* she said. *"Miss Young says you should call me E-vonne."*

Yvonne, the sibling Mirabelle became closest to, had no memory of that other father, the one not her own, the one who gave Mirabelle her colour and her charm. There was no comfort of shared memory for Mirabelle. She had to let him go a little. Had to get on with life without him, though she never forgot him.

But oceans and islands were no obstacle now. No matter where in the world, people could be traced, could be reached. The only thing her eight-year-old self thought she knew for sure about her father was he had gone back to Jamaica. But Summer had no passport, no mother in a far-away land. The likelihood was she was much nearer home: under her finger rather than beyond her hands.

There was still no evidence to suggest foul play, no body in the mortuary, no sign of suicide or murder. The kitchen whiteboard bore testimony she'd been alive and well up to eight months after she'd disappeared. In all likelihood, Summer was still alive somewhere. She needed to keep looking, no matter everyone's well-intentioned wish for her to 'move on.'

Mirabelle knew Sam had just about had enough, seemed to be pushing for her to make a choice. She shrugged her shoulders and hardened her heart. Her choice was made the day Summer was born.

Chapter Twenty

Rather than helping her to move on as Sam intended, the trip to the ballet sent Mirabelle spiralling backwards. Where she had been beginning to climb out of the abyss she had been in, she felt herself tumble back into it, losing the foothold she had on the way forward.

She felt badly that she had started enjoying herself before she had proof positive that Summer was okay. That's all she'd need. Just to know for certain her daughter was safe and well and had total freedom of choice. Mirabelle tried to convince herself she'd be okay with whichever choice Summer made, as long as it was free of coercion or threat.

No amount of discussion and reasoning by Sam or Yvonne could convince her Summer had that freedom.

It felt more important than ever that she find her, because Summer must be in trouble. If she hadn't been in trouble, she would have been at the Saturday matinee. Of this, Mirabelle felt certain.

"That really doesn't follow," Yvonne said. "She just might not have known it was on. Or been busy that day."

"Or in trouble," Mirabelle insisted. "I have a bad feeling. I just know she would have been there if she could have been."

Yvonne shook her head and left Mirabelle to her deliberations.

Where she had been unable to do anything about searching for her father, Mirabelle felt there was still plenty she could do about searching for Summer. There were still stones to be turned, still plenty to check again since the early days of the search. Using the whiteboard, Mirabelle started to list the things she had done, the facts she had checked, working along under the timeline, making sure everything had been covered.

The police had long since lost interest in the case. They had closed the casebook on it, confident it had been a teenager falling out with Mum and leaving home, nothing to follow up, no action needed. She was over sixteen. It was her choice.

Even Sam had to back off. There was enough going on in Edinburgh that did need his attention, and this was something that clearly didn't, so it was up to Mirabelle and Mirabelle alone. She would do this. She would find her daughter.

She would turn detective. A reluctant one, but a detective none the less.

Thinking it through, she came to the conclusion if Summer was still using drugs and alcohol, it seemed likely she was still in a pitiable condition and an unenviable place.

At Lena's suggestion, Mirabelle checked and found the letter allocating Summer a National Insurance number. It was still in among the piles of papers filed haphazardly into Mirabelle's kitchen drawer.

Without it, Summer would be unable to get a regular job, apply for Social Security Benefits or any other state help.

Without it, she couldn't apply for a council house, and most rented accommodation required proof the prospective tenant had an income and could pay the rent, making it very difficult for her to find somewhere to live.

Mirabelle's theory was, with no job, therefore no income, Summer would almost certainly still be homeless, so, with a distinct sense of déja vu, she took to the streets again, started making regular check-ins with the various agencies who try to help youngsters in difficult circumstances, even calling in at her old office. Greeted kindly by those she had worked with, she wondered about returning, but the dedication had gone, that feeling of commitment to her career, her clients, was not there. It would just be a job, and her clients deserved better.

Her mood was different: less bitter, less resentful. Something had shifted when Summer didn't appear at the ballet, causing Mirabelle to look at the whole situation from a new perspective. Instead of concentrating on her own pain, she needed to be looking to relieve Summer's. The way to do that hadn't changed so very much. She still needed to find her.

She took to lingering in parks and cemeteries, looking at faces, standing in shadows watching for ones that moved. As the sun went down on regiments of tulips standing to attention for Taps, Mirabelle looked beyond them for the denim jacket, the red hair.

Leaving the one in the wash-house, she retrieved the other sleeping bag from the back of the hall cupboard and spent some nights sleeping rough. Derelict buildings, empty churches, tenement squats, Mirabelle tried them all, settling down to semi-sleep with one eye open, leaving notes behind when she moved on after a few nights. Notes to Summer in case she followed.

"Have You Seen My Daughter?" she asked any others with whom she bunked. "If you see her, please can you tell her I'm looking for her?"

She got to know some of the 'skippers' she shared shelter with. Knew some of them already. Knew some of them could get nasty, be violent when roused, were prone to sudden outbursts of bizarre behaviour. Some of them were young people she had already previously tried to help, some of them out-patients at the psychiatric hospital. She knew what she was doing was not without danger, and she was not without fear and not without caution.

But, among the skippers, there were gems: kindly souls, lost souls, and she listened to their stories, told her own.

Promises were given: "I'll keep my eye out, hen."

"Give us a copy of that photie. I'll keep it in ma pocket. Help me remember who I'm looking for."

"I'll ask around when I move on, dear."

"She bella, you daughter, no? I look for her. I help you."

Although she checked in with them regularly, her enquiries were always met with a sad shake of the head, sometimes a comforting hand on her shoulder. And it *was* a comfort to feel she was not alone in her search. There was a large team of helpers: eyes all over Edinburgh.

Lying in her sleeping bag and under a couple of thin blankets in the cemetery, rousing herself every time there was a sound, a rustling in the trees, every time a shadow flitted across her face, she knew this was a place often favoured by those who sought invisibility. Who else would be in a graveyard during the night? Hardly a place for a moonlight stroll. A cold, flat gravestone with cardboard spread over it made a hard bed, but less damp than the grass around it and her bunkmates could make no complaint.

Night after night, in a corner, enclosed on two sides by high walls, where the wind was less likely to find unprotected flesh, she made herself a cosy nest and semi-slept till daybreak. Often there'd be one or two others sharing her hideaway and they'd chat before they slept or give no more than a nod of acknowledgement, sometimes, but not always, companionable in their silence. Not an easy place to sleep alone.

Sam was understandably shocked at what she was doing and had to be dissuaded from standing guard over her at night.

"She'd only have to catch a glimpse of you standing there, on guard, and she'd be off before you could say, 'Evening all!'" Mirabelle complained.

"These skippers are not just cold and sad, you know. Some of them need to be watched, approached with caution. Some of them would steal your coat off your back while you slept if they could."

"Don't you think I know that? I didn't sail up the Forth in a banana boat, you know!"

"But this is crazy, Belle. Crazy, unwise and, as far as I can see, pointless."

"Well, it won't be the first crazy thing I've ever done," she told him as she pushed him away.

Mirabelle felt there was point to the exercise. Even if she didn't stumble on her daughter, she was building a list of contacts among the homeless population of Edinburgh and many of them were willing to be extra eyes and ears for her.

As Sam predicted, Summer didn't show. No traces of red on a stone pillow.

However, a few nights after starting her cemetery watch, Mirabelle shared her food and, later, her makeshift bed with a young girl no older than Summer.

"What's your name, pet?" Mirabelle asked over a shared packet of sandwiches for supper.

"Mela."

Mirabelle looked at the small bag hung across the girl's body. "Didn't plan on sleeping out here, then?"

Mela shook her head and drew her knees up to her chin, wrapping her arms round them to try to keep warm.

"Would you like a share of my blankets and stuff?"

"'S okay."

"Promise I'll not snore. Or fart in the night."

Mela smiled.

"Mind you, that might help us stay warm. Centrally heated sleeping bag. Could catch on, eh?" Mirabelle tucked a blanket round the huddled girl and made room on the cardboard mattress. "If you change your mind."

Sun-up found them trussed together in the cold blankets, trying to stop one another shivering.

"Homeless shelter for us tonight, I think, yes?"

Mela nodded.

"Still too cold for the great outdoors." Mirabelle shrugged. "Got any plans for breakfast?"

A shake of the head.

"Come on, then. McDonald's. My treat." And she linked her arm through Mela's and pulled her towards the cemetery gates without leaving room for refusal.

Mela put up little resistance as Mirabelle hustled her from breakfast to lunch to dinner to shelter for the next few days. The child had no more idea of how to live rough than she had money for food in her purse.

"Enough?" Mirabelle asked after another long, cold, sleepless night outdoors. They'd been too late getting to the hostel, missing out on minimally warmer beds. "Time to give up?"

Mela nodded. "But I can't go home. I just can't."

"Want to tell me about it?"

And, when Mela did, Mirabelle had to agree, from personal experience, going home to her alcoholic mother was probably not the best option. "Let me take you down to the Children and Families Department. I used to work there and they're not such a bad lot," she said when Mela drew back. "They'll help you sort out what's best to do. Get your mum some help."

"I'd like that," Mela said. "I'd like if Mum got some help." For the first time since they'd teamed up, Mela's eyes filled with tears. "I did try, like. I tried to get her to go to the doctor, but she just said I was overreacting and she'd be all right if I just gave her time to sort herself out and she was just sad 'cos of my dad leaving and that, like, and I don't even know where he went but she thinks he's gone off with someone and I don't know if that's true but they'd been arguing all the time and he kept sending me to my room and I could still hear them even if I turned my music up." She took the tissue Mirabelle offered and blew her nose mightily.

"Better?"

"It was a bit better after he went 'cos at least there wasn't all the shouting and that but then the drinking got worse and that's mostly what they argued about before and I thought if she stopped drinking so much maybe Dad'd come back but when I asked her not to drink so much she said she was just needing a bit of space and I was nagging her too much and needed to leave her in peace, like."

Mirabelle handed her another tissue, needing one herself.

"And then it all got worse and worse until she was just drunk nearly all the time and there was no food and the house was getting filthy and she wouldn't let me clean it up and then she told me to get lost and I got out the house and went to see my pal but she was out and I didn't know where else to go, like, 'cos she said she'd kill me if I said anything to my nan or the teachers or anybody and I went back home but I was really scared, like, 'cos she kept waving the kitchen knife at me and she came at me and I ran back out the door and she locked me out of the house and I just walked and walked till you found me and, and …"

"Okay," Mirabelle soothed, gathering the child to her. "It's okay. We're gonna get this mess all sorted out for you. It's going to be okay."

This time, she knew what to do.

"And it is okay, in as much as anything can be okay when life has become unbearable and people turn to the bottle," Mirabelle told Sam a few weeks later. "It's not the storybook happy-ever-after ending, but Mela's being cared for by her grandmother while her mother goes into rehab and I'll look out for her now and again when I pass the school at lunchtime or that. We could always share a sandwich or something."

Sam smiled.

"Huh! Better than sharing a stone slab, I can tell you."

"Yeah. Well. You know how I feel about that."

"Oops! Sorry I brought it up."

"Bet you are. But bet it'll not stop you anyway, will it?"

"Mmm," she mumbled, knowing it wouldn't.

"A timeline. That's what we need," Mirabelle said to Mela when Mela asked help to find her dad as they chatted outside the school gates. "We need to chart where and when your dad was last seen."

"Like in *Without a Trace*?"

"Just like that, only there's only you and me to do the detective work. So, first question, does your dad have any brothers or sisters he could be with?"

"There's only Auntie Ally and he's not there. I went round. She hasn't seen him since before he went off."

"His mum and dad?"

"No. Granny died about a year ago and Gramps doesn't know where *he* is, like, never mind where Dad is." Mela made a gesture to her head. "Dementia, like."

"Right. So, where did your dad work at the time he left?"

"In a garage somewhere. Belfast Garage? Something like that, like? He's a mechanic."

"D'you mean Belmont's?"

Mela shook her head.

"Beauford's?"

"Y-e-a-h. Maybe. Yeah, I think so. Beauford. Yeah that sounds like it."

"Right. In which case, I'll look in there this afternoon, see what I can dig up and report back to you later."

Mela offered a high-five.

"Okay," Mirabelle said as she returned the salute. "Since we've not got an office, my kitchen will have to do. Ask your nan if you can come over to my place to do your homework tonight and I'll get hold of another whiteboard."

But, in the event, they didn't need another whiteboard.

Mirabelle found Mela's father before she could even buy one. She asked around in a few garages, all beginning with a 'B', until she found the one where he used to work. He had changed job but only to another garage just outside Edinburgh, so Mirabelle settled herself on the bus and went to see him.

"He's managed to rent a flat in Haddington," she told Mela later. "He was hoping you'd like to live there with him once he's sorted everything out with the school and your nan. He didn't know you were on your own or he'd've got in touch sooner. He was trying to get set up for you first."

"Oh, thank you, Mirabelle. Thank you! Thank you! Thank you!" Mela flung her arms round Mirabelle's waist and hugged her.

"Nothing to thank me for." But she relished the embrace. Eyes closed, it could almost be Summer.

The weeks and months were moving on, despite her longing for time to stop, to hold still while she examined the past in order to change the future.

With each season, the city changed its dress: from winter downfalls, carpeting the parks and gardens with green, wet grass or soft white snow, and cold east winds sweeping the trees bare; through gardens and window boxes adorned with the freshness of spring, blossom fluttering from trees to confetti the streets and parks; to summer with its colourful fill of tourists and awnings, rose gardens and bandstand concerts, fading into autumn with the grace of rustic colours blending with the brick and stone of elegant buildings.

This year was no different, though she wished it so.

Mirabelle watched as the seasons marched with no heed for her pain as they passed.

Unable to halt the flow of time, unable to know the truth about her father or her daughter, unable to accept the evidence as it accrued, Mirabelle wandered the streets of her city, not quite aimlessly, but with no defined destination, only a driving, desperate need to find traces of her daughter where she had found none of her father. Loss of the two most important people in her life had twined together and grown into a choking vine, climbing and clinging painfully.

Some days, she stopped at the top of Leith Walk, at the tiny fast-food kiosk there, before taking a wander along the east end of Princes Street and into the gardens, guessing she might meet one of her growing army of helpers.

"Ah bella, bella, bella! My beautiful Bella. What can I do for you today?"

"Hi, Tomas. Got something for you." Mirabelle handed

over the warm, brown package, the promise of hot pie wafting up as Tomas opened it.

"Ah!" He breathed in the delicious smell. "Delizioso! Something to wash it down?" he asked, more in hope than expectation.

She held out the Styrofoam cup. "Coffee? Not Italian, I'm afraid. From the kiosk round the corner."

He took it from her and wrapped his hands around the cup. "Ah, Bella," he said. "Always kind, always practical." He looked up, shaking his head. "But never anything stronger to warm the heart of a poor old man."

Mirabelle grinned. "I've brought you something else to warm you, though, Tomas." And she drew from the depths of her bag a beautiful cashmere scarf. "Got it in the charity shop for a song and a sixpence."

Tomas fondled the soft, dark blush of burgundy in his hands. "Canzone d'angelo, I think, to win you such eleganti each time." He winked up her. "Mia fidanzata."

"You wish," Mirabelle said with a grin.

He wound the scarf round his wrinkled neck. "So, what can I do in return, mia Bella, to deserve such a fine omaggio?"

"There's nothing you could do to deserve it, you old rogue." She pushed her fist into the shoulder of his coat. "It's no use to me. Too dark a red."

"You no found you her yet?"

"No, Tomas. Not yet," she said on a long sigh. She heaved herself to her feet, looking up at the sky. "I'll speak to Milly at the shelter. She'll save you a place tonight. It's going to pour. Enjoy your pie, mi amigo."

washing dishes

After leaving Tomas, her wanderings took her down to the Stockbridge area, in and out of charity shops and bookstores, dodging heavy showers of rain, and now she was nearly home. She was laden with wonderful treasures and interesting volumes: an oriental fan, its Geisha smiling shyly out at her when opened, and another bag to join her collection, this one beaded and embroidered in swirls of purple and lilac, its handles long and soft, comfortable on her shoulder. She'd found a biography of PG Wodehouse, in good condition but obviously read and enjoyed, its pages well thumbed, its spine like a well-oiled joint. And her prize: an ancient volume of Shakespeare's Sonnets, its brown leather binding caressed and worn, speaking as eloquently of love as its contents.

As she went, she had been asking in hotels and restaurants, "Do you have this girl working here?"

Showing the photo. "Waitressing?"

"In the kitchens perhaps?"

"Cleaning up?"

Then, at one of the small hotels not far from home, "Yeah, I've seen that kid. She used to wash dishes here." He lifted a grubby cloth to his head, wiping sweat and steam from his brow. "Bout a year ago." He shrugged. "Maybe more."

"She was here?" Mirabelle was so used to getting no response to her questions she had started to walk away, to continue up the alley looking for the next staff door. Now she turned and walked back, her breath held in her chest. She held out the photo again. "This girl? She was here?"

"Yeah, she was here. Good wee worker. Sorry when she

moved on." The chef took a last draw on his cigarette and threw down the stub.

"And you remember her? After all this time? Almost a year?"

"Sure. Like I say. A good wee worker. Good looking kid." He looked about himself. "Bit younger than I'm used to but fair fancied that red hair lying across my chest."

"You are remembering this is my daughter I'm looking for?"

He laughed. A course laugh. His tobacco-laden breath catching in her throat.

"How long did she work here?"

"Six, seven weeks?"

"Six or seven weeks? And you're sure it was her?"

"Listen darlin." He leant in closer and tapped the photo Mirabelle still held in her hand. "You don't forget hair like that in a hurry." And he turned into the back door of the hotel kitchen.

"Wait!" Mirabelle held his arm.

He looked at her hand on his sleeve.

"Sorry," she said, removing it. "Just another minute. Please?"

He looked into the busy kitchen. "Half a minute, then. I've to work magic with a poor wee chicken or two."

"Would you have any record of when she worked here? You? Or someone else?"

"A payslip you mean?"

"Anything. Yes. A payslip."

He shook his head. "Casual work, that. Washing dishes." He looked around. "Between you and me, boss doesn't worry too much about putting everything through the books. Cash in hand every night. No questions asked. Simpler that way. They come and go all the time. Students looking for a few bob usually. Too much hassle to do it all official like. I mean, nothing illegal or anything, like. He just puts it all under extras."

"So there's nothing? No contact address?"

"No paperwork. Sorry, dear." He pushed the door open. "Good wee worker, she was," he said, turning back to Mirabelle. "Tell you what, if you catch up with her, tell her we'd have her back anytime. Better than some of the shirkers we've got just now."

Mirabelle leant against the wall, her feet refusing to walk away from the doorway. Blood drained from her head and pooled in her feet, rooting her to the ground. Turning her face to the wall, her body doubled over in pain as she tried to stifle the howl rising in her throat. She had been here. Summer had been here. So close. So close.

Mirabelle was drowning. Waves of nausea engulfed her. She was choking on the gall. The need to see her daughter, to touch her, to beg her to come home was so great it was crushing her. And she'd been so close.

How could she have been working here for weeks, six or seven weeks, and not come home? What was it that stopped her from walking the ten minutes or so up the road, drag her tired body up the stairs and fall into her own bed?

It seemed almost perverse, to choose to be so near home and not to make that extra effort. Would it really have been so difficult? What kind of welcome did she think she would get?

Mirabelle lowered herself to the ground, heedless of the dirt she sat in. There was no strength in her legs to move. She sat with her head bowed waiting until the angry, raging howl inside her bled out through her tears.

How many times did Summer walk in and out that same door? She closed her eyes and tried to imagine her lovely daughter, sleeves rolled up, hands in steaming-hot water.

"I hope she wore rubber gloves," she said to Sam the next day when they met for lunch in the new Bistro Restaurant on Leith Walk.

"Never mind that," Sam said. "Have you any idea what this means?"

Mirabelle stared at him. "Do you?"

"Statistically, the more sightings we have of Summer, the longer she is known to be alive, the less chance her disappearance was anything other than choice."

"And that's supposed to comfort me?"

"Think about it, Belle. Listen to what I said. Okay, so it's hard to believe she really did choose to leave home. Crazy she would choose to work a stone's throw away. I know, I know."

"It's not just crazy. It's downright cruel."

"As I've been trying to tell you all along."

"Yeah, yeah, yeah. So, you were right. Now what?"

"Well, it's confirmation of what we thought. Each sighting increases the probability she's still alive. That has to be good, doesn't it?"

Mirabelle sighed. "Yes, of course it is, if that's what it means."

"Of course it is. It's the statistics."

"Okay," Mirabelle said as she took the plate from the waiter and nodded her thanks. "So you think I should stop worrying about her?"

"Yes, I do, Belle." He smiled in thanks to the waiter too. "So, knowing that — knowing Summer's alive and kicking, what about us, Belle?"

"What about us?" Mirabelle said through a mouthful of

tuna mayo panini.

"Us. You and me. Is there an us?"

Mirabelle chewed on.

"Do we have a relationship?"

Mirabelle shrugged.

"Please, Belle. Put the damn sandwich down and talk to me."

With exaggerated care, Mirabelle placed the panini on its plate, licked each finger in turn, finished chewing and ran her tongue carefully around her mouth to check it was empty. "Better?" she said.

Sam unclenched his fingers. "You know you drive me crazy, don't you?"

She laughed.

"But, I do love to hear you laugh," he said with a smile.

Mirabelle sat forward, her elbows on the table, her hands clasped under her chin, the few bangles and rings she'd begun to wear again sparkling. "You do know if you want to have a serious conversation with me, it had better be quick. The smell of this tuna is hard to resist."

"Never mind the serious conversation ..."

She reached for the panini again.

Sam restrained her hand.

"No! What I mean is ... what I want to know is, do we have a serious *relationship* here or not? We've been going out for a long time, Belle. I want to know — need to know — is this relationship going somewhere?"

"Like?"

"Like marriage. You must know that's what I want."

"And you must know I can't, not while Summer's still missing."

"But you know she's all right."

"No. I don't. Knowing she's alive is not the same as knowing she's all right. Correction; knowing she was alive *a year ago,*" Mirabelle leant across the table to add emphasis, "is not the same as knowing she's alive and well now. She's still missing."

Sam thumped the table, causing the café owner to look over, eyes narrowed, on the alert for trouble. "Not missing, Belle. Absent."

"The difference being?"

"Choice! She doesn't want to come home. She's choosing to be away."

"So? Away, absent — whatever you want to call it, she's still missing as far as I'm concerned."

"And you won't marry me till she comes home? Is that what you're saying?"

Mirabelle sighed. "That's exactly what I'm saying. It's what I've been saying since you first asked. It's what I'll keep saying till Summer's back." She picked up the panini and bit into it.

"Will you put that damn thing down!"

The owner stopped, the plate he held poised above a customer's table, his eyes flashing at the sound of the raised voice.

"This conversation is not over," Sam hissed.

"Well, it doesn't seem as though there's much more to be said." Mirabelle took yet another bite.

"So? What? What now? I'm tired of all this, Belle."

"All what?"

"This!" He shrugged. "I'm tired of watching you destroy yourself, your health, any chance of happiness you might have — *we* might have. And for what? Looking for someone who patently doesn't want to be found. You're letting Summer — searching for Summer — take over your life. In fact, you don't *have* a life any more. And neither do I! Everything's on hold. Has been since Summer went missing." He thumped his fist on the table. "No!" he said, leaning forward, his face pushed close to hers. "Since Summer *left home!*"

Mirabelle drew back.

"Because that's what she did, Belle. She left home. She didn't go missing. She *left home!*"

Mirabelle felt his heat prickle on her skin, making her

shiver.

He stared her down.

She knew he expected her to dissolve. To say she was sorry. Shock tactics, that's what he'd call it. She sat up straighter in her chair and stared right back at him. Slowly, with deliberate care, she picked up the panini and stuffed the last of it into her mouth.

"Do you expect me to just hang around forever? Like your pet poodle?"

"Don't have a poodle," she said through the food.

"At your beck and call? Sitting up and begging whenever you click your fingers?"

"Never could click my fingers," Mirabelle said, wiping them on her skirt and having another ineffectual try.

Sam pushed his chair back and stood up. "And I never could sit up and beg!"

'Let him go.' There was a voice in her head kept saying, *'Let him go. You don't need him. Just let him go.'* But she knew it was lying.

She told Yvonne about their row.

"Oh, no! That's awful."

"Och, he'll soon calm down," she said.

"You hope."

Mirabelle handed Yvonne a mug of tea. "He will. He's not hung around all this time just to walk out on me now."

Yvonne shook her head. "It's been done before. Plenty couples break up after years together."

"But not Sam and me. We'll be all right, you'll see."

"I wouldn't be so cocky, if I were you. You'd miss him if he didn't come back."

"Truth is, I miss him already," Mirabelle sighed as she put the biscuit tin on the table beside her. "But I know Sam. He can't stay angry with me for long."

"What if he's right?"

"About?"

"About Summer. About it being time you stopped looking for her. And you can stop looking at me like I've just stabbed you in the back. I'm not saying he *is* right, I'm just asking, 'What if?' I mean, maybe he's right. Maybe Summer doesn't want you to find her."

"Well, I *know* that! Of course she doesn't want me to find her. But that's no reason for me not to try. She's my daughter, for heaven's sake!" Mirabelle snatched a biscuit from the tin and crammed it into her mouth.

"So you'll just go on as before?"

"I'll just go on as before." She sprayed crumbs as she spoke.

"Even if it means losing Sam?"

Mirabelle hesitated. Swallowed the last of her biscuit.

"Even if it means losing Sam. But it won't. He'll come round in time, you'll see."

So Mirabelle continued looking for Summer. And Sam stayed away.

Sam stomped out his frustration in the Pentland Hills. Too deep in winter yet to go anywhere further afield, he settled for a few days tramping across the hills he could see from the windows of his mother's nursing home. He didn't bother with a tent, but returned home to sleep in the warmth of his own bed each night, but for three days, he set out early each morning before it was light, parked somewhere in Ratho or Currie, pulled a woollen hat on, zipped up his coat and walked.

Mirabelle was driving him crazy. He loved her. He'd always loved her. But she was the most infuriating, frustrating, stubborn woman… He kicked a tuft of frozen grass. Why could she not accept that Summer had upped and gone. Kids do that. They grow up and, one way or another, they leave home. That's the way of things. That's life.

She needed to get over herself.

He swiped at the frozen skeleton of a beech tree.

She needed to forget about the how and why Summer had gone and just accept the fact. She had left home.

A skein of geese wrote across the sky. Heading North, probably to their nesting site up in the Montrose Basin. They'd be Pink-Footed Geese, wintering there, heading back to the Arctic Circle in the spring no doubt. He looked at his watch. Yeah, getting on a bit, time to head back to the car if he didn't want to get caught out here in the dark. He watched how the geese changed position in the V, the rested ones taking over from the leaders as they tired, looking out for one another, sheltering one another from the icy wind.

"Eaaagh!" he shouted to the sky. Why did he have to feel

so damn responsible all the time? Why did he have to be the one who did all the caring?

Looking after the good citizens of Edinburgh. Trying to keep them safe.

Looking after Mother. Worrying about her. Making sure she had all she needed.

Looking after Mirabelle.

None of them were grateful. They all just accepted it as their due.

"What about me?" he shouted. "What about what I need? What about what I want?" He pummelled his chest with his fist.

What he wanted to do was take a swing at someone. Anyone. What he wanted to do was shout and swear, curse the world and all that was in it.

Shaking his head at the futility of it all, he started the walk back to his car.

Back to his job.

Back to the responsibilities of his work.

Back to his mother, to the regular visits of a stranger who'd been a son.

But not back to Mirabelle.

Chapter Twenty-One

Mirabelle had never seen Dermot Wilson, let alone met him, yet she recognised him as soon as he passed through her line of vision. Sam's description was etched in the grey matter of her brain.

It was not her habit to take the bus, but she was weary this morning, weary of life, weary of wandering.

A lightning flash cut through the fug in which she sat. Shaven head displaying lightning streak tattoo walking up Leith Walk. That was him, the tattoo the clue, the swagger and the leather jacket all the confirmation she needed.

Energised by the sighting, she jumped from her seat and pressed the bell to stop the bus, twisting her head, trying to keep her quarry in sight, muttering curses when the bus took too long to stop and he was lost from her view.

Clutching her bag to her chest, she jumped from the bus as soon as the doors opened and hit the pavement already running back to where she'd seen him, scanning the pavement as she ran. "Sorry! Sorry!" apologies to those she pushed past. "Excuse me!"

Lorne Street. Across the road, not much further down, Balfour Street. Her mission focused her mind. Dermot Wilson lived in Balfour Street. She looked across and there he was, turning off the Walk into Balfour Street.

Dodging between cars, parked and moving, she hurried across the road, her vision fixed on the blouson-style leather jacket, the cocky swagger as he made his way along the street. When he fished in his pocket for the key to the outer door of the stair, she drew into the scant shelter of another doorway, praying he wouldn't recognise her as he looked round himself before pushing the door open and stepping inside.

She moved her bulk faster than she knew she could to stop the door from slamming shut behind him, thankful for the slow, measured, door closer.

Then she hesitated, unsure of her next move.

Her mother's instinct was to rush into the stair and confront him, demand he tell her where Summer was, what he'd done to her, if he'd harmed her, why he thought it a good idea to give her drugs, tell him why she thought it wasn't, what she thought of scumbags like him, what she wanted to do to him. So much burned inside her, pushing her to recklessness.

She knew Sam would not want her to confront him at all, to ask anything, to tell him anything. Knew what Sam would say, what he had said already. "He's dangerous. Leave it to the professionals," he'd say. "We're watching him. The drug squad are watching," he'd tell her. "We're closing in on him. On his whole operation. If he had any contact with Summer, we'd know, Belle. We'd have seen it. Trust me."

She could hear his voice in her head, clear as though he was standing beside her just inside the stair, but the voice in her heart shouted louder. "He was with Summer," it said. "He introduced her to drugs. He took her to clubs, casinos. Heaven only knows where else and what else he's introduced her to. Get him!"

She launched herself up the stairs, taking them two at a time until her legs were shaking.

"Leave it! Get out of here!" Sam's voice in her head.

"Get him!" her heart shouted. "You're here. He's home. You may never get this chance again!"

"Get out!"

"Go for it!"

She went for it, found his door, thumped on it.

This was it.

Taking a deep breath, she banged again, halting the noises from within.

A shuffle, a scuffle, an eye at the peephole, the door opened a fraction. A woman. She tried to open it further but a man's hand caught her by the shoulder and pulled her roughly out of the way.

"What?" Dermot said, anger sparking from him. He looked at Mirabelle, tried to slam the door shut, but, once again, Mirabelle was too fleet of foot and she stuck her size seven in the door.

Pain shot up her leg, but she held the foot firm, adding her shoulder to the door, pushing it wider. "Ah," she said. "I take it you know who I am, then." She pushed harder as he tried again to close the door, her sheer bulk and determination more than a match for his puny muscles.

The door began to open.

With gargantuan effort, Mirabelle gave it all her pent up fury, all her mother's rage.

Dermot gave up the unequal struggle and jumped from behind it.

The door smashed against the wall of the hallway.

Mirabelle fell forward, off balance.

Dermot punched his fist into the side of her head as she fell.

Giving her a kick as he went, he stepped over her and crashed down the stairs, cursing her with the full extent of his wide vocabulary as he ran.

By the time she'd picked herself up and started for the top of the stairs, she heard the slam of the back door.

Leaning over the bannister, she could see the empty stairwell and felt defeated.

"What's going on?" The woman of the peephole had stepped out of the doorway. "What did you want with our Dermot?"

Turning to look at her, Mirabelle started to explain, then saw the woman's face and stopped, her mouth open, her own pain forgotten. "What happened…" she started to say, pointing to the swelling round the other woman's eyes, the bruising on her cheek. "Was that him? Was that your son?" she said, nodding in the direction Dermot had taken. "Did he do that to you?"

Mrs Wilson's hand went to her split lip and the cut on her chin.

"Good grief, what kind of animal is he?"

"He's my son."

"And this is the thanks you get for the privilege of changing his nappies and wiping his bum?"

"None of your business." She started to close the door. "Who are you anyway?"

"Sorry!" Mirabelle put out her hand. "I'm Mirabelle Milligan. I'm here because I think your son knows what happened to my daughter."

Mrs Wilson held the door, opened it another inch. "Oh," she said. "You're the mum of that girl who went missing."

"Summer. Yes."

"The polis were here."

"Yes."

Mrs Wilson hesitated, her hand on the door, almost opening it, almost closing it. "I don't know what to say to you."

"No."

She stepped back a little. "Maybe..." and a little more. "Maybe you should come in," she said at last. "I'll give you something to put on that bruise." She pointed to the swelling on Mirabelle's face.

Mirabelle smiled. "After you get something to put on your own," she said.

Mrs Wilson nodded and started to shuffle down the hall, leaving Mirabelle to follow.

"You're limping. Your leg ..."

"Hurt it on the fireplace. When I fell."

"Right. Is it broken?'

She shrugged. "Just bruised, I think." She lifted her trouser leg and examined the fresh gash on her leg.

"Mmm. More than bruised, I think. Looks like you'll need stitches."

Another shrug. "It'll heal." Mrs Wilson went through to the kitchen, put the kettle on and drew a First Aid box out of the cupboard. "Here, have a look through that," she said, handing it to Mirabelle. "There should be some Arnica tablets in there. I'll get an ice pack from the freezer."

"Keep a few handy do you?" Mirabelle gave her a rueful smile as she took the pack and held it to her face. "Does he often do this to you?"

"How d'you take your tea?"

"Two and the coo."

Mrs Wilson made the tea in silence and brought it through to the living room, pulling out the smallest of a nest of tables beside Mirabelle to put her cup on. "I put in an extra sugar," she said. "For the shock. You took a bit of a tumble when the door gave."

Mirabelle handed her the bottle of Arnica pills. "Here, you could do with some of these too, I guess."

"I told the polis months ago, I don't know anything about your girl. Only saw her the once since then."

"You saw my Summer?"

"Aye! She came looking for Dermot. Months ago. But ah tell her he wasnae home."

"When? When was this?" Mirabelle wanted to know.

"Right after the polis turned the flat over. They was looking for drugs, but this is no where he keeps them. No since they done him for possession years back."

"But he still deals them."

Dermot's mother shook her head and sighed. "It's no the way I wanted him to turn out."

Mirabelle leant forward. "I know. They seldom do turn out as we plan." She sighed too and they nodded at one another in sympathy.

"I dinnae like him dealing and all the rest. Always asking him to get a proper job and clean his life up." She touched her face. "Like you say, this is what I get for my trouble."

"It was him then?"

"Course it was." She looked round the room. "No-one else here."

"It's not the first time?"

Mrs Wilson looked at her. "Look, I haven't even told you my name. You're Mirabelle, you said. Well, I'm Sheila."

They nodded at one another again, in recognition this time, the occasion unsuited to a handshake somehow.

"Sheila, I know it's none of my business, but shouldn't you report him if he keeps battering you like this?"

Sheila laughed. "And get another?"

"But you could get an injunction, change the locks, keep him away from your house."

"That's the trouble, it's no ma house. It's his. Bought and

paid for from his takings no doubt, but a roof over ma head just the same."

"Is there nowhere else you could go?"

"Look, I don't know what your situation is, Mirabelle." She took a deep breath. "But ah work hard just to feed and clothe maself. couldn't afford tae rent a place or nothing. For all he's no all I wished for in a son, he's all I've got, an he does me a favour letting me stay here."

Mirabelle shrugged. "Like I said, it's not really my business. It just seems a strange way of showing his affection for you." She looked at the cuts and bruises on Sheila's face.

"Aye, maybe you're right. And maybe ah will do something about it sometime. But, right now, I'm too damn tired."

And she looked it. Under the colourful signs of his mistreatment, she was grey and haggard, with dark rings showing along with the redness and swelling round her eyes.

"In fact, I'm wore out." She stood up. "If ye've finished yer tea an ye dinnae mind, I'd like to head to ma bed. I start work again at eight o'clock."

Mirabelle put the teacup down and got to her feet. "Of course, sorry. Where is it you work?"

"Well, the night, I'm at the tills in the supermarket down the road. That's till midnight. But ah do some cleaning for Dermot, first thing, in his office and then in the afternoon in his other flat."

"He has an office?"

"Aye, well least, he shares it with some other guy. They rent out flats and stuff. All legal, like, he tells me."

"Well that's something."

"Yeah, well."

"And another flat?"

Sheila looked at her feet. "I think you better go now. I think I might have said more than's good for me."

Mirabelle started walking to the door. "Please, this other flat. Could Summer be there?"

Sheila shrugged. "Let's hope not," she said.

"Oh!"

"I'd not want any daughter of mine doing what he's got they girls doing."

"Oh!"

Sheila opened the door. "Look, I'm sorry, but really, I can't say any more. If he finds out...." Her hand wandered again to her face.

"Yes. I'm sorry. Thank you." Mirabelle walked past Sheila and out of the door.

"She's a nice kid, your girl. Or leastways, she was before he wasted her."

From inside the communal stair, letting the front stair door go, even giving it a push, there was a click — no way you could call the noise a slam. The door-closer-thingy at the top ensured that. Mirabelle thought back to the sound she'd heard as Dermot left the building. The back door. It had to have been the back door. She walked down the close and tried it, letting it go as she had the other. The slam resounded through the close. That was it. That's what she heard.

So where was he off to, going out that way? The park at the end of the street, maybe?

Mirabelle knew it was a bit of a hang-out for neds and dealers, that park, and she wondered if that's where he might have headed, but her interest in finding the man himself had waned somewhat with the information he had another flat somewhere. Around here, she wondered?

Opening the door, she stepped into the back yard. It looked a lot like the one at home. A communal area made up of various patches of grass and paving stones. Some of it well kept, some of it less so. She walked across the path and onto the grass directly outside the door she'd come through. There was a worn pathway cutting diagonally across, leading to a fence that separated this garden from the one belonging to the flat whose back door she could see across a paved yard. Measuring herself against the fence, she decided she couldn't vault it, it wasn't strong enough to support her weight to permit climbing, so it became an impassable barrier.

The backs of the tenement properties she looked across at would front onto Cambridge Street, so she retraced her steps across the grass, walked through the close and re-emerged on Balfour Street, before walking round the block to check her local geography.

She found the tenement property easily enough, checked it by gaining entrance with the use of the service button and checking where the back door led, at which point it occurred to her even if he cut across the grass using the worn trail she'd noticed, climbed the fence and crossed the yard beyond it, there was no guarantee this was the close he'd entered.

Climbing the stairs, she checked the names on each door, listened outside them for any sound that might provide a clue to the occupants. With a sigh, she admitted the futility of the exercise, and descended to street level again.

As she emerged from the stair door onto the street, she almost bumped into Sam. "What on earth are you doing here?" she asked, her hand on her chest to stop the pounding of her heart. "You gave me a fright."

"I might ask the same question," he retorted. "What are you doing here?"

"Since when do I have to answer to you for where my feet take me?"

"Since you started following one Master Dermot Wilson, of dubious character and dangerous nature."

Mirabelle stared at him. "But who says ... How could I ... What do you mean?"

"You still don't trust me, do you, Belle," Sam said, taking her arm, his grasp rough, firmer than she felt necessary, leading her firmly towards his car. "I told you. We're watching him." He opened the car door and waited, fury in his face, while she got in, slamming the door when she was, taking a moment before walking round to the driver's side.

When he was sitting beside her and had started the engine, "When the guys from the drug squad, the ones who were on watch today, when they saw first him, then you, go in his stair, they gave me a heads-up," he told her. "Mistakenly thinking I cared tuppence, I suppose," he muttered as he checked his mirror. "They didn't think it too clever of you, funnily enough. Plus they were raging that you might get in the way of what they are doing."

"Oh."

"Decided just to keep an eye on things from across the street till I showed up."

"Oh!"

"Yes, oh! You do realise you just might have put months of work up the spout for them?"

"But I don't think …"

"That's just the trouble, Belle. You don't think. You never stop to think about what's best, what's sensible, what makes good sense. What makes any kind of sense at all!"

"Okay! Okay, I'm sorry, right? I'm sorry." She put her hands over her ears. "There's no need to shout."

Sam drove in silence, shaking his head, taking very obvious large, deep breaths.

After a while, he nodded at the bruise on the side of her face. "I see you've found out what kind of character our Master Wilson is, then?"

She rubbed the pain.

"You know it could have been far worse?" he said as he drove.

Nodding, "You should see what he's done to his mother," she told him.

"Nice guy!"

"Creep!"

"Is she going to report him?"

"Doubt it."

"Didn't think so. Doubt if that was the first time, but maybe we can make it the last."

"And how are you going to do that?"

He held up his hand, the first two fingers indicating a centimetre at most. "We're this close to nailing him and those higher up the food chain."

"You know he's running some kind of brothel?"

"And you know this because?"

"His mother said as much. She hinted that's where he

300

keeps his drugs as well."

Sam nodded. "Thought so. That would make sense. Drug squad reckon he's providing storage and taking delivery for himself and a bunch of other dealers. They've had their suspicions for a while, but he's a slippery customer and they haven't been able to fix where he disappears to. Couple of times they thought they had him, but they were just empty flats. Seems he was looking to buy one."

"Or he knew your guys were following him."

Sam shrugged. "Or he knew he was being followed. Like I say, he's a slippery customer. Reckon he doubles back on himself, weaves about a bit, drug squad's not quite worked him out yet. But they will." He didn't shut off the engine but turned to face Mirabelle as he leant across to unclip her seat belt. "He's just a minnow, but they reckon he could lead them to the big fish. They've nearly got him and the outfit sussed, so do us a favour, Belle, and just keep out of the way, before you get really hurt. He's an animal. Won't think twice about knocking you down if you get in his way. None of them would."

"Yeah," she said, holding the pain in her shoulder. "Found that out."

"Yeah. Gonna leave it to the pros now?" he said as he prepared to drive off, hardly giving her time to climb out of the car.

Mirabelle nodded as he drove off, but neither of them believed she could leave it, though he certainly seemed to have left her.

"I'm more scared for Summer now than I've ever been," she admitted to Yvonne later. "Having met the slime-bag she's been associating with, makes it feel far worse. He's violent, Vonnie. Beats his mother up regularly, by the sound of it."

"Doesn't mean he's touched Summer." She looked at Mirabelle. "Okay, okay. No need to look at me like I'm an idiot. He might not have. Summer might be able to control him."

"Pah! You didn't cross paths with him."

"True, but you don't *know* he's done something to her."

"Yeah! Nor do I know he ain't." Mirabelle shuddered. "It's terrifying me what he's capable of. Plus, he's got this flat ..." Her voice tailed off and she swallowed hard. "She might be ... His mother said ..."

Yvonne knelt by her chair. "It's okay, Belle." She put her arms round her sister. "We don't know Summer's there. We don't know she's with him anywhere. Or in any sense of the word."

Mirabelle looked up at her sister. "But I need to know, Vonnie. Don't you see, I need to know."

"Yes, I do see that." Yvonne held her close and smiled. "How about if I tell you my plan?"

Chapter Twenty-Two

They waited across the street until he came out of the tenement.

"That's him," Mirabelle hissed.

"The one with the jacket?"

She nodded.

"Okay. You know what to do?"

"And you?"

They shared a quick hug.

"Right! Phase one," Yvonne said. "Game on!" She walked over to the bus stop and waited. When the bus came, she got on after Dermot and sat near the door. He had gone upstairs. As the bus pulled away from the bus stop, she didn't turn her head. Didn't show any sign of recognition as it passed Mirabelle waiting to cross the street, and Mirabelle noted Yvonne didn't even look into the supermarket on the other side as the bus passed it.

Mirabelle, however did. Looking through the glass door, she could see Dermot's mother was at one of the tills. She went into the shop and wandered round the aisles, picking up a few bits and pieces: some milk, bread, some biscuits, a couple of apples and some pink toilet rolls. "Oooh!" she mumbled, putting the toilet rolls back. "Pretty!" She took a pack of palest lilac ones instead. "New colour."

When she got to the checkouts, she joined the queue waiting at Sheila Wilson's till, studiously avoiding looking at her, toying with the items in her basket. Only after she had placed them on the conveyer belt did she look up and pretend surprise and delighted recognition. "Oh, hi!" she said. "Forgot you said you worked here." She smiled. "Mirabelle Milligan," she said. "In case you've forgotten."

Sheila returned her smile. "No, not forgotten." She scanned the purchases through, and told Mirabelle the total price.

"Thanks," Mirabelle said, as she placed them into the bags she had brought. "What time do you finish?" she asked.

"Not till twelve the night," Sheila answered.

Looking up at the clock, "Not too long now, then," Mirabelle said. "Half-eleven."

Sighing, Sheila took Mirabelle's money and counted it into the till. "Thank goodness."

"Hey, you did well with the make-up," Mirabelle whispered, leaning in a bit as though checking something on the receipt. "Really well."

Sheila grinned at her. "Thanks," she said. "Practice."

They exchanged a conspiratorial smile.

Just as Mirabelle turned to leave, she stopped as though she'd just had a thought. "Hey, don't suppose you fancy having a cuppa or something to eat with me after you finish? That wee restaurant across the road stays open till the wee small hours."

Sheila looked at her hands as she started scanning through the next customer's shopping.

"I don't do so well at night," Mirabelle said, her voice low and sad. "Get a bit lonely without Summer." She swallowed. She had stepped aside to let Sheila get on with her work, but lingered behind. When the customer was served and Sheila still didn't say anything, Mirabelle continued, "Anyway," she said as she stepped forward. "I'll be across there if you fancy it." She patted her stomach. "Ready for a bit of supper." Smiling, she touched Sheila's arm in a gesture of friendship, solidarity. "See you!" she said. "Bye!"

Choosing a table for two as close to the window as possible, and with a view across to the shop doorway, Mirabelle settled herself in, her bags at her feet and made a show of searching the menu for something she'd enjoy. In truth, she was too tense to eat, so she took her time and, having made her choice, ordered a ham and mushroom

304

omelette and chips.

She smiled to herself as she thought of the horror on Sam's face should he happen to see her right now. The idea of eating something cooked, a cooked meal, at this time of night was repugnant to him. "How can you sleep after eating all that?" he'd ask. "How can you digest it at this time of night? Chips?" He'd shudder. "You know it's the worst time to eat a meal, don't you?"

"How could I not know," she'd retort. "You tell me often enough. Anyway, it won't make any difference. I don't sleep."

Her expression changing to a grimace, she acknowledged to herself he'd be unlikely to care what she was eating or not eating these days, since he was still keeping a cold distance from her.

She knew too, that's not all Sam would have to say if he knew what she and Yvonne were up to tonight.

phase two

The bell was pressed by someone upstairs. Yvonne could see his long, pointed winkle-pickers and jeans coming down the stairs, so she prepared herself to get off the bus, making a great show of rooting through her handbag until he had stepped off ahead of her.

"Thanks," she said to the driver as she passed.

"Have a good night," he said with a smile.

"Thanks, you too."

A good night. Grief! How long was it since she'd been out at this time of night, dolled up to the nines, make-up inches thick on her face, nails painted, the works?

Never, actually, she decided. It wasn't really her style, and these shoes were killing her feet as a reminder.

Keeping a safe distance, she followed Dermot down the street to the nightclub.

"Good old Bellabear," she thought. "Right first time."

She lingered outside the door as though waiting for someone, just to make sure Dermot had plenty of time to get settled in before she followed. Once inside, she scanned the room, struggling in the dim lighting until her eyes grew accustomed to it. Once she spotted where he was, she found herself a seat at the bar where she could watch him without looking too obvious, and ordered herself a glass of tonic water with a slice of lime and ice. "Just wave the gin bottle at it without taking the top off, will you?" she asked the barman.

Grinning, he did just that and they shared a laugh about it.

"And that's my drink for the evening, if anyone should ask," she told him, paying well for her drink and waving the over generous tip his way. "Thanks."

With an understanding nod, he pocketed the change and moved to his next customer.

It wasn't long before she had company, a great bear of a man who sat beside her at the bar and offered to buy her a drink. "Whatever the lady's having," he ordered the barman. "And another Jack for me," he said.

She tolerated his slurred speech and his foul breath, but when he started to paw her backside, she downed the rest of her drink and excused herself with a sweet smile and headed for the ladies' room, dodging out of sight before getting there, keeping Dermot in view. Once Barney Bear had sauntered back onto the dance floor to paw someone else, she moved back to the bar.

After similar encounters with Wally Weasel and Stanley Stoat, she saw from her vantage point at the bar Dermot was making a move. Feigning a drunken stagger, wobbling precariously on her four inch heels — what on earth made her think she'd ever be able to walk in these things — she followed him out of the nightclub door, witnessed the pseudo friendly, backslapping, hail-fellow-well-met, farewells for the benefit of onlookers and the more sneaky exchange of money with Stanley Stoat, who leered delightedly at his purchases, pocketed the packet and grabbed hold of Dolly Bird.

"Scored at last, Stanley," Yvonne said under her breath. "With body odour like yours, that's the only way you were likely to."

When The Stoat slunk into a taxi with his catch, she hailed one herself and took great delight in telling the driver to "Follow that cab!" in true clichéd film style.

The driver turned in his seat as she climbed in. "Seriously?" he said with a huge grin.

"Go for it," she grinned back.

The driver did well and stopped at a discreet distance when the other taxi stopped outside a tenement property somewhere in Portobello. Yvonne asked him to wait for her and she followed The Stoat and his Dolly Bird into the stair.

307

Guessing they were respectively too drunk and too occupied with the business in hand to notice her, she hung about just inside the open close, pretending to be texting on her mobile, till she saw which flat they entered, using Dolly's key. A cloud of sweet perfume and soft music wafted out as the door opened, lingering in the air after it closed.

"Job done." She smiled as she noted the address in the notebook she carried in her clutch bag, went back to the waiting taxi and headed for Mirabelle's.

phase three

Mirabelle's patience had been rewarded, when Sheila joined her in the restaurant after work. Mirabelle had watched her say goodnight to the manager as he closed up the shop, watched her huddle into her coat and start to walk away. For a moment, it looked as though Sheila was heading straight home and Mirabelle felt a stab of disappointment. But no, second thoughts registered in Sheila's body language and she turned towards the restaurant with her shoulders squared ready for the new experience.

"Oh, hi!" Mirabelle looked up from the book she'd been pretending to read as she toyed with her omelette. "I'm so glad you decided to come. This book is not proving to be much company tonight." She held up the cheap detective novel she'd bought earlier in the thrift shop. "I guessed who dun it in the third chapter." She waited till Sheila, having hovered at the side of the table, decided she would sit down. "Can I get you something?" she said, passing over the menu. "My treat."

"Ta," Sheila said, taking it but not looking at it. "I wasnae sure I would come."

"I can recommend the omelette. And the chips were not too bad."

"I'm not sure why you're doing this."

Mirabelle shrugged. "Think I'll have another cup of tea and a muffin."

"What you expect of me."

"Nothing." Mirabelle said. "I don't expect anything of you. Just a bit of company for a while to break up a lonely night." She smiled at Sheila and tried to look as welcoming and needy as she could.

The waiter had appeared at their table. "Can I get you something, ladies?"

"Yes," Mirabelle said. "Cup of tea and a chocolate chip muffin for me, and…"

"Just a cup of tea for me," Sheila said.

"Really? Nothing to eat?" Mirabelle said, disbelief in her voice.

"Ta, but no at this time o' night. To be honest I dinnae really like much after work. I'm usually too tired tae bother. Besides, I'd no sleep."

"Oh, you sound just like my friend. He's always on at me. Reckons that's why I don't sleep. I eat far too much in the evening according to him."

While they waited for the waiter to return with their order, Mirabelle kept up a stream of chatter. "Listen to me," she said after a while. "You'll be thinking you must've ordered waffles!"

Sheila laughed. "You're all right," she said. "It's nice to hear a bit o' a chat of an evening. I usually go straight to bed."

"I'm afraid I'm a terrible stop up. I hate my bed at night-time, can't get to sleep, think too much I suppose. Think too much about Summer." She stirred some sugar into the cup of tea the waiter had put in front of her. "Huh! Then I can't get up in the morning once I do drag myself off to try for sleep."

"It must be worrying for you. Your daughter. Not knowing where she is an' that. What age is she?"

And before long, Mirabelle had told her all about Summer, how hard she was trying to find her, the places she'd looked, the people she'd asked to look out for her.

"What makes you so sure she's still in Edinburgh?"

"One or two sightings, places she's worked, places she's stayed over the months. That's if she's still alive," Mirabelle said, looking up from pulling apart her muffin. She held her breath, willing Sheila to take pity on her. "I don't know where else to look."

Sheila pushed her cup away from herself and gathered

her things. "I'll keep my eye peeled for her too if you like."

"I would like. Thank you, Sheila. That would be so very kind if you wouldn't mind."

"I could ask in Dermot's flat. Some o' they girls hang around during the day when I go in to clean. Huh! Usually still in whatever they were nearly wearing in bed, no matter I don't go in till late afternoon. I'll ask them if they ken anything."

Mirabelle reached across the table and put her hand on Sheila's arm. "Thank you, Sheila. I would be so grateful if you would do that." Genuine tears rolled down her cheeks. No pretence. No plotting for pity. Only the relief another avenue of help was opening up.

"Well done!" Mirabelle hugged her sister. "You did great!"

"And so did you."

They high-fived.

"I hardly recognise you in that get-up," Mirabelle said, looking at the make-up and party clothes Yvonne was sporting.

"Hardly recognise myself. Haven't worn any of this stuff in years. You're lucky I still had it at the back of the wardrobe."

"And you're lucky you could still get into it." Mirabelle looked at her own full figure and then at Yvonne's slim silhouette.

"Thanks, sis." Yvonne smiled. "Anyway, honey, I'd better be getting home," she said with a yawn. "Up early tomorrow."

"Sorry," Mirabelle said. "But thanks a billion. We made real progress tonight, I think."

"Yup! We did." They high-fived again as Yvonne prepared to go. "I'll leave this address here for you to pass on to Sam." Yvonne placed a piece of paper on the kitchen worktop.

Mirabelle picked it up and studied it. "I think I'll leave it for a bit," she said. "Give Sheila a chance to find out what she can first. If Sam decides to raid the place or something, they'll all clam up."

"But it might mean they can catch The Rat in his nest and winkle out his stash of goodies. He'll get done big time."

"Yeah, I know. But I think I want to wait a bit."

"You mean I put up with sweaty hands pawing me all night for nothing?"

"No, I mean I just want to give Sheila a chance first to get some info on whether Summer's in that house, been in that house or if they know where else she might be. Or if something happened to her."

Yvonne hugged her sister. "Nothing's happened to Summer."

"You can't know that, Vonnie. She's not been keeping good company. That rat's capable of anything."

"Think on it, Belle. It's not in his best interest to do anything to her. As long as she's around, she's dependent on him supplying her. She represents income to him. Like every other rat, he's greedy."

Covering her face with her hands, "I don't know what part of this conversation you think is comforting, Vonnie. As long as she has anything to do with him, she's in danger and she's sinking deeper into the sewer with him." She shuddered and shook her head. "I just need Sheila to find out if she's still anywhere near him. Then I'll let Sam bust him."

"Is that wise? Should you not tell Sam what you've got?"

"Why? The police have closed Summer's case. They're not interested."

"That's not really true, Belle. Sam says the drug squad are keeping a watch on Dermot."

"Yes, to catch him dealing drugs. Not that he's anything. Small fry. There's a thousand Dermot's in Edinburgh. It's the bigger fish they're really after. They're watching him to catch them." She sighed. "They don't care tuppence about my Summer."

"Sam does."

Mirabelle closed her eyes against the tears that threatened.

"Okay, honey. You do what you think best." Yvonne headed for the door. "I'm off home before Hugh thinks I've left him." She kicked off her shoes and wiped away some of the make-up with a tissue. "Better not scare the you-know-what out of him. You got a pair of boots I can borrow and I'll pick the heels up tomorrow?"

Chapter Twenty-Three

Mirabelle was rushing up Broughton Street to get a bus, clutching her side through the folds of her long nightdress. No time to stop and catch her breath.

The bus was signalling, waiting to move out into the stream of traffic.

With barely a pause, she jumped on the bus, leaving behind the last shreds of her dignity.

As the bus trundled on, she closed her eyes to shut out the pitying looks and sniggering comments occasioned by her nightdress and slippers. She hardly dared to imagine the sight she was and cared even less. Concentrated instead on trying to ward off the nagging doubts niggling away at her.

Sam had called at eight o'clock in the morning, awakened her from what passed as sleep. "We've got this girl, late teens, early twenties, but she's badly hurt. Unconscious. Been in a car accident. A hit and run. She has no identification on her."

"You think it's Summer?" She clutched the phone, afraid to breathe.

Sam paused. "I don't know, Belle. I really don't know."

"But you've got the photograph."

"Yes, but you know I've never met Summer. This girl has reddish hair. I just don't know if it's the right colour. Hard to be sure from a photograph. And it's a mess."

"A mess?"

"Unwashed. She looks like she's been living rough for quite a while. Her clothes and everything."

"But her face?"

Another pause, longer this time. "Like I said, Belle, she's been in an accident. She's still unconscious. Her face is a bit of a mess."

Mirabelle gripped the phone tighter, closed her eyes, fell against the wall. "Is she...?" There was a whole, rough, scratchy walnut, shell and all, lodged in her throat. She tried to swallow it down. "Is she going to be all right?"

"Hmmm! Well, she's alive anyway."

"I'm on my way." Without thinking of anything else, she reached for her bag where it hung nearby.

"It might not be Summer. You know it might not be Summer?"

"But you think it might be?"

"An outside chance, that's all, Belle. An outside chance."

So here she was, her heart pounding in her chest, people staring at her state of undress, her hair matted to her forehead by the sweat of her fear, on a bus, a frustratingly slow bus, creeping through the morning traffic, inching closer, minute by agonising minute to Edinburgh Royal Infirmary, to sweet reunion or bitter disappointment.

"Please God," she prayed. "Let her be all right." The phrase repeated again and again to the thrum of the engine. "Let her be all right."

At last, the bus stopped outside the hospital.

Sam was waiting for her.

"No comment!" she warned, holding out the skirt of her nightdress.

He shook his head.

"No time," she explained.

"No hurry. She's not going anywhere."

"But I have to know."

"Yes." Sam led the way to the ward.

Patients, visitors and nurses smiled as she passed, but she guessed their smiles were for her long cotton nightdress, the one with lace at the neckline and cuffs. A touch of Victoriana in the hospital corridors.

The room was small, only one bed in it. Not bright, a small window, blinds drawn, on the far side of the bed. There were curtains round the bed and Sam held them aside for Mirabelle to step through.

But she couldn't.

Sam waited.

"What if it's not?"

"What if it is?"

"But what if it's not?"

He put his arm round her waist. "Take your time, Belle." He looked about. "Look, there's a chair over there. D'you want to sit for a minute? Compose yourself? You're shaking."

Mirabelle took a deep breath and shook her head. "No. It's okay. Let's do this." And she walked through the opening.

There were various monitors and machines.

They may have been beeping and whirring.

All Mirabelle heard was the swishing and rushing of the blood thumping in her head. It was so loud. She closed her eyes, waited till the noise stilled a little, waited till she could bear to look.

There was a light above the bed. Not a very bright one but enough for the staff to work. They were tidying the bed, making their patient comfortable. Smoothing the hospital cover over the cage protecting her legs, moving in slow motion, Mirabelle's brain the remote controlling them.

Somewhere far away, a voice said they'd just brought their patient up from the theatre. She was still sleepy. The nurses moved away.

Mirabelle's finger slipped on the remote.

Suddenly it was all happening fast, too fast.

Red hair. Tangled and tousled.

Sunshine streaked through it. Lighter. Much lighter.

Too light.

And straighter.

Young face. Battered and bruised.

Stitches stretching from eyebrow to ear, covered by fresh bandaging.

Jaw scraped and cut.

Sorry, sweet face.

But not Summer.

She shook her head. "Not Summer."

Mirabelle felt the floor drop away.

A chair was pushed in behind her legs, and she sat down.

Noises rushed in on her. Voices. People talking. Footsteps in the corridor. Machines beeping and whirring.

Sam's voice. "Oh, Belle. I'm so sorry." Kneeling on the floor beside her, arms round her. Holding her tightly, all indication of their recent estrangement disappearing in his compassion.

It only took a moment.

One moment, her world was hopeful.

The next, the light was switched off and she was in familiar darkness.

She'd arrived at the hospital certain her quest had ended, anxious, but relieved to have found her daughter. Even though Summer was injured, she was alive. Alive and found.

It only took a moment.

The curtain was pulled aside, she stepped through to claim her daughter, her heart pounding. In that one moment everything was lost, hope evaporated.

"It's not Summer," she croaked, looking up at Sam. "It's not Summer." And she started to weep as he pulled her head against his shoulder.

Someone brought Mirabelle a hospital dressing gown, belted it round her as Sam led her from the ward. She hugged its collar as they sat in the hospital cafeteria having a cup of tea.

"Who is she?" she asked, then, shaking her head, "No, obviously you don't know that."

"Haven't a clue," Sam said with a sigh.

"Where did you say she was found?"

"Down the Cowgate. We think she's been sleeping rough. Her clothes were pretty grubby and torn. Looks like she'd been living in them, sleeping in them for weeks."

"Poor kid."

"Yeah. Shoes worn into holes. Probably been wandering Edinburgh for long enough. That's why I thought it might have been Summer. Sorry."

"No purse?"

Sam shook his head.

"Nothing on her at all?"

"Nothing."

"You'd think she'd have *something*, wouldn't you?"

"You'd think."

"Must be someone's kid. Some poor soul's looking ..." Mirabelle choked on the thought.

"We'll go through all the missing person reports. Maybe come up with someone."

"Down the Cowgate, you said? That's Izzie's territory."

"Izzie?"

"Yeah." Mirabelle frowned. "I met Izzie when I worked at the soup kitchen down Cowgate months ago. There was a bit of trouble and I helped her out. Made a friend, though she never has much to say, poor soul. She does, however, see everything that goes on around there." She stood up, ready to go. "Can you give me a lift down that way?"

"Even better. I can give you a lift back home."

"But I thought I could ..."

"And I think you could get dressed before you do anything else."

"Oh, yes. Oops! Forgot I wasn't." She pulled the dressing gown closed, tucking it round her legs and bottom. "Wondered where the draught was coming from."

Mirabelle knew where she'd find Izzie when the winter sun was shining. Better dressed now, in a colourful dress with a warm woollen shawl round her shoulders, she piled on a load of bracelets, conscious of the unaccustomed weight, and headed for The Meadows.

Sure enough, there was Izzie sitting on a bench, feeding crumbs of bread to some pigeons.

"Hi Belle." Izzie looked up as Mirabelle approached. "You're looking tired. Want a seat?" She shuffled to one side, putting her carrier bags behind her feet, and patted the seat beside her.

"Thanks Izzie." She'd met Izzie not long after Summer disappeared. Mirabelle won Izzie's trust when she rescued her from a couple of young thugs one night as she walked home.

They'd been taunting Izzie, trying to get her carrier bags from her.

"What you got in there, Missus?"

"The kitchen sink?" asked the other, poking the bag.

Mirabelle flew at them, swinging her own bag. It was heavy with books and all manner of things she'd bought at the charity shop earlier and she managed to land a good thud on the first boy's shoulder. "Get away from her," she yelled at them. "I've called the police. They're on their way." She hadn't, of course. She rarely remembered to carry her mobile phone. But they weren't to know that and had scarpered just in case. Off to find some other victim.

Izzie had accepted her intervention wordlessly and tolerated her company whenever Mirabelle happened upon her.

She continued feeding the pigeons, every now and then taking little nibbles of the bread herself.

"You hungry, Izzie?"

"Birds are too."

"I'm sure they are. It's kind of you to share."

"Good to share."

Mirabelle took a cellophane carton of sandwiches from her bag. "Want a share of my lunch?" She opened it and held the packet out.

Izzie nodded and took a sandwich, breaking off a crust for the birds before biting into it herself. "Ham and pickle. Good choice."

Mirabelle took the other sandwich and started to eat too, each bite accompanied by the jingle of her myriad bracelets as they travelled up and down her arm. She shook them free when they settled, making sure the sun sparkled off them. "Pretty, aren't they?" she said in response to the admiration in Izzie's eyes. "You like them?"

Izzie nodded, her eyes never leaving them as she ate.

"I can share them too, if you'd like?" Mirabelle took several of them off and held them in her hand. "Here, you can have them."

Izzie snatched them from her.

"You can put them with your treasure," Mirabelle said. "Can I see your treasure? You know I won't touch anything."

"Shown you before."

"Yes. But I'd love to see it again." She leant forward as Izzie retrieved one of the bags from under the bench. "Anything new since the last time?"

Izzie grinned up at her. "Got this," she said, holding up a sweet little hair clasp.

"Oh, that's beautiful. Anything else? A wallet, perhaps? Or a purse?"

"How'd you know?" Izzie eyed her suspiciously.

"Just guessing."

"Got this." A red and white striped purse. The kind with a coin purse on one side and a wallet for notes and cards on the other. The kind a young girl might carry. It was grubby and frayed.

"Hey, that's cool. Who shared that one with you?"

"Someone."

"Sleeping, was she? Last night? In the road?"

Izzie nodded. "Didn't need it any more."

"She told you that, did she?"

"Wasn't talking. Didn't need it any more."

"Can I touch it? Just for a minute? I'd really like to look inside it."

With great reluctance, Izzie handed over the wallet.

"You don't really need that bit, do you, Izzie?" Mirabelle pointed to the identification card inside the wallet. Isla Arthur. Dalkeith. Midlothian. A phone number too, she noticed. "Would you share it with me? For the bracelets?"

Mirabelle didn't really want to be there for the grand reunion, but Marlyn Arthur sent flowers and a card expressing her gratitude for the part Mirabelle played in finding her daughter. "I can't thank you enough," she wrote. "You could *never* imagine how desperately worried I've been since Isla went missing."

Summer hadn't thought seriously about running away. Oh, she'd talked about it on Facebook and Twitter, but that was just talk. She'd had no intentions of leaving home when she'd set out that Friday morning. She just wanted to have her own celebration, a last fling before preparing to go to uni. She'd leave home soon enough. She'd get a flat second year at uni. Take the first year to suss things out, then, boom! She'd be off.

No, it hadn't been planned. But events overtook her. She got herself in a bit of a mess doing all the things her mother would disapprove of. Feasting on forbidden fruit. Some of it she'd already tasted, but, that day, the day she got her acceptance letter for uni, she gobbled a whole fruit-bowl. Thought she'd enjoy it more than she did.

When she stumbled out of the hotel room the next afternoon, forbidden fruit sour in her stomach, shame hot in her heart, she knew she couldn't go home. There'd be hell to pay and she was broke.

So she'd gone to the only person who really knew what she had been up to in the months before she left, the only person who saw the whole extent of her double life.

Dermot offered a place in his flat, and she tried it for a few nights, but found she was not willing to pay the price, and she wasn't talking about money. Sleaze bucket! She was in enough of a mess without making a career out of it.

Ended up in a dive of a hostel. She'd given a false name, but, put on the spot, it wasn't a very imaginative one. Sally Red. She smiled at it all the same. Always liked the name Sally. Used to have a doll called Sally. Wonder if Mirabelle's

322

still got it somewhere tucked away. She was such a horrific hoarder.

Slept rough, here and there, deadening the cold and discomfort with alcohol and drugs till the money and the pills ran out and Dermot got nasty.

After washing dishes for a few weeks, she made friends with one of the waitresses, and crashed on her couch for a bit, but Edinburgh began to feel small. She knew Mirabelle would be looking all over for her. It was only a matter of time till she'd find her and she wasn't ready for that.

She saw her own face on every lamp-post, the television appeal on TV sets in shop windows, heard them tell about police enquiries.

"Hell's teeth!" No going home while all that's going down!

Made the decision she had to get out, lose herself, become invisible.

Physical appearance not the big problem: all too easy to do a complete makeover back in Dermot's flat, girls there to help her. Bright, burnished-red hair became dull, lack-lustre black at the shake of a bottle. Same for eyebrows and lashes.

Long, shining waves lay on the floor in heaps, and there, staring back from the mirror was a pale, elfin creature with a black swim-cap on.

Thick white pan-stick make-up to cover the freckles, black kohl and mascara — who was going to look into those eyes? Eyebrow piercings added to the 'keep your distance' effect, though she balked at nose or lip piercings, her sense of hygiene just not permitting it.

Black school skirt, cut really short and worn with thick black tights. Anonymous.

Changed her appearance as much as she could, but, when she saw her friends patrolling the streets, looking in all her favourite haunts, she decided she had to leg it.

Easy decision.

More difficult, the problem of where the heck to go.

London seemed too obvious, too copy-cat. No passport,

so going abroad not on. Glasgow, too near. If she knew where her father lived, she'd go find him, but that had proved impossible. Her beloved Internet had let her down, though, in fairness, it had little to work with. Mirabelle was for giving nothing away. Claimed it was a one-night stand and she didn't know his name. Slut! Or liar?

Settled for Liverpool, hitching her way there one wet weekend. Two nights huddled at the corner tables in all-night transport cafes, three days trudging across-country along muddy grass verges with her thumb out. There were other places nearer, easier to reach, but Liverpool caught her imagination. Home of Frankie Goes to Hollywood and The Beatles, groups she'd grown up with, their sound belting out from Mirabelle's second-hand hi-fi system. The Mersey called her.

Most problematic was money. The thirty-five pounds she'd saved and stashed in a pair of shoes in her closet seemed a fortune when all it was expected to purchase was an occasional coke or pair of tights. Add to that a few pounds, taken from here and there around the house, retrieved on a clandestine raid when Mirabelle was out.

There was always money lying about in the house. Mirabelle was careless with her money, knowing it would be useful to Summer when she herself wasn't home or forgot to shop. She never knew how much dosh there was stashed here and there. Didn't seem to care. Sometimes made the difference between feast and famine. Often bought things Mirabelle knew nothing about, but least said about that the better.

Knew the stash wouldn't last long and she'd have to find work again.

Her first taste of working life had been washing dishes in a half-decent hotel in Edinburgh, her next, the same job in a sleazy pub in Liverpool's dockland area. It didn't pay much but it had left-over food as perks and a cosy corner to sleep in if she managed to hang back at closing time and get locked in.

She'd shout 'Bye!' at the door then watch for the moment

she could slip back inside and into the big double cupboard under the sink along with scrap buckets and stinking floor cloths. No one else ever opened those filthy metal doors, so she knew she'd be safe enough. The dirty washing hamper in the corner of the kitchen made a soft, if smelly, cot once the key turned in the lock of the pub door.

A bit of carefully timed dodging and she appeared right behind whoever opened up in the morning.

Once again: not glamorous. Not the stuff of dreams. But she managed to replenish her dwindling money bag by the time she was ready to move on after a couple of weeks.

Visited the Cavern. No longer the original: she learned it didn't survive the building of the underground railway. Seen where Lennon and McCartney grew up. Visited Penny Lane and Strawberry Fields.

Romantic notions satisfied, the Mersey no longer held mystique. Besides, people at work were becoming suspicious about her sleeping arrangements.

Manchester, Macclesfield and Birmingham; Nottingham, Sheffield and Leeds. The next wee while read like a road-map.

Sitting in a tiny, rented bed-sit in one city, a room in a shared flat in another, a hostel here, a park bench there, she felt two-dimensional, as though the atmosphere allowed no space for her existence, the air didn't part for her to pass. She slid through it like a black and white photograph, discarded from the album, falling through a crack in the floorboards, unnoticed and un-missed because it had never occupied a space on the page.

Middlesbrough, Sunderland and Newcastle...

If she could make some permanent mark on life: drive in a nail, chisel a groove, something someone could run their fingers over and know she'd been there.

Only one person would remember the tiny dent she made in the surface of existence: one person knew her, knew she lived, cared she continue. A longing for Mirabelle took root in her after a bad bout of bronchitis. Weakened and lonely, she decided to go home. Lying back on a narrow bed with her eyes closed, her breath rattling in her chest, she rehearsed what she would do, what she would say.

At first, she had been jubilant she'd done it. She'd run away from home. Escaped. Huh! That'll teach her. A shudder ran through her with the memory of her childish jubilation. Mirabelle may or may not be her birth mother — something she often doubted, given the huge disparity in their ethnic origins — but she was the only mother she'd known, and the only one who'd shown any sign of claiming her. The months had softened Summer's disdain for Mirabelle.

When she first got back to Edinburgh, she fully intended to walk up the stairs and in the ever-open door. But, as Summer turned up at the top of Broughton Street, Mirabelle started to walk down to the bottom. Summer recognised her immediately: her bright, flowing clothes, her untamed hair, her bags and shawls. Pain washed through her in a flash-flood of nostalgia. The flamboyance that used to embarrass her suddenly seemed endearing. Her mother looked delicious in her eccentricity: an overblown rose, faded petals dressing a vibrant heart. She decided to follow, watch from a distance before making herself known.

Walking down Broughton Street, familiar shops smiled out a welcome home — until she looked in the butcher's window and saw a witch look back at her. Ghostly white with matted black hair and tattered clothing, she was shocked to meet her stare, disgusted to realise it was her own reflection. With heavy tread, she spun away and disappeared.

going home, always going home

She came so close to going home several times after that.

So close to revealing herself to Mirabelle: months ago, at the ice-rink, then at the ballet. Other times too. Lost count of the times her hand lay poised on the outside stair door, ready to push it open, ready to feel the smooth bannister as she ran up the stairs. Stopping herself for one reason or another. So many reasons not to do it. So many better ones to do it.

And here she was again.

She braced herself.

This was it. Nothing was going to stop her this time.

She'd cleaned herself up, made herself look more like she used to, though it would take more than a bottle of shampoo and conditioner for her red hair to resurface, despite the fact there were traces of it showing here and there. Years of golden growth lay on the floor of Dermot's miserable flat, where she'd found herself all those months ago. But, scrubbed clean of make-up and grime, her face hadn't changed so very much. Thinner perhaps, more grown up, but certainly recognisable.

Even found herself a semi-decent boyfriend. Turned out to be married, mind, but, hey, if he could stomach the deception, so could she. At least he put a roof over her head. Seemed he factored a heap of flats around the city, installed her in one and left her pretty much to her own devices most of the time. She knew she was just his bit of rough, but that was fine. All she wanted was somewhere to sleep after her cleaning work, somewhere to get herself sorted.

Summer walked confidently down the street and was

about to cross the road when Mirabelle appeared at the mouth of the close, spewn out too early, the night still in her hair, her face, her clothes. She started to run. She was crying. Even from across the street, Summer could hear the gulping sobs.

Summer froze against the wall. "She's lost it!" she thought, a sluggish milk-shake of guilt and embarrassment filling her.

Watched as Mirabelle hurried up the hill, followed her for a little, her face contorted in disgust at Mirabelle's eccentricity.

Really, who else would wander about, outside, in public, in her slippers and a long cotton nightdress, no coat, no dressing gown, nothing to cover its old-fashioned frills and flounces. Summer gritted her teeth, trying to remember how much she'd missed her, but years of similar public humiliations rose in her throat, leaving a bad taste in her mouth.

When she saw Mirabelle jump on a bus, she turned away, shaking her head, glad no-one knew she had anything to do with the madwoman.

Her homecoming plans wiped away with the swish of a cotton nightdress, Summer didn't know what to do with herself at first, and started to wander about in the shops on Princes Street, but she had no money and no interest in buying the things she looked at.

Every time she thought of Mirabelle, she got that sick feeling again. Crazy, crazy, crazy! The woman was off her head.

Without a lot of thought, Summer found herself heading back to Broughton Street, not knowing what she meant to do, but angry enough to do anything, angry enough with the crazy woman who had ruined her life. When she got there, she slammed into the flat, grabbed her backpack from the cupboard, filled it with underwear, socks, jeans, her hair straighteners, even some books and her laptop. No need to fear discovery. She just didn't care any more.

Raked around for any money Mirabelle had left lying. Stupid woman never knew how much she had in her purse or in her hoard of bags. A fact that had often come in handy when Summer came home from school to an empty house and an empty fridge.

Was almost undone when she entered Mirabelle's bedroom. Piles of tangled beads and bangles lay neglected on the dressing table, rings caught among them. The sudden stab of knowing these baubles should be strung around Mirabelle's neck, sliding up and down her wrists as she moved around, her fingers decorated and dazzling. It wasn't right they should be lying like that, uncared for, discarded. Summer fingered the pile for a bit, tears threatening behind her eyes. Selecting one of her favourite rings, she pushed it firmly on her thumb, since that was the only digit it fitted, and turned away from the sad collection.

Satisfied with her raid, afraid to linger longer in case her disgust subsided and she'd be overcome with longing, Summer pushed out the door and down the stairs.

Was almost at the bottom when she heard the outside door open. Looking down through the banister, she caught sight of Mirabelle's black curls, her flowing nightdress.

Freeze.

Retreat. Back. Quietly. Back up the stairs. Past the door she'd just closed behind her. Up another flight. And another. Up to the top.

Fist pressed to her mouth, the ring on her thumb smooth against her lips, Summer closed her eyes and waited, forbidding tears, swallowing utterance.

Waiting. Waiting.

Until she heard the flat door close, then quickly, quickly, on quaking legs, down the stairs. All the way down.

Down and out.

Shock, denial, pain, guilt, anger, loneliness, depression, Mirabelle had tasted them all. Alone or in combination, they'd forced themselves upon her in overwhelming doses. She'd even come close to supping acceptance. When she thought she could move past the table, acceptance in her cup, something always sat her back down to start the meal again.

The body dredged out of the river, the Saturday matinee, the sight of a redheaded girl, identifying Isla Arthur, the triggers were varied, but they all had the same result.

The day after she identified Isla Arthur, was one of those triggers. Bad enough the crushing disappointment it wasn't Summer found and in need of her loving care, hard enough to reunite a mother and daughter that was not her and Summer, weary enough from all the months of searching for her, what finished Mirabelle off was walking past Summer's bedroom in the early morning and catching sight of an open drawer.

Cold, cold water rushed through her veins.

Summer had been here.

She knew it as surely as though her daughter was still standing in the middle of the room, felt her presence through her fingers as she opened the drawer wider and saw the depleted stock of underwear, felt her absence in the space where her rucksack no longer sat in the cupboard.

While she paraded her desperation in a cotton nightdress in the streets of Edinburgh, her daughter was ransacking through drawers, stealing the last vestiges of her trust and hopes, taking what she wanted, leaving nothing in return.

Mirabelle wanted to taste anger, but shame was on her plate too.

Guilt, isolation, depression, despair: familiar fare. Sitting on Summer's bed, a pair of discarded socks in her hands, she had to gulp down these emotions again.

Then, when she could swallow no more, she curled up in the foetal position on Summer's bed and cried herself to sleep.

Chapter Twenty-Four

When Summer returned to Edinburgh, she had nowhere to live, no job and no contacts.

She knew her disguise worked. She'd managed to be right there, standing beside Mirabelle without Mirabelle knowing.

The day that autistic man took ill.

Mirabelle's hand had brushed hers as she gave her the phone.

A shiver of emotion quivered through Summer. She felt like crying whenever she thought about it.

She'd been walking through the gardens on her way home from one of her cleaning jobs. It wasn't her quickest route but it was the one she preferred. She often spotted Mirabelle here or hereabouts.

Not usually running. That had been a shocker. Couldn't remember the last time she'd seen her mother run.

Another shiver of emotion: disappointment this time.

Her mother didn't have a clue. How could a mother not know her own daughter up that close? She'd seen her face, for pity's sake! Touched her hand!

Okay, so she wouldn't recognise her from the hair. She wasn't her natural ginge, and it was cropped, but she hadn't had time to straighten the bits that insisted on curling. Even through the pan-stick and mascara, shouldn't Mirabelle have recognised her own daughter? She's spent enough time looking for her!

Summer laughed as she walked past the Omni Centre, jumping to slap the tall giraffe's butt and stroke the side of the wee one, as was her habit, forgetting she carried the weight of her raid. Cursing as it thumped against her back.

Ironic, isn't it? How long Mirabelle spends searching for something that's a heartbeat away and she can't see it. Like she's looking through a veil: a veil of memory and expectation.

Not that she'd made it easy for her mother, she knew. No eye contact, no questioning smile, no lingering look.

After that, she'd often followed Mirabelle. Seemed the easiest way not to be surprised by Mirabelle finding her was never to be where she looked. Who spent their time looking behind them?

Hitching the heavy rucksack up her back a bit where it dragged under the weigh of the laptop, the straighteners and everything else she'd stuffed into it, she tossed her head to rid herself of the image of Mirabelle's beads and stuff lying in a tangled, neglected heap in her bedroom.

Chapter Twenty-Five

"Got him!" Sam said, crashing the phone down. "Elliot!" he shouted.

PC Elliot came to the open door. "Sir?"

"Drug squad picked Wilson up. Got his suppliers, importers, the lot." Sam punched the air, weaving and parrying round his desk like a boxer in the ring. "We're getting a go at him this afternoon. Wants to get everything sorted on the one charge sheet, try and keep his sentence down."

"Think he was supplying Mirabelle's girl, sir?"

"Let's find out, shall we?" PC Elliot held the door for Sam and they headed to the interview room.

"So? What's the story, son?" Sam asked as he drew out a chair and Elliot clicked on the recorder.

"'S no a story. Just what happened."

"Tell us what happened to Summer Milligan."

"Ah dinae ken what happened tae her, no all of it anyways. Just when she came tae me after."

"After?"

"Aye. Weeks after."

"After what?"

"After she'd gone off."

"Gone off?"

"Left home. Done a bunk, ken?"

"So, you're saying she came to you? Now, why would she do that, d'you think?"

Dermot leant forward, his elbows on the table. "Ah'm no a mind reader. D'you wanna hear this stuff or no?"

"We're all ears, son."

"Aye! Could yer mammy no hae done somethin' aboot

that when ye were a bairn?" Dermot placed his hands over his own ears. "Pinned them back or something?"

Sam chose to ignore the cheek. "So, Summer Milligan came to you after she'd been missing a few weeks?"

Dermot turned to PC Elliot. "Good, your boss, eh? Quick on the uptake."

"So, she came to you, for a chat? For company?"

He shifted in his chair. "No exactly."

"No. Of course not. She'd finished with you, hadn't she? So, why else would that wee lassie come to you, son?"

"Aye, well. She was using, like. Nothing hard, like. Just a few pills and that."

"And what happened when Summer Milligan came to you?"

"Well, ah asked her where she'd been, like, and she told me to mind ma own business and just give her what she wanted."

"So she didn't want to chat?"

"She just wanted a fix."

"And you gave her something?"

Dermot nodded.

"Was she shooting up?"

"Naw, she couldnae go near sharps."

"Just tabs?"

"Aye."

"And that was it? She left and you haven't seen her since?"

"Aye."

"And what would you say if I told you we had evidence you were her pimp?"

Dermot shook his head. "Naw! Ah telt ye. Jist the tabs."

"That time?"

"Aye."

"What about the night she went missing?"

He looked to his lawyer, who nodded. Dermot sighed and nodded too. "Jist the once, aye." He leant forward on the table. "But just that once!"

"You sure?" Sam drew a folder closer and opened it, shuffling through the papers. "Now, where's that witness statement?"

"Okay, okay. Maybe no just the once."

"She'd been coming to you regularly?"

Dermot nodded.

Sam looked at the recording machine.

"Aye!" Dermot almost shouted into it. "She came tae me regular."

"You'd been supplying her?"

"Yes!"

"And pimping for her?"

"Naw! Well, no really."

"Yes, or no?"

"Just the night she went missing and a few after that, like. Then she wisnae having any of it. Didnae want to dae that." he pulled a face. "Not that kinda girl. Huh! A choosy slag."

"Okay," Sam said. "So let's move on a few weeks. She came to you for tabs."

Dermot looked ready to protest, but once again, his lawyer encouraged him with a nod. "Aye," he said.

"Tell me all about it, son. Tell me about the last time you helped her out. What she said, what you said, what you gave her, all of it. Take your time. Just start at the beginning."

She was sick of Dermot. He'd been useful: getting her into pubs, clubs and casinos. But he was a jerk, heavy-handed and demanding. She'd held him at bay for a while, but, once she was hooked on the pills he provided, he could get what he wanted from her by withholding them. They rowed, she was sick on his trainers and they parted company. He had tired of her too. So he introduced her to some of his acquaintances and spent their gratitude in the casino.

She had new habits. She knew it was only a matter of time till Mirabelle found out and she couldn't face the lectures, the disapproval, the disappointment on her face.

She hadn't meant to leave home when she did, but, when she woke up in a dingy hotel room with little or no memory of how she got there and who she'd been with, she couldn't go home. Scared she might be pregnant, aware she looked wrecked and knowing she needed to sort herself out, she decided she couldn't face Mirabelle.

Initially, Summer thought a few weeks would just about do the job: give Mirabelle time to be so glad to see her she'd not care what she'd done. Make her feel bad, make her realise she'd been neglectful, change the dynamics in their relationship. But it became too difficult to casually waltz back home. There'd be questions to answer, counselling, recriminations: she wasn't ready to face it. Jubilation had very quickly become nervous uncertainty.

No longer sure of what she hoped to achieve or how long she should stay away to make her point, she nearly went home several times, but just couldn't face the fuss. Plus, she needed to do a bit of research on the whole birth parents

337

thing, and she needed time to get sorted.

"What'd'ye mean, get sorted?" Drae asked her with a sneer. "You're in too far. Had a taste of life. You gonnae go back to ordinary?"

"Look, I'm not asking your advice, slime-bag. Just gimme the stuff and let me outa here."

"Ooo!" He grabbed her chin, his fingers and thumb digging into her cheeks. "You need to talk nice to Drae, or Drae might just tell Mummy what her little girl's been up to."

She twisted free, pain ripping at her face. "You talk to my mother, I talk to the police."

"You widnae be that stupid. Don't suppose Mummy would bother anyways."

"What's that supposed to mean?"

"Bit of a hippie herself. Maybe she'd like to share what you got," he said, holding up the tiny poly bag.

"You know nothing about my mother." She snatched the bag from him and pushed the money at his chest.

"She's looking for you," Dermot said with a smirk. "Maybe I should just tell her where to find you."

"Maybe I should just tell the police where to find your stash." And she stomped away.

The next time she looked for him, he'd not been home.

"Polis been watching him, questioning him," his mother told her. "Don't know what about but they turned this place over," she said, looking dismally around her at the chaos she called home. "Don't know if they found all what they was looking for." She looked at Summer through narrowed eyes. "You that girl that's missing?"

Summer backed away. "Missing?" She laughed. "Me?" She held her arms out to show she was here. "Hardly!"

Dermot's mother shrugged. "Shall I tell him you were looking for him?"

"Nah!" Summer shook her head. "Don't bother. I'll catch him another time."

Or not! Summer hugged her arms round herself in a vain attempt to stop shivering. There goes her supplier, then.

The next few days gathered before her like thunder clouds.

What was the saying? Or was it a song? 'Drugs, sex and rock'n'roll': something like that. Not glamorous.

Neither was living rough. Park benches and cemeteries. Freezing cold, uncomfortable and filthy. Not glamorous.

Not the lifestyle she'd dreamt about.

She huddled against the cemetery wall that night and decided she'd had enough of this. "And enough of this," she told herself, tossing the now unhelpfully empty poly bag from her. "Gonna be a long hard night." And she hunkered down, ready to take the horrors of a night without pharmaceutical help.

"Why don't you go home, dear?" some old baggie said to her. "Nice young girl like you should be tucked up warm in bed by your mother." She raised the bottle to her mouth. "Do it now, before you can't."

"Soon," she told her. "Need to get sorted first." And she huddled down, cravings shaking her body, clutching her jacket round her, trying to hold herself together. "Need a job," she said, more to herself than her companion. "Need some money."

"Need the booze?"

She closed her eyes, shook her head. "Need to get clean. Like you say, before I can't."

"Bennie always looking for dishwashers."

"Bennie?"

"Restaurant down Leith. Show you tomorrow."

"Why don't you do it?"

The woman held out her shaking hands.

"Sorry."

"Like I say, before it's too late."

Chapter Twenty-Six

The police were able to verify as much of Wilson's story as mattered. He was charged and, since the evidence against him was compelling, his lawyer had advised him to plead guilty to eight counts of trafficking and procurement.

Mirabelle had passed on the address Yvonne had given her and the police had watched the flat and timed their raid to catch Wilson, the drugs, the girls, the guns and the bigger fish. There was much celebration in the police station.

Sam's celebrations were tempered by the fact the whole operation told him nothing about Summer's whereabouts, because, although her case was officially not ongoing, his personal search was. In Scots law, Summer was over sixteen and deemed an adult with the right to leave home. In Mirabelle's eyes, and to an extent in Sam's as well, she was a child, Mirabelle's child, and he had hoped to find her for her mother.

Sam knew she had gone willingly with Ricky Horner and his brother, so they were out of the picture as far as she was concerned. While his colleagues had been watching Wilson, there had been no further sign of involvement with Summer after the encounter Wilson described. And that was it.

Another lead followed and ticked off Sam's private list.

Another lead leading no closer to finding Summer.

Enough.

Mirabelle had had enough.

She had relinquished the address of Dermot's flat to the police not caring any more whether it would inhibit any flow of information about Summer and her whereabouts.

She had had enough.

To know Summer had worked for weeks just a short walk down the road, but hadn't let her know she was alive and well, couldn't even put a note through the letterbox. Didn't care enough to knock on the door and say she was leaving home, didn't want to live with Mirabelle any more. Anything. To be so near and yet do nothing to put Mirabelle out of her misery. Mirabelle found that hard to stomach.

She had swallowed it when first she learned of it, noted it on the timeline, where it mocked her every time she looked at it. With every day, every week, every month, the hurt grew, the bitterness built up.

To know Summer had gone to Lexie the day after she disappeared, to keep in touch via email for months afterwards, but didn't let her know she was alive and well, wouldn't allow Lexie to pass a message to tell her she was safe. Couldn't find it in her heart to phone the house and ease the fear in her mother's heart.

She had tried to understand, had tried to be happy that at least someone knew, but the more she thought about it the more it rankled.

To know Summer had kept up her association with a known criminal, a no-good scumbag who cared nothing about her welfare, but didn't choose to meet with her mother; preferred the company of drug addicts and prostitutes to an evening by the fire with her mother. Mirabelle felt diminished.

Through the months, she had tried not to let it get to her, but the floodgates had been opened and her sense of injustice flared.

To know Summer had slept in hostels and flats in Edinburgh, within a few streets of where they had lived together for most of her life, without letting her mother know that life continued. It was thoughtless.

No.

It was cruel.

All of it.

It was tearing into Mirabelle's soul with vicious thrusts.

And now, for Summer to enter Mirabelle's home knowing she would not be there.

It was too much.

Too much.

Summer's cruelty lacerated deep down into her gut, slashing this way and that, wounding her to her very core.

Humiliation inhibited her from sharing her pain.

Feeling acutely conscious of all that she had given up, her job, her life-style, the relationship she had thrown away to search for Summer, all the advice she'd been given not to become obsessed with her search, she felt humiliated.

She avoided everyone, stopped answering the phone and made sure she was out of the house as much as possible and couldn't be found home.

She took on 'clients', strangers who were looking for strangers who belonged to them, people who had heard Mirabelle had contacts, could sometimes find missing people.

It kept her busy, stopped her thinking, allowed her to avoid those she knew while working on behalf of those she didn't.

As far as she could, she worked without her contacts, checking in with them only as a last resort, preferring to speak only to new contacts as she could make them. People who knew nothing of Summer.

Sam would be pleased if he knew her obsession was

cured, she wasn't still looking for someone who made it abundantly clear she didn't want to be found.

But Sam was gone.

Out of her life.

Though she still saw him, they still spoke, and he was still around, he was no longer her companion, no longer her lover, or her friend.

Mirabelle was alone.

She felt compelled to be out of the house.

Wandering the streets of Edinburgh had a new purpose; not to find Summer, but to lose herself.

On one such wandering, she met Sheila Wilson on Leith Walk.

"Oh, I'm glad ah bumped into ye," Sheila said. "Was hoping ah would. Been asking about your girl, like I said ah would."

Looking up from the study of her feet, Mirabelle tried not to care. "Oh. Hi. Sorry, didn't see you there." If she had, she would have crossed the street, having no energy for news of Summer.

"Aye, yer looking kinda miserable, but this'll maybe cheer ye up a tad. Yer girl's no in yon flat Dermot had. One of the lassies reckons she was only there a couple nights here and there."

Mirabelle nodded. "Oh. Good. That's good."

"She called herself Sally Red. It didn't dawn on me till now it was the same girl, your daughter, till I showed the girls her photie."

"Yes. Sally Red. Of course."

"Come to think of it, ye'll not find her using that photie you gave me," Sheila said, taking it from her pocket and handing it back to Mirabelle. "Left a bucket-full of hair in the shower room when she left. Huge long hanks of it. I'd forgot till the girls reminded me."

"Oh!"

"Aye, apologised for the mess she made with the hair dye too."

"Dye?"

"Aye, black. Black as night. It'll be a devil to keep black when the roots grow in. Cheap home dye kits ruin your hair, I reckon, unless it's one of those wash-in-wash-out kind of

344

things."

"Black?"

"Aye. Coal black. Told her when she apologised that she needs to be thinking of a new name, 'Sally Black,' I said. She just laughed. Said she'd need to give that some thought, 'Maybe Sally Raven,' she said. 'Since I must've been raving to do this to myself last night,' she said. Gave me a laugh, so it did."

"Thanks." Mirabelle made to move past.

Sheila halted her with a hand on her arm. "But one of the other lassies thinks she might be in a flat somewhere down the Walk here. Says she's seen her with a bairn."

"A baby?"

"Aye. Maybes isn't hers, but Gloria, that's the lassie I'm meaning, she thinks it might be. Says she's seen her a few times. Seems this other guy Dermot's in business with, he's got flats of his own, nothing to do with Dermot. She thinks she's in one of them."

Mirabelle stared at her. "Wait a minute. Can you just say all that again, slowly?"

Sheila laughed. "Aye, hen, looks like maybes you're a granny."

She sat in the kitchen, her purse in her hand. "I've been a fool!" she told Yvonne. "Summer's made a fool of me."

"What d'you mean?"

"She's been here."

"What d'you mean, here?"

"Here. In the house. She's been in the house."

Yvonne shook her head. "No! She can't have been."

"Yes," said Mirabelle. "She's been here while I was out."

"How on earth can you know that?"

"She left a note."

"A note?"

Mirabelle nodded her head in the direction of the whiteboard. "Look."

There, written neatly at the end of the timeline:

'Thanks, M. See you sometime. xxx'

Yvonne put her hands to her mouth. "Oh my giddy aunt! When did she leave that?"

"I'm not sure. Sometime while I was out today."

"And, of course, you never lock the door." Yvonne turned to Mirabelle. "I couldn't do that." She shook her head. "I'm not like you. I would be afraid to leave it in case I got burgled or something."

"Well, I was."

"Burgled? No!"

"She was here. She took my rainy-day savings." Mirabelle pointed to the empty jug on the worktop. "And she left a note."

"Oh my giddy aunt!"

"It suddenly caught my eye. I hadn't noticed it at first when I came in, and now it's all I can see in the whole

346

blooming kitchen."

"I don't believe it."

"And it wasn't the first time she'd been here. There were other things that went missing before."

"Why on earth didn't you say?"

Mirabelle shrugged. "Well, I wasn't sure at first. You know what I'm like." She looked around at the untidy kitchen. "It's quite easy to lose things."

Yvonne sat down. "What's gone?"

"Oh, just bits and pieces. Jewellery, rings and stuff."

"How d'you know it was Summer. Oh! The note, I suppose."

"And the fact she's taken more of her clothes. I checked after I saw the note. I checked in her room. In her drawers. She's taken the rest of her underwear and jumpers and stuff."

Yvonne frowned. "What d'you mean, more of her clothes? The rest of her stuff? Has this happened before?"

"A couple of weeks ago. After that time at the hospital."

"The nightdress day?"

Mirabelle nodded.

"You never said. Why didn't you say?"

She studied the rings on her fingers. "I was ashamed. Humiliated."

"That has to have hurt."

Nodded again.

"Oh, Belle." Yvonne's eyes filled up. "How awful. I can't believe she'd do that."

Mirabelle lifted her purse. "I'd left out money to pay the stair-cleaner." She shook her head. "I *know* I took it out of my purse." She got up from her seat at the table. "I left it here." She touched the worktop. "But when the cleaner knocked for it, it wasn't there. I thought perhaps I'd imagined I'd put it out. Every Monday. The stairs get swept and washed every Monday. I leave the money out on the kitchen worktop Sunday night." She patted the place she always put it. "It's the only thing I'm ever organised with. It's so I don't have to fumble about looking for change while Mrs B has to wait. She likes to get away sharpish so she can get the kids from school."

"Maybe you forgot."

"That's what I thought — the first time. But then it happened again today. And I *know* I left it out. Now I've found the note, I know. I just know Summer's been taking it."

"Why would she do that?"

Mirabelle shrugged. "I left extra money lying beside it last night with a packet of those biscuits Summer was so fond of. You know, the American ones? Oriels, or something?" She shrugged. "Whatever they're called. And I went out, like I do. Just to see if I was right. Sure enough. Gone when I got back. Just a few minutes before you came." Her hand trailed across the empty space on the counter.

The air in the room felt heavy, oppressive.

"It's awful," Yvonne said in a whisper.

"I don't care about the money. Summer knows that. She knows she'd only have to ask."

"But it's awful she came when you weren't here."

"She must watch me." Mirabelle walked to the window. "She must slip in when she sees me go out." She turned from it in disgust, her voice thickening as the full import of it all began to dawn on her. "She's been watching me."

"Oh my giddy aunt!"

A thought crashed in on her consciousness and Mirabelle hurried to Summer's bedroom. She searched on, in and around Summer's dressing table. "They're gone. Her straighteners are gone." She checked in the drawer where she had put it. "And her phone charger." Looked around. "And her laptop. Sheila Wilson must be right. Summer's not homeless. Summer's not homeless at all." She threw herself across the bed, screaming into the pillows, thumping the mattress with her fists. "All those nights I slept on cold hard gravestones, she's been tucked up cosy in some man's bed."

Yvonne stood in the doorway, her hands covering her

348

mouth, tears trickling down her face. "Oh, Mirabelle," she said, "This is awful. It's too awful."

"It's cruel!" Mirabelle shouted. "That's what it is. It's downright, damn-well cruel!" She tore at the bedding, got up and ripped it from the bed, then kicked at the heap she'd thrown to the floor. "She must have seen me head up the road. *Watched* me walk up the road, heaven only knows how many times."

"But she wouldn't know how long you'd be out. She really took a risk you wouldn't come home and find her here."

"Oh, she'd know all right. She'd know." Mirabelle stomped back through to the kitchen. "There!" she said, her arm outstretched to the traitorous calendar on the kitchen wall. "See! I'd written across the calendar. I'm out! Not home to anyone! I did it in a temper after the hospital debacle." She ripped the calendar from the wall and threw it in the direction of the bucket. "She knew all right."

"Oh my giddy aunt!"

"Never mind your aunt. It makes *me* giddy. Sick, in fact. It makes me sick." Mirabelle slumped onto a chair. "I can't believe she could do this to me." She clutched at her heart. "Oh! It hurts. It really, really hurts, Yvonne." She wept with frustration and disappointment, and sheer, raw, undiluted pain. She shrugged Yvonne away as she tried to hold her. "I don't know what to do," she cried. "I don't know what to do." Restless now, she started to pace the kitchen.

Yvonne put the kettle on.

Mirabelle paced and ranted and screamed and cried until she was exhausted.

"I'm done with her." She said at last, as she blew her nose and dried her eyes, swiping reams of paper towel from the roll in its holder next to the cooker. She stamped on the lever that opened the bin, threw the soggy mass of paper into it and let it crash shut. She washed her hands and dried them on the towel that hung behind the door, wiping them until they were red and glowing. "That's it! I'm done with her," she said again.

349

Yvonne dropped teabags and poured hot water into two mugs.

"If that wee besom can watch me going out to search for her. If she can stand out there and watch me. Knowing how much I'm trying. Knowing how much it hurts." Clutching the pain in her chest, she turned to Yvonne. "I'm done with her," she said yet again. "Finished. That's it. If she wants to come home now, she's gonna have to ring the damn doorbell and ask. I'm changing the locks tomorrow, and that's it. I'm done looking for her. Finished. Caput. Done."

"You don't mean that," Yvonne said. "You're upset."

"Upset? Upset? You're damn right I'm upset." Mirabelle started to pace the kitchen again. "I'm absolutely furious." She paused and thumped her fist on the kitchen table, spilling the tea from the cup Yvonne had set beside her. "She has the cheek, the impudence, the … the … the … the sheer *wickedness* to walk out of this house and disappear, leaving me to fall to pieces, leaving me to search for her, to drive me crazy, to … to break my heart! And then to have the *gall* to sneak back in when I'm *out*, when she's *watched* me go out. When she's *spied* on me going out. She sneaks back in my home like a thief. How dare she. How *dare* she make a fool of me like this." She swung round to Yvonne. "Upset? D'you think? Upset? I'm incandescent!"

The fire of Mirabelle's rage continued to blaze and, true to her word, she engaged a locksmith the next day to change the lock on the door.

"You can't do that!" Yvonne was horrified. "What if Summer wants to come home?"

Mirabelle demonstrated how well the doorbell rang.

"She'll feel rejected. Shut out."

She demonstrated the doorbell again. And how easily she could open the door in answer.

"And you're really not going to look for her any more?"

"Nup!"

"But she must be here, somewhere close by." Yvonne stood at the window, scanning the street.

"Yup!"

"But we *can't* stop looking for her."

"Yup!"

"Is that all you're going to say?"

She shrugged.

"Well, *I'm* not going to stop looking for her."

"Be my guest. Just make sure you close the door properly on your way out."

Sam's office door was pushed open, letting in the noise of laughter. "There's been a break-in down the Walk, sir. Squad car picking up couple of suspects as we speak."

He reached for his jacket. "What's the merriment about, then, Elliot?"

"Having a bit of a carry-on out at the desk, sir."

"Is that some kind of music I can hear?"

"Bit of a jig going on. Oh! And there's someone to see you, sir," Elliot said with a smile.

"Hi, Sam!" Mirabelle breezed in, bracelets jingling as she waved her kazoo at him, mischief twinkling in her eyes. "Entertaining the troops!" she laughed, her large body jiggling with merriment, no trace of the angry mood she'd been in for weeks, or the sleepless nights of self-examination, of building herself up to rebuilding her life, no reference to the fact she hadn't seen him socially for months, hadn't seen him at all for weeks.

With a sweep of her arm, she cleared the papers on his desk to one side, opened her bag and upturned it. A multi-coloured waterfall of Mars bars, Snickers, Twix, Dairy Milk and various other confectioneries cascaded from its depths. "You can take these into custody," she said, laughing up at Sam. "I've made a decision. The answer is 'Yes!' Thank you, yes."

Sam frowned. "Yes?"

"Yes, I'll marry you. If you still want me, I'll marry you."

Because she'd promised Sam she'd marry him if she found Summer; because she had decided, through those long sleepless nights of the past few weeks, that yes, 'life did go on' and it was time hers did; because she'd promised

352

Sam she'd stop eating so much junk when she found Summer, she'd gathered her secret stashes of chocolate bars of every persuasion and poured them out on his desk as an offering of joy.

"What?" Sam asked. "I don't understand. You said ... We haven't found ..."

Mirabelle leant across his desk. "Well, effectively, we have found Summer. She's right here in Edinburgh playing silly beggars with me. So, if you still want me, we can get married and Summer can rejoin the family if she asks nicely."

Sam shook his head. "But ..."

"You were right, Sam. All along, you were right. She's been getting on with her life. Doing whatever she liked. Not caring tuppence I couldn't do the same. Well, I've seen the light. The penny's dropped. I've cottoned on. Whichever cliché you want to use. You were right. To hang with Summer, I'm moving on."

"I don't understand." Sam scratched his head. "What's this about?"

"She's been spying on me, stealing from the house when I go out. She even had the gall to sleep in her old bed when I was away last weekend."

"You were away?"

"Long story for another time." Mirabelle dismissed the last seven weeks of hard work with a wave of her hand. "A case." This wasn't the moment to fill him in on all that had happened since he'd stormed out of her life. "I'm done looking for Summer. You were right. Looking for her was an obsession, so I've quit. Gone cold turkey. I've done a heap of serious thinking and I'm ready to move on with my life. Start a new chapter."

"You don't mean that. You're just angry with her."

"Justifiably!"

"Yes, but what about when you simmer down?"

"I have simmered down." She threw her arms wide. "Look at me. Look at my face. Do I look angry?"

Sam looked at her: the glow in her cheeks, the bright

smile in her eyes, the unmistakeable happiness in her smile. He smiled back.

"So? Are you gonna marry me or what?"

He grinned.

Mirabelle took that as a 'Yes,' and put the kazoo to her lips. "Here comes the bride," she kazood. "Fifty metres wide," she sang. She raised her arms above her head, the kazoo waved in triumph. "But not any more," she said, picking up handfuls of confectionery from his desk and throwing it in the air, letting it fall around her like confetti as she twirled and waltzed across the room. "It's raining sweets, Hallelujah! It's raining sweets. Yeah! Yeah! Yeah!" she sang, throwing them up, letting them fall. "I'm getting married, Hallelujah! We're getting hitched. Yeah! Yeah! Yeah!"

Sam watched her victory dance, a smile spreading from his face to his heart despite his natural caution.

She paused in her celebration long enough to lean across the desk, take his face in her hands and kiss his mouth. Still holding his face, she looked into his eyes. "Never mind a new chapter. This, my dear, sweet, patient Sam, this is a whole new book," she told him.

~~~

*If you enjoyed Searching for Summer,
you will be pleased to know*

~~~Traces Of Red ~~~

*the second book in The Reluctant Detective series,
will be coming soon.*

Traces of Red

*Mirabelle never set out to run an informal Missing Person's
Agency, but she seems to have a talent for finding missing
people — except for the one missing person she set out to
find in the first place — her daughter, Summer.
Summer is still missing but, following information she has
received, Mirabelle is certain she is on her trail and closing
in.
Meanwhile, people keep coming to her, asking for help and
she becomes known as, 'Yon woman that runs The Agency
down Broughton Street.'
Although reluctant to play detective, she becomes involved
with searching for someone's missing husband, someone
else's daughter, the mother of an abandoned baby, and how
they are all connected with the body in the burn.*

~~~

Can't wait?

*There are four other novels published by the same
author. These four are individual novels, and not part of the
Reluctant Detective series.
You can find their details in the following pages.*

*Christine would be delighted if you could leave a **review** of this or any of her other novels on Amazon or Goodreads.*

http://www.amazon.com/Christine-Campbell/e/B00BRGC0C2

https://www.goodreads.com/Cic1947

Thank you.

the author
christine campbell

a novelist, who also enjoys writing poetry and short stories.

You can follow Christine on her blog

http://cicampbellblog.wordpress.com

Facebook

https://www.facebook.com/WriteWhereYouAre

Goodreads

https://www.goodreads.com/Cic1947

Twitter @Campbama

https://twitter.com/Campbama

or YouTube

http://www.youtube.com/watch?v=lcJCfT1nHHQ

the books

also by christine campbell

Family Matters

http://a-fwd.com/asin-com=B00BR9JUV8

Making It Home

http://a-fwd.com/asin-com=B00BR9YS0G

Flying Free

http://a-fwd.com/asin-com=B00HUHGQW2

Here at the Gate

http://a-fwd.com/asin-com=B00KIW95OW

Amazon Author Page

http://www.amazon.com/Christine-Campbell/e/B00BRGC0C2

Sarah's husband, Tom, disappeared without trace eleven years ago. Now her son, Peter has died.

Tom appears at Peter's funeral and tries to reestablish contact, which Sarah refuses but Kate, her daughter accepts. The growing closeness between Kate and her father worries Sarah because she believes that Tom is dishonest and unreliable, at best.

Then Sarah finds Peter's diary and follows the steps he took in search of his father. It becomes a journey of self-discovery: what she uncovers forces Sarah to reassess her view of herself, her origins and her certainties.

A relationship novel, but also a detection novel with a difference: this story traces a woman's drive to uncover and understand the truth about a family she thought she knew … her own.

http://a-fwd.com/asin-com=B00BR9JUV8

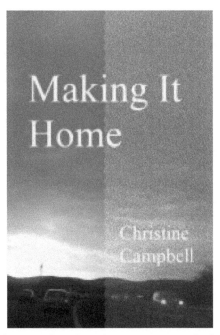

Kate had a home, but her heart wasn't in it … or in her marriage. So she left them both.

Phillis had a home … and her heart was in it … but she wanted something more. So she shopped.

Naomi had no home and her heart was in cold storage, frozen by grief and fear. So she shopped.

They found one another in a department store. Shopping. The problem with 'retail therapy': you can overdose.

As friendship grows between these three women, they help one another face up to their problems, realising along the way, that every heart needs a home and it takes more than a house to make one.

A contemporary novel about women who want more.

<u>http://a-fwd.com/asin-com=B00BR9YS0G</u>

When Tom asks Jayne to marry him, he unwittingly opens her personal Pandora's Box, and she can't seem to close the lid on all that rushes out at her, whirling her into a cycle of self-sabotage.

Unable to commit to a relationship, she pushes Tom away, along with everything else important in her life.

Then she finds someone to help her make sense of what's happening, but, instead of slamming the lid shut on all that has been let loose, he helps her open it wider and face her fears in order to overcome them.

Remembering the past helps her make sense of the present and allows her to begin the process of healing and she finds that, as in the fable, there is one last thing left in the Box. That thing is hope.

But, when she is ready to commit to, will Tom still be waiting?

This novel traces a woman's struggle to become the woman she wants to be in order to marry the man she loves.

A contemporary novel about someone who could be your neighbour, your friend, or even you.

http://a-fwd.com/asin-com=B00HUHGQW2

Christine Campbell

Here at the Gate

Mhairi had worked hard to build herself a normal, stable life, but there had always been a dark fear inside her. No matter how happy she was, it was always there.

It followed her about like a black bat, haunting her nights, hiding in a corner during her days, flapping out at odd moments, scaring the wits out of her.

It was as though she was standing outside a high-walled garden, barred from the secret of her past by the wrought-iron gate. She could see all the bushes and trees, the rhododendron and hydrangea. She could even smell the roses and the honeysuckle, but then the gate would swing shut and she was outside and it was dark.

Now her happy, settled life was being threatened by her own daughter and she knew she had to force through the darkness. She needed to remember what she had spent a lifetime forgetting.

http://a-fwd.com/asin-com=B00KIW95OW

Lightning Source UK Ltd.
Milton Keynes UK
UKHW041919090419
340750UK00001B/125/P